ACCOLADES FOR THE SERPENTS OF BLISSFULL

"Bruce Pratt knows the  s of the backwoods, and in this l nny and brilliant portrait of a dow ling for a toehold in life's craggy h runners, and snake-handling re. late the ridges and valleys around Blissfull, West Virginia may be an idiosyncratic bunch, but they have much to teach us about endurance, loyalty, and love. Not since *The Beans of Egypt Maine* has there been a book so true to it sense of place. *The Serpents of Blissfull* is an absolute winner."

— **Clint McCown** has published three novels and three volumes of poems that have won numerous awards. He teaches a creative writing program at Virginia Commonwealth Univ.

"*The Serpents of Blissfull* is a wonderful read--well-drawn characters, intriguing setting, strong but subtle writing. The narrator, Isaac "Ize" Butts--no'count drunkard, veteran, and born-again Christian who joins the snake-handling Star of Morning Church--has a marvelous voice, a voice at once gritty and poetic, earthy and insightful, a voice that is as real and unique as the mountain "hollers" from which it came. Though the novel travels some familiar territory--moonshine-running hillbillies, psalm-singing, river-baptizing Christians, and the backwoods culture of Dickey's *Deliverance*--in Pratt's skillful and sympathetic hands, Butts' narrative is completely fresh, filled with insight, compassion, subtlety, and power."

— **Dr. Michael White**, Professor of English and Program Director MFA in Creative Writing; Fairfield University and author of four *New York Times* notable novels.

"Bruce Pratt writes with the ear of a musician, the insight of a poet, the heart of a dramatist, and the sparkle of a fireside storyteller. He is every one of these men and more, and he brings them all to the table in his debut novel, a brilliant, literary page-turner called *The Serpents of Blissfull*, a fiercely American saga that dances between hilarity and pathos as we shadow a wild-eyed hero with a damn-fool dream up and down the mountains of West Virginia. Hard-drinking, hard-loving, hard-living Isaac Butts never gives up, and he never lets down. Neither does this book."

— **Michael Kimball** is a novelist, playwright, and screenwriter. His novel **Undone** received the Fresh Talent Award in the U.K. and remained on the London Times' top ten bestseller list for two months in 1996. Stage plays include **Ghosts of Ocean House**, nominated for the 2007 Edgar Award by the Mystery Writers of America, and the award-winning short play **Say No More**, which has been produced by more than 25 companies across the country. Michael has sold original screenplays and adaptations to movie companies and written episodes for television series. He teaches popular fiction and scriptwriting in Maine, at Stonecoast MFA.

"Like the people in Bruce Pratt's hardscrabble heaven of Blissfull, West Virginia and its environs, you may or may not want to live there, but it hardly matters because once you get Isaac Butts' voice in your ear, you can't leave. In Butts, Pratt has created a smart and soulful narrator whom we'll gladly listen to all night and into the morning. *The Serpents of Blissfull* is a grand feat of storytelling. Bravo!"

— **Richard Hoffman** Author of *Half the House: A Memoir*, and *Interference & Other Stories*

THE SERPENTS OF BLISSFULL

THE SERPENTS OF BLISSFULL

BRUCE PRATT

And these signs will accompany those who believe: in my name they will cast out demons; they will speak in new tongues; they will pick up serpents, and if they drink any deadly thing it will not hurt them; they will lay their hands on the sick, and they will recover.

Mark 16:17

THE SERPENTS OF BLISSFULL

BRUCE PRATT

MOUNTAIN STATE PRESS, INC.
CHARLESTON, WEST VIRGINIA

© Bruce Pratt 2010. All rights reserved. No portion of this book may be reproduced in any form whatsoever, except for brief quotations in reviews, without the prior written permission of both the copyright owner and the publisher.

International Standard Book Number: 978-0-941092-58-6

Library of Congress Control Number: 2010933191

1 2 3 4 5 6 7 8 9 0

Cover Photos: Joe's Eyes and The Country Church by Deanna Kizer
Serpent by Jonathan Mays
Front Cover Design by: Deanna Kizer
Cover Design by: Mark S. Phillips
Book Design by: Mark S. Phillips

Previously Published Works and Awards:

Boreal, Poems by Bruce Pratt; Antrim House
    Nominated in 2008 for a Pushcart Prize in Fiction
    Winner in 2007 Andre Dubus Award, Words and Images
    Winner 2007 Ellipsis Poetry Award, Judge James Galvin for *A distant ship tiding home*

This is a work of fiction. Any references to historical events; to real people, living or dead; or to real locales are intended only to give the fiction a sense of reality and authenticity. Names, characters, places, and incidents either are a product of the author's imagination or are used fictitiously, and their resemblance, if any, to real-life counterparts is entirely coincidental.

Mountain State Press, Inc.
2300 MacCorkle Avenue SE
Charleston, West Virginia 25304
www.mountainstatepress.org

Printed in United States of America

DEDICATION

I dedicate this book, and any other I may write, to the late Welch Everman, mentor, friend, husband, musician, writer, and as fine a teacher as I have ever known. Welch, I miss you every day.

And to the late Dr. Fred G. Jones, Jr., the brightest man and scholar, and most influential teacher, I have ever known. For seventeen years Fred guided me with his generous wisdom and led me to understand that learning never ends.

And to my loving wife Janet, as loving, intelligent, and decent a person as inhabits this planet, who kindly married me thirty-seven Bloomsdays ago

Cover Design and Photo Credits

Front cover design and photos of *Joe's Eyes* and *The Country Church* by Deanna Kizer. Front cover serpent photo courtesy of Jonathan Mays.

Back cover photo by Janet Pratt.

CHAPTER ONE

Reverend Willis first saw me the day Riley got the ostrich. Fred Hicks had been towing the bird in his homemade trailer when he felt the tongue grinding up the gravel behind his pickup. A one-and-seven-eighths ball will usually work with a two-inch hitch, but his cup was worn, and even though Fred had put a rag on the ball, the only thing holding the trailer to the truck, when he shuddered to a stop in front of my brother's house, were the chains.

When Fred picked up the trailer hitch the ostrich slid to the back and broke through the gate of one-by-two pine slats, and the rope Fred had looped around his neck slipped off the tie-down. Fred tried to catch the bird, but the ostrich fought him. Hoping to get some help he reached into the cab and leaned on the horn. Riley looked out the window and hollered for me to get dressed. By the time I had my boots on and got out to the end of the driveway, Fred's forehead and face were bloody, Riley was trying to lasso the ostrich with an old length of frayed, slip-knotted hemp rope, and his two dogs were barking and running circles around the terrified bird.

I tried to help but I was drunk, and even sober I'd have no idea how to wrestle a seven-foot, three-hundred and fifty pound ostrich. By the looks of it, neither did Fred. The three of us chased the bird around in the driveway and along the ditch, but didn't get control of him before I passed out from the heat, the commotion, and the pint of my late father's best ten-year-old whiskey I'd had with my breakfast to chase the one I'd sipped through the night.

Fred had bought the ostrich after reading that they could be raised here, and were a hot item in the exotic pet trade. The problem was they didn't like the mountain climate, you needed two to breed, his female had died from a snakebite, and no one in southern West Virginia, especially Blissfull, craved exotic pets. When the trailer hitch uncoupled, he was taking the bird to a llama dealer over in Beckley who said he might be able to sell him to a petting zoo. Since Fred had welded a cap to the bed of the truck, and the ostrich was taller than most men, he had to tow him when he took him anyplace, and the bird resented it. Having never cottoned to riding on the washboard roads in these parts, the ostrich was most reluctant to get back in the trailer.

I was supposed to ride with Fred because Riley had to watch his kids that day and he wanted me out of the house because his ex-wife, Lillian, with whom he desperately wished to reconcile, had been threatening to complain to the social services people about me. After seeing the bird batter Fred's cheeks and hands with his beak, I didn't consider a petting zoo a good home for such a beast, and I'd lost the itch to ride over to Beckley long before I passed out in the high weeds.

Fred told me later that Riley had fetched his 22 and was going to shoot the bird, which was poking along the edge of the broken rail fence in the yard, when a van pulled up and a man got out and began to talk to the ostrich. I think I remember some of that, but I know I was out before he took over the chase. Fred said it was the holiest thing he'd ever seen. The man had Riley put the dogs in the house, and then bade everyone stand still and eventually the bird began to calm down and peck in the weeds where I was snoring. Fred said the man hummed some hymn or old gospel tune to the bird and soon had a hold on the piece of rope around the ostrich's neck and was leading it into the small fenced area where the Old Man used to keep hogs. "Let it rest here awhile," the man said. Only other words he said, according to Riley, were, "He is one of the Lord's creatures, frightened and taken from his home. Do not kill him."

The man got in the van and drove away down the ridge.

I woke up after the bird was exploring the field and Riley had mended Fred's broken tailgate. Riley helped Fred put me in the trailer—Fred was afraid I'd be sick in the cab—and Fred ran me over to his place, parked under a shady maple, and let me sleep it off.

Reverend Willis isn't like the prayer and peas preachers at

the Sally. Besides extensive passages of the Bible that he's memorized, and the names of every bird you find in these hills, he understands snakes, which he calls serpents. He knows every den on every ridge around here, and can fill a sack with as many rattlers and copperheads in a day as most mountain people would need a week to catch. He can shout up a ball of lazy rattlers on a frigid February night and croon low and sweet to a fidgety copperhead on a blazing July Sunday when he knows the serpents can smell the fear in the ones he calls the non-anointed, and I've seen him handle a full-size rattler and a copperhead at the same time, and not be bitten. No one I ever saw could handle like Reverend Willis, which is why so many believe that God also gave him the power to heal.

Selling snakes is not always legal by the laws of man, but handling them, some believe, is commanded by God. At the Star of Morning Church, which is like a holiness church in that there are serpents at services, they believe that everyone can feel God's anointment and protection when handling, not just a few chosen ones, and as soon as anyone feels the need to handle they take a serpent or two out of the boxes at the back of the stage. However, they never pass them to any who is afraid or who doesn't feel the Word on them, and never drink poisons like some holiness folks do.

Star of Morning is poor. It raises money like most churches with bake sales and free will offerings, but also by selling serpents to churches in Maine and other states where it's too cold for them to live, and to congregations in cities in New England where there are no snakes at all. Reverend Willis has convinced his congregation at Star of Morning to make it its mission to provide serpents to those who cannot catch their own. West Virginia is one of the only states where handling snakes at a religious service is not outlawed and persecuted, which is why Reverend Willis came here from Tennessee where he first received the call to preach. He calls himself a signs preacher according to Mark 16.

I didn't grow up in the church. Mama quit when she was carrying Riley. She wasn't married yet and her Daddy let the preacher, who said she'd been possessed, take a switch to her to cast out the devil. She never went back. When I told Reverend Willis about that he said that preacher had been wrong. "To believe, you must believe in forgiveness," he says, "Love and forgiveness are necessary to receive grace."

My father was a moonshiner, poacher, and tree farmer, and though he had no use for any church, prospered because of an age-old alliance between the whiskey makers and the local Baptists that once kept our county dry. He walked with a hitch as a result of being hit by a jeep in the army, and his limp got worse when he went to town because he was getting a disability near as good as some of the miners with black lung were getting, and he didn't want to make them feel bad. Their problems would be killing them soon enough, and he could live a long time with a balky hip.

When Riley was fourteen and I was almost twelve, Mama left us and went up with some of her distant relations in Detroit. She left a note for Riley and me, saying that she'd be gone for a month or two, which I endeavored to believe was true, but the first night she was gone Riley said, "We ain't never gonna see her again. The Old Bastard drove her off."

Mama had finished high school and learned to type well enough to get an office job at a Ford plant. After she'd been there a few years, she re-married and sent money home asking Daddy to let us ride up there on the bus to visit her. He'd not allow it, so a few times a year she would drive down home and visit us for a few days. She'd stay in a motel over in Welch, and come out in her car early each morning and wait for us at the end of the gravel and ride us to school, or, if it was summertime, she'd come up to the house and bring a picnic to eat in the hills. She'd ask Riley and me if we were okay and we'd always tell her we were, though I ached to find a way to go back with her. It wasn't just that I missed her, and I did, but I wanted to see what she was like living with someone else. I never did meet, Alvin, her new husband, as he never came with her, and in time I suspected that the reason we didn't move up with Mama was as much Alvin not wanting to take us

4

on as it was the Old Man's refusal to give us up. Daddy was a fierce man. He'd killed men in the war and in the mountains, and taken the strap to everyone in the house, even Mama. The Old Man loathed her car, and would have whipped us all if he knew we were catching rides to school. I'll recall for eternity the sneer creasing his face the first time Mama drove up the ridge in her own vehicle. He'd told her, "Take the boys in that car, I'll come kill you for sure. You take nothing of mine with you when you gone." Still, I was always aware that she had ample opportunity to grab us, and for all his bluster and meanness, the Old Man wouldn't have bothered to track us down. She knew that, too.

Sometimes, in high school, when I was staring out the windows at the mountains, I fancied hitchhiking to Michigan and arriving on Mama's doorstep unannounced, but I never got to Detroit, once I was free to go. I feared I might not be welcomed and I knew that if I was turned away by Mama that it would be an abrasion on my heart no amount of time or whiskey could heal.

When we'd climb up the ridge to her family's burying ground for a picnic, she'd leave her keys in the ignition, in part, I believe, because she hoped the Old Man might steal it and disappear, but he had nowhere to go, having seen everything of the world he'd yearned to see and more while he was in the army. Still, though Mama never tried to run off with us, I know she searched her being for the strength to do it from the way she'd look at us each time she left for Detroit. The defeat in her eyes was a sign for me that the strap and its meanness had broken her, and I knew, even as a kid, that it had broken me a bit, too. Riley's different. It hardened him, but he doesn't pass the meanness on, and he's never let it break him. Reverend Willis says, "Spare not the rod, but never use it in anger." He says that it is reasonable to believe that God didn't intend actual hitting with the rod, and he's tried to explain what he means when he says, "There are many signs we have yet to know," but I have never mustered the concentration to follow the finer points of his religious musings.

5

When I woke up in the back of Fred's trailer, I had ostrich shit on my shirt, a terrible thirst, and a vicious headache. One of Fred's kids was hanging upside down by his knees in the tree staring at me and looking at him made me sick. I puked over the side of the trailer, which attracted Fred's dogs who began to fight over the spoils.

As my stomach worked on towards the dry heaves, I knew it was time for me to head back to the VA to dry out. Twice, I'd been in Beckley Vet Center, but I never could get straightened out there, perhaps because it's where the Old Man died, his limbs pruned away like branches off a sick tree, diabetes ravaging his kidneys, his liver turning to stone. As a rule, moonshiners and their kids don't drink much, not because it eats up the profits but because they've seen how their product corrodes their best customers. The Old Man and I are alike only as exceptions to that rule.

Blinking up at the gapped-tooth grin of Fred's youngest, I decided it was time to fetch my backpack, enough hooch for a three-day hitch, and head out for a hospital up north. I waited at Fred's fighting the shakes and scouring my guts with black coffee until I was sure Lillian couldn't use my condition against me in case she was there, and had Fred tote me back up to the old place. I cleaned the ostrich shit from my shirt, showered, shoved three quarts of the Old Man's best and most of my clothes into my backpack, loaded my shaving kit on top, tied a warm coat to the frame, headed down the gravel toward the asphalt and stuck out my thumb. Riley had staked me to a twenty, and that, along with two rolls of quarters I'd been saving, was all the cash I had.

It was coming on dark when I looked back at my home ridge, wondering as I always do when I'm leaving if I'll ever be back, and, as I stared into the purpling shadows, I remembered the first time I'd left home—the judge offering me two years in the pen for possession of illegal whiskey with intent to distribute, or an enlistment in the army. For most of my hitch, I was stationed in El Paso, and I thought I had sweated all the corn out of my system in the west Texas sun, but once I came home and traded my fatigues for Dickies and jeans, and the motor pool for the Krogers' loading dock, I fell into my old ways.

After I got fired from Krogers, I got work parting-out cars for a junkyard. It was spring and working outside inspired me. I hopped on the wagon, cold turkey, for a brief ride, but when the Old Man went in the hospital for good, and I got to fighting with Riley because he wouldn't visit him when they called to say that his, "death was imminent," I crawled back into the booze and slunk off the mountain again.

Reverend Willis has come to call my next years, "The journey of a soul looking for God." I leave the religious things to him, but if I was looking for The Lord, it was in some odd places. He says my problem was that I was trying to find God, "Without believing in Him." I wasn't always drunk in those years. Rather my life was a series of lengthy sober stretches followed by brief, but spectacular, binges. Sober I'd get a job and a decent room or apartment, but if something set me off: a fight with a woman, some Yankee insulting the way I talk, an incest joke about West Virginia, or just the piling up of sorrows that happens when you're poor, I'd get liquored up, get in a fight, get locked in the drunk tank, and, once I'd gotten past the worst shakes, get shipped to the nearest VA hospital to dry out.

It took me three days to reach Bangor Maine, about as far north as I had ever been, courtesy of some kids in a van who picked me up in Connecticut on their way to a concert. They offered me a place on the floor of their motel room, which I accepted, but when they pulled out a stash of reefer and enough coke to put us all away, I stumbled off in search of a poor man's bar. I found one near the bus station, got drunk, and then got bounced out the door with my pack hurled after me.

When I couldn't find my way back to the motel, I wandered down toward the dark ribbon of the Penobscot River to find a place to sleep in the weeds at the water's edge. Though September, the night was cold, a chilly fog cloaking the river, and I scuttled into a small hole in the bank. I awoke to the pop and rumble of traffic on the interstate and the salty smell of the river rising on the tide. I had one roll of quarters in my pocket and one bottle left in my backpack.

I can't remember anything else until I found myself in the Northampton, Massachusetts jail. The cops later explained to me that I'd been found passed out in the bed of a student's pick-up truck in a Smith College parking lot and been hauled to the drunk tank.

After I got released from the Veterans' Hospital in Holyoke, I got one of the best jobs of my life working at Plourde's Funeral Home as a custodian and handy man. The job came with a room with my own bath on the top floor, and featured an unobstructed view of the Connecticut River. At night I'd watch the abandoned warehouses and factories in the section of the city the locals call The Flats burn a bright orange against the black sky. I backslid a few times, but if I kept the drinking down to two or three sixteen-ounce beers, and stayed away from it during the day, I could coast along, sharing the third floor with a family of reluctant ghosts, and my Friday and Saturday nights with a girl named Ella from Kentucky, who worked downtown in a shoe store and had a place on the third floor of the same building.

I might still be there with Ella, except for a tumble I took from a ladder on a windy late October day, six months after I'd dried out. I was decorating the boss's house, which stood above the river north of town on the way to Easthampton, for a Halloween party, tacking cardboard witches to the side of his garage, when I reached too far and rode the ladder to the driveway. I was out for a couple of hours, and when I woke up in the hospital I thought I'd gone on a bender. Turned out I have some syndrome I can't pronounce, that gives me the whirlies. In the past, when I got dizzy, I figured it was the effects of all my drinking, but the doctor said that wasn't, "What compromised my balance."

I was in Mercy Hospital in Springfield for two weeks, the

first time in my adult life that I'd been in any medical facility other than an emergency room that didn't belong to the VA. While I was there, I heard that charity cases were often shipped to Mercy, because they didn't insist on being paid as part of some broader mission, but other than a few crucifixes and some nuns in the hallways, the main difference from the VA that I noticed was that the patients at Mercy seemed to be on the mend.

A hospital volunteer drove me in a van back to Holyoke along with a young Hispanic guy in a wheelchair headed to a nursing home. I had the driver drop me off downtown and I headed straight for Ella's place. It was late Sunday morning; the hills above the Connecticut Valley were draped in fog, and a thin stream of brown water ran in the gutters. I paused a minute in front of an empty storefront window, my reflection distorted by a fine mist collected on the filmy glass. Purple and yellow rings surrounded my eyes, and though the stitches were gone and my hair had already begun to grow back, the slash across the back of my head was nubbly to the touch.

The initial lucid thing I'd done when I came to after my fall was to ask Mrs. Plourde to contact Ella at the shoe store, which she took pains to do that very afternoon. But when she tried to visit me, because she couldn't prove she was kin and I was just out of the ICU, they wouldn't allow her in.

After that, we spoke most evenings when she got home from the store, but she had to use a pay phone and we couldn't talk long. Brief as they were, each conversation was a comfort, the ragged sound of Ella's voice as sweet in my ears as it was the first time I heard it one wet April Sunday morning, soft, southern, and shy among the hard clatter of Yankee speak rattling around Kelly's Diner. I'd sprinted through a quick, hard shower and was shaking the rain off my denim jacket when I heard someone say to the counter waitress, "I'd be obliged to ye for some sugar, ma'am." The use of ye for you, something I've never heard outside of the southern hills, warmed my cold bones. Though I hadn't seen who'd said those words, when I scanned the backs of the patrons seated at the counter, I knew by the simple ponytail and the way she hunched over her food that the voice belonged to the short thin woman at the end of the counter.

I was on my second cup of coffee and third doughnut when a seat opened up next to her. I sidled over and said, "Morning miss, long way from home are ye?"

Ella lifted her head and straightened her shoulders. "You be as well?" she said, turning on her stool to regard me with her black eyes.

Though we talked for over an hour that morning, gleaning any information from Ella other than her name, where she worked, that Monday was her day off, and how long she'd been in the north, was as difficult as wrestling a snarl of fishhooks out of your pant's pocket. She didn't give me the name of the town she was from, saying only that she "Hailed from a ridge in East Kentucky that don't have a true name," and the only promise I could earn from her about seeing her again was an invitation to meet her at the store when she got off work at six on the following Tuesday.

After that, I stopped by the store every evening I could, and we'd either stroll to Kelly's for coffee, or, if the weather was nice, wander the streets peeking in store windows at things we'd never buy, until we arrived back at the entrance to her building. It was two weeks before she asked me up, and before she unlocked the door to her room, she took my hand, riveted those black eyes on me and told me the story of her arrival in Holyoke. "I come up here three years ago with a boy from home said a friend from the army had construction work for him," she said, "But I got pregnant and he got fired, so he left me. The rest is between me and the Lord." Standing again in front of her building, I remembered the way she undressed that first time under the covers, and how she said as she turned out the lone lamp in her room, "You don't need no protection. I can't have no babies now," as I fumbled to open a condom I'd had at the ready for a week.

A wave of sorrow sloshed in my guts, as I recalled the concise way she told me that part of her past, as if such defeats were the normal course of living for everyone, and I trudged once around the block to clear the darkness from my heart before going up.

"I could have fetched you in a cab," Ella said, opening the door to my knock.

"I only found out I was leaving a few hours ago," I said, "I didn't want to wake you."

"Look like you been in a fight," she said, reaching for my hand.

"Must be a sight," I said.

"I met a guy in the Elm Street Tavern," Ella said, "Says you could sue Plourde for plenty."

I stared a moment into her black eyes, searching for the hatch marks of a hangover, but her whites were clear. "I've done best in life when I've avoided the law," I said.

Ella stepped back from the door to allow me in. I set the paper sack I was carrying on the floor by the bed, and she said, "What's in that?"

"Medicine," I said.

"Painkillers?" Ella asked.

"No," I said. "An antibiotic and an anti-inflammatory."

Ella shrugged. She strode across the room and sat on the bed, dangling her legs like a kid on a dock. "Least talk to legal aid," she said. "They helped me once."

"Maybe," I said, sitting beside her.

When I draped my arm around her, she hurled herself into my chest and began sobbing. "I feared you'd die," she said.

I started back to work at Plourde's, but two weeks before Thanksgiving Ella scurried home to her people, the southernness that had joined us together sundering us in the end. We were lying in her bed on a Sunday morning, the radiator in her room groaning against the fall chill, when the pay phone rang in the hallway and we heard Gus Blanding, an old man on disability answer. Seconds later he was beating on Ella's door. I rose on an elbow and watched her cinch her robe around her waist, brush her hair with her fingers, and step out into the hall.

When Ella pushed back into the room a few minutes later she said, "My Daddy's ailing. I couldn't abide not seeing him afore he passes." It didn't take a seer to know she'd be on a southbound bus that day, and that neither the shoe store nor me would be enough of a reason for her to come back.

As Ella gathered her things into a suitcase and a duffel bag, it occurred to me that though we had spent much of our time together, I didn't know her birthday or even how old she was or if she had brothers or sisters, and though she went by Ella Marks, she'd once said to me, "That ain't my born name."

Though I can't imagine what the VA shrinks would have to say about it, as I sat on the edge of the bed pulling on my jeans, the finality of Ella's leaving brought on the memory of my mother heading off to Detroit, and though Mama had made the effort for years to see Riley and me, I knew that if I was ever to see Ella again, I would have to find her.

"Write to me at Plourde's," I said, as the driver stowed Ella's luggage under the bus, "To let me know when you'll be back."

"My Mama may need me," she said, mounting the first step and turning so we stood eye to eye. "I'll miss ye."

When I kissed her she pulled away as if she was embarrassed, and wandered down the aisle to the rear of the bus without looking back.

As the bus backed out of the bay, I thought about how both of us had been abandoned in our time, and how I should have offered to go south with her, though had Ella wanted me to do so, I knew that she have mentioned it. Then, as I watched the bus disappear, it occurred to me that I'd have been more of an outsider on her ridge than either of us were on the streets of Holyoke.

I sauntered back to Plourde's, the morning chill eased by a bright November sun firing the last color on the hills, wondering how long it would take for her landlord to realize that Ella was gone, and what he'd do with the things she'd left behind that didn't fit in her suitcase or duffel: a hotplate, some dishes and silverware, several pair of shoes, and an empty candy sampler box where she stored needles and thread. I wondered how long the shoe store would wait to advertise her job, or if anyone would stop by her room to see if she was sick.

As the sun warmed my neck, I admitted to myself that I knew what would happen to Ella. She'd tell her people that she would stay until her father was well, but even if he survived she'd convince herself that her life among her kin was better than what she could ever cobble together off her home ridge. As soon as she set foot in her family place, she'd have forsaken the world outside it, no less than a monk committing to his cell. As I imagined her resigning herself to a life she'd once run away from, I thought about my mother up in Detroit, and wondered how often she ached to see the mist rising off the field or the snow piling up in the dooryard at home, as she listened to the sounds of the city or inched along in a traffic jam on a flat stretch of Michigan interstate.

Climbing the back stairs to my room, my eyes welled and my throat hurt as if I'd run hard on a cold day. On the landing outside my room, I had an attack of the whirlies, and latched onto the banister with one hand and the knob to my door with the other, then lowered myself to the hallway floor. The bells in one of the Catholic churches began to ring, reminding me that it was Sunday, the liquor stores were closed, and that if I wanted to get drunk that I'd have to find a bar where I could do it on five bucks. Saliva filled my mouth and I sensed the stab of despair that has so often driven me to whiskey surging in my guts, as I rose to open my door. I flung myself onto the bed, hoping to awaken in the dark after the bars were closed.

After Ella left, the ghosts at Plourde's, the shorter, darker days, and the empty hours of each evening, harrowed my heart, tugging at me with the same longing that had wrenched her from my life. We didn't have many interments, which Mr. Plourde explained one gray afternoon was because, "Old folks hang on thorough the holidays. We'll get busy after New

Year's or if the weather turns bad," he said, slapping me on the shoulder. "Until then, we wait." The days continued to crawl along, the idle time poisoning my mood, and a week later, while shoveling the first snow of December from the funeral home walkways, I resolved to head home.

It isn't the south, or the mountains, or sweet memories of childhood that lure me back, but the way people talk, and the way they don't need to talk to say something most of the time, and the way most folks don't throw your failings and weaknesses into your face every time you see them. Though the Old Man's scent and Mama's scared-shitless eyes are there, Riley's improved the home place, and there are hungers satisfied only by being with kin. The difference between sadness away from home and family is that on your home ridge there is someone to be sad with you, someone willing to let you steep in your sorrows without trying to cheer you up or remind you that they are of your own doing.

The night before I left, I lay curled up on my bed, the season's first sleet rattling on the windows. I missed Ella, wanting to hear her voice as much as to feel her flesh, cursing myself for not asking to go with her, or at least learning how to contact her. Each hour she'd been gone, the battle to keep myself from cashing out and hitting the bars until my money was gone became a more pernicious ache in my throat. The thought of living rough in the Yankee winter terrified me, and, burrowing deep into the covers, I considered suicide, rather than risking freezing to death in an alley to be eaten at by stray dogs, or be found frozen to a park bench.

Once I could imagine taking my own life, the methods available to me rioted in my mind. I'm far too claustrophobic and plagued by the whirlies to hang myself, and the thought of botching it with pills and booze and ending up a vegetable in the back ward of the Beckley VA was too morose to consider, as was the notion of slitting my wrists in the bathtub where someone would be forced to find me.

Eliminating jumping off a bridge, or stepping in front of an Amtrak train, meant using a gun, something that would be difficult to acquire in Massachusetts. A long barrel wouldn't work. I couldn't conjure mouthing the barrel of a twelve gauge like some bankrupt farmer, or aiming a rifle at my heart, deciding that the best solution, one that assured success and minimized pain, would be a thirty-eight slug in the soft spot in the roof of my mouth. Once home, I'd pry down the board in the ceiling of my nephew's room and get the revolver I'd snuck home from the service and stored there years before.

The second part was more daunting, and that was to pull the trigger when I was sober. I couldn't risk having the shakes because they might make me mess up the job, and if I did it when the numbing sting of whiskey didn't impair my judgment it wouldn't look like a drunken blunder, some mistake or brief lapse in sanity. If I was going out this way, it would have to be by deliberate choice.

I drew the covers over my head and resolved to retrieve the gun, clean it, fire off a few rounds up on the ridge to make sure that it worked, and then, sometime after Christmas, hike far enough into the woods above the old place that a single shot wouldn't be heard by anyone except the crows and deer. If I took my backpack and some booze, Riley would assume I had gone off on another jag, and when I didn't return, he'd come to believe that I'd shit the bed in a gutter or gone the way of the Old Man in a VA ward. Not knowing my fate would be nettlesome for Riley at times, but finding your brother with the top of his skull splattered against the trunk of a tree would have to be worse, and I owed him better. If I snuck off far enough into the winter hills, unless a hunter or another bootlegger found me, the coyotes would get what little I had to offer in the way of nutrition before the thaw exposed my bones to the birds.

CHAPTER TWO

I started hitching at two-thirty on a Friday afternoon. I'd intended to get an earlier start, but Mr. Plourde was out fetching a body in Bernardston up near the Vermont line, and as I had worked under the table since returning from my fall, I had to wait for him to go to the bank to get the cash to pay me. When he rolled up in front of the home in the hearse, I was sitting in the main lobby. He strolled in the door, handed me an envelope, which I later discovered contained an extra twenty dollars, and said, "You're a good worker, Isaac, and I'll hold your job until after the holidays. Just call me if you're not coming back. If not, I wish you well."

As I shook his hand, I could see in his face that he knew I was as gone as I knew Ella was. All I could muster to say was, "Thank you."

I hoofed it downtown to the Sally thrift store to buy some decent clothes and a winter jacket for the trip, then took my new threads into a Dunkin' Donuts, changed in the rest room, and headed for the highway.

A sparse, gritty snow was gusting up the Interstate 91 ramp and running over the tops of the snow banks, as I waited for a lift. It's been my experience that Yankees don't stop for strangers like southerners do, and I believe that's because they only get in the car to go somewhere. I don't know if every kid in the southern mountains spent as much time in cars going nowhere as my friends and I did, but, often, three or four of us would buy some beer and a pint of bonded whiskey, then ride around the hills and coal towns waiting to see if something would happen. In good weather, when Riley and I could get the Old Man's station wagon and had a few bucks for gas, we'd drive around picking up friends until the car was bursting with people with no place to be and no time to be there, often as not, picking up hitchhikers and running them to where they were going, even if it meant being gone all day or riding over into another state.

The sun faded and the cold deepened with a rising wind.

I dug a red wool hat I'd found in the funeral home's lost and found that said, Ski Bousquet, out of my new coat's pocket, and turned up the collar to keep my nose and neck warm. I know booze makes you colder, and the VA docs tell me it dehydrates you, too, but as the mercury dropped I contemplated spending a few hours getting warm in a saloon, or even heading back to Plourde's and saying I'd had second thoughts, and twice started down the ramp toward town, but each time something gnawed at me, a voice promising me that a good ride was coming soon, and I marched back into place.

As the dark fell, the cold burrowed bone deep. I paced, I sang, windmilled my arms to keep warm, and tried to remember prayers I'd heard as a kid, or hymns I'd sung at the Sally, not only to keep my mind occupied, but as part of my preparations for what might be waiting for me down the line if I decided on an early exit. All I could summon up to sing was, Throw Out the Lifeline, but I couldn't remember what came after, "Someone is drifting away," so I sang the first two lines over and over and hummed the rest until my voice grew as hoarse and raspy as the wind slicing through my jeans.

When I got weary of pacing, I leaned against a light pole playing a game with the license plates passing by me that I'd first made up on the bus in high school. I'd sit alone, always on the driver's side, and take the first letter of a passing plate and think of a vocabulary word that began with it. Vocabulary tests were one thing I excelled at because I could memorize anything I set up in my mind as a list. Though I might not remember them all a week later, I could learn twenty words and definitions in ten minutes before the test. A, assiduous, V, vertiginous, S, salubrious, D, distaff. Song lyrics, street names, historical dates all leave my head seconds after I hear them, unless I can envision them written down on lined paper in my own handwriting.

A little after nine a van rolled to a stop twenty feet up the ramp. A tall, bony kid eased down from the passenger's seat, opened the door, and told to me to sit up front as he was going into the back to nap. As I settled into the shotgun seat, the driver flipped on the dome light so the kid could see his way to fix up his sleeping bag and blankets and stow my pack. I peered over my left shoulder into the back of the van and saw the kid rest my gear against a stack of shallow wooden boxes with small round holes in the top and fitted with bright brass corners, that rose up on either side of his pallet. The driver was humming, low and quiet, and I thought he looked familiar, but as frozen as I was, and after all the booze I've had and all the places I've wandered, most everyone looks like someone I've seen before. The man turned to me, stared a moment and smiled. "Had any ostrich trouble lately?" he said.

"Reverend?" I said, not remembering his name.

He reached out his hand and I shook it. "If you're headed home son, we're going that way."

"Yes sir, I am," I said, the sound of the way he'd said home surging in my heart.

"That's Lucius Farrell," he said pointing to the kid in the back. "Might be you know some of his kin."

"I knew a Winifred Farrell," I said, looking back at the kid settling into his sleeping bag.

"She's my mama," the kid said, his voice muffled by a blanket he'd pulled over his head, "She's a Cooley from Lanks Holler."

I opened my jacket and stuffed my hat in a pocket, my hair sparking as I ran my hand through it, my scalp itchy. "I know some Cooleys," I said. "And I worked at Krogers with a girl from Lanks, Sarah Crimpton, but she moved to Ohio to live with her brother."

The kid sat up, pushing the blanket from his face, and seemed to stare past me to my reflection in the windshield. "Ain't you Riley Butts' brother? The moonshiner's boy?" he said.

I didn't know how to answer that. I'd never thought that Riley and I looked that much alike, I'm darker and able to grow a beard in a week, while Riley's fair-haired and can go a month without shaving, but I guess we're similar enough to the folks down home who remember every family's peculiar features and tics. I said, "Riley's my brother. My father's dead."

Reverend Willis didn't say anything. He checked the side mirror and eased the van back onto the ramp and out onto the highway. Snow devils swirled over the black pavement, but the snow was dry and the wind from the traffic kept it from sticking to the asphalt. It felt as good on my tongue as any whiskey I'd ever drunk to hear my own accent again and the names of places I knew. Even the names of the dead, like my father, and the long lost, like Sarah Crimpton, spoken in Lucius's sonorous mountain drawl, were a comfort to my soul, and as I heard them again in my head I felt the Yankee winter slipping from my shoulders.

The van rattled, and the wind buffeting the butterfly window on the driver's side pierced the cabin with a low whistle like someone signaling in the dark. My fingertips tingled as they thawed, and my throat, raw from singing in the frigid wind, ached. The loose rocking of the van in the wind and the rushing heat made me drowsy, but I got a brief attack of the whirlies whenever I closed my eyes. Soon, the kid was snoring, and Reverend Willis backed the heat down when I began to sniffle. I didn't say much, and neither did Reverend Willis until we were slowed down by an accident near Hartford." I hope we can get back for tomorrow's service," he said, his voice firm but quiet. "I promised the congregation I'd be there."

I don't know why, but I turned to him and blurted out, "We'll make it. I can feel it."

He smiled and said, "Do you often feel things, Mr. Butts?"

"As much as most folks, I imagine," I said. Then I said, "My name's Isaac, but all my life I've been called Ize, on account of how when my Daddy used to ask me to do something if I didn't get right on it he'd make fun of me and say, 'Ize gonna do it Daddy, Ize is.'"

"Do you believe you see things others don't?" the Reverend asked.

I laughed. I've always done that when I've wanted an extra second to answer a question. "On a bender," I said. "I've seen

19

beautiful sights, but later, in the hospital when the DT's were on me hard, I've seen all kinds of terrible visions. Spiders, snakes."

"What about when you're sober?"

"Then I see what most folks see, I guess."

Reverend Willis began to describe miracles he said he'd witnessed: the blind seeing, the deaf hearing, twisted legs healed, tumors shrunk away, demons cast out—"All," he said, "By God's power and grace." Leaning toward me, his eyes still focused on the highway he said, "No whiskey vision can compare with a glimpse of God's eternal love and power."

Reverend Willis spoke, low and steady, about the next world and while I loved the lilt in his ragged drawl, I was swelled with a sudden sorrow for Ella, for Riley and all his troubles with Lillian, and for my mother. I also felt a sudden and stinging sorrow for the two men the Old Man had shot and buried in an abandoned mine shaft and for all the dead I'd known and those never met. As Reverend Willis's voice, more music than speech, laved my ears, I even began to pity Fred's ostrich, and wondered if it were dead, too.

The Reverend kept talking and humming as he drove, sometimes taking his right hand off the steering wheel to flex his fingers, his eyes riveted to the road ahead. He told me, without raising his voice more than necessary to be heard over the wind and traffic, that though I'd had one father die, I had another in heaven and a savior in Jesus Christ, waiting to take me in. When I didn't say anything, Reverend Wills sat up straight in his seat and began to sing, What a Friend We Have In Jesus, asking me to sing each line back to him, as he tapped time on the dash with his right hand. When we'd sung the song three times, the last time in unison, my voice as creaky as a thirteen-year old boy, Reverend Willis began to pray for me. "Lord, I ask You to send the Holy Ghost to Isaac, Your child, made in Your image," he said. "Cleanse his soul, bring him peace from his travails. Maranatha, come, Jesus, come." Then he said, "Close your eyes, Isaac, remember the faith of your namesake's father, embrace the true belief of Abraham."

Though I had no clear idea of what he meant, I shut my eyes. He hummed and the whirlies subsided as a freight train rush of adrenaline spiked up and down my legs and burned in the tips of my fingers. I kept my eyes shut, and though my body ached, and I had to swallow down a sea of yawns, I didn't want to sleep. Reverend Willis crooned hymns and spoke to me for hours, pausing only to ask if I understood what he said, until outside Scranton, Pennsylvania, when we stopped to add oil to the engine on the stony shoulder of Interstate 81, I promised my life to God.

Since that moment I have tried to recall the ocean of relief that swamped me then. I cried as hard as I had as a kid when the Old Man had worn out my ass with his strap, or when I was real little and I'd heard him take it to Mama. I didn't sob out loud, but my stomach and chest heaved and my temples throbbed. As Reverend Willis prayed, I remembered Fred telling me about how he had crooned to the ostrich until he was able to lead it into the field, and I remembered the stormy sorrow scratched into Ella's face when she'd said that her father was sick, and when she'd told me about her baby's father running off. Even now, I can't recall the exact words Reverend Willis said that persuaded me to promise to follow the Lord as best I could, but the feeling they engendered in me, the soothing, boiling warmth in my heart and groin and head and soul are seared deeper into my memory than the shock of April creek water on my naked flesh.

Reverend Willis leaned against the van and pointed out the morning star emerging from a small spill of moonlit cloud in the chilled night sky, dipped the tip of his little finger into the mouth of the empty bottle of Castrol 30 weight, and anointed my forehead with an oily cross. Lucius, who'd been jarred awake as the van crossed the rumble strip onto the breakdown lane, emerged to take a leak, and when Reverend Willis told him what had happened, he cried, too, repeating, "Jesus, oh sweet, Jesus," over and over between snuffles. They knelt next to me, arms laid on my shoulders, as Reverend Willis prayed for a few minutes among the weeds and litter beside the highway, semis storming past us, and the van's engine clicking in the dark as I felt my heart hurry and my blood surge against my skin.

Rolling south toward home, the thrumming of the van on the pavement, the whistle of the vent window, the resonant steady cadence of Reverend Willis thanking the Lord for my deliverance, the throb in my heart, and Lucius' snoring, surrounded me as sweet and close as a cloak of honey.

As we descended from the interstate, a soft fog, like the one I'd seen rise off the river in Bangor, hovered over Blissfull. Reverend Willis coasted the van down the deserted grade, taking the curves wide and slow, as if not to upset the boxes in the back or bounce Lucius around as he sat cross-legged on his pallet.

Reverend Willis dropped Lucius at the end of his road, and, as I watched his lanky frame disappear into the mist toting a small duffel bag, I thought about Ella trudging up her Kentucky ridge, or calling her kin from the bus station hoping someone might fetch her home, a cold lump rising up into my parched throat. As the last trace of the kid was absorbed into the fog, I realized that I had stayed up all night and tried to remember the last time I'd done that sober, but couldn't.

While helping Reverend Willis unload the van, I learned the reason for his trip north, which had taken him as far as Maine. Each of the brass-edged boxes had held a serpent. He told me that it had been his last trip north for the year, and he'd been unable to provide each of the congregations with as many serpents as they'd hoped for. "There are so many who needed them that I could have sold a hundred more," he said. "Now the serpents have gone deep into their dens. I caught the last I could spare during a sunny spell in early October."

Reverend Willis and I sat side by side in gray folding chairs for an hour in the Star of Morning Church, housed in the long-vacant former Blissfull Auto Parts store, while he explained to me about the peace of Jesus, and the way God will forgive any sin to a true believer. He quoted a little scripture, but mostly he talked about the strength he'd gained, "When he committed himself to the Lord, and was born again into faith."

Reverend Willis wasn't like the holiness preachers I'd seen around Blissfull; wiry farmers and miners who got the call to preach and held their services in people's houses or in tiny wood-framed churches they punched into the hillside at the head a holler. He didn't seem self-taught like the men that Riley and I loved sneaking down to the creek on Sunday afternoons to spy on as they baptized the converted. Those scrawny crow-voiced hill preachers, cracked-leather Bibles clutched to their chests, or hands above their heads waving like hay in the wind, would call upon Jesus at the top of their lungs to baptize and heal those they were dunking beneath the dark water, and the gathered would shout their amens and praises so they'd echo along the ridge line like gunshots. Sometimes those being baptized would wear white robes, but just as often they'd stride into the current in their everyday clothes, get dunked, and come up sputtering and praising Jesus, while the saved clapped and prayed on the creek bank. Except for the lack of cussing such gatherings could have been mistaken for a turkey shoot. I remember one cool Sunday in September, near the end of the outdoor baptizing season when we were hidden in a maze of mountain laurel, suggesting to Riley that it might be fun to skip a few stones across the pool at them, but he said the Old Man would flay us alive if we did anything to rile any of the religious folk up against him. "Bootleggers and Primitive Baptists got to get along he'd said, "Because one way or the other it behooves us both to keep this county dry."

Dusty light began to stream through the filmy store front windows casting grainy shadows across the stage and altar, and I knew that the fog was burning off, that the light was rising above the hills, and that the sun would soon crest the higher peaks to the east. Reverend Wills, his face drawn and eyes cross-hatched with fatigue, stifled a yawn with his hand. "I need to rest awhile," he said, "But I'd be pleased to run you up the ridge," he said.

I'd always walked up the ridge when I'd come home before, so I said, "I'd be pleased if you could drop me at the gravel."

As I hopped down from the van Reverend Willis said, "You're always welcomed at Star of Morning, Isaac," and pressed a business card into my hand that read, Reverend Theobald Willis, Signs Preacher. "Trust in Jesus, Ize," he said, "There is no greater love in this world than God's. We know that because He gave us His only son to redeem us."

I waved as he turned around and headed down into Blissfull.

The hike up the ridge is pretty at any time of the year. That morning, the peaks of the higher mountains, flecked white, contrasted with the dark, leafless trees and brown grass in the fields. The creek ran hard and flocks of birds hovered in the low bushes like bugs hatching over a pond in the spring. Wherever I looked, I saw signs or traces of my life along the road. I passed the clump of bushes where I'd first seen a naked girl, Lorena Whipple, the place where the creek washes out the road every spring, the brace of pines where I'd shot my first deer, and the bent hickory tree I hit when Riley was teaching me to drive the Old Man's truck, which reminded me of the whipping I'd gotten for bending up the fender, and the whipping reminded me of the way Daddy took the strap to Mama for telling Riley it was okay to show me how to drive in the first place, and the way he stopped hitting any of us when Riley opened his forehead with a wrench and his blood had dripped down into his craggy face.

Pausing to catch my breath and to gaze back into the valley, I remembered a VA psychiatrist in Beckley who said I drank and ran away from people because of what my father had done, and because Mama had never fetched me and Riley. But over time I have realized that's just shrink shit. I know now that I drank because I liked the taste of whiskey, and I liked being drunk better than being in school, or the army, or working for the Old Man. I drank because the ghosts who pester you at night when you're sober can't find you when you're passed out. I also knew, as I cast my eyes over the broad gap in the mountains that is Blissfull, that I was going home, one way or the other for the last time, that I was in the end no different than Ella, because though I'd tried to live away from where my blood was born, I had never discovered the means to sever the cord.

I was a quarter mile below the house when Riley's dog, Patches, scented me, and bounded down the hill. A good dog never forgets you, and we'd been keeping one from every bitch's litter who'd descended from the Old Man's best watchdog, Devil, a, black and tan mixed-breed with a nose for friend and foe, for as long as I could remember. Patches jumped up all around me kicking up dust, covering ten feet for each of my strides, sprinting on ahead then doubling back to be sure I was really coming home.

I stood on the porch petting Patches, who'd ceased barking, and Roxie, Riley's breeding bitch, staring a long time at the hills, before I knocked. It was early still, not yet full light, which takes its time to sneak into and illuminate the narrow hollers and balds on the steeper hills, especially in the cold months. Summoning the courage to waken the house, I peered down the ridge watching the day crack open over the valley, listening to the creek singing and the wind grating the tops of the dead grass in the field.

I gave a soft shave-and-a-hair-cut-two-bits knock, and Lillian, barefoot and in her nightgown, answered the door. It had been three weeks since Ella had gone and I felt the first great temptation of my new Christian life avoiding staring at the soft curve of my former sister-in-law's calves and the outlines of her nipples. She looked me up and down, and it was easy to see again why Riley had been so crazy to marry her, and why he'd been fighting to win her back, but the expression on her face was less than welcoming. "Your Mama's sick," she said, "Riley rode the bus to Detroit, because his truck is down at Earl's Garage. I'm staying with the kids till he gets back." Then peering hard into my eyes she said, "You sober?"

"I've been saved." I said.

"Jesus fucking Christ," Lillian said, retreating a step into the

25

house, "The god damned Prodigal Son. I hope you're a less tedious Christian than you were a drunk, as I generally like drunks better. Come in before I freeze my butt off out here."

As I stepped through the door, the kids, Annie and Carleton, leaped up from the couch where they'd been watching TV and rushed me. When I bent down to hug them they shied away from my smell, but as I stood up they each grabbed me by a leg. On the days Riley had them, during the stretches I lived at the old place, life was pretty loose. Annie, particularly, complained that Lillian was too strict with them so after school, when Riley generally wasn't home, I'd just about give them the run of the place, which had not endeared me to their mother. As I lowered my pack off my back, the kids clung to me like burrs, asking me where I'd been, and telling me about an upcoming Christmas pageant until something on the television captured their attention and they threw themselves back on the couch.

I straightened my back and turned to Lillian, "How sick is my mother?" I asked.

She motioned me toward the kitchen, and I followed her. "Female cancer," she said in a half-whisper. "Best get at your praying if you expect to see her again."

I didn't have time for the news to find my heart before the kids, distracted from the show by a commercial, tore into the kitchen and began peppering me with questions and asking if I'd stay for Christmas. "If you want Uncle Ize to tell you about that, turn off the TV," Lillian said, "I've got to shower."

I slumped on the couch and told the kids stories about Holyoke and the ghosts I'd seen at Plourde's, which prompted Annie to howl and Carleton to spit out, "boo" and raise his fingers like claws and growl. Though I'd been gone more than a year, the kids didn't seem any older to me, and the way they sat close to me on the couch, though I was near as fragrant as picked skunk cabbage, felt as good as a hot shower and clean socks after a week on the bum. Sitting between them and fighting to keep from listing in either direction, my back cramped up, and weariness, deep as the Massachusetts cold, shuddered through me. I'd slammed my eyelids tight against the brightness of the morning firing the front window to wrestle with the whirlies. My mind began drifting back to the highway and Reverend Willis's singing, when Annie punched my shoulder and said, "Wake up sleepyhead," which sent her brother into gales of laughter, and I bolted up straight.

In the few minutes that I'd been asleep, I dreamed of my mother, young, sitting on the porch step with Riley and me, watching a kettle of hawks rise on a spring thermal and drift from sight. I have no idea whether it was a memory I'd conjured or a fantasy, but in the dream my mother's face wore none of the weariness I was accustomed to seeing there before she left, and I pondered a moment if the vision was what Reverend Willis meant when he asked me if I saw things, things that maybe not everyone saw. I blinked to wet my eyes, dry from the long night in the van and from the dry heat of the woodstove, wondering what my mother's last conscious thoughts would be and hoped they might be a vision of the view from the ridge and that my brother and I might be there.

Lillian got dressed and fixed breakfast. The coffee was strong, the ham crisp on the edges, and the eggs runny as she remembered I prefer them. The kids tore through their food then ran back to the living room while Lillian and I lingered at the table. When I started to get up for more coffee Lillian said, "Be still, you've had a long night. I'll get it." I sat back down as if following an order. "Kids are glad to see you," she said, refilling my mug. Those words and the perfection of the meal made me feel as if I'd been granted an absolution or at least a truce, but all I could muster was, "Thanks, Lillian."

I craved sleep, but Annie was sprawled across the couch fiddling with the TV remote, Carleton was sitting in the recliner coloring in a book, and there was no spare bed now that each of them had their own room. I stood in front of the front window watching the sun climb over the ridges to the south and gazing over the valley toward Blissfull. I imagined my mother dying in a Detroit hospital, the nurses assuring her in their flat Midwestern voices that the pain would pass, and I realized that I didn't even know if her husband, Alvin, was still alive. Barbs of sorrow snagged in my heart, and I felt a darkness welling in me, the kind that has often sent me to the bottle searching for some oblivion. I felt my eyes welling up, and, as I didn't want to tear up in front of Lillian or the kids, I announced that I was going out for a walk.

"You'd rather sleep," Lillian said, "Get in our bed. I'm washing sheets today anyway."

The full thrust of sorrow invaded in my guts when Lillian said our bed, because she and Riley were, as far as I knew, still divorced, and because I'd helped Riley haul it in the house and set it up—a canopied, queen-size, four-poster he'd found in an antique store over in Virginia. Riley had been so proud of it that I knew that I couldn't crawl in there and smell Lillian's scent in the sheets. "Maybe later," I said, "I need some air."

I didn't have to tell Lillian why I was going for a walk. Riley and I, whenever vexed by death, or illness, or trouble with the law, or to avoid the Old Man, have gone for walks in the hills. It's easier to think there and sometimes steeping in your own darkness is the best way out of it. I set out through the field, west toward a place where the creek races through a narrow gorge, the thunder of the water blocking out the sounds of the world.

I crashed a half hour later on a flat sunny spot, the roar of the water as soothing as late night radio static. It wasn't that warm, but when you've dropped off in the weeds as often as I have you can sleep anywhere. I've been rousted by the cops after passing out on the main drag sidewalks and alleys of dozens of towns and cities, so when I can find a soft spot on the ground, with some shelter, even a scrubby bush in a public park, I can slumber on like a baby in a bassinette. I guess I'm a little bit like a rattlesnake I once saw on a cool morning wrapped around an old pot near one of Daddy's stills dozing in the sun, drawing the warmth from the copper. I can find comfort in hostile places.

As I conked out, I thought about Riley and Lillian and the kids, wondering if I should have spared them a last look at me, if all I had done was come home to die. Thinking

I'd been selfish and gutless to bring my personal darkness home to the ridge, I pondered a moment if Reverend Willis and his religion, in some tangible sense, might save me from my own hand.

Lillian is a registered nurse. She got her schooling at Morgantown and met Riley at the hospital after he'd stepped on a rotten board and driven a rusty spike clean through the top of his foot. I know why Riley is crazy for Lillian, but I can't begin to see what she saw in him. With all the young doctors who work off their medical school loans down here then move away, odds are good that she could have married one of them and long departed these parts for the suburbs of Atlanta or Chicago or New York. But I guess the hills get into just about everyone who grows up here, and she has one of the few jobs that survive about any economic misery or setback. As for Riley, he believes that he has some inherent mountain magnetism, that's his phrase for it, that Lillian finds sexy and irresistible, despite the fact that when the kids were still little she divorced him and took them to her own place in town. Whatever his charm is, Lillian's been able to resist its pull for long stretches of time, and I had no reason to believe that she would succumb to it again for very long.

Riley's his own boss, selling firewood and hauling logs for the local sawmills, picking up skidder work and other odd jobs like clearing lots, and, traditionally, tends a discrete but lucrative crop of high-class weed. It was the dope that sent Lillian packing. He promised her that he was long done with that before they got married, but she found out a few months before the debacle with Fred's ostrich, when she discovered six grand cached in a plastic bag at the bottom of the flour canister, that it was an ongoing enterprise. That night after the kids were asleep, the creek running hard in the distance and an owl hooting up the dark, I listened as she dragged him out to the porch and said, "I'll work my tail off, content to be poor, but I'll not allow my children to be raised around any goddamn weed or fucking moonshine, Riley," she'd said, "You swore you were out of all that and you fucking lied to me. Choice is yours, no bullshit, no more, or you can live up here all alone."

Riley insisted that he was in the process of getting out of the business, and mustered his best effort at soothing her rage, but I could tell by the silence, which greeted each of his excuses and promises, that Lillian was resisting his charm. Riley doesn't have the Old Man's meanness. He would never raise a hand to Lillian or the kids, but I believe he'd add a crop poacher to Daddy's pile of enemies at the bottom of the mine, if he thought his freedom depended on it. I know Lillian sensed that about him and it terrified her. That fear, and the fact that she's as fierce as a she owl about Carleton and Annie, hovering over them till she about smothers them in concern, unlike Riley who indulges them, fomented more than one spat between them and, after months of pitched battles, coaxed her off the ridge.

When I got back to the house, Lillian, dressed in jeans and a sweatshirt, was standing on the porch talking on the cordless phone. I'd been intercepted by Patches and Roxie, and stood stroking their heads and reading Lillian's face. I knew before she held her hand over the mouthpiece and said, "Ize, I'm sorry," that Mama was gone.

I slumped on the steps and listened to her side of the conversation with Riley, but I didn't really hear what she said. I wanted a drink, one I could already feel blistering my toes, a hard long gulp of 'shine, but I knew I wouldn't have one, at least not until Riley had come home. I kicked at small stones in the dooryard stunned to think that I'd become an orphan and a Christian in an eye blink, and I figured that if Reverend Willis was to be believed that The Lord must have intended both to happen to me. I remembered the relief, almost happiness, I'd felt when the hospital called and I knew that the Old Man was off to hell, and though I figured God had taken Mama to heaven away from her worldly sorrows, I wasn't prepared for the terrible ache, or the salty tears, and dark remorse roiling in the core of my soul, knowing she died so far away, in a place where I had never mustered the courage to go and find her.

Lillian laid the phone on the porch railing. "Riley says he'll be home in a few days. He's bringing your Mama with him. He wants to bury her here. I couldn't talk him out of it."

"How's he going do that?" I asked

"Didn't say," she said. "He just insisted he was going to bury her on the ridge in her family plot."

As the sun warmed my face, I recalled how The Old Man had asked to be cremated and buried on the ridge. Riley made the arrangements and I'd offered to help him spread the ashes up in the hills, but he kept putting it off. While I was at the VA dentist in Beckley, he fed the ash and bone to Fred's pigs. I'd have just tossed him into the wind and let it go at that, and when I asked Riley why he'd done it that way, he said, "He called all of us worthless as shit a million times, so turning him into pig shit was fair enough." I understood that, but I wasn't convinced that Mama would want her final resting place to be this ridge regardless of the final disposal of her first husband's remains.

CHAPTER THREE

The following Thursday at three-thirty in the afternoon, the sun a descending glimmer behind the ridge, Riley backed into the yard in a four wheel drive, F-150, long bed pickup with a tonneau cover, front-mounted winch, sporting temporary Michigan plates, and sounded the horn. Spying the new red rig through the window, it took me a micro-second to infer that he'd bought it with the profits from the bounty of a good harvest, having left West Virginia intent on bringing Mama home in style, and in a Ford at that. I eased up from the kitchen table where I'd been helping Lillian peel carrots for a stew, grabbed my coat from the peg on the door and went outside.

The first thing I noticed as Riley opened the tailgate to fish his suitcase from the bed, was that Mama's coffin wasn't there, and all I could think of was the time Fred lost the ostrich. "Where's Mama?" I said before saying hello.

"I intended to haul her myself," Riley said, "But Michigan law don't allow it so I spent three damn days and a pile of cash to arrange for her to be shipped down to Beckley." He let that settle before adding, "She's due at the train station Saturday."

The kids bounced out of the house behind Lillian, both screaming, "What did you bring us?" only to be disappointed to discover that Riley hadn't returned with gifts. He said, "The new truck is a present for the whole family," slipping his arm around Lillian's waist. She moved off with a frown, and Riley donned a pout that seemed to say, "You could be nice to me after my Mama died and I drove nine hours to get home," but what he did say was, "We'll all go for a ride later on."

Lillian and Riley headed inside, the kids racing ahead of them, while I lingered in the dooryard admiring the truck. Leaning on the hood and staring back at the house, I saw Lillian and Riley in the kitchen and envied my brother. He was divorced from a beautiful woman with a good job, but even the pale flicker of hope in his heart that he might get Lillian back trumped any of my prospects. I cringed to think at how little she'd be impressed by the new truck, and I knew she'd damn sure grill him on how he got the money to pay for it, but I hoped that she'd temper her desire to know until we'd had a chance to give Mama a decent burial.

I was in the bone chilled, as the sun cached itself behind the ridge, but didn't rush inside in order to allow Riley time with Lillian and the kids before he sought me out to discover what had brought me home. Encountering my chalky face in the truck's side view mirror, pierced with a four-day stubble, I wondered if anyone in Blissfull would ever give me a job, something I knew I'd need if I were to finally settle on the ridge. I'd worn out my local favors, and even if someone didn't know me, they'd learn soon enough from the grapevine that I was the drunken son of the dead moonshiner, Burleigh Butts. But in that bleak moment, I was cheered by the odd calm that had swamped me since Reverend Willis had anointed me, and I was soothed by the sound of my kin in my ears. Gazing up at the white and purple peaks to the west, I realized that I didn't want to leave home again, either as crow bait on a snowy hillside, or as a drunken traveler stumbling toward his final end, but that it would take more than a job to keep me in Blissfull. No matter how strong a hold the Lord had on me, the pull of women has long fought for control of my soul with the sweet sting of whiskey, and though I might learn to live without hooch, my other preferred pleasure of the flesh, if ignored, would drive me back to the bottle. If Lillian were to be around regularly, the situation could only be worse.

I shivered down into my coat and closed my eyes. Listening to the creek racing over the old stones, I imagined building my own place beyond the edge of the field, letting the daydream run until I saw a vision of Ella trudging alone up a long gravel grade, her facing morphing into my mother's, and wondered how, with all the old ghosts who haunt me, I would survive the trials ahead.

As the dark deepened, I could make out Lillian and Riley in the kitchen, and could tell by the way he gestured with his arms and hands that he was telling her about some difficulty he'd had to overcome in making the arrangements to get Mama home, but I also knew by the squint in Lillian's eyes and the pucker in her cheeks that Riley's mountain magnetism was having little effect.

I swung my eyes toward the front room, the blue glow of the TV cast against the drawn curtains as if a movie was being projected on them. Carleton's face emerged between a slit in the curtains, his breath fogging the pane as he peered out the front window. Seeing his nose flat against the window, my heart was washed again with the terror that hits me each time I limp home, the fear that when I next leave it will be for the final time, and in that instant, I remembered the revolver stashed in the ceiling of his room.

As they sat across the table from each other lit up by the kitchen lights, my brother leaning forward on his elbows and Lillian tilted back in her chair, I marveled at how much of the time since I'd come back that I'd sinned by dreaming about her. Four days of living in the house with only Lillian and the kids had taxed my new faith, especially as each day she displayed an increasing respect for my sobriety and I pondered on how on the second morning I was back, when she had ascertained that I was in "a sober period," as she put it, Lillian worked a double shift, and trusted me with the kids. The phone had rung at six, and a minute later Lillian awakened me from a dream about Ella, by nearly yanking me off the couch. "Ize, I need you to help me get the kids going. There's been a bad wreck in the fog on the interstate, they're sending some of the injured to us," she said, her hair still wet from the shower, her breath sweet with toothpaste. "If you'll get breakfast going, I'll lay out their clothes."

I fished the milk from the fridge, grabbed a few boxes of cereal from the cupboard and set two places on the table. I popped bread in the toaster, poured milk into a sauce pan for cocoa, and was buttering the first slice of toast when Carleton and Annie slunk into the kitchen rubbing the sand and sleep from their eyes. Lillian swept into the room behind them snugging up her jeans and rummaging in her purse for her keys. "Annie Elizabeth and Carleton Louis, you help Uncle Ize make your lunches and do as he says. Do not miss the bus," she said. "Mama may be home late."

I trailed Lillian into the living room where, as she sat on the couch lacing up her boots, she gave me last minute instructions, then bolted up, took a deep breath, kissed me on the cheek as she might have done to Riley once and said, "Thanks, Ize," and hustled out the door.

Twelve and ten, Annie and Carleton mostly take care of themselves. They went to school and came home on time. Annie adores being the oldest and watches her little brother about as well as a grownup, though she does tend to give him cookies when he acts up, which just riles him up more. When Lillian was home, and Riley was in Michigan, she did things with them to lure them away from the television—a distraction Riley and I never had as kids—but once they were in bed she would sit in the kitchen drinking tea and reading a magazine or newspaper, or talk with me.

A few times the subject of my new faith came up, but she didn't want to really talk about it. She said she'd seen plenty of jailhouse and deathbed conversions, and she said, "Time will tell the story," preferring to share hospital gossip, or the details of spectacular highway wrecks or mining accidents. Lillian loved the house warm like the hospital, and kept the woodstove stoked and the furnace chugging along as well. Even in her baggy nurse greens, a man could see the curves of her hips and backside, and my longing for Ella, or someone like her, became physically painful. I remembered from a Sally preacher that I was not supposed to alleviate it myself, but I figured that sin was less offensive to God than sneaking down to the Delbert Hotel and scaring up one of the three or four local semi-pros who work out of the bar there—not that I could have afforded it or would have stayed sober enough to fully enjoy it.

I turned my back to the house and stared out over a dark Blissfull, reclining deep into remembering, the cold gnawing at my ears, visions of Lillian in her scrubs and of Ella, bony and naked with a weak spear of the October afternoon light stabbing at the sheets and glinting on her toes, plaguing my heart. I was shocked from my visions when Riley bounced out the door. "Good to see you back, Ize," he said, slapping me on my shoulder. "Let me show you the new rig."

The truck featured an AM/FM radio, CD player, built-in phone, which he didn't have any service for yet and wouldn't have worked on the ridge if he did, and two jump seats behind the front seat for the kids. When he showed me those seats and "their individual storage bins" sounding as I imagined the salesman who'd sold him the rig did, I knew he was imagining riding front up Lillian, Annie and Carleton ensconced in the back. That depressed me because I knew Lillian had been seeing a guy named Rob, a manager at Krogers, something she trusted me with when I'd asked her if she was back to stay. "I don't know what will happen, Ize," she'd said. "And lord don't tell Riley. We're not going together, and we haven't done anything—I just get squirrelly in town by myself."

When Riley had finished explaining all the bells and whistles on the truck, which I knew was a dress rehearsal for showing them off to Lillian, I asked him if he would run me into town. I figured if he was going to have any chance with Lillian, he'd need some privacy to assert his mountain magnetism, and between my lust for Lillian and missing Ella, I wanted be somewhere without any booze handy.

As I inched the Star of Morning door open, I heard Reverend Willis singing, but in the room's darkness I couldn't make out where he was. "Come in Ize," he said, "And close the door." It took a few seconds for my eyes to get acclimated to the light and to spy Reverend Willis standing on the altar stage. He stepped down off the platform and said, "Follow me." He pointed to a door to the left of the altar on the opposite side of the room from the piano and organ. Reverend Willis opened it and I followed him down a flight of stairs. The basement was one large room with hewn chestnut beams, a concrete floor, brick walls, and a half-dozen steel support columns. Along the back wall were a series of shelves with serpent boxes. I detected a faint rattling and felt a chill, though the room was warmed by a coal furnace. "Low light makes the serpents happier," Reverend Willis said, "In the winter we have to feed them. In the warm months we only keep them a few weeks, returning them to their dens to multiply."

The next few minutes seemed to last an hour as Reverend Willis plucked white mice from a cage on one of the shelves, held them by their tails in his left hand, opened some of the serpent boxes with his right, and dropped them in. "I keep only one serpent per box. Other signs people keep many together, but as it is hard to know the males from the females, and I do not mix the ox and the ass, so to speak, mine live in their own boxes. I believe it makes them more difficult to handle."

My throat was as swelled with sour bile as if I'd thrown up some Antabuse. With a sudden shudder, I recalled when I was twelve and the Old Man called me to see a copperhead he'd pinned against a stump with an iron rake. He ordered me to kill it with an Army machete. I lopped of its head with a fierce swing and the rest of the body wriggled free from the rake tines. "Pick it up, can't hurt you now," the Old Man said. When I balked, he grabbed the writhing tail and flailed it like a whip across my back and head, laughing the entire time. I backed away from him, but I knew that I'd get a whipping if I ran. "Here," he said thrusting the twitching tail toward me, "Hold in your teeth like a knife you damn cornholer pansy." In the end he'd forced the dead snake inside my shirt and pushed me to the ground, my face landing near the bloody head. Even though it was freshly dead, the snake was cold and hard against my skin and when I flinched, the Old Man cackled and tried to trap me on the ground with his foot. I wriggled away and pulled the dead snake from beneath my shirt and flung it as far from me as I could. "Fetch it back here, now," the Old Man snarled at me. I searched in the brush as if I was looking for it, though when I spied headless body, I kept kicking it further from me toward the ditch alongside the road. I doubled back as if I'd missed it and after a while the Old Man called my name. When I looked up, he stared through me for a few seconds and said, "Couldn't find your dick with both hands or know what to do with it if you did," and turned away and walked off.

My jaw tensed and my mouth watered as I watched Reverend Willis seize another mouse. "Sometimes we will see the miracle of serpent birth right here in our church, but not often," Reverend Willis said as he dropped the squirming mouse into a serpent box and fastened the lid. I watched in silence as he worked. When he was done he turned to me and said, "Has the Lord continued to watch over you?"

I didn't know what to say. I glanced at the serpent boxes and heard the tick of the coal fire. After a few seconds I managed to spit out, "I haven't backslid into drinking."

Revered Willis's face crinkled into a smile. "Let's go upstairs, Ize," he said, his voice low and hoarse, "I want to show you something."

Reverend Willis had a small office behind the altar in what had likely been a closet or storeroom. There were bookcases, a desk, a computer, and piles of newspapers and magazines. He motioned for me to sit in the chair. "Look up toward heaven, Ize," he said. I leaned back in the chair and on the gleaming white tin of the ceiling above me was stenciled:

And these signs shall follow them that believe; In my name they shall cast out devils; they shall speak with new tongues; They shall take up serpents; and if they drink any deadly thing, it shall not hurt them; they shall lay hands on the sick, and they shall recover. Mark 16.

I felt Reverend Willis's hands on my shoulders. "Those words are the basis of our church, Ize," he said. "Many other well-meaning people believe we are ignorant and foolish, but I know the power of my belief and the great forgiveness of God. Even other serpent handlers have not noticed the subtle beauty of God's grace in those words. It says we will cast out devils, take up serpents and lay on hands to heal. It says, if we drink poison, we will not be hurt. It doesn't say we have to do that, it is not commanded of us, but if we should be poisoned by an enemy of the Lord, He will deliver us."

I felt the Reverend's grip tighten on me, and a sweet, sleepy torpor invade my body, the way a shot of whisky does when you're beset by the shakes. Taking a sip from a glass on his desk he said. "I drink only water, pure as I can find. No poisons, alcohol, carbonation, or sugar." He paused and raised the glass to his lips again and said, "I drink only what the serpent drinks."

Reverend Willis released his hands from my shoulders and I stood up. He stared at me and said that I had the eyes of a changed man. "You're not sure of yourself, Ize, but Jesus will change that."

Reverend Willis gave me a King James Bible, fresh from its wrapper, and told me to begin reading it. I asked him if I should just begin on page one and try to slog my way to the end, but he said, "Open it and read. God will guide you. Head home now and find a quiet place to study His Word."

It was full dark when I got home, the sky above the ridge littered with stars and the great swath of The Milky Way. Two planes blinked along the far horizon. Lillian's car was gone. Riley was sitting in the truck, the window cracked to the night, listening to a Conway and Loretta CD. Through a part in the living room curtains, I could see the faint blue glow of the television. Riley looked up when Patches began to bark to welcome me. He popped out of the truck and turned to meet me. "Lillian says you got religion from that snake handler," he said.

"Hey to you, too," I said.

"I don't care what you believe, but Lillian will get my joint custody revoked if you start bringing snakes in here. I won't have it."

"You sell reefer, but you won't have snakes?"

"I'm out of that. I'm working on getting Lillian back. Put most all of last year's profits into the truck and thirty acres of timber down ridge."

"I stopped drinking and you stopped growing herb. The Old Man must be turning over in hell," I said.

Riley leaned back against the truck. He picked at something

in the palm of his left hand. "I don't care what that bastard does in hell, but tomorrow we're going to dig Mama's grave in her family plot up on the ridge. Put her between her grandfolks. There's room there."

"How are we going get her up there?"

"That's why I bought the truck," Riley said.

It was a hard slog to the burial plot. Mama's family's place had burned down when I was about six, probably torched by the Old Man. It wasn't much to begin with, real old style, hide windows in the winter, homemade screens in the summer, just a shed roof, like a lean to, with one big room and a half loft. The water was gravity-fed from a spring, and they kept a fire year round in a cast iron stove for heat and cooking. It was about four miles up the ridgeline and another mile into the woods from our place. If Mama's people hadn't gone regular to church, Daddy might never have seen her passing by the house on Sundays, and might never have eloped with her to Kentucky.

Riley and I worked to make an opening in a stonewall the Old Man had forced us to build to hide the way in to one of his stills, then took the chainsaw to some deadfalls to open enough road for the truck. It had been a few years since anyone had driven there, the ruts matted with frost-killed thatch, though the track was still evident. Where the sun shone there was mud, but in the shaded-over spots the puddles were sheeted in shell ice. The graying, sugary remains of a late November snow were blown up into rippled waves in the woods, and lay several inches deep in the dark holds of the thickets.

Mama's family plot held just two graves, her mother's parents, Evangeline and Virgil Thurl. I never knew them, and Riley has only a vague memory of them as they were both carried off by a spring flu when he was four. A year or two after Mama and the Old Man eloped, her parents and her lone sister, leaving her grandparents behind, moved north and she lost contact with them. If, once she was in Detroit, Mama ever located them, she never told us.

I'd loaded the truck bed with shovels, a pick, a peavey, a come-along in case we had to heft any logs up, and an extra thirty feet of chain for the winch, having buried enough whiskey to know that West Virginia is a damn rocky place that gets rockier by the foot as you climb up out of the bottomlands.

The digging was miserable and Riley and I got to fighting over the whole thing. I told him that I intended to ask Reverend Willis to say some words over Mama, but he said she'd long left the church and he took pains to remind me about the preacher who'd beat her. When I told him that Reverend Willis had said that preacher was wrong, Riley exploded saying, "You should never have told anyone outside the family 'bout what had happened to her. You been with Yankees too fucking long, Ize," he said, slamming his shovel into the stony earth.

"Bullshit," I said, standing up to stretch. "Every soul deserves some words said over them by a preacher."

Riley flung his shovel across the grave at me, but I dodged it. "This ain't no damn snake handler's business, and I don't give a fuck what you think about that," he said.

"She'd have it done for you," I said.

"I brought her home," Riley said, "That'll give her more peace than any damn preacher."

Riley will never concede a point, and I didn't want to get run off the ridge by a disagreement, so I didn't answer. Instead, I tossed him his shovel, and resumed digging.

My hands blistered quickly, and my back ached, but I was glad to be out in the mountain air. Once, when I was resting on my shovel, I looked off toward Blissfull where the sun cast an orange glow over the valley that reminded me of the nighttime fires in Holyoke, which got me to thinking about Ella. The images that swirled in my mind of the fires recalled the muzzle flash of the rifles we fired on the night ranges in Texas, and that got me to thinking about the revolver in the ceiling of Carleton's room, and envisioning him glued to toy ads on the TV reminded me that it was less than two weeks to Christmas, which got me to thinking about Lillian, so I threw myself back at hacking through roots and scouring out stones.

By noon, we were but half done. We had one big rock to dig out that would gain us considerable depth that Riley had managed to work a foot or so of a long crowbar under. I had fixed the come-along to a big oak stump so that once we got the chain around the grey boulder we could rock it up enough to winch it out with the truck.

The sun sat overhead, crows were squawking at us from the trees, the air was as still as a summer dawn. When Riley insisted on a break, we shared water from a thermos and ate sliced ham and bread. I didn't want to stop for long because I knew I'd tighten up, and when that happens I often get the whirlies, but Riley was slow to eat and even stretched his legs out straight as if he was going to lean back against a tree and doze. As his eyes closed, I said. "Let's finish before I can't bend anymore," I said.

"You're out of shape brother, " Riley said, "but I suppose we may as well get this over and done with."

There is no flat in our part of West Virginia. The boulder was embedded in the earth so our grave sloped down hill from head to foot, and though we pried and cursed, in the end could only winch the rock to the foot of Mama's final home. As the afternoon's darkness gathered and the wind snaked through our coats, we'd managed to dig a four wide by six-foot deep, open-ended trench that you could have walked directly into from below were it not for the rock. "It'll do," Riley said." My back knotted and my head drifty, I had no strength to argue.

Riley eased along in second gear, careful not to rip open the oil pan on the rocks and stumps. I know that television has made people believe that all moonshiners and mountain people drive like crazy, but that isn't the case. If chased, you have to run, but if you wreck with a load of hooch you can burst into flames, so we're naturally cautious drivers. Any criminal will tell you that the ability to go unnoticed is your best friend. I've managed to be invisible most of my life.

As we bumped along, Riley spun me the tale of the trouble he'd had arranging Mama's shipment to Beckley, saying, "Cost me a damn pile of money," explaining that some of that was cash in hand to a woman at the medical examiner's office. She was, "A skinny, big-toothed broad," he said. "Looked like a redheaded Whipple."

There'd been six Whipple girls and they all had names beginning with L; I know that Riley's first sex was with Leotta, and my first was with Lorena. If we'd had other brothers likely they'd have first done it with a Whipple, too. The girls were bony blondes left to wander as they pleased by their mother, Lenora, who, after her husband coughed out his lungs and died, spent her nights at the Delbert looking for a man who'd marry her and take on raising a half dozen wild girls without being after them himself. By then, Lenora's looks were gone. Six children and a side hill farm on a miner's death benefit will do that. Water rushing down a trace works the slate smooth, but grinding along broke and alone, trying to keep clothes on your kids and food in their bellies, chisels the sorrow into your face, and Lenora Whipple's was as weary and as sorrowful face as I ever saw.

When we'd nearly reached the break in the wall I asked Riley, "Any Whipples still around?"

"Don't know about now, but used to be two or three of them around and a shit load of new ones. It's funny, Ize, but it seems like they needed to get older before they could get knocked up. Many times as I banged ol' Leotta, and as easily as I got Lillian up the pole, I guess I'd have to count myself lucky." Riley stopped the truck for a second and said, "Must be I have a weakness for women whose names begin with L. Leotta, Leslie Crooms, wasn't I some disappointed when she moved up to Ohio, and Lillian. Damn glad I found the best one last."

My gut spasmed and I stared out the window so Riley couldn't read my face, "Lillian is a fine woman," I said.

Riley eased the truck through the opening and back onto the gravel. The valley spread before us with that pinkish glow you see at sunset in the mountains or in the sooty skies over big cities, and I wondered what life would have been like if my brother and I had both ended up with a string of kids out of the Whipple girls. Lillian was a long way from a Whipple, none of whom I imagined had ever finished high school, no less nursing school, and she had a fullness to her that these stony hills had denied Lorena, but I would have given anything, as the truck bumped downhill toward the house, to have her flinty Whipple grin waiting for me.

After supper, I was alone. Lillian had taken the kids with her to do some food shopping in town, and Riley was out walking. I knew what he was thinking about. He was trying to hone his plan to win Lillian back fulltime, searching for an angle among the details of setting Mama in the ground with her kin that would endear him to her again. I guessed that even after the divorce Riley and Lillian might have still been sharing the bed we'd bought at the antique shop, because she seemed to have her own drawer in the bathroom and her red night shirt that said, "I Only Sleep With The Best," which Riley bought her at South of the Border on their honeymoon trip to Florida, hung on the back of the bedroom door. Still, I doubted that he was going to get her back permanently. She might sleep with him, but I couldn't believe that she'd ever live back up on the ridge fulltime, and I knew he would never leave here. I also knew that without his cash crop his wallet would be in tough shape. The Old Man used to say that the only decent work around here was for miners, bootleggers, and whores, and believed that whiskey making was the safest of those occupations. Riley may be more of an entrepreneur than the Old Man was, and is surely worldlier, but Blissfull is no Eden of enterprise, and I couldn't imagine him ever working for anyone else except as a contractor.

Weary of my Bible, I searched for something else to read and realized for the first time since I'd been home that all my old books were gone. The most treasured of the meager few I'd saved from my childhood, novels and biographies mostly, paperbacks I'd gotten from the Scholastic Book Club or hard covers with ragged dust jackets I'd rescued from Sally stores, had been the unabridged dictionary Mama bought me when I was in the sixth grade. The only subjects I'd truly cottoned to were English and History, and of the two I liked English the better. I may have been the only kid in the sixth grade that adored diagramming sentences, discovering an awesome symmetry in grammar and syntax. I scoured that dictionary in bed at night and when I first got up in the morning, as part of a game I played with myself to learn new words. I'd have a twenty-six day cycle where I would try to memorize a new word each day starting the first day with an A word and going through the alphabet until it was time to start over. I'd write the word down on a tablet I kept in our room but not the definition then, at the end of the cycle, I'd test myself to see how many I remembered. Later, books kept me warm. When you're walking around until the Sally opens, two of the few places you don't get chased out of the minute they spot you for a bum are the Goodwill and St. Vincent de Paul stores. Purchasing a twenty-five cent book can buy an hour's warmth.

Patches barked as Riley came up the road. I could see his breath ghosting in the dark as he ambled into the dooryard, and I got off the couch to let him in, but he and the dog piled into the truck and drove off. I wondered if he'd go looking for Lillian, or if he'd just ride the dark hills, thinking. Neither Riley nor I talk much to each other. We never have. The Old Man did most of the talking when he was around, and my recollection of Mama is that she spoke little and sang a lot; old hill tunes, like Barbry Allen or Ernest Tubbs and Patsy Cline songs. At night, or if we were sick, she'd told us stories of travail with happy endings, or tales that required the intervention of handsome princes to save a young girl from an evil villain. The Old Man, when he decided to spin a yarn, preferred the ghost stories handed down from the old folks, grisly horrors about bogeymen and coal black mountain lions.

Mama used to say, "You can say nothing and seem like a fool or open your mouth and prove you're one," so in school I never said much either. When you don't know the answers you don't volunteer, and except for English and History I often didn't have a clue as to what was going on. The one book I can recall wanting to discuss in school was Moby Dick, which makes sense to me now when I think about how much I've wandered. At the time, I couldn't decide who you were supposed to root for, Ahab or the whale, and I'd never seen the ocean so I had a hard time imagining some of the setting. When Mrs. McCall asked questions about the plot, I knew the answers, but I preferred the anonymity of the back row and did not raise my hand. Like I said before, invisibility has served me well.

Mountain people don't need much light to see by at night. The Old Man had taught us to see without the moon or flashlights because the law used them. I'd turned out the porch light, after I'd helped Lillian and the kids put the groceries away, something we'd always done as kids when everyone was inside for the night as it makes it easier to see anyone approaching the house, and by ten had fallen asleep on the couch, so I had no idea what time it was when Riley came in. I did know, by the tickle in my nose and by the way he went through the kitchen cupboards and refrigerator, that he hadn't sold his entire crop. Though I was always a whiskey man, marijuana emits as pleasant a scent as any flower I know. I'd been in Riley's drying shed a few times, and it exuded a fragrance rivaling a smokehouse full of hams, or the soap and shampoo smell of a just-bathed woman. When Lorena and I used to have sex and then skinny dip in the creek, she'd swim down to the end of the pool above the waterfall, where she kept a stash of soap and shampoo, and wash up. Nuzzling her afterward, the scent of the soap on her cool skin and the lemony smell in her hair, I'd get right and ready to have a second go at it. Even now, if I get a whiff of lemon I get the old tingle down below.

CHAPTER FOUR

I woke up early on Saturday, pulled on my clothes and boots, and went out to pee in the ditch. It's one of the few habits, other than whiskey, in which I take after my father. Peeing inside never seemed natural. As for the other function, I admit a fondness for the indoor plumbing Riley's put in the place. Sitting down in the outhouse, all the Old Man's tales of porcupines, black widow spiders, and rattlesnakes used to pester my courage. Even mice scritching in the walls unnerved me, affecting my ability to finish what I'd come out to do. Peeing, I feel less vulnerable to such things, though in the wind of winter I don't linger at that either.

I'd heard Riley go out early and assumed it was for a walk, but his truck was gone. I hadn't heard him drive off and figured that he must have coasted down the road until he was out of earshot so as not to awaken Lillian or the kids. The glow of town was fading, the first pale streaks of dawn strafing the sky over the valley, a sliver of moon visible through a notch in the ridge. In the brief time since my conversion, my spirits lifted by the knowledge that I wasn't hungover, I had come to love daybreak as much as I had as a kid on the summer mornings I'd been able to sneak off into the hills and out of the Old Man's range before he could hitch me to a day-long task. I'd grab a piece of bread and slice off a slab of ham and be gone all morning, careful to avoid the Old Man's stills and the entrances to the hand-dug, played-out mines where he stored his inventory. If I was lucky, when I'd get back he would have gone off to tend to his business, and though that might earn me a slap across the face or a few welts, it beat a day of work for the sake of its exhaustion.

The field was bone white with a hard frost, the air full of wood smoke rising behind me in the hard light, curling away up the mountainside like dispersing fog. I stretched my arms and shook the last of sleep from my body and gazed about the dooryard a final minute before heading inside.

I'd fallen asleep reading my Bible. I had decided to start

again at the beginning and read on through hoping it would make more sense to me that way, but after Genesis and Exodus, I skipped ahead. I could follow the stories, but all the laws and begats made me sleepy. Before nodding off, I'd been reading about old Job's troubles and thinking about Riley and Lillian, trying to comprehend how God could be such a bastard as to bet the devil that he could ruin a man and still have him love him. Though Job gets a new family and riches, what about all the loved ones he lost? Some hurts don't go away. I know. I've tried to drink away, fight away, love away, and piss away a mountain of sorrows, but no amount of time dulls the sword of some pain. I decided that if I was going to understand Job's faith in such an unfair God, I would have to see Reverend Willis.

The road was quiet. I spotted several skittish doe in a clump of birches nosing up the wind, but the crows announced my presence and they scampered off. At the end of the gravel, I gazed back up at the mountain, still dark and brittle, wondering how long I'd be able to stay before I had to have work. A log truck roared past me, spitting sand and fumes into the air, as it geared down for the grade, the driver waving to me as if to apologize for rupturing the morning's calm. I waved back, and began my descent into the valley.

When I crossed over the creek at Graver's Corners, I remembered Malcolm Greaves who'd died there. Everyone who knew him was of one of two opinions about his death. I always believed it was an accident, but most folks preferred to believe that he drove into the creek because he was unable to cope with the sorrow from his last high school basketball game. Malcolm, college scouts believed, was as good as Jerry West had been in high school, and he was recruited by dozens of top basketball schools. The town lived and died with every one of his games and when Malcolm went his whole senior year without missing a foul shot and led us to the state title game, even the national press picked up on it. He could date near any girl he wanted, never paid for food at the diner or fill-ups at the Texaco, and wasn't obligated to open a book to get

A's in school. He was two years ahead of me and only spoke to me when wanted some of the Old Man's best.

Riley and I had piled into Shep Petty's station wagon with five other guys and ridden up to Charleston for the state game against Wilton Consolidated. For three quarters we trailed by anywhere from four to ten points. We'd get on a run only to have Wilton jump back up by a few buckets. Shep said that the one thing in our favor was that we were country boys used to long days of hard work, and in the last few minutes he appeared to be a sage as Wilton wore down from our relentless press, turning the ball over several times. Malcolm kept drawing fouls by driving to the basket, and hit every free throw, adding to his record. Then, with fifteen seconds to go, he nailed a twelve-foot jump shot to narrow it to a three-point game. Shep nearly decapitated me with a bear hug, and said, "We gonna get there now."

On the inbounds play, Malcolm stole the pass, and called a time out. Our side of the gym went crazy, chanting "Malcolm, Malcolm," then "Blissfull, Blissfull."

During the time out, I could see in the expression on Malcolm's face that he believed we'd win. Staring at the dark creek water rolling and foaming down through the rapids, I recalled the exact color of his eyes, the sweaty furrows creasing his forehead, which was so big Riley had once called it a five head, and the surly curl of his mouth.

Malcolm took the inbounds pass and got fouled hard with ten seconds left. No one on our side of the gym was sitting, and everyone was clapping and screaming. Wilton took a time out, during which Shep explained that Coach Culver would want Malcolm to make the first shot, then bounce the second one off the rim so Dave Wooley, our six foot seven center, could grab the rebound and lay one in to tie it.

"Ol' Malcolm'll make one, all net, then he'll miss the next one. Ol' Wooley'll pull it off the ceiling if he has to," Shep said. "Money in the bank."

Malcolm hit the first one, but swished the next one, too. When we didn't steal the inbounds we had to foul. The Wilton kid made them both. Since it was before the three point shot, even when Malcolm nailed a jumper from near half court we lost 77-76.

We argued all the way home about what happened. Shep said Malcolm only cared about his consecutive free throw record, I said he probably hadn't missed in so long that he forgot how, and Riley was convinced that Malcolm had done it to get even with Coach Culver for calling him a fairy at practice, something he said he'd heard had happened the week before.

Malcolm went to Morgantown but he quit basketball in February of his first year, lost his scholarship, and was back home by March. In April, on a night full of fat wet snow, he drove his father's truck through the same guardrail I was leaning against and into the creek. The coroner said he was drunk, and I figured it was on whiskey I'd sold him the day before. I went to the funeral and stayed away from school for the next three days, spending my time watching the swollen creek run down into town, imagining it tumbling into the river and down into the ocean, wishing I could do the same.

Back at the same spot, I contemplated easing out of town after Mama was buried and seeking a sober fortune somewhere else, afraid Malcolm and the other ghosts of Blissfull would overcome my resolve. I thought about Ella. It would be a tall order to locate her with no more information than her name and that she was a hillbilly from eastern Kentucky, and I knew that I'd as likely get killed as find her in those hollers and ridges. I even thought about calling up Plourdes and seeing if I really could get my job back after Christmas. Though these thoughts terrified me, they did keep the revolver out of my mind, as if I were offering myself a plea bargain of sorts.

The sound of the creek and the rising of the wind sang in my ears. Crows kept shouting at me to move me along, and standing on the bridge I wondered if I'd ever discover where I belonged in this world. Wandering the hills to figure out a problem is one thing, but wandering the earth looking for a home is another.

The door to Star Of Morning was open, but there was no one inside. I sauntered down Main Street past the Delbert Hotel and the empty store fronts where there used to be a Western Auto, Woolworth's, Blissfull Feed and Seed Company, and Slatterly's Dry Goods, until I got to the square and the Miners Bank and Trust. I stood under their marquee, which advertised Free Checking for Seniors and Students, which is all that's really left here, and watched the town wake up.

Across the street, Riddley's Diner was open, but I only had a few bucks and Riddley's coffee, as I recalled, was old and harsh even at five in the morning. I reckoned it had gotten no better with time. Besides, the last full meal I'd ever eaten at Riddley's was just after Mama left for Detroit. The Old Man took Riley and me into town for the blue plate special, "Open faced Turkey and Gravy with Mashed Potatoes, Peas and Blueberry Cobbler." I don't think the Old Man was feeling guilty or fatherly, but he wanted to show us that he didn't need Mama to take care of us. He was probably trying to show us the value in toeing his line as well.

I'd been in Riddley's a few times after that afternoon, usually to sober up on their sludgy coffee, and a few times when I worked graveyard at Krogers the crew would come in for breakfast on payday, most of us half lit. Standing at the bank looking at a nearly deserted downtown, I was struck by how few of the buildings on the square I'd actually been in. I guess I just never had business in those places: Gilroy's Home Finance, Mountaineer Timber and Land, The Blissfull Crier Gazette, Carrie's Academy of Cosmetology, Sullivan's Driving School, Lane and Carver Furniture. Even when I got arrested, I was taken in the back way to the lockup behind the Municipal Offices and Public Safety Department building on the south side of the square, and when Daddy bailed me out we left the same way.

Pigeons were flapping around the little park in the center island of the square, where the monuments to the town's war dead from the Revolution through Vietnam were just catching the December light. A squad car circled three times, slowing as it passed the bank. I had a local address and enough money to avoid being picked up as a vagrant, but I wanted no part of the law so I began ambling toward the river and the train station.

I was strolling along the broken sidewalk on Elevator Street when Riley honked, waking me from a daydream about Ella. He eased the power window down and hollered to me to get in. As I closed the door I smelled reefer, and when I looked at him I could see that his eyes were like two red coals. "Your stuff?" I asked.

"I told you. Ain't much of it left after this rig. Where the hell you headed? You ain't leaving on me before we bury Mama, are you?"

"You must be fucked-up brother, I ain't even got my pack."

"The train station is this way," he said, as if he'd made a great discovery.

"And where would I get the money for a ticket?" I said. "And have I ever left, except for the army, any way but hitching?"

Riley didn't answer.

When we'd been riding for about ten minutes he said, "We're goin' to Beckley to fetch Mama."

I'd expected to see a coffin, but Mama was in a big wooden box marked, "Saw Parts," with a bill of lading taped to the top. I didn't ask Riley why this had been necessary, but he volunteered that he'd had to, "Make arrangements." I've never held more than a few hundred dollars in my hands that belonged to me. A couple of times I'd made deliveries for the Old Man that brought in several thousand bucks, but it was not mine. I'd had a few Kroger's checks that included overtime that put a fair jag in my pocket, but I'd never had enough cash to buy something that I wasn't supposed to have. Riley's pot business was cash intensive, and I was sure that he'd slipped someone a big wad of green to get Mama home, even if she was labeled as parts.

Riley took it easy on the way back up the ridge, careful not to draw the attention of the police by speeding on the highway, and driving as if Mama could feel all the bumps and potholes in the gravel road. He played ZZ Top and Hank Jr. CDs, and huffed quick hits off a thick roach he kept snuffing out in the ashtray. By the time the home place came into sight, he'd drunk most of a half gallon of spring water.

When we got back Lillian and the kids were on the porch, Lillian dressed for work and the kids dressed up for the school holiday concert. "Shit, goddamn shit," Riley said as we pulled into the dooryard. He'd forgotten that Lillian was going in at four for an over-night double shift, and that he'd promised to take care of the kids. We weren't late yet, it was just three, but Riley didn't want to leave Mama unattended in the school lot, and we had no place ready to unload her crate. Using the best of his mountain magnetism, he persuaded Lillian to let him use her car to drop her at the hospital, take the kids to the show, and promised to fetch her in the morning. Lillian wasn't happy, but she seemed to cut Riley some slack at the sight of our mother's rough casket, and if she smelled the reefer on him, let that go, too. I did wonder why she'd signed up for a shift that meant she'd miss the show, but decided that she was making sure that Riley understood that she was committed to staying on the ridge past Christmas.

Ten minutes later, the four of them looking like a family again—the kids spruced up, Riley's hair still wet from the shower, Lillian with her overcoat draped over her greens and a stethoscope around her neck—pulled out of the dooryard with a tiny squeal of tire.

I sat on the porch steps as the night gathered over me. In the western sky, the new moon was holding the old one over its head. The dogs panted next to me. I took turns stroking their ears, and, as I listened to the night, I was flooded with grief for Mama. She'd had to die to come home and I couldn't be sure that was what she wanted. The meanness and relentless sorrow of her life here sunk its talons into my shoulders the way the clammy bitterness of a concrete sidewalk seeps into your bones. I wondered if when I died, I'd be anywhere where anyone would know to send me home. The dogs whimpered to be fed and I went inside, careful to switch on the porch light.

The house empty, I opened the door to Carleton's room, determined to locate my revolver. Before Riley worked on the house, it had been laid out on one floor, though as the roof is pitched to allow the snow would slide off in the winter, our room consisted of an open area with a loft where we slept stuffed into the eaves. Over time, Riley trussed the roof, added a board ceiling and a set of drop down stairs, so he can use the space for storage. Above Carleton's closet there was a board resting on the molding and the door header that had never been nailed down, where I'd hidden the revolver wrapped inside of an old hunting shirt.

Standing on a kitchen chair, I pushed up on the board but it wouldn't budge. I ran back to the kitchen, grabbed the flashlight from off of the top of the refrigerator, pulled down the stairs and climbed into the attic. Pausing on the top step, I shined the light around the room, noticing that there was no floor, only boards and pieces of plywood laid randomly across the joists in places, and most of those were covered with boxes. Creeping on my hands and knees, around the kids' old crib, I got close enough to the corner to see by the flashlight's beam that neither the shirt nor the gun were still there.

My first reaction was to curse my brother, but as I mulled over what Riley might have done with the gun, it occurred to me that he'd likely hidden it elsewhere to be sure neither Lillian nor the kids found it. Sitting in the opening for the stairs, I decided that if it was still in the house, logic would indicate that it was stashed in his room, where I was reluctant to forage for it for fear he or Lillian would notice. I climbed down, swung the stairs back up into the ceiling, and resolved to ask Riley where the gun was when I got him by himself.

I stood a minute taking note of the room, when it occurred to me that I might have been looking in the wrong place, as the closet in Carleton's room mirrored Annie's. In making Carleton's room over as he did, Riley hadn't just modernized it; he'd made the house more efficient. He'd also hidden the loft and all the demons and bitter memories of what we'd heard and learned up there. In Annie's half of the old room he'd insulated between the rafters and covered them with boards from an old barn he'd been paid to take down, leaving a high ceiling over most of the room, though he had fashioned a small loft that ran the length of the wall and closed in the top of her closet.

I cleared some space, set the chair down, and poked at the ceiling with the flashlight until I located the loose board. Pushing it to one side, I shined the light into the opening and felt around until I got a purchase on a cloth bag, which I fought to ease it down between the boards. Massaging the bag's contents to make them fit through the opening, I remembered a picture from my tenth grade biology book that showed a snake bloated from swallowing a small pig that we learned would take the snake a week to digest. I had the bag three quarters out when it fetched up. I gave a yank and when it came free I had to grab the back of the chair with one hand to prevent falling of it, as the weighted bag slipped from my hands and thudded to the floor. I sat a minute on the chair, closing my eyes against the whirlies, picking at the knot in the drawstrings. When the spinning ceased, I opened my eyes and spread open the mouth of the bag.

As I emptied the bag's contents onto the floor, my youth fell out before me: a red flannel shirt I'd worn until you could read a book through it, a photograph of me and Lorena Whipple sitting on a stump, my high school diploma, my senior year yearbook—the only one I'd bought, my Army discharge papers, Moby Dick, an envelope with letters to me from my mother, a half dozen pictures of her with Riley or me, but never the three of us together, and at the bottom, the thing which had been so difficult to wrench through the opening, my unabridged dictionary, my mother's inscription, To Isaac, Merry Christmas, Love Mama, printed in her hand on the inside cover. Had the revolver been in the bag, I might well have tromped up the ridge and ended it right then.

Seeing Mama young and smiling, then imagining her as

an old woman wracked with cancer, seared my heart. So did the realization that Riley had saved these things, I believed had been lost or destroyed, for me. I began to understand the pains he'd taken to bring Mama home. Though we'd never sung for her with those brotherly harmonies like the Louvin's or The Everly's as she was convinced we could have done, Riley had managed to bring her home where we could lay her to rest without fear of the Old Man hurting her again.

Save for a picture of Mama and Riley standing beside her car that I stowed in my wallet, I packed everything into the bag, forced it back into the space above Annie's closet, and replaced the board. I was beset with waves of the whirlies as I replaced the flashlight and the chair in the kitchen, and I collapsed on the couch, my pulse a jackhammer in my ears, my body invaded by sorrow and nostalgia.

Taking my Bible off the side table, I slammed it to my chest and resolved to never backslide, so I wouldn't die lost in some city where I'd be sent to the nearest medical school to be some future sawbones' cadaver. I tried as hard as I'd ever tried at anything in my life to remember the details of Mama's face and voice and touch that I would conjure in the nights after she first left Blissfull, and while I could hear her singing to us and I could smell her sweet breath, I kept seeing the Old Man's face next to hers and she would recede from me.

I decided to see her one more time.

Black metal bands girdled the packing crate and the lid fastened with wood screws. The bands broke easily when I pried against them with the point of the peavey, but the screws had been set with a drill and I had to lock the vice grips on the shaft of a screwdriver to work them out. Even then, I found that the corners had been secured with twelve penny nails and it took me some time to dig up one of Riley's pry bars to loosen them up enough to pull them out. I levered up the crate with the peavey and pulled the broken metal bands out from under it. I decided that if Riley noticed the bands were gone I would tell him that they made me sad and made Mama's remains look too much like freight. I wondered for a moment how her second husband could have let her come back here on a train to a place where she'd known little peace and contentment, but I decided that it must have been her wish.

Once the lid was free, I paused. I wondered what she'd look like after the cancer had shriveled her up, and I wasn't sure that I'd be able to look at her, even though I've seen some scarred and shrunken old men dying from diabetes, cirrhosis, or emphysema in the VA, watched kids walk right by fathers they didn't recognize, and heard mothers refuse to believe that the ashen face hooked to the oxygen bottle was their own flesh. Still, I knew that if I was to see Mama again, I only had a short time before Riley and the kids came back, and I flipped the lid over onto the ground.

Inside the crate was a large metal box with a hinged lid. I opened it, pulled out a blanket laid on top and discovered two assault rifles, a thin sheet of plywood, and, when I removed that, what looked like a million pills in quart sized, sealed plastic bags. In one corner of the box there was a small rectangular box marked, Mama's Ashes. Something like the whirlies passed over me and I gripped the edge of the box for support.

The Old Man would have been proud of Riley, turning a tragedy into an opportunity to make a buck, but I was as furious with him as I imagined Lillian had ever been, despite having just been touched by his kindness in saving my things. I didn't object to Mama being cremated, but sending her home with enough drugs to send us to prison for life, not to mention storing her ashes beside the guns, was cruel. If he'd ridden her in the cab, I might have understood it, but Mama deserved more respect after all she'd borne in this life than to be shipped home like that. I took her ashes into the living room and stored them under the couch, then ran outside, panting, and screwed down the top of the crate in the hope that Riley wouldn't notice anything amiss when he got back.

Riley scurried into the house to fix the kids some dinner and the smell of frying hamburgers made me realize that I hadn't eaten all day, something drunks often do, and something, that even sober, I'm prone to forget. Riley ate two burgers, the reefer clearly goading his appetite. I chewed slowly, fueling myself for the battle I knew we would have when the kids had gone to bed.

I auditioned a dozen opening lines in my head, but only managed to ask, "What happened to Mama's husband?"

"He's senile," Riley said. "He don't understand she's dead."

"How'd you know she was sick then?"

"Hospital called. Mama listed me as next of kin."

"None of her new kin had anything to say about this?" I asked

"What the fuck you drivin' at Ize," Riley said gripping the edge of the table, his eyes red-veined as old porcelain.

"Just wondered why you thought it was okay to stuff her ashes into a crate of dope and guns."

"It's simple dipshit," Riley snarled, "Not that you were there to offer another opinion. I called Pervis Meeker up in Detroit to see if I could stay with him. He moves a little painkiller on the side, and a few other things you can't waltz down to the K Mart to pick up."

"So you had her cremated to create more room in the crate?"

"Fuck no," Riley said. "I had her cremated because the doctors told me she looked real rough at the end. But, goddammit, we're going bury her in this box in the grave we dug."

"You're not planning to feed her to Fred's hogs?" I said, my voice breaking like a schoolboy's.

"This ain't like that," Riley thundered. "The Old Man got better than he deserved. Listen, I want to get Lillian back in this house where she belongs. I move this oxy and I clear nearly fifty thousand. I'm through with small time shit. I got fifty grand stashed, add this deal to it, and I'm going to build Lillian a nice new place on the timber lot. While you were flopping in every fucking gutter from here to hell and back, I been trying to get ahead. Don't fuck this up, I swear."

"That what the guns are for?" I said. "To add me to the pile of bones in the mine?"

"Listen, peckerhead," Riley said, "Don't make me ponder killing my own kin."

I saw the Old Man's stare in his eyes, and I could finally recall Mama's face. "I won't fuck it up," I said, "But you could have told me I was riding around on ten to twenty in the pen."

"Less you know the better for you and for me," Riley said, pushing his chair back from the table and storming out the front door with me in pursuit.

I didn't ask how he was going to move that many pills in these hills, but I knew he had a plan and that he'd been fine tuning during his late night drives and walks. I also figured he had a partner or two. I have no idea what the mark up on dope is, but I knew that up north the stuff sold for as much as twenty dollars a pop on the street, and that junkies and entrepreneurs were breaking into pharmacies and doctor's offices all the time to get their hands on it. Pills never appealed to me. Booze is a better addiction, because it's legal. If you're willing to find a place to drink that's hidden from the public view, you can stay wrecked as long as your money holds out

Riley stomped out to the shed and grabbed a drill attached to a long orange extension cord, which he plugged into the outlet on the porch. He removed the rifles from the crate and zipped the lid tight. "In the morning," he said in a slow deliberate voice, "A guy is coming by, first light, to pick this up. He knows to open the lid, take the oxy and leave the cash. "These," he said patting one of the rifles, "are insurance. Put 'em in the shed. I'll get them later."

I took the guns from Riley and watched him take the porch steps two at a time. I couldn't believe that he hadn't noticed Mama missing, and I knew then, if I hadn't realized it before, that he was for sure more the Old Man's child than I was. I also realized that my fingerprints were now on the guns.

A Snap-On tool calendar hung on the wall in the shed, with a leggy blonde in a bikini leaning against a racecar. For some reason it looked like her head had been added to someone else's body. She was holding a wrench in one hand and a spark plug in the other, and looked down over the workbench like she was ready to leap off the page and help with a tune-up. The calendar was five years old, but I could see why Riley kept it. The blonde bore more than a little resemblance to Lillian, and I imagined Riley sitting in the shed on summer nights scheming for ways to take advantage of his mountain magnetism to reel her back up onto the ridge.

The longer I stared at it, the more the picture unnerved me. Though I missed Ella, I had a stinging longing for Lorena Whipple, too. Maybe the thinness of the soil on the shed floor where the old pine boards had rotted away, or the raggedness of the December light, helped me recall her sinewy, knobby body. Never coy or shy, Lorena adored sex, and lived to please and be pleased. I admired that in her. It wasn't just because I was the one enjoying the benefits of her hunger for life's carnal delights, but was as much that she was so confident, so unlike me. It may be from Lorena that I came to understand hunger of all kinds, but it's through my own trials that I came to understand how often one mistake or misstep mushrooms into an engulfing disaster.

Unsettled from stewing on the details of the argument with Riley, I rubbed down the guns with a rag I found hanging on a nail, hoping to smudge my prints beyond recognition. I considered that if Riley was really out of the weed business, and if this was one last big score, it would only work if he got Lillian back. If he didn't there was no telling what the next project would be. I was stung by the realization that I would likely have to move on either way; the vision of my body slumped against a tree and my brains running into the snow ripped through my heart. I shook my head against the dream and realized that if Lillian came back, I'd be in the way. If she didn't, I couldn't face what would come next. God only knew what would happen if she married Bob from Krogers, especially now that Riley had an assault rifle. For a minute or two, I thought about grabbing the guns and a few bottles of whiskey and taking off, but I realized that even broken down the rifles would be impossible to hide in my pack, and the thought of another detox burned like lye in my guts. I hadn't had the shakes in more than a week, and I feared that if I slid off the wagon this time that I'd be crushed beneath its wheels.

Reverend Willis says you have to recognize when the Lord calls, and pray to Him to be sure it's not Satan seducing your soul. I clasped my hands until my fingers went numb as I tried to pray—searching to recall any of the words I'd heard a preacher say, be it at the Sally, or from Reverend Willis himself, but all I could summon were those few words of Throw Out the Lifeline, I'd squawked to hoarseness in the Massachusetts night.

I bolted the shed door then sat on the porch steps until the cold worked into my skin. I wanted to see Reverend Willis, but didn't have the energy to go to town. I wanted a deep pull on a bottle of the Old Man's well-aged, almost golden-colored whiskey, but refused to be tempted at least until Mama's ashes had been buried. Mostly, I wanted to know what to do, so I walked.

When I came back, it was after midnight. I peeked in the window and saw Riley sacked out in the recliner, the two rifles at his feet. I creaked open the door and the dogs scuttled toward me. Using the signal we'd used as kids, a low imitation of a whip-poor-will. I whistled to wake Riley. He bolted up and reached for one of the guns. I froze and he laughed. "Patches heard you half mile up the road. Played a little possum."

I slumped on the couch and tried to sleep.

At five, long before the dawn had wended its way up the valley, a blue Chevy Sierra with Virginia tags pulled into the dooryard and two men, both bundled into gray ski parkas, got out. I'd been awake for about half an hour. Riley was in the bathroom peeing, when I whistled to him. He'd left the door open as a precaution, and, after zipping up, snapped a clip into one of the guns. He didn't bother loading one for me, and moved to the window. He petted Patches and Roxie, who'd alerted us to the men's arrival with low growls, calming them so they wouldn't wake the kids. Riley peered into the dooryard through the slit between the curtains. "Lying fucker promised to come alone," he said, flicking the safety off on the gun. He laid the rifle against the door and fished a small walkie-talkie, no larger than a pack of cigarettes, from his pants pocket, and turned it on. "Ize, keep your eyes on the taller one," Riley said, "This ain't fully as planned."

While Riley fiddled with the dials on the radio, I fixed my gaze on the two men as they opened the crate with a cordless drill and examined in the contents. "There are two of them," I heard Riley say into the radio, "Was only supposed to be one."

A voice squawked back, "It's fine."

"Better be," Riley said, returning the radio to his pocket.

It took the pair less than five minutes to transfer the load into a series of picnic coolers, Riley keeping them in his sights the entire time. "Who are they?" I whispered.

"Better you don't ever know that, brother," Riley said.

The woodstove clinked, the fire out, the metal cooling. Roxie grumbled out a low growl and Riley hushed her. The house grew silent. One of the kids coughed and my bowels froze, but Riley stood in the window with the rifle to his shoulder as if waiting for an open shot at a buck following a doe into a clearing. "Get the fucking money, assholes," Riley said in a half whisper, his eyes narrowing as if taking aim.

My brother has balls the size of grapefruit, and is a meticulous planner, but I was sweating like I had the DT's, imagining the worst. The thought that Annie and Carleton might wake up to a shoot out sundered my soul, but I was more fearful that I'd have to shoot someone in defense of my brother, a deed I had no conviction I could do.

When the men finished transferring the coolers to the Sierra, they tossed the type of pouch I've seen folks carry into a bank into the box, and set the lid back on top without screwing it down. As the truck eased out of the dooryard and slunk down the gravel. Riley switched on the porch lights, ran out to the crate and drew out the pouch. I never saw anyone, even a bank teller, rifle through a stack of bills as quickly as he did. He counted it twice then came inside, keyed the black walkie-talkie and said, "Let 'em pass."

Riley counted the money again, and placed it in piles. Stacks of one hundred dollar bills sat on the table like the currency in a kid's game. He pushed some bills he fished from his wallet across the table to me. "Here's five hundred. You deserve a cut for helping me dig the grave," he said, "And for helping get her in it tomorrow."

I pocketed the cash, sorrowed that Riley had called Mama her and angered that he thought he had to pay me for digging my own mother's grave. But what sliced me the deepest was the thought that the money might be intended to get me to the next place I'd be going. It was becoming clear to me, if not to Lillian, that Riley believed she would be his again. Imagining there would be little room for a fifth wheel, my eyes watered up and my tongue conjured the body-firing shock of a mouthful of whiskey swallowed into a naked stomach.

Riley stuffed the bills back in the pouch and sidled toward his room. "I got a strong box up top of the closet. Something happens," he said, "You see Lillian gets this."

"Born to fret," the Old Man had once said of me, and fretful I was, the two words something happens, striking my heart like a bullet, as if the deal wasn't complete, the deed not yet done, that some serious danger lay ahead. A persistent itch plagued my scalp as it had in the night I rode home to Blissfull in the Star of Morning van, and my legs and backed ached.

But if Riley was apprehensive, he hid it in a manic delight. When he strode back into the kitchen he was whistling. Parking himself behind my chair he said, "Ize, when I get the new house built, and I'll have to do it slowly so's not to arouse suspicion, this place is yours. I'll carry you for a while, but you might need to get you a job, for appearances, so it will look like you can sustain yourself. You ain't beholden here. We're orphans now and kin needs to protect kin."

For Riley, that speech amounted to an oration. I tried to

respond in kind, but I was so dry-tongued and stunned by the extent of what he'd said in the light of what I had been considering, that I managed nothing better than to mutter "Thanks, Riley," over and over until he begged me to shut up.

Slapping me on the shoulder and spinning on his heels as if he were dancing, Riley strolled to the living room and flung open the curtains to the morning. "What a goddamn perfect West by God Virginia Day," he said, something I'd heard the Old Man utter the few mornings I remember him in a decent mood.

An hour and two pots of coffee later, Annie and Carleton stumbled into the kitchen and Riley and I made them breakfast. While they slurped down French toast drowned in molasses and honey, Riley described in detail how we were going to go up the mountain in the truck and bury their grandmother, making it sound as much like a picnic or a trip to the fair in Beckley as he could. Carleton glanced up from his plate, his chin lathered with the commingled honey and molasses and said, "But isn't she in heaven?"

I peeked over at Riley to see how he'd handle that one, but he drove the question back at me. "Uncle Ize is the religious man in the family," he said. "He can explain it better than I can."

"Well?" Annie said, scraping her spoon along the plate to get the last of the liquid.

"It's like this," I said stalling. "Your grandmother's soul is in heaven, but her body is here. God doesn't have enough room for all the bodies, so we go up there, if we've been good, as souls."

"Are souls littler?" Carleton asked.

"I don't know that Carleton," I said, "But I think they just take up less room."

"So," he said, "You need to be good to be made into a soul when you die, just like you need to be good so you don't get coal in your stocking from Santa. Right?"

"Yes," I said, "I would say that's right."

"But what happens to the body?" Carleton asked.

Annie shrieked, "I know. The worms crawl in the worms..."

"Annie Elizabeth that's enough," Riley said, which, for reasons I still can't understand, set her brother to crying. If Carleton had ever seen Mama, I'd have understood, but she couldn't have been any more real to him than one of the cartoon characters he enjoys witnessing getting flattened by trucks or riddled with bullets in the mornings before school.

"Hey Carleton," I said, "When the soul goes to heaven, the body can't feel or know a thing."

"Then why bury it?" he said, looking at Riley. "Why not keep it and pretend that it's alive?"

"It would stink, silly," Annie said holding her nose.

Carleton's eyes started to well up, so I said, "Because God wants us to bury the person in the ground, because he made the first people from the ground."

"He did?" Carleton said.

"He sure did," Riley said. "Maybe your favorite Uncle will read that story to you before bed."

Carleton considered that a moment and said, "Can I have more French toast?"

While Riley dipped and fried up another piece of bread, I sat on the couch thinking about Mama down there in her box with the dust balls, dog hair, and mouse shit, unsettled about her crate rotting away, her ashes saturated by seeping rainwater, and resolved that it would be up to me to ensure that she received a decent farewell.

I knew Riley wouldn't agree to have Reverend Willis at the grave, not because he'd begrudge Mama a few words of the Bible's comfort, but he'd made it clear that he didn't want anyone to know where we'd put her. I hoped to persuade Reverend Willis to come later, after Mama had been there a while, but I knew that would never happen with Riley's approval, because I'd heard him tell the kids that the whole affair would be a lifelong secret, and that even if tortured they'd need to keep silent about their grandmother's resting place.

It was a speech adapted for kids from Daddy's family-first repertoire. While we are a clannish people, Daddy never gave a shit about family. What he wanted were servants, the kind you can beat fear and loyalty into. Riley had the gift to talk you into what Daddy strapped you into. He told the kids that folks have a right to be buried where they want, if it's their land—in this case he was only stretching the truth a bit, as it was ours in every sense save for the fact that we had ceased to pay taxes on it years ago—and that we'd have been able to do as we pleased only some, "Mean old lawyers made up a law says you have to be buried in a cemetery." It was the perfect blend of truth and fiction a kid would eat up, but I really think it succeeded because he went on so long the kids would have agreed to anything to get back to the television.

When Annie and Carleton were done with breakfast, Riley sent them out to tip some pine trees to make Christmas wreaths, which I knew must be part of his scheme to woo Lillian back to the ridge fulltime. I wondered if he'd go so far as to get some lights and a reindeer or two, and try to make the place look like one of the houses in the subdivisions south of town where the last of the Blissfull's middle class and the disabled and pensioned-off miners lived.

Annie and Carleton looked like illustrations from a book of fairy tales we'd had when Riley and I were little, dressed in boots and gloves, necks wound with scarves, their hats pulled tight over their heads. I didn't figure the kids to be up to the chore, but Riley seemed convinced they'd want to do it. "There are plenty of boughs you can reach down the road by the creek crossing," he told them. "Just don't get wet or don't lose any fingers."

Annie rolled her eyes. "Dad, I'm practically a grown-up and I can watch Carleton," she said. The pair trooped out the door singing a song about cutting down a Christmas tree, Annie cradling the lopping shears and Carleton trailing a burlap sack.

When the kids were gone, Riley went to lay out their clothes for the burial. I snatched Mama from her spot under the couch and set her just outside the door on the porch, having decided to rush her down to Reverend Willis for the benefit of a few of the Lord's words. I was also worried about her being cremated, because in the early parts of the Bible, and I hadn't read too much further, the old Hebrews had always been gathering the bones of their ancestors and putting them in the same cave that they bought from the Hittites. I didn't know if ashes were the same as bones, but I figured Reverend Willis would know. I was also a bit vexed about dropping into the Star of Morning on a Sunday, because I didn't know when the Holiness-style churches held services, worried that they might run all day and into the night, and I couldn't keep Mama that long.

When Riley had laid out the kid's clothes, he leaned his head into the living room and said he was going to lie down for a bit. I told him I thought I'd walk into town, and he said I could take the truck, if I was back by eleven.

I stalled the first two times I let out the clutch and realized that I'd never driven a new truck, or any new vehicle for that matter, except in the army. The Ford's suspension absorbed the ruts and potholes in the road, and it was quieter in the cab than it is on top of the ridge on a hot summer afternoon. I eased along, unsure of when I might find Reverend Willis, and unsure of what I wanted to tell him about why I had Mama's ashes with me.

When I passed the kids near the tree I'd hit learning to drive, I saw Carleton holding down a spruce bough with both hands so Annie could snip it off. I would have honked but I didn't want to startle them.

CHAPTER FIVE

When I cracked open the front door to Star of Morning, Reverend Willis was sitting on the stage, his hands folded, feet dangling. "Hello, Isaac," he said.

I tried to slip into the story, but once I started it all stormed out until I was as breathless as a man with the dry heaves. I told him about Daddy's meanness and Mama leaving for Detroit and Riley fetching her home, and being worried about her being cremated, and how I wanted him to speak over her. Reverend Willis waited for me to finish, then pushed off the edge of the stage, stood beside me, his hand gripping my shoulder and said, "Let's pray together."

I placed Mama's box between the Reverend and me and we knelt right there on the floor. He prayed, keeping an arm draped around my shoulders, telling God all that I had told him as if it were his own story, then asking Him to take Mama into His care and to admit her into the glories of heaven and eternal life. When he'd prayed a long time in full voice, he put his free hand on Mama's box and commended, "A worthy soul to its immortal home in heaven." When the Reverend Willis said, "Thank you Jesus, Amen," I felt a surge of warmth bolt through my veins like the one I'd get when Ella and I, sober and rested, would start to make love on a Sunday morning, no hurry to be done, and no need to be anywhere in this world but her room. That such thoughts had come to me in a church, my mother's last remains beside me, shamed me, and I began to cry, but Reverend Willis said, "Ize, be filled with gladness that your mother's trials are over and that she has gone to be with the Lord." When we stood up, Reverend Willis hugged me close to him and invited me to sit with him for a while. It would have felt strange to me to be embraced for so long by a man, but Reverend Willis has a way of making you feel like that's all right.

As we sat side by side on the edge of the stage, he told me that once my mother's soul had passed from this world that her earthly remains were just, "Like the dust from whence we were created." His words made me feel better, especially since that was about what I'd told Carleton, and I asked him if he would come up to the plot sometime after we'd buried Mama to say a few words over her grave. I told him how Riley still held a grudge with all preachers on account of the one who'd beat Mama, and he said, shaking my hand, "The Lord knows all and in the spring we'll hunt up some serpents and visit your Mama's earthly grave, where I'll be proud to say a few words."

When Reverend Willis released me from his grip, I thanked him for his prayers and comfort, relieved that he'd said the Lord needed no more words to receive Mama's soul, and I knew that if I explained to the Reverend how to get to the plot, even if Riley's plan blew up and I had to leave Blissfull, that he'd find a way to honor my request.

I stayed until some women from the church began to arrive with food for the service and a man with a serpent box came in and set it on the floor near Mama. I thanked Reverend Willis, who hugged me again, and I promised to return to see him. As I was walking up the aisle to the front door, I heard a woman say, "Reverend, ain't that a Butts boy?"

On the ride home, overcome by the imminent final commitment of my mother's remains to the rocky earth of the ridge, I recalled a line from a song I'd often heard her sing that goes, "Don't mind so much the dying, but the laying in the grave so long." After living so many years of her life hidden from the sun in the shadows on the ridge, and after running off without her children, whom I believed she loved, only to die alone far from where she was born, I resolved that I couldn't put Mama to rest in the trench we'd dug on the ridge.

I eased the truck to the shoulder at the spot by the creek where Malcolm died, and where local kids say his spirit haunts the bridge. They tell a typical mountain ghost story embellished with strange lights and voices, the sounds of a basketball dribbled on the pavement, and visions of Malcolm in his uniform wandering about the water's edge crying. It's a story of the kind Daddy favored, except in his version Malcolm would be dribbling his severed head.

I remembered sitting there on the replaced guardrail after Malcolm died, imagining that if you slid into the creek that you could float all the way to the sea, and decided that such a journey would be my present to Mama. I fetched her box from the seat and slit the packing tape across the folds with a piece of sharp shale I found on the bank. Her ashes were packed in a clear plastic bag closed with a twist tie. Flecked with tiny bits of bone, they didn't look like stove ashes, the mixture, coarse and grainy to the touch, were not enough to fill a Quaker Oatmeal box. The small amount of Mama that remained, less than a child's pailful of sand, seemed a terrible reduction of a life, and I wished that no matter how shrunken or gaunt she'd become that I'd seen her before they put her body in the oven. I cursed my father aloud and wished that I could have taken the shard and cut him, as he used to say he'd do to anyone who crossed him, "Deep, wide, and again."

The creek was running slower than the last time I'd stopped at the bridge, but it was still muddied the color of strong tea, the current surging white where the bed narrowed between two gray boulders that sat like giant turtles regarding one another. I slid down the bank and nearly pitched into the creek, coming to rest when my foot snagged up on a large tree root. I'd managed to hold onto Mama, and once I was steady, I opened the box, untied the bag and, after repeating some of the words Reverend Willis had said in the church, I poured Mama into the creek, the dark current carrying her gray-white remains toward the Atlantic Ocean. A few bits of bone and ash clung to the plastic and I decided that those, along with some small stones and a few handfuls of the clay and dirt from the creek bank would go back into the crate.

I listened to the creek sing until I was sure Mama was well out of sight and beyond the sound of my voice, then headed back up the ridge.

Riley was standing on the porch and I could tell by the scowl creasing his face that he had discovered the box missing. I got out of the truck and showed it to him. "I wanted to take her for one more ride around town before we laid her to rest," I said.

"Bullshit," he said. "You took her to that preacher and now somebody besides kin knows she was cremated. That was a big fucking mistake Ize, a big fucking mistake."

I thought about lying, but said, "All he said was a few words over her. I told him we'd be spreading the ashes on the ridge." Riley contemplated that for a second then said, "Might save your ass, might not. Then," as if the storm had cleared he said, "Need you to help me with something."

I followed him inside, where the kids were weaving pine tips around a metal wreath maker's frame. Pinecones, a spool of wire, and some cutters lay on the table, and the kids worked as if it was a project they'd done before. When I asked them how many they planned to make, Annie said, "We get four dollars each from the wreath lady who sells them at the tree lighting in the square, and Daddy lets us keep it all."

We'd only been inside a minute before Riley said to the kids, "Uncle Isaac and I have an errand to do. We'll be back in half an hour."

I followed Riley outside, surprised that he'd leave the kids alone for so long. When he swung up into the passenger seat of the truck, I hustled around to the driver's side and started it up. "Drive down toward the old Whipple place and stop by the washout," Riley said, glancing back at the house.

I managed to work the clutch without stalling, pulled out onto the gravel, and headed downhill. At the washout, Riley directed me to turn onto a road at the edge of the former Whipple farm and we eased by the house and barn long fallen to the elements. The road, too, had been abandoned and I worried aloud that the truck might bottom out, but Riley assured me that we had plenty of clearance. Fifty yards beyond the Whipple's former dooryard, Riley said, "Park here, Ize."

We got out and Riley grabbed two shovels from the bed. "This way," he said, pointing toward the remains of a smokehouse, battered and sagging beneath the encroachment of a brace of pines and the ravages of the mountain weather.

The day was cooling and I smelled snow. I get a buzzing sensation in my nostrils and my nose hairs cling together whenever a storm is imminent. The door to the smoke house, long ripped from its hinges had been nailed to the jamb. Riley wrenched it free with one sharp motion of a pry bar he'd grabbed from beneath his seat. He took the end of his shovel, pried up some rotting boards, and began digging in loose, disturbed soil, uncovering what looked like a shower curtain. When he tired from digging he stepped back and I knew to take his place. "Don't tear nothin'," he said. Cold as it was, he was sweating.

"What am I digging up?" I asked.

"I told you best to know as little as possible. It ain't what, but who, and I don't know the answer to that."

I didn't say another word. I figured that if narcotics and illegal weapons weren't enough to land me in prison, a dead body might just clinch it. Though Riley had enough of the Old Man in him to make me worry, there was no way to turn away from the task at hand. The shower curtain turned out to be a garment bag, and inside were human bones. I made that discovery when I slipped and drove the tip of my shovel through the plastic and struck a skull. "Jesus, Riley, when did you kill this guy?" I said.

"I ain't never killed anyone, he said. "When my shed floor rotted away, I started digging to replace the sills and there he was. Figure the Old Man must have put him there. Then I remembered something from when I was real little and you were likely no more than three or four."

I waited for Riley to say more, but he grabbed one end of the bag, dragged it from the hole, and started filling in the old grave. When we'd tamped down the soil and nailed the door back to the jamb with a rock, I broke off a pine bough to sweep away our tracks, but Riley was only concerned with getting the bones into the truck bed and pulling the tonneau cover over them. Though I have sacrificed far too many millions of brain cells to booze, I was beginning to see where this was going.

We were going back up the road to home, Riley driving,

when I asked him, "These bones going in with Mama?"

"I believe she'll enjoy the company."

"How's that?"

Riley settled back into the seat. He unzipped his jacket and turned the heat down. "You know how Daddy always took us to the shed for a whipping, and how those wouldn't be so bad as the ones we'd get if we ran and he had to catch us."

I nodded, as my privates tightened and a tremor passed along my legs.

"Once, long before I got the balls to open his head with that wrench, he dragged Mama out there. He was cussin' her and saying that if she ever again looked at some guy he thought she'd been making eyes at in town that he and she'd both end up, and he said this part clear as day, 'under the shed with the other one.' I figure maybe it's somebody she wouldn't mind spending eternity with."

I couldn't tell Riley that if this guy was going to spend eternity next to Mama that he wasn't going to have much company. The meager bits of her in the bag, mixed in with the clay and stones of the creek bank, weren't more than the size of a pack of cards, but I knew he believed that no opportunity to make a buck, or settle a score, should ever be missed.

When I coasted into the dooryard, Riley said, "Keep the kids distracted while I put this guy in the crate. Leave Mama on the seat."

I went inside where the kids were working on a third wreath, praying that Riley wouldn't examine Mama's box, as it had traces of the creek bank on the sides, and I hadn't resealed the top, just folded the box flaps so it would stay shut. I wondered why Riley was going to such ends to bury the bones we'd dug up, and why he didn't just dump them down in an old mine the way the Old Man disposed of his enemies, but I guessed he'd decided that by doing something memorable for Mama he would increase his chances of reconciling with Lillian. As for Mama, she'd lived with two husbands, and neither my brother nor I could ever know whether either one had ever made her happy. Maybe Riley figured he'd found the remains of someone who could, or that he had to atone for his sins by fixing those of others. As I stewed on all the possibilities and intricacies of the situation, I was as perplexed as I'd ever been sober.

I determined that the hole in Riley's thinking was this; Daddy might have killed the guy just because he didn't like him. That a feud might become deadly over a woman made sense, yet the Old Man never acted like he minded Mama leaving, or seemed shamed by it as a failure on his part. She'd left, too weak, too disloyal to stay. That he'd kill a man to save his own hide, or livelihood, I believe, but I can't see him ever risking his freedom over jealousy. In those days, a missing hillbilly didn't rouse much interest from the cops either, as plenty of despairing souls quit these hills for the north with no more than what was on their backs. That doesn't happen so much now, but it used to. Broken by the mines or the grind of scratching for a living, men just left. Some sent for their kin, or reappeared, but plenty vanished and no one of importance felt they were worth finding.

I'm sure the Old Man would have made Mama pay if he thought she was showing too much attention to another man, but I believe that he'd have killed her before he would have killed to keep her. It was the same way he'd never hit one of us in the face where it might show, or the way he took the strap to Mama's legs so she'd wear long skirts like the holiness women, or pants that didn't show how pretty those welted legs might have been.

It's hard for folks who didn't grow up like we did to imagine that if the Old Man had killed the guy, and Mama knew it, that she would have let it pass, but it's also hard to imagine how much we feared him. I think about the years she endured an impossible situation, and how miserable she had to be to leave us, about the look she carried in her eyes like she was peering into some other world, a kind of panic that came into them every time I knew she was afraid for herself or her kids. All I remember about Mama is sweetness. I can't recall her raising a hand to Riley or me, but that may be because of the pieces of my memory I burned away with the hooch that has trickled down my gullet. One of the VA doctors, the one I'd been most honest with, told me that I'd confused my mother's affection for me with reality. He said she must have not only been afraid, but also been a part of what happened to us. I thought he was full of shit, but visiting with him saved me from group therapy and all the AA stuff I can't swallow. What I do know is that once Riley proved with one swing of that wrench that the Old Man couldn't hurt us anymore, Mama was free to go.

I was sitting with the kids and trying to help with a wreath, but I was distracted by Riley placing chains and shovels and the peavey into the truck, the metal clunking against the plastic bed liner. I looked at the clock and realized that it was past noon, and that in an hour we'd be trucking a scintilla of Mama and the old bones up the ridge and into the woods. I hoped that Mama was enjoying her journey toward the sea.

Lillian's car swept into the dooryard and skidded to a halt as if she'd arrived with some dire news. I looked up from the table as she cut the motor and saw a few fat flakes drifting down from the half-clouded sky. Riley was putting the come-along into the bed and snapping the cover down over the crate, and Lillian didn't stop to speak with him. She carried a wine-red garment bag over her shoulder, and I noticed that her hair was wet from a recent shower. The kids jumped up from the table, spilling boughs and tips onto the floor and ran to her gabbling and shrieking and asking when they could sell their wares to the wreath lady.

"Hush," Lillian said, letting each of the kids grab a piece of her waist, "I been up most of the night, had to pull a double plus because of a church bus wrecking on its way to Florida. I'm beat tired. Your father will take care of toting you and the wreaths to Mrs. Drybeek's tomorrow. I'm gonna lie down for an hour." She passed into the bedroom with a simple, "Hey, Ize."

Bone tired, almost haggard, she was as sexy as any woman you'd see. I know that nurse's clothes make women look that way, even the loose scrubs they wear now, but the thought of her warming the sheets with her body, and her hair leaving a cool spot on the pillow was too much for me. I could understand killing a man over her.

Riley was as animated and as cheerful a pallbearer as I'd ever seen. Other than the service for Malcolm Greaves, and a few other kids I'd known who died in wrecks, I hadn't been to many funerals. I'd seen the preparations for dozens of them when I worked at Plourdes, but I never was in a room during a wake or a service. The few I had been to in Blissfull had been full of wailing and hymn singing and preachers ranting about the glories of heaven and freedom from sin.

Our funeral was being held for a mother neither of her surviving children had seen in years, and attended by an ex-daughter-in-law and two grandchildren who'd never laid eyes on the deceased. I couldn't tell whether Riley was more pleased about burying what he thought were Mama's remains in the old plot along with the bones of an old lover, or with having his family together in his new truck. Thinking about the mud and stones in Mama's box, I nearly took to laughing at the thought of burying dirt under dirt

I listed against the passenger door and Lillian sat with a leg on either side of the shift. Each time Riley changed gears I turned more toward the door and raised up my left leg. We crawled up the ridge under glowering skies, streaked with pink and yellow clouds back lit by the sun, as if Riley was trying to make the experience last. He kept asking the kids if they were comfortable in the back seats, and pointed out deer at the edge of a clearing and a twisted, lightning-scarred tree that looked a man carrying a sign. The kids hadn't been raised to tramp over the hills the way Riley and I had been, and hadn't needed to learn the hollers and creeks, caves and old mines, the way we did so we could hide from the law, or Daddy, or hole up in a safe spot when caught out in a thunderstorm. It was if the kids were on vacation, as if we were in a mystery or play.

With just the decaying bones and the box of creek mud flecked with a few of Mama's ashes in the crate, it was easy to set the box above the grave we'd dug, though Riley groaned as if we were moving a Sherman tank, which I guessed was not to arouse Lillian's suspicions. A little water had seeped into the hole, but not so much as to splash as we slid the crate over the edge. I'd felt it would have been more respectful to pull it in from the front with the come-along, but Riley was eager to get that part of the day's chore completed. The problem came when the crate slid too far toward the open end of the hole and Riley and I had to put our shoulders into the task of pushing it back up the slight incline. We braced it with some rocks, and once it stopped moving we crawled up the bank, stones, roots and balls of wet soil falling behind us, and stood above the grave. Lillian and the kids scampered up beside us, and I could tell that Annie and Carleton were beginning to see that this was supposed to be a somber occasion. Riley glanced over at me. The look on his face was clear; he had done his part and now I was supposed to take over, but I had no idea what to say.

Riley shifted his weight, scratched his head, and cleared his throat. "Since Uncle Ize has become a church man," he said, "I think he should say a few words so the Lord knows that Mama is coming."

I knew she had long been in heaven, if such a place existed, but I also knew that Riley was determined that I lead us in a prayer, so I tried to remember what Reverend Willis had said. "Dear Lord," I began, "We commend the soul of our dear mother, Anne, to Your eternal care in the hopes that one day we might, too, sit with You and our Lord Jesus, and see her again. She had many trials in this life." I couldn't think of anything more to say, so I just added, "Amen."

Now I had heard, even as a boy, about the resurrection and the stone being rolled away from the tomb, so as we piled the thin mountain soil, rocks, and clumpy roots on top of the crate, I had to force down a chuckle. It wasn't that I figured Mama or her grave mate to rise from the dead, but I did imagine someone stumbling across the strange sepulcher we'd dug into the hillside and taking it for a stash of whiskey or weed, and I had to suppress a laugh as I imagined the look on the ghouls' faces when they found what was inside the box. When we fixed the chain around the boulder at the foot of the grave and tugged it tight to the freshly piled earth and rock, I damn near burst out laughing, imagining Riley coming up here to find the stone rolled away and the crate empty, like something from the Old Man's collection of ghost stories. It took Riley and I more than an hour to seal up the grave. Annie and Carleton helped at first by tossing clumps of dirt and root onto the pile, but, freed from the task once we got to serious shoveling, were excited to romp around in the woods. They didn't get far enough off to cause any worry, and most of the time Lillian trailed behind them. Riley and I stamped the earth as hard as we could and packed it with shovels. For a minute, we could have been a family on a picnic, except for the chill in the air and the nature of our work.

On the way back down the mountain, Riley played a Patsy Cline CD—music he said Mama loved—and pointed out sights from our childhood to Annie and Carleton, places we'd made forts, paths that led to caves and spots in the creek where the trout holed up in deep pools during the heat of August, the best places to hunt berries. The way he spoke and waved his hands you'd have thought our childhood would have made a great kid's book, a mountain boy's version of Tom Sawyer, a book I remembered well. What I recall most about it is the part where Tom and Becky go into the cave and get lost. I just remember thinking that a girl in a cave would be a nice thing.

All afternoon the air had been worried by flurries, but as evening settled on the mountain, a steadier snow began to stick on the grass and fence posts and I decided that God was snugging a blanket over the last bits of Mama.

Lillian sat slumped on the couch drifting in and out of sleep, occasionally startling herself from her rest with a loud snort, which threw the kids, who were sitting cross-legged on the floor watching TV, into fits of laughter. Riley, who'd slept as little as any of us, had put all the tools away, and swept the bed liner clean before pulling the cover back down tight on the truck. I'd watched him standing up in the truck bed, the snow falling and sticking in his hair, savoring his chore. I knew what he was thinking, and I prayed that Lillian, even if she wanted to dismiss him outright, would not slam the door on him. Though I was sitting in the only place I'd ever called home, and felt for the first time in years that I might belong there, I still felt a bit like a refugee waiting for a ticket to a new country.

In the night I awoke. At first I wasn't sure where I was, and as many times as I've experienced that fear, I've learned to first establish control of my breathing and pulse. I relaxed and let my eyes acclimate to the light. The porch light had been left on and I could see a half a foot of snow glistening on the hood of Lillian's car. The wind was still and the house cold. I'd gathered all the quilts around me, and as I came fully awake I realized that I'd been awakened by the sound of Riley and Lillian making love. The creak of the antique bed and the sound of Lillian's voice, full of surprise and joy, filled my ears in the otherwise soundless house. I heard Riley say, "Lily, Jesus, Lily." I'd never heard him call her that before.

CHAPTER SIX

Riley's mountain magnetism seemed to be working, at least for the moment. Lillian stayed on the ridge each night and began to help the kids decorate the house for Christmas. I liked her being around, except at night when I could hear her making love with Riley. It was strange that she'd be so free with him in the bedroom, but never hold his hand or touch him when the kids could see them, especially since, if sex and companionship were all Lillian wanted, even in a backwater like Blissfull, she'd have been able to do all right.

I remembered Christmas as a truce of sorts when I was young. The Old Man would be occupied fetching stock from his caches around the ridge for holiday delivery, and what wasn't being sold for the season had to be stored where it wouldn't freeze. The revenue people aren't fools, and they'll set to tracking in the winter because the snow makes their job much easier. Most of the winter Daddy sat around the fire, or, in good weather, hunted squirrels. It wasn't that we ate much squirrel, or that he enjoyed hunting, but it gave him an excuse to see who might be snooping around the ridge. As kids, it was a quiet time. If we stayed out of the way, even if the Old Man was sampling a batch of the fall's best, he'd leave us be. As long as the wood box was filled and the steps and dooryard were shoveled, he was easy until spring.

When I'd watch the kids stringing cranberries or making paper loops to hang on the tree, I'd be infused with hope, but I was frightened, too. I didn't want to consider how many Christmas Eves had triggered the start of a bender. The Sally Santas ringing those bells, the constant barrage of sappy Christmas songs that blast at you all day and night in every city I've ever been in, would find that touch-tender spot in my heart and rip away all the protective scar tissue I'd built up there. Watching Carleton color a red nose on a snowman in one of his books, I remembered a story we read in elementary school about an old woman who wrapped up presents for herself that she set under her tree. About the only holiday present I used

80

to give myself was a hangover and the shakes.

At night, when Lillian would pour herself a modest nightcap, I'd be sorely tempted to join her, but I swear that each time I really felt the pull—the knot in my gut, the peppery saliva washing the inside of my cheeks—I would hear Reverend Willis, singing in the Star of Morning van, and see the swirling snow on the highway the night he picked me up, and I'd whip the curse one more time.

A few days before Christmas on a blinding, sunny, calm day, when the ditches flowed a little, I took a hundred bucks from the money Riley had given me and hiked into town to buy gifts for the kids. When he saw me putting on my pack, Riley asked, "You ain't leavin' are you?"

When I told him I was just going to town to buy a few things he offered to drive me, and when I said I'd rather walk, he asked what was troubling me.

"Nothing," I told him, "I feel like a walk and this might be the last good day for one for awhile."

I could tell by his hard stare that he wasn't sure I was telling him the whole story, but I headed down the hill without saying another word. I stopped at the bridge and said a quick prayer for Mama, the sun firing the water, and the current singing. I said what came to me, "Dear God, grant my mother peace in heaven," and no more. I'd tried to think of something I'd written down in my notebook, but I'd pretty much stopped reading the Bible because all the stuff about following the laws precisely was confusing me. After I said my prayer, I felt like running.

When you don't have kids of your own it's hard to know what to buy them. All Annie and Carleton seemed to like was watching TV and making wreaths—they'd finished ten and had split the forty bucks. I thought about getting them cards and putting a twenty in each one, but I knew that might get Lillian suspicious as to where I got that kind of cash. It didn't seem right anyway. It was the kind of thing Mama did after she moved off the ridge. She never sent it to us, but each time she came down she brought us an envelope with some kind of sentimental message written on a card with money taped to it. She'd tell Daddy she'd given us ten bucks each, but usually there was another ten she didn't let on to him about. It wasn't as if these were presents for any specific holiday or birthday, just something she had to do to feel that she was taking part in raising us, I guess. Daddy wouldn't have a phone, said that the feds would just tap it, and Mama wasn't one to write with regularity. The money Riley had given me seemed to be like that, too. I was paid for being part of the family business, whatever that was now, not so much blood money as kin money, something to be shared.

Dudley's Toy and Pet Emporium had long been replaced by a Rite Aid. When I walked in, I was slain by sadness. I missed the smelly pet department with its yappy puppies, the long rows of bicycles with colored plastic streamers attached to the hand grips, the stacks of archery sets, the sweet-smelling baseball gloves, the bright tropical fish in the huge tanks with sunken ships and spidery plants, the racks of dolls and trucks, but what floored me most was the sameness. The store was laid out just like the one in Holyoke around the corner from Plourde's. There wasn't a thing West Virginia about the place. Even the cashiers looked like Yankees, their eyes going straight through you, not a one saying, "Hey," or "Need some help?" Except for the accents, I might have been in Massachusetts.

I'd have left straight off if I'd thought there was another place to find something for the kids. I knew there was a new mall south of town and that I could take a bus there, but I was sure that mall would be just like every mall I'd ever been in, not that I'd ever had money to spend in them. I used to like malls in the winter if I was between jobs or flops. They were warm, and you could see a whole town pass by in a day. Early, there'd be the old guys who walk loops to keep their hearts fit, and the Spanish-speaking girls who clean those places up, and the security guys who reload the cameras and remind you that you can't sleep on the benches or in the corners, and that the bathrooms are off limits to hooch and drugs. Later the women, mostly mothers with kids in strollers, arrive, then in the afternoon the high school kids, then at night the people who have homes but still need a place to get away from the loneliness.

I roamed the aisles looking for gifts, settling on three sketchbooks, a bag of markers and a box of colored pencils for Carleton. I also bought him one of those watercolor sets that come in a long tin box with colors like cerulean and burnt umber. I'd had one of those and a color-by-number picture book when I was a kid. I'd get an old jar lid with a bit of water and dip the skinny brush in it then rub it across the square of paint. I'd follow the directions, but I always seemed to get too much water on the brush, or didn't squeeze out enough of the excess against the rim of the lid and all my paintings ran together, the mountains dripping into the trees that ran like melted chocolate into the brook or ocean. I'd seen Carleton coloring and drawing and knew he liked to read the comics, so I guessed he'd at least think I was paying some attention.

Annie was a lot harder. She seemed too old for a doll, and all the other toys seemed to be geared to boys. I spied a pink plastic box like Mama's old sewing case, advertised as the Ultimate Teen Beauty Kit, and wondered if it was appropriate for Annie who'd told me most everyday since I'd arrived home that she'd be thirteen in March. I wondered if she'd be glad that I regarded her as more than a little kid, but I fretted that Lillian might think it was out of line. I picked it up and put it back on the shelf a half-dozen times as I'd often done with a bottle of whiskey in the past. It was the same kind of decision—something final about it. If I open a bottle, I'll finish it. If I wrapped that present and put it under the tree she'd open it, and if I'd done the wrong thing we'd both be paying for it.

I left the case on the shelf and made another circuit of the store. I realized that the Rite Aid had taken over more than the toy store. Dudley's had six aisles and, as a kid, I had memorized the order and contents of each one. The Rite-Aid had twelve aisles, and I was coming down number ten, where they had the cold remedies, pain killers, skin lotions, and dental supplies, when I began to think that I would have to take the bus to the mall if I was going to find an appropriate Christmas present for Annie. It had also occurred to me that I would need to get something for Riley and Lillian as well. I started toward the front of the store with Carleton's presents in my basket when I saw Lorena Whipple reaching up to get a tube of toothpaste from the top shelf.

The years had fleshed her in a sexy way, and she'd developed a round backside that filled her jeans. If it hadn't been for the almost white blonde hair and the lanky legs, I might have not noticed who it was. Never suave, all I could think to say was, "Lorena?"

She turned to see who it was that asked her the question and the old, hard Whipple mouth and eyes gave me a quick once over before she smiled. "Isaac. Sure as shit still alive. If I hadn't heard from my brother-in-law that you were back I wouldn't have believed it was you."

I didn't answer at first, trying to figure out who her brother-in-law was, and how he knew I was home. There aren't many secrets around Blissfull except the ones you hide up on the mountain or store deep in your heart, but I had been trying to keep a low profile. I looked at her hands for rings and saw none, but I noticed her cart had a box of diapers and a case of baby formula. "You heard I was back?"

"Hell, my brother-in-law rode you back here," she said.

"Reverend Willis? He's married to one of your sisters?"

"Was married to Lenora, the one named after Mama."

"They divorced?"

Lorena stared at me with a steely smile then down at her cart. "Lenora's dead. Snakebite. She was living out in Tennessee when she met him. They were hunting snakes and she got bit. They were too far up in the hills to get her to a doctor on time."

I couldn't quite digest what I'd just heard and all I could think to say was that I was sorry. I was about to ask Lorena about herself, when she launched into more details about the

Reverend—the old enthusiastic Lorena breaking out all over her face.

"Reverend Willis went to Jolo after Lenora's funeral and stayed with the holiness people over there. They say he handled and prayed for four days without sleep, disappeared in the hills for the summer and then decided that he would stay here and start a new church. Hiram, my first husband, offered to let him stay with us for a bit, being neighborly, but Theo, Reverend Willis, he just camped out in the hills that whole summer, searching for snakes—they call them—serpents, and praying. Come fall he went away for a few days and come back with a new van and his clothes. He bought the store and opened Star of Morning."

I wanted to ask who Hiram was and what Lenora was doing in Tennessee hunting snakes, and about a hundred other questions, but what I most wanted was to be skinny-dipping with Lorena and smelling her hair, and running my hands up and down those legs. I asked her where she lived and how old her baby was and she told me she had a house in Pine Hills, which I guessed was one of the developments south of town, and that the diapers and such were part of a collection she'd taken up at work for a young miner's widow. "Took two divorces and two sets of twins, she said, "But I got a place and it's paid up. I work in the City Clerk's office thirty hours a week, and Mama watches the kids."

I may not be the swiftest bird in the flock, but it seemed to me that Lorena had indicated that she was amenable to fairly personal questions. I decided to ask her if she might like to go out, but I'd never been on a real date having met most every woman I'd slept with, other than Lorena, either in a saloon or in the weeds somewhere. Even Ella, who was as refined and sweet a girl as I'd ever been with, was someone I'd met in a diner. Lorena looked at me as if I should speak and I did. "Would you like to go out sometime?" I asked.

"Maybe," she said, flashing me a wide smile. "How about taking me to church, Star of Morning next Sunday?"

"Sure," I said, without thinking.

"210 Carolina Drive," she said.

"What time should I come by?" I asked, unsure that I'd even be able to borrow Riley's truck.

"Service begins at ten. Come by at nine and we can have some breakfast. Mama will like to see you."

I stared at Lorena's backside as she headed to the checkout. I waited to pay for Carleton's things until she'd gone, then holding my plastic Rite-Aid bag I headed for the bus stop.

The ride out to the Mountain View Mall would take five minutes in a car, but on the bus takes twenty because of all the stops it makes. Rich people don't ride the bus, so it coils along a winding circuit of the raggy, older neighborhoods on its way out toward the highway, beginning and ending its loop in front of the city hall where the courthouse, jail, and motor vehicle offices are.

I found presents for everybody. I bought Riley a red chamois shirt like one he used to have, but I hadn't seen on him since I'd been back. I almost settled on a gift certificate for Annie to The Gap, because I'd heard her say that it was her favorite store, but because I wanted her to have more than an envelope to open I bought her a blue jean jacket instead. It had big buttons and looked as if it were already old, something the sales lady said kids preferred.

Lillian was the hardest to shop for. I saw lots of clothes I'd have liked to see her wear, but I knew I couldn't give a nightgown or a dress to my brother's wife. I realized that I really didn't know my sister-in-law very well, and that I'd spent so little time around her when I was sober, that it was as if I was shopping for a stranger. I thought about getting her a gift certificate, or buying her a fluffy bathrobe, but I didn't want to look like I was in on Riley's plan to get her to move back in with him. Lillian is so naturally beautiful and indifferent to what people think or notice about her, that she doesn't mess with much make up or spend time fixing her hair, and has never developed any vanity that I can detect. If I couldn't buy her personal items, the only things other than booze I'd ever bought for a woman, I was at a loss for what to do.

In a store called, Mountain Woman's Home, which peddled clothes, furniture, and crafts made in various parts of Appalachia, I spied a sign hung near the rear of the store that said, "Gift Consultant." Seated at a table beneath the sign was the least West Virginia-looking woman I'd ever seen. She had short gray hair that appeared to be shellacked into place and huge gold-hoop earrings. She was wearing a sweater, though it had to have been seventy in the mall, and a long woolen dress. I must have stared at her a second too long because she looked up at me and said, "May I help you select a gift for someone?"

She didn't sound like a West Virginian either, her voice dry and even, but I decided that I had nothing to lose so I told her I needed a gift for my sister-in-law. "Evelyn," she said, hanging out a heavily moistened hand, which I shook. She asked me how old Lillian was and what she liked and what she did for a living, and ended up recommending a special foot spa that you attached to the bathtub because it was good for people who spend their day on their feet, or, she said, "a complete selection of hand and body oils and natural lotions for every type of skin condition." As I pondered both choices it seemed to me that using either of them involved a level of nakedness on Lillian's part that would surely upset Riley. I ended up buying five cedar boxes that nested inside each other, that Evelyn said, "Every woman needs, for jewelry, old love letters, and keepsakes." Even though I was sure Lillian had no love letters from Riley, and rarely wore jewelry, the little boxes with their tiny gold hinges and clasps smelled nice and would fit in my pack.

Evelyn offered to have the gold plate on the lid of the biggest box monogrammed, but as Lillian seemed to be going by her maiden name, Stalls, I asked if I could bring it back later and get it done. Evelyn said that would be fine. She gift-wrapped the boxes with bright red and gold foil and added a white bow. She placed the package into a shopping bag, and I hung it on my pack frame.

Walking up the ridge road, I remembered that it was December 21st, the shortest day of the year. It wasn't yet three o'clock, but the sun was down behind the mountains the temperature was dropping, the world shadowless. I was about a quarter mile up the road when I heard the whine of the school bus behind me. I knew that Annie and Carleton would be looking out the windows and thinking about how glad they were that vacation had begun. I don't want to sound like an old fossil, but when I was Annie and Carleton's age the bus didn't come up the road. The county never did much work on it besides plowing it after a storm, and if you didn't know the washouts it was an axle buster. I crossed from the left to the right side of the road, because I knew the driver would swerve that way to avoid a heaved-up culvert just ahead of me.

The bus growled to a stop when it drew up alongside of me and the door squeaked open. A stocky, gray-headed woman spilled across the driver's seat asked if I'd like a ride. I was about to say, "No thank you," when Annie ran up to the front of the bus and hollered, "Sit with me, Uncle Ize." I held my pack in one hand and the shopping bag in the other, and stepped up into the cab.

There were only four kids on the bus. I sat with Annie, though Carleton insisted on getting on my lap. The driver said, "Don't allow that normally, but seeing as how it's near Christmas he can sit there if he don't move around or fuss none." We inched up the hill, the woman downshifting each time she slowed to avoid a pothole or rock.

Several times, the kids attempted to peer into the bags and my pack, but I told them they wouldn't get any presents, even from Santa, if they peeked.

The bus gasped to a stop at a new, rain-rutted road that ran down the east face of the valley. I'd noticed it when I'd climbed by it the day I came home, but, because it descended into a thick stand of oaks, I'd assumed it was only a tote road. A woman, as reedy as the driver was thick, stood waiting for the bus, and when her two kids got off she tousled each of their heads, then shambled down the road with an arm around each one.

Mama had met the bus sometimes where it turned around just a few hundred yards above the end of the gravel whenever Daddy was in a bad mood or raving drunk. She'd take our books and lunch sacks, hand Riley and I some kind of a snack, and tell us to go off for a walk. We didn't have to worry about stopping to change like some of the town kids. We didn't have play clothes and school clothes, we just had shirts and jeans and shoes.

The sight of the woman and her kids disappearing into the woods snagged in my throat as I remembered that I hadn't stopped at the bridge on the way back to the ridge to say a few words to Mama. Then I thought of Lorena Whipple, naked, upstream where we swam in the deep pool and had sex. She'd had two husbands and four kids. The scrawny, hungry, half-wild girl from our ridge had a house and a job with the city clerk's office, while I had a few hundred bucks, no prospects, and lived on my brother's couch. I wondered what we'd talk about and where we'd go if she'd let me take her somewhere besides Star Of Morning.

When the bus got to Riley's place, Lillian was on the porch, dressed as if she was leaving for work.

"Thank God you're here, Ize," she said. There's been an accident at the Forsythe Trace. Bunch of stove-up boys and I'm needed at the hospital."

I didn't hear what Lillian said to the kids, because Lillian had never been so grateful for my presence before. Sobriety is full of wonders. I'd been off the juice for less than a month, but already my brain was working quicker, and I was finding an ability to speak to people who were also not drunk. I told Lillian that I'd take good care of the kids. She smiled at me, then about slew me when she gave me a quick hug and said to the kids, "Mind Ize for me now," raced to her car and drove off.

The kids and I worked on making wreaths. They had orders for four more that were going to be hung Christmas Eve at the Episcopal Church where Lillian used to go, and I preferred helping them snip the wire and choose bough tips to refereeing their afternoon bouts over which TV show to watch. Carleton was still young enough to like cartoons, especially if they involved a lot of fighting and sound effects, but Annie had become fond of movies. Lillian had rigged up the satellite TV so the kids couldn't watch the sexy stuff, and though she'd showed me how to work those features with the remote, I couldn't get the hang of it. I feared that if I unblocked any channels that I wouldn't know how to set the controls again, and I felt a horrible sureness that would result in the kids seeing something they shouldn't—the kind of thing bound to infuriate Lillian and piss off Riley as well.

It was fully dark at four, the house scented with pine boughs, a fine heat cranking from the fire I'd built in the stove. No matter how high the furnace is set, nothing warms like wood, or a good red coal fire; they're just drier and warmer. When the kids finished the wreaths, they headed for the TV, and I waited for the battle to begin, but the first thing they found was a Christmas movie they both declared to be their favorite. I didn't recognize it, but they knew each line and said them before the actors did, erupting into those little kid belly laughs where they curl up into themselves, clutch their stomachs and roll from side to side on the couch. I wondered if Lorena's kids were watching the same show, and I wished I'd asked her about them—how old they were, their names, anything to have made the conversation last.

I was sitting at the table drinking a cup of coffee when the phone rang. I jumped and rushed to pick it up, not quite knowing why I was in such a hurry. It was Lillian and she said that she was going to be home late, maybe one or two in the morning, and to tell Riley that she'd be as quick as she could. She couldn't talk long, and I didn't get to tell her about how well the kids were doing, and about the wreaths, and when I hung up I knew that I needed to find some woman company soon.

When I was with Ella, I didn't get wrecked all the time. The softness of a kind woman is the greatest enemy of the hooch. The truth is I'd rather have sex than do anything else in this world, but I'd always been so clumsy around women, other than Lorena, when I was young, that I wouldn't even try to get close to them when I was sober. Sometimes I'd drink a powerful fill of courage before I'd get up the nerve to ask a woman out, or even to dance. The results were rarely good, and I tended to wake up with women who had less of an idea about what had occurred on the previous night than I did. I can remember Ella, not with the searing intensity I remember Lorena and the creek, but most of the others are like the smoky fog that cloaks these hills on summer mornings.

Riley came in at five and he'd brought a huge pizza, and two quarts of Pepsi. Carleton shrieked when he spied the soda, and Annie began fetching plates and glasses down from the cupboards. Normally you can't pry them away from the tube, but the sight of the red and white Apollo Pizzeria box sent them into a tizzy.

Sober, food tastes much better than when you're drunk. Drunk, food is just the fuel you need to keep living. That's why true drunks are often reed thin, save for a small paunch. I knew I'd gained weight, because my clothes didn't hang from me the way they had in Holyoke. I was getting plenty of exercise walking into town and around the ridge, but that seemed to goose up my appetite as well. The pizza tasted great, though the crust was thicker and doughier than the kind you get up north, and as the kids don't cotton to a lot of toppings, Riley had ordered just cheese and sausage. After two glasses of soda, the kids were both wound right up, and I knew that if Lillian saw the Pepsi bottles she'd give Riley some grief about it, so after dinner I flattened the empties and, when no one was looking, popped them into the fire.

When I told Riley that Lillian had called from the hospital to say that she would be working until after midnight, I could tell that he was pleased. "She says she's gonna surely stay with us through Christmas, for the kids," he whispered to me.

The look in Riley's eyes scared me a little. I could tell that he thought his mountain magnetism had worked its full magic, but I figured that Lillian didn't want to be alone for the holidays any more than he did. I didn't say anything, and as soon as the kids had gone off kicking and screaming to bed, complaining that it was vacation and they could stay up, I fell asleep on the couch, my belly and my mind full. From time to time, I'd stir as I heard Riley move around in the leather recliner, or when he yelled back at the players in the basketball game he was watching on the TV, but mostly I was out until I heard Lillian drive in.

In the quick seconds that her headlights shone in the kitchen window, I saw on the wall clock that it was after two. Though Lillian was trying to come in unnoticed, I switched on a light and said, "Hey, Lillian, I'm awake."

"I'm sorry, Ize," she said.

"Rough night?"

"Yeah," she said, her voice ragged and hoarse, "Three old boys died, six'll make it, but there're going to be some miserable Christmases 'round here."

"I'm sorry, Lillian," I said.

"They were all young. It was horrible," she said pulling off her gloves a finger at a time. "Kind of night makes me want to be most anywhere else in this world."

I was glad Riley hadn't heard those words. Lillian slumped herself down at the kitchen table, leaned her head back and rolled her neck from side to side as if to work out a crick. "What'd you'all have for dinner?"

"Pizza."

Lillian leaned on the table with her elbows. "Soda, I'll bet, too."

I didn't answer. Lillian looked up at the ceiling and yawned, then flexed her arms above her head. "Well they're good kids and it won't kill them every now and then. You know, I just don't want them to be like all those baggy kids you see hanging around the school, lumpy and fat, all pasty-faced, and looking like they might puke at any minute. 'Fore people began eating all this sugared shit, folks around here were generally so skinny their pockets met in the back of their pants. Now there's all this asthma and diabetes, and just plain fat little shits everywhere. I don't know."

"They didn't have much," I said, wanting to keep Lillian talking. The sound of a tired woman's voice has always soothed me, and I don't know why, except that tired women are just sexier to me. Maybe that's because except for Lorena and Ella, so many of the woman I've had sex with were verging on sleep, or passing out. Though I knew the answer, I asked Lillian if she was going to stay around for the holidays.

"I got no place to go, the kids will like it, and Riley and me are getting on pretty well," she said, enunciating pretty. "I never plan too far ahead anymore." When she'd said that, Lillian got up and opened the cupboard above the refrigerator. "If it won't be a problem," Lillian said, "I'd like to have nightcap before I go in."

I wondered if it was a test, or if she detected some new reason to worry that seeing the bottle might send me back into the weeds. "I'm done with booze," I said. "Some of us can't have any, all our tickets have been punched, but that's no reason for you not to."

Lillian poured out bourbon, neat, then went to the fridge and fished out one cube from the ice tray. She'd poured out less than a decent bar shot, and sipped it over the next few minutes, as the cube shriveled and disappeared. She talked, as much to herself as to me, about what she'd make for Christmas dinner, and when she had to work, and what she'd bought for the kids. I was going to tell her what I'd bought for the kids, but I was afraid to let her know I had that much cash, so I said I had a few small things for each of them. She told me she thought I'd been real sweet to the kids, rinsed her glass in the sink, set it in the drainer, and walked over and kissed me on top of my head. I smelled hospital soap on her clean nurse's hands, and when her ponytail swung by my face, the scent of lemon in her hair, and, though I knew it violated a commandment, I coveted my brother's ex-wife with a searing lust.

Saturday, Lillian took the kids to town to deliver their wreaths and to do their last minute shopping. I was having coffee with Riley, when I told him about Lorena. He said he could let me have the truck for a few hours, but that he had some errands to do Sunday afternoon. After a minute, he said, "Yeah, Lorena. Isn't she the one with the nice ass? The one married Hiram Potter, and then left him for some guy…Roger was his name… who got killed in a wreck? Believe she has four tow-headed kids and she's the Whipple who works in city hall, handles the tax liens and the like."

"She was married to guy named Hiram and she works in the city clerk's office," I said. "Must be her."

"The one you used to spend time with at the creek?" Riley asked. Before I could answer he said, "Do you some good to straighten your old lizard out."

"I'm taking her to church. Star of Morning," I said.

"She don't seem like the snake handling type, one-eyed trouser snakes maybe, but not rattlers and copperheads," Riley said, laughing at his joke.

"Reverend Willis is her brother-in-law."

Riley, who'd been hunched over a cup of coffee at the table, sat up straight and said, "That Whipple girl died of snakebite over in Tennessee somewhere. She'd married some old miner, twenty years older 'n her from over near Welch. She started goin' out on him, and he caught her in some guy's car. Tarbox, that was the husband, Ray Ed Tarbox. Pulled a gun on the guy, made him drive off, then pulled every stitch off a Lenora, took a damn stick to her and made her walk in front of the car all the way into town. Said he shoot her dead if she stopped. Pulled right into the police back lot. He got two years and when he come out he tore her up again and got sent back. That's when she went away. I'd forgotten all about that when you asked about those girls before. Lorena is a looker, but I'd stay away from them serpent handlers or you'll end up over to Jolo snake bit dead for sure. I wouldn't handle no snake no matter how someone might dare me." Riley paused, then said, "I need to take a leak, be back in a minute."

As a kid, I'd been in trouble for taking dares, and while Riley was gone, I relived some of the fully foolish stunts I'd pulled long before I'd had my first sip of the Old Man's best, chuckling aloud at the memories. In third grade, I ate an earthworm that had come up after a rain and was wriggling on the asphalt section of the playground during recess. When I got sent home, the Old Man made me dig up and eat five more, then wore out my backside with his belt, not for eating worms but for getting caught and thus drawing attention to myself. Later, I drew the attention of the Blissfull cops who nailed me for standing on the hood of Billy Fairbanks's truck holding up a plastic statue of a naked Venus he'd found at the dump, while he drove through the square downtown, which earned me another thrashing. Even when I was still a little kid, I'd been willing to jump off a high place or across a spot in the creek no else dared to try, but my biggest stunt was the time, on a dare from Shep Petty, I cut down the lone tree in the high school courtyard.

It was a few years after the new high school had been built to replace the one that had stood downtown since the turn of the century. A modern, one story brick building, it was designed with lots of angles and rooflines, some as sharp as the narrowest mountain valleys, some, like the gym roof, humped like a whale. The science wing was jammed into the hillside so with a boost and strong arms you could pull yourself up onto the roof from the teacher's parking lot. The night I cut the tree down, Shep pulled his truck alongside the back wall and I scrambled up onto the roof with an axe.

To get into the courtyard, I had to sneak along the gym roof. There was a basketball game going on so we knew no one would hear us, and as I passed over the gym, I could feel the school vibrating with the rhythmic cheers of the crowd. Stars were splashed across the winter sky and my breath ghosted in the cold. While I waited for the game to end and the building to clear, I sipped from a flask of the Old Man's hooch and tried to imagine the scene in the gym: the cheerleaders doing splits, coach sitting half on and half off the end of the bench tossing a roll of athletic tape from hand to hand, Malcolm Greaves at the foul line, face frozen, bouncing the ball and settling into his crouch before swishing another free throw.

When the game ended, I heard the crowd exhale through the double doors at each end of the gym and cars squeal out of the lot in a victory dance. I knew that, cold as it was, there would be parties and bonfires, and that as soon as the team had showered that the guys would be slipping rubbers into their varsity jackets and popping celebration beers in the cabs of their trucks. I'd been to a few of those gatherings, but someone had always tried to buy liquor from me.

After the visiting team's bus had coughed up the hill to the highway, and the last straggler's cars had abandoned the lot, I dropped down into the courtyard.

I had to make a cut that ensured that the tree, a twelve foot spruce, would fall against the roof so I'd have something to shinny up to get out of the courtyard, because all the doors to the inside hallways were locked. It took me half an hour to hack through the tree, I was about half-saturated at the time, but with the drunk's luck it fell with its bushy crown landing on the roof at a corner of the courtyard. Before I crawled up the trunk I carved three initials in the stump with my Barlow knife. L for Lorena, I for Isaac, and E for Ever.

Shep's truck was gone, and thinking he'd forgotten about me, I started walking home, the sweat freezing along my spine. Orion hung above me and I thought about the poem, Mrs. Ingalls, our English teacher, had read that day about a "patient ethersied upon a table." I'd liked the poem. When she read it I felt like I did when I was just feeling the whiskey move my mood, when my skin was warm and my mind clear. I know booze fogs your thinking, but there's a moment, just before the numbness starts, where everything is lucid and you understand the things you're about to forget. If I could pause at that instant, I would do so every time. That's the curse in drinking, that you can't keep that perfect second when all is understood. Half a mile up the road, Shep pulled alongside and said, "She fall right?"

"Perfect," I said, jumping into the passenger seat. "Where you been?"

"Cops was riding around the school, I was the last one so I figured if I drove out they'd leave."

The next morning the principal, Mr. Cowfeller, got all teary as he told everyone over the intercom that, "That tree had hurt no one," and that, "Anyone who'd commit such a terrible act of vandalism was beneath contempt." I could have just let it be a great mystery, but a sudden craving for attention and a status as something other than a bootlegger's kid, compelled me to stand up in my home room, over Mrs. Marshall's protests and say, "I cannot tell a lie. I chopped down the tree with my little axe." At first no one believed me, though they all laughed, but when I persisted, Mrs. Marshall said, "If that is the case, Mr. Butts, go tell the principal." I got suspended for two weeks. After that, I rarely called attention to myself.

It was stuff like that that encouraged the belief in people that I'd somehow kill myself long before I got gray. It might have been the end of me anyway, except Mama intercepted the suspension letter, and told me to head off for school each morning and stay in the woods away from the Old Man, until the suspension was over, which was what I was thinking about when Riley returned.

"Just to be clear, it's no snakes," he said. "Not ever."

Dares are one thing, snakes are another, and along the way life and booze have worn the edge of my courage and tempered any desire for notoriety. "Riley," I said, looking him as straight in the eye as I could, "They've scared the shit out of me my entire life. I ain't never handling any damn snakes."

Riley said, "Thought you were all born again, Ize," then grinning like a little kid laughed and added, "But look out for Lorena. Soon as she gets your snake in her hands again you'll be doing whatever she wants. That's the thing about women. They got what we can't get ourselves and because of that a man will do most anything to get or keep it. Hell, I given up both my natural businesses, whiskey and reefer, just to try and keep the one woman I can't live without."

"You make a point," I said. "But I'd bet that Tarbox guy felt the same way about Lenora being the only woman for him, too. Look at the grief it caused him."

"No. That was just mountain mean. I'm sure he was just as pissed at the guy as at Lenora, but he didn't blame him for getting some. That was about pride. Keeping his and taking Lenora's." Riley paused for a minute and stared at the grounds in his cup. When he started to speak again his voice was softer. "I don't blame you for wanting to get up with Lorena again, for she has become quite the looker, filled out in the best places, but women with religion is trouble. Jesus will whup your ass for them every time they want him to."

I'd rarely heard Riley talk so freely in a long time. It felt like when we were kids, allies again against the Old Man, two skittish boys who shared a bedroom haunted by the dark sounds of the house in the night, talking to each other to keep the nightmares away.

I thought about what Riley had said about there being a mountain mean, and I knew what he meant. All the old feuds, and all the killing the Old Man had done was mountain mean, a stony hardness, a sharp knife-edged, slit-your-throat-for-looking–at her, meanness. Once, a professor had come to our tenth grade civics class to tell us about our heritage, all those Scots-Irish clan types who'd found these hills to be like the ones they'd been driven out of in Europe, and loved so much that they drove out the Cherokee. He said we'd inherited many of their customs, good and bad. He said feuding and violence were the bad ones, and that music and family were the good ones, or something like that. What I still remember about the guy was that he was shiny bald with drooping cheeks like a cartoon dog, and that he spoke with that funny accent they have in the Tidewater section of Virginia. He said those early white settlers made log hooses using methods they had seen in the highlands of Scotland, and a bunch of other stuff I've forgotten, but all he said about the blood feuds might have been summed up as mountain mean. If so, it had to hum somewhere in our blood because we'd been begat by as mean a mountaineer as there ever was, and all of Mama's sweet helplessness couldn't wash that away.

"Let's go for a ride," Riley said, "I need to get out of here."

We put away our dishes and mugs, stepped outside, pissed out the coffee into the ditch, and headed down the gravel in the truck. Riley didn't offer as to where we were going and I didn't ask. Some rules don't ever change—Saturday is the traditional day to just drive. My memories of riding with Riley are pretty steeped in booze, a cold Pabst Blue Ribbon between my legs and a pint of hooch in one hand; riding slumped against the passenger door. In the summer we'd have the windows open and my right arm would get browner than my left one did. We'd ride the hills and hollers peeking in the nooks and crannies of the mountains for something we hadn't seen before, or something we'd missed the hundred other times we'd wandered up a certain gravel road. This time Riley headed over to the interstate and drove north for about an hour, turned around and drove south, got off on a side road and navigated back to town by his natural sense of direction. That, too, was part of the ritual. I can't ever remember us having a road atlas in the car. If we got lost we asked someone for directions, or took our cues from the sun. We were so honestly local, so purely hill people, that no one ever turned us down, or displayed any sincere suspicion. Sometimes we'd pick up a hitchhiker just to find our way to a familiar place. I guess those skills are why I'm still alive. I've navigated a good part of this land, sometimes nearly blind with drink, and made it home when I had to. I never had a map, and I guess that the only sense I have is a sense of direction.

The creeks were burbling beneath a dull sun warm enough to melt the snow in the valleys and towns into brown slush, though the mountaintops looked like they'd been draped with fresh-off-the-line sheets, and the pines up in the high valleys drooped beneath the wet snow. West Virginia is the most northern of the southern states, not just by geography, but also in climate. We learned about that back in school, too, how our altitude supported flowers and birds that you usually only saw far to our north. We learned how parts of Maryland and Delaware never got as cold as our highest valleys, and how our rivers plunged faster and steeper than most any of the ones in the New England mountains.

When Riley steered the mud-splashed truck into the dooryard, Lillian and the kids came out to greet us. The porch had been strung with colored lights, and a freshly killed Christmas tree stood in the window, untrimmed, but shiny in the light. I had to hide the fact that I was fighting off tears, that I was both as sad as I could remember being, and as hopeful as I imagined I might be again. Lillian kissed Riley hello and the kids tugged at my arm and entreated me to come in and taste the cookies they'd made. I felt at home and I felt like an intruder. I belonged and I feared that I would have to go. And I had no idea where.

CHAPTER SEVEN

Most of the religious singing I remember was croaked out by the reluctant raspy voices of the career drunks at the Sally, droning renditions of Throw Out the Lifeline, or Nearer My God to Thee, accompanied by a veteran of the flops on a poorly tuned spinet or foot-pumped organ; hymns sung by men who were swapping a feigned interest in the Lord for a square meal and a bed. A few times in the winter when I was on the bum up north, I'd crawled into a dark corner of a Catholic cathedral and listened to the chanting and singing, trying not to freeze. But nothing prepared me for the music at Star Of Morning.

A piano and an electric organ, both of which had been covered with sheets when I'd been in the church before, sat off to the left of the stage, which was strewn with tambourines, guitars, basses, amplifiers, and serpent boxes. The service never really seemed to have a starting place it just sort of erupted. Folks leaped up to take turns with the singing and shouting, while Reverend Willis, stood in the center of the activity, Bible held above his head, eyes closed, talking about Jesus being, "Born of a Virgin," and "God's only begotten Son," and describing the Wise Men and their gifts and the perfection of God's love. The vibrations from the instruments were enough to shake a man from his chair, but Reverend Willis, as if oblivious to the exuberance around him, stood tall and nearly motionless, his voice rising with each new line of prayer and testifying.

I never got nearer to the stage than the fifth row of chairs where Lorena and I had first sat down. Despite the shouting and singing and Reverend Willis's ever-louder exhortations, my eyes were focused on the serpent boxes, as I imagined that the rattlers and copperheads would be coming out at some point soon and would be more than a bit agitated by the din.

After what had to be an hour of uninterrupted preaching and hymn singing, Reverend Willis's white shirt was saturated with sweat, and I could delineate the outline of his sleeveless t-shirt each time he swelled his lungs full of air, yet he showed no sign of fatigue. From time to time, he would open his eyes and stare straight up as if trying to glimpse heaven through the roof of the building and cry out, "Maranatha!" and a hymn would erupt and he'd join in, verse after verse, never needing a hymnal, his voice soaring above the congregation. During one of the hymns, I cast my attention on a half-dozen heavy-set women twirling in front of the stage with their arms held above their heads as if poised to catch a beach ball, and it occurred to me that there might be no limit on how long their energy or the service itself might last.

To keep my mind off the snakes, which were no more than twenty feet from me, each time someone rattled a tambourine I snuck peeks at Lorena, who rocked side to side in rhythm with the music, eyes riveted to the show. She'd worn a blue, long-sleeved, mid-calf dress and low-heeled shoes, her hair loose, not tied up in a ponytail, as it had been when I saw her at the Rite Aid, and she hadn't put on any makeup. I glanced at a few of the other women and noticed that all of them were without lipstick, and all had long unfettered hair. In so plain an outfit, another woman might have looked dowdy, but Lorena's eyes, their ember blue enhanced by the dress, and the sight of her body as she swayed to the holy jam session, flooded me with as vibrant a spirit as the saved and anointed.

I was ogling Lorena as she spun twice in front of her chair, the hem of her dress brushing my leg, the creeping heat in the church and the blast of the band making me dizzy. When the Reverend Willis shrieked out, "Maranatha, come Jesus come," then ceased to move or speak, Bible in his right hand, his left palm forward and raised well above his head, silence invaded the congregation. Eyes closed, Reverend Willis drew an audible gust of breath and shouted, "I feel the Holy Spirit in this place." The organ held a long low chord, and the ladies began to hum as one. As soon as the women had their note, the men droned one beneath it and a new vibration rattled through Star of Morning. After a bit, some of the women took hold of a higher note and the chord swelled. The organist added an even higher note but played softer and the singers eased down to a near whisper.

Reverend Willis began to speak. "Maranatha, Lord come," he said. "Lord will come, Jesus, come by here." I noticed everyone, including Lorena, had their faces upturned toward the ceiling, their hands raised, and were swaying side to side with their eyes closed, though I kept mine open. I heard snakes rattling in their boxes, and a shooting chill grabbed my privates as if I'd plunged naked into a snow bank. The chord swelled again, modulated a tone higher. I jumped as Lorena grabbed my hand and held it as if she wanted to wring water from it. Reverend Willis began to speak again, calling to Jesus to come, "Into this unworthy vessel, so that those who believe may be healed," his voice, soft and ragged, discernible as a whisper above the hum. He bent forward, placed his Bible on the stage floor, stood up, spread his arms as if to embrace a small child running to jump into them, and called out, "Ye who believe on Me come to be healed of your afflictions."

The voices of the chord swelled, louder; women shrieked and cried out, "Come, Jesus." The organist modulated the chord again and the congregation clawed up to it. Lorena squeezed my hand so hard my elbow tingled. She was shifting her weight from foot to foot and taking deep breaths that would have made me hyperventilate, and holding the alto note for what seemed like minutes at a time. I could not avert my gaze from Reverend Willis; sweat pulsing off the tip of his nose, his cropped hair obsidian black in the dim light. He rocked on his heels, arms raised and said, "Oh Lord, oh Jesus, Savior and King, healer of the afflicted body and mind, I see here today people who are sick and in pain, and I ask You to help lead them to You and Your grace." He paused, flicked the sweat from his nose with a finger, and raised his arms again. "I sense among us this morning," he said, "A sister in Christ whose rheumatism and arthritis makes each step, each simple chore, each stair a moment of misery, and I ask that she come forward to be healed, to find the magic grace in Your love." He paused again, and a torrent of shouts of "Jesus," and "Cast out the Devil," broke over the room, the keening and praising rising decibel by decibel until it boiled in my chest. Reverend Willis's voice thundered, "And I sense a brother in Christ whose back is weakened by pain, who cannot sleep at night, nor rest during the day, and I pray that he will come forward to feel the love of loves. Praise God."

Choruses of "Amen" and "Praise Him," erupted as the music swelled again, the reedy, beaked-nosed organist opening the stops and the teenaged girl on the bass adding a bone-rattling throb. Slowly, some of the older and larger women began to form a line in front of Reverend Willis. He grabbed a full glass of water that had been sitting on a serpent box and drained it, and dried his face and neck with a towel. Two young men, maybe twenty, bounded up onto the stage and flanked him, edgy as a dictator's bodyguards.

Reverend Willis and both of his assistants struggled to lug the first woman in line up the two narrow steps to the stage. She'd attempted get herself up by setting her right hand on the edge of the stage for balance, but was unable to bend down that far. All my life I'd seen women like her in these hills, pushing three-hundred pounds, glasses as thick as jelly jars, skin the color of burlap and papery as rotten birch logs, ankles swelling out of their shoes like rising bread dough. I could hear her mumbling praises, but she didn't open her mouth beyond a slit like folks I've known who've lost their teeth or have worn them down to black-pitted stumps. Her hair, the color of old, wet hay, fell thin and tangled to her waist. As Reverend Willis stood behind her, hands on her shoulders, she kept worrying her glasses up on the bridge of her nose, but, swathed in sweat, as soon as she'd punch them up with her stubby index finger, they'd slide down again.

Reverend Willis spun her to him and she seemed to whisper into his ear. He patted her head and stroked her back as he hugged her, then he stepped back from her and raised his arms, the dark stains under his arms oily in the half-light. The woman handed her glasses to one of the assistants and stood in front of Reverend Willis with her head bowed and her arms raised above her head. He gazed up to the heavens and cried out, "Jesus heal this woman whose feet pain her to walk. Bring comfort from her distress with Your infinite love which we sinners are unworthy to know." One hand on the woman's forehead and the other on the back of her neck, Reverend Willis shouted in a voice louder than July thunder, "Come, Holy Spirit. Heal they servant."

The woman's knees buckled and the assistants helped her slump to the floor like a sack of half-set cement. I'd expected her to crash in a heap, but the world moved at half-speed until she'd oozed onto the stage in a sprawl. When she rolled to her back and began to shake like a kid with the giggles, the congregation hollered and the organ and bass were joined by a guitarist and several women with tambourines, shouting, "Glory, Glory, All Glory to God."

The woman went rigid and I thought she had passed out or died, but she rolled to her knees and sprang to her feet, shrieked, and began to speak in tongues, her voice rushing from her throat with the sound of ice sliding off a metal roof. Her wail sent a jolt through Star of Morning and I swear that Lorena's fingers dug into my arm so hard that I nearly passed out. Once the woman was steady on her feet, she swirled and spun around the stage like a kid in the rain, holding her hands above her head and shouting words I couldn't understand, her long hair whipping her florid face, which sparked a parade of believers to the stage.

I'd lost track of the time and was slammed with panic, afraid Riley would be angry with me for keeping the truck, but I was more terrified that Lorena might drag me up to the front to be healed. I'd knocked myself out enough times to know that I had no desire to be knocked out by Reverend Willis. My nose was suddenly assaulted by the odor of human sweat, and I wondered if Reverend Willis had thrown a second sack of coal on the fire, because the windows were fogged and the air was as dry as October meadow grass, making me as light-headed as breakfast beer. Maybe the heat was for the serpents, or maybe just a way to make the poor folks who comprised his flock warm for a few winter hours, but the room was as blazing as an August sidewalk.

Half the congregation queued up to be healed in two lines that snaked through the aisles and up to the stage. A few times, as he stepped back from a collapsing believer, I swear Reverend Willis stared through me, and I grew deathly afraid he'd call to me to come forward so he could lay on hands. Each time our eyes met, I felt as trapped as I did in algebra class when Mrs. Laneworthy called on me even when she knew I hadn't done my work. I peered at Lorena's wrist to make out the time, but she was wearing a woman's watch with miniscule hands you'd be hard pressed to see in full noon sun, and in the low light of Star of Morning it was impossible to read them.

Lorena had said little since we'd entered the church, though on the ride over she'd been talkative as hell, and I'd been convinced that she was pleased to see me even though she hadn't invited me into the house. It wasn't a real cold morning, but I'd been surprised to find her waiting on the porch with a mug of coffee after she'd said I was invited for breakfast, and wondered if my dizziness was from a lack of food or a spell of the whirlies coming on. She glanced at me for just a second and smiled, her right hand gripping my arm above my wrist as if she was taking my pulse. I thought it looked like the smile she used to give me when I walked her back to her place when we were kids, when we were both still damp from the creek and my balls had shriveled to tiny pits after our love-making.

The music quickened. Lorena rocked side to side, and I recalled what a guy had told me once when we were sitting around a fire we'd built in the woods off the side of the interstate near Brattleboro, Vermont. "You want to find the horniest chicks in any town," he said, "Find a Baptist church. All that talk about sin fires them right up. You'll find more pussy at a revival meeting than any saloon in America." Remembering that talk, I was glad that Reverend Willis couldn't read my mind.

The big woman who'd been the first to be healed appeared to be losing steam or getting woozy. She ceased twirling, lowered her hands, her chest heaving, and staggered to the back of the stage, settling for a moment under the stenciled sign containing the words of Mark 16. Without her glasses, she appeared to be navigating by touch. I don't know why I fixed my gaze on her, maybe to avoid making further eye contact with Reverend Willis, but I watched her huge body disappear behind the two assistants, Reverend Willis, and a crumpling, hump-backed old miner. When she came back into view she was holding two serpents, and this time I squeezed Lorena so hard she gasped.

One of my chores as a boy was to keep the grass mowed close around the house and to cut away the weeds along all the buildings to make sure that there was no place for snakes to hide. I'd slept in the weeds on the bum, but I had to be thoroughly drunk and convinced that I wasn't in snake country. Seeing that woman let the two rattlers roll over her body frightened me deeper than the Old Man ever had. I wondered how Lorena could stand to see them when she'd lost a sister to snakebite. As soon as it was clear that the woman wasn't coming down off the stage, my fear ebbed, but did not disappear.

Reverend Willis, took up a rattler and a then a copperhead, and held them both over his head. Lorena moved closer to me. As I was about to ask Lorena what time it was, Reverend Willis began to sing to the serpents, and held their heads to his face. Lorena rose on tiptoe and whispered, "Mama wasn't well this morning. The kids will be making her crazy by now, take me home, please."

I didn't see anyone take notice of our leaving, the appearance of the serpents having garnered everyone else's attention. We got our coats from the rack, and as I helped Lorena into hers, it took every ounce of my new resolve not to wrap my arms around her.

As we walked to the truck, Lorena told me that the service would go on into the afternoon, break for a communal meal, and conclude at night. "Sometimes," she said, "They meet till dawn. I go to support Theo. He's been good to us." She paused a minute then stared hard into my eyes, "Lenora's dying wasn't his fault," she said, "He tried to save her."

Though I thought Lorena was opening a door for me to talk, I wasn't sure enough of myself to go any further. "I believe that he's trying to save me, too," I said.

I turned the ignition and pulled out into the street. I'd been gone two and a half hours, and though I knew that Riley might be antsy about his truck, I hoped that Lorena would invite me in when we got to her place. "I hope your mama isn't too sick," I said.

"She's old, Isaac, that's all. Never took care of herself." Lorena said. "I took her with me 'cause I needed the help with the kids, and because she was afraid of ending up in a home. What ever happened to your Mama?"

I knew that at some point I'd have to tell someone about Mama, but I wasn't sure how much I could say. "She died in Michigan," I said. "Riley had her shipped home. We buried her on the ridge with her people, least the ones that stayed long enough to die here."

My guess is that there was something in my tone of voice that Lorena interpreted as final, because she changed the subject to how Lenora had simply stumbled on a snake and been too far from town to get medical help in time. "Some can be bitten and live, for some it's fatal. I don't believe it's a sign of the Lord's, but the people at Star of Morning are believers and I respect that, respect their way of seeing things," she said. "I won't be handling, that's for sure." I stewed on what she said, because it was my understanding that believers don't accept medical help when they're bitten, but rather trust God to let them live or call them home as he sees fit, and I was relieved to know that Lorena cared no more for the serpents than I did.

Lorena's house was immaculate and modern and I was struck by its vivid contrast to the side hill disaster she'd been raised in. Her mother limped out into the living room when the kids, towheads like Lorena and her sisters, hollered hello to their mother. Mrs. Whipple was as shrunken as an old apple core, hunched and gnarly-fingered, with a skein of hair as white as a fresh line on the highway. When Lorena said, "Momma, you remember Isaac?" she allowed that she did, but I knew it was only when Lorena told her my last name that she understood that her daughter had brought home the bootlegger's boy.

Old mountain women, even when they've been lugged to the safety of town by a child in the waning light of their days, are a wily, suspicious lot. Lorena's mother's weary gray eyes bored through me with a probing intensity rivaling Reverend Willis's.

Mustering her natural hospitality, Mrs. Whipple invited me to have coffee and a biscuit, and though it was hard to pass up, I had to return Riley's truck and I knew she'd felt beholden to make the offer.

Lorena escorted me outside. She stood a minute leaning against the truck, hugging herself against the chill, having left her coat inside. I asked her if she'd like me to bring her to church the next Sunday. "Maybe," she said. "But first take me somewhere next Friday," she said.

"Name the place," I said, having no clue where to go.

"Just be here at eight," she said, unveiling a mouthful of Whipple teeth, "If you can't get the truck, call me and I'll fetch you."

Before I could answer she was sprinting back toward the house. I sat a moment in the cab memorizing the wiggle in her jog, hoping it would sustain me through a Christmas that risked becoming a train wreck.

When I backed out of Lorena's driveway, I figured I could get Riley to lend me the truck as he might not want a Whipple back up on the ridge so soon after we'd dug up the bones from their old smokehouse.

By the time I got home the last of the snow had melted in the dooryard, though it clung in wet lumps to the fence posts and covered all the humped back stones in the sloping pasture. Nothing, save for Fred's ostrich, which Riley said Fred had managed to sell to a displaced Yankee potter with a female one of her own, had grazed in the field for years, and it had become pocked with clumps of softwood saplings and small fir trees. The kids had tromped paths through it and where they made repeated crossings the white had become a muddy brown.

I lingered a minute while the engine ticked and cooled and thought about the fact that I could not recall the past several Christmas Eves and wondered what year it had been that I had sat the night with an old priest in a cavernous stone cathedral up north after the late mass, telling him all my troubles and the dark stories of my family. I did recall how he'd trusted me to sleep in the church, covering me with jackets and sweaters from the lost and found, and how, in the morning, he brought me coffee and warm rolls, offered me a shower at the school next door and some fresh clothes from the mission donations, without once asking me to commit to anything, while gently warning me about the evils of the drink which he said he himself had struggled with as a young man. I could faintly conjure his face, ruddy cheeks full of checkered blue lines and his eyelids drooping and moist. He'd smelled like soap and starch, and he told me that Christmas was a fine time to turn one's life around, that like Easter it was a time of birth and new opportunities. His resonant voice urged me from the dulled edge of a hard spree like a thermos of black coffee. I felt life running back into me as the raw edges of flesh on my palms, ripped open by the pavement of the sidewalk where I'd fallen with the whirlies, pulsed and throbbed, and the anvils and hammers in my temples pounded out their penance. "I'm not Catholic, Father," I said.

"As not all who are sick in their souls are," he answered. "Only God can tend to all those who need his help. I can only help set you on a path to His will, a journey of discovery you must make. I hope that you look for His grace before you face more trials like those you have told me about. You need not be a Catholic to be here son."

I could not remember much else, what happened after I showered that morning, put on the new clothes, and stepped out into the bitter sun of a Christmas Day, but I could imagine it. I am sure that the old priest gave me a few coins, and I know I had on a decent coat, so I guess I sold or hocked it for a lesser rag and hit the skids again when the despair of Christmas up north smothered me. I've done that every time my fortunes improved—except with Ella who ran away for her own lonely reasons—and sitting in Riley's truck, our kin money in my coat pocket, the sight of Lorena moving way from me into her house seared into my mind, all my demons rose in front of me, leaping up from the woody clusters in the pasture, springing from the shadows cast across the snow by the late morning light, and rising from the grave up on the hill where tiny flecks of my mother lay with the bones of someone she might never have known. In my mind's eye, I envisioned the Old Man sweating and cursing as he dragged the stiffening body of a man without a face into the mouth of an old mine and down the passage to a deep shaft where he heaved one mighty time and paused to hear the corpse fall against the decaying one he'd already laid there. I imagined the scent of cordite followed by the muffled thud of the small charge he'd set to cause the cave in that would forever inter those men— my soul slain by the cruel difference between being hidden as they were, and having your mortal bones gathered unto your ancestors, as I'd read about in Genesis, to be enshrined in the cave of Machpelah in the field Abraham bought from Ephron the Hittite for four hundred shekels of silver.

As I stared at the front door of the house, I ached to rush inside and be with Riley and Lillian and Carleton and Annie, but I also longed to flee as far from West Virginia and the ridge as I could, discover a place I could drink until I was invisible or dead, a cave in a field without memories, somewhere far from the revolver, which had, as I imagined the remains of those dead men, again developed a voice of its own in my conscience.

I was staring up at the shadows skimming across the

mountaintops when I heard the front door open, and noticed Patches and Roxie rush out ahead of the kids. Annie and Carleton, each toting a bundle of wreaths linked with a piece of string, raced ahead of Lillian and Riley to the truck. I jumped down from the cab and said, "Hope I wasn't gone too long."

Riley laughed. "I was worried you might have gotten snake bit. We're off to take the kids' wreaths to Mrs. Drybeek, and then do some food shopping."

Before I could say anything, Carleton said, "Can I ride on Uncle Ize's lap?"

Riley said, "I don't know if Uncle Ize is coming with us."

It was too blatant a clue to miss, and though another time I might have made Riley sweat a bit, I couldn't bring myself to piss on his parade. "Sorry Carleton," I said. "I have to do a few things around here to make sure Santa can find the place."

"He knows where we live," Annie said.

"I just want to make sure," I said, as Riley bundled both kids into the rear seats of the truck. "We wouldn't want him to miss us."

As they drove off the ridge, the dogs running for the first hundred yards behind them, I wondered if I had hit that final low point, the underside of the bottom as a counselor once told me, that place they say all drunks have to find before they can begin to claw their way back up out of the sewers they've made of their lives. I hoped so, for I felt my resolve waning, and my throat ached with anticipation, as it might at the sound of a bottle's seal being broken, though it made no sense for me to be gripped by despair. I scoured the horizon, wishing that I could peer down into the crevices of Blissfull so I could watch Lorena and her kids eat their Sunday dinner, Riley and Lillian fill their shopping cart, and Annie and Carleton collect their money from Mrs. Drybeek, but most of all I wished that I could see clear to the ocean.

The dogs sauntered back up the road, Roxie pausing to rub her head against my shin, and I turned my back on the valley and went inside.

I'd fallen asleep on the couch watching "It's A Wonderful Life" and only realized that Riley, Lillian, and the kids were home after the door had been opened and an icy winter finger jerked at my collar. The four of them were red-faced and laughing and there was fresh powdery snow on their coats and in Lillian's hair.

"Close the door so it doesn't follow us," Annie shouted.

This brought on inspired laughter from her little brother who was holding his nose and roaring at the same time. "Look out, Ize," Lillian shouted, "Something crawled up your brother's butt and died, I swear." Riley was waving the back of his winter jacket like he was fanning his backside, and making a face like he was being choked. Seeing this, the kids collapsed into giggling, an octave lower than normal, that gut-shaking laughter that makes you think they'll pass out before they catch their breath. "God," Lillian said, "I thought you'd melt the damned dashboard."

Riley kept making his faces, puffing out his cheeks and waving his arms like a dumbstruck pigeon, to the kids continued shrieking delight. Riley had toted in a canvas sack with a gift-wrapped package and a large loaf of French bread peeking over the top, which he nearly tripped over as he wobbled around, arms out to his side like a cartoon airplane spiraling to earth. It was clear that he was happy and proud, his eyes laser blue, and at that moment he looked no different than an insurance man or the owner of a small factory, a full-blooded member of Rotary and The Chamber of Commerce, the kind of man no one in our family had ever been confused with by anyone who knew any of the truths of this ridge.

Lillian was beaming at the kids, paying no attention to Riley's goofy faces or exaggerated antics, and I knew that a family was beginning to flicker again in a place that had not been kind to family in the past. My father had never played with us in the way that Riley and Lillian were playing with Annie and Carleton, including them in their own jokes and silliness. If my mother had said what Lillian said, she'd have been hauled off to the barn and strapped, and if we'd dare to laugh at the Old Man he'd have made sure we didn't laugh at anyone for a long time to come.

Though I was rooting hard for Riley and Lillian to reconcile, I knew the house well, and the only respites it had ever witnessed before in its domestic wars were an occasional nighttime truce, when a glimmer of satisfaction in the Old Man's eyes offered us a rare release from our fear of making a mistake. As I observed Lillian watching the kids, I saw in her eyes an appreciation of their happiness, and believed Riley had a chance if his mountain magnetism rode herd on his hint of mountain meanness.

Exhausted from laughing, the four of them slumped around onto the couch, Riley and Lillian resting like tilted bookends on either side of the kids. If I hadn't been sleeping on that couch each night, and if I hadn't spent hours staring up at the painting of a waterfall that Lillian had hung there when she and Riley were first married, I could have believed the scene was from a catalogue, the kind where the kids are dressed like miniature adults and the adults look too self-absorbed to be parents. For a moment, I could have believed I was up north in one of those leafy towns with a prestigious college, where people have dogs that cost more money than I've ever made in a single paycheck, where the kids have last names as first names, where my stumbling presence on their streets drew a visit from the squad car and a ride to the outskirts of Springfield or Hartford, anywhere away from their lawns or houses or gutters that might be soiled by my sorry passed-out body and rags.

"God, that was awful, Riley," Lillian said, with a peacefulness in her voice. "But I haven't laughed that hard in a long time." She unbuttoned her coat and tugged off her hat and gloves. As she rubbed her hands together, I wondered how many bodies those fingers had touched, how many times her soft alto had soothed a hurt child or a stove-up miner who knew he was about to lose his life or a piece of his body. "I'm gonna change," she said slumping back into the couch, "Then I'll scare up some lunch."

"Don't give Daddy any beans," Annie cried out, and she and Carleton laughed, but this time it was like the polite laughter a bad joke gets the tenth time you've heard it.

"That's enough now, guys," Lillian said, "Get washed up. I want you both to try and nap after lunch so you can stay up for the tree-lighting and the pageant at church."

The kids ran off to their rooms, blowing on their arms and laughing each time it sounded like someone passing gas. Lillian didn't get right up off the couch. Riley wasn't saying a word and she leaned into him and said, "That was fun. It was real good for the kids."

"Just the kids?" he said.

She didn't answer right off, but stood up, kissed Riley on the head, and said, "Let's have a good Christmas."

Seeing how well things were going just then, and not wanting my dark mood to sunder that, I decided it best provide Riley and Lillian some privacy. If the kids napped, I figured they might like to rest a bit themselves, so after lunch I went out to the woodshed.

I scrounged a file from the toolbox on the workbench, and grabbed one of the three splitting axes hanging on the shed wall. I've never favored the maul and wedge system for splitting stove wood, preferring to drive a well-sharpened axe blade into the round hunks of oak and beech that we dried in the shed. After I had a nice edge on the blade, I de-burred it with a whetstone and honed it with emery paper.

I pulled a dozen or so seasoned rounds from the pile, set one on the splitting stump, and reacquainted myself with what had been my favorite childhood chore. I used to pretend that the unsplit logs were the Old Man and that each clean stroke cleaved him perfectly in two, the blade slicing through the middle of his nose and between both balls. It was a task I'd busy myself with whenever I worried he was gunning for me, knowing he'd be reticent to come at me swinging if I had a well-honed blade in my hands.

It took me awhile, but I got my old swing back, when I remembered to let the head of the axe do the work and to extend my arms so I hit squarely on the midpoint of the wood. In the cold, the hardwood split easily, and soon I had more than thirty pieces.

For the first time in a long time my sweat didn't smell like booze and flop houses and tobacco. I didn't mind the coolness under my arms or across my back when I stopped, and the soreness in my muscles felt as right as the first brush of a woman's nipples against your cheek.

I went back to the shed to fetch more logs, remembering times the Old Man had complimented me when I had split a cord of wood without being asked and times he'd taught me to hone an axe, patient with my nervous beginner's mistakes. But when I spied a long leather cord, the kind Riley used to use to bind up his pot for drying, the snap and the cut of the strap came back to me with a rush of the whirlies. I dropped the axe and sat on the stump until it passed.

It took a half-dozen trips with the wheelbarrow to get the split logs onto the porch. I filled the wood box and covered the rest, which I had stacked against the wall on the porch, with a ragged blue tarp I'd found in the shed. When I came in the house it was quiet, save for someone snoring in Riley and Lillian's bedroom.

I showered and dressed in my best jeans and a dress shirt. I had a wool sport coat I'd picked up at the thrift store for ten bucks, but I wasn't sure if it was ridiculously out of style. I decided to ask Lillian when she woke up. The only decent shoes I had were a pair of western boots I'd bought in the service and left behind each time I left the ridge, knowing I'd hock them on the bum. I'd polished them up one night while taking a break from Leviticus and actually felt like I might pass for a respected citizen at the tree lighting.

Clouds crept over the tops of the hills to the west and the weak light of the winter afternoon dimmed to a faint glow. I turned on a few lights, stoked up the stove, and sat on the couch trying to remember what it's like to be a kid at Christmas. I remembered a year when the miners had been locked out just after Thanksgiving and Mama had made rag dolls for their kids, and that Daddy had given me and Riley each a twenty dollar bill to put in the offering at a benefit supper organized by the union relief fund that he'd taken us to. He told me to be sure to hold the bill in the middle when I dropped it into the bucket, so the people could see how much we gave. At the time, I thought he was being kind. He'd often said that the lowest people in these hills, after the revenue men, were the coal bosses, and he declared them his mortal enemies. Later, I realized that his business was the only that hadn't slowed down when the bosses sealed the gates.

CHAPTER EIGHT

Lillian woke from her nap first. "Your brother is out cold," she said as she swept into the living room, hair up in a towel, wearing a red terry-cloth robe. "He can sleep like the dead, or be as fidgety as a two-year old with croup, depending upon what's on his mind, I guess."

"As a kid he'd talk in his sleep," I said.

"Still does sometimes, but I can never understand him," Lillian said, opening the damper a bit on the stove. "Course that's not all I can't make sense of about him."

I didn't know if I was supposed to offer some insight or make a comment, so I excused myself to use the bathroom. When I came back, Lillian was standing on the slate in front of the stove gazing out the front window, rocking on her bare feet and cinching the sash on her robe. When she stretched her arms and yawned, it struck me that she'd had less sleep than all of us. As she unwrapped her hair, shook it loose, and began to rub it with the towel, I remembered how she'd told me once that she didn't need a clock to wake up when she needed to. "Ten hours or ten minutes," she'd said, "I've got an internal alarm that wakes me up. I close my eyes and it goes off on time."

After half a minute of drying her hair, Lillian tossed the towel on her shoulder and said, "As often as I've stared out of this window, I've never committed the view to memory. It changes, the angle of the sun, the cast of the shadows. Every hour it's different. I don't believe I could ever weary of it."

"He loves you," I said.

Without turning, Lillian said, "I know that, Ize. It's been a good week. But like the AA folks say, one day at a time, right?"

"Sorry," I said.

"It's okay."

I pushed up from the couch and said. "Will you give me your opinion on something,"

"Depends," she said, pivoting toward me.

"I want to know if this jacket is okay."

I opened the closet door and slipped the sport coat on. It was a heathery blue tweed, and I couldn't find anything wrong with it when I bought it. "The lady at the thrift store said it was in style, that it was from some guy who'd died in a wreck, about my age."

"Looks fine, actually it looks quite nice. Got a date with Lorena Whipple?"

I must have blushed to the roots of my hair, because Lillian parsed me up and down and said, "Tell you what. Take off the coat and shirt and grab a towel from the bathroom and I'll make that mop of yours more presentable."

I sat in a chair in the kitchen while Lillian combed out the snarls and snipped away at my hair. Thinking about Lorena, and feeling Lillian's hands on my head and neck, I was forced to sit with my hands in my lap. Some women know when they are lighting you up, they'll slip their foot in and out of their shoe, or lift the hem of their dress to scratch an itch on their thigh, but all Lillian needs to do to fire me up is touch me.

I was dumping a dustpan load of dirt I'd swept up by the front door into the trash and Lillian was pouring coffee when Riley stumbled into the kitchen wobbly as a new colt, his eyes narrowed to slits against the light, and said, "Jesus I hate falling asleep in the middle of the day. Messes up your night, too."

"No one dragged you in there," Lillian said.

It was Riley's turn to blush, "That is a fact," he said. He splashed cold water on his face at the sink and squinted at me. "Best threads I've seen on you in years," he said. "Your hair trimmed, you look shit sure like a new man, Ize."

Grinning more than I wanted to, I said, "Lillian did the best with what she had to work with."

A fierce scowl slashed across Riley's face. I wasn't sure what I'd said to prompt it, but I feared that all the holiday happiness was about to explode in my face as most of my brief spells of decent luck had done before. I glanced at Lillian, but her eyes told me nothing.

"Honey," she said to Riley, "Would you get the kids up?"

Riley's face brightened at the sound of her endearment, and I exhaled an audible breath as he left the room.

A few minutes later, the kids trudged out to the kitchen as bleary-eyed as Riley had been. Carleton crawled up into Lillian's lap at the table and nearly fell back to sleep, while Annie groped in the refrigerator for the orange juice, poured a glass and oozed into a chair. No one spoke. I could hear Riley fussing with the stove in the living room, and Carleton's sleepy rasp as his eyes flickered open and shut. Lillian kissed the top of his head and said "Who's going to decorate the tree, sleepyheads?" which startled both kids awake.

"You mean now?" Annie said.

"Can't think of a better time," Lillian said.

Riley scrambled up the trapdoor stairs to the attic and handed down to me the boxes of lights and ornaments, and if he noticed that I'd moved any of them, he didn't say so. As I passed the boxes, one by one to Lillian, I wondered which one contained the silver star Riley had made for Mama in tenth-grade shop class. He'd never shown it to her, and when I asked him why he hadn't he said, "It's hers' if she fetches us up to Detroit."

While the kids unpacked the ornaments and tinsel, I helped Riley center the tree in the stand, while Lillian dialed in the West Virginia Public Radio Christmas special on the stereo. I didn't recognize the carols, and I've never liked the sound of a boy's choir since having to lie still once for two hours while one performed at the VA when I was recuperating from my fall at old man Plourde's house. Lillian, raised Episcopalian, sang along with every one. I couldn't recall her singing before, and was surprised at the strength of her voice in the lower register, and the fact that she knew so many verses by heart.

Once Riley and the kids were in the rhythm of decorating, Lillian fixed up a quick dinner, lugging out trays of cheeses and slices of sausages, and mushroom caps filled with diced beef and onion in a sauce I'd never tasted before.

"When did you make all this?" I asked her.

"Didn't. Came from that gourmet shop at the mall. Place likely won't last long, so I figured to give it a try before they fold up," she said, loading a cracker with a slice of cheddar.

Reveling in my newfound ability to discern the subtle differences in food, I sampled all six of the cheeses Lillian had spread across the big platter with the Thanksgiving turkey painted on it, each one's distinct taste lingering on my tongue like the sweetness of a late summer blackberry.

By the time I'd untangled the lights and replaced the burned-out bulbs, and Riley had straightened the star on the top of the tree, Lillian announced that it was time to head into town for the tree lighting. She made the kids wash their hands and brush their teeth, and she took the hairbrush from her pocketbook to make a few last minute adjustments on my head. Re-knotting Riley's tie, she pronounced us both handsome and presentable. I know if we had been alone I would have kissed her.

The kids rode in the back. All bundled up in their coats and hats they rubbed against each other, which might have sparked an argument another time, but with Christmas on their minds they buckled their belts over their layers of clothes and said nothing ugly. I offered to sit in the middle, but Lillian insisted on taking that place, and I noticed that she snuggled as close to Riley as she could. She was wearing a long wool dress, dark tights and nice boots. To straddle the shift, she hiked her skirt and slip up and I noticed that she did not push Riley's right hand away from her left knee.

The tree lighting was in the square. We parked behind the courthouse near the entrance to city hall. They used to have meters in the lot and for six blocks along all the streets off the square, but they'd disappeared. I mentioned it to Riley and he told me that once the mall came along the merchants' association forced the city to take the meters down so they could try to compete. When we got into the square there were already hundreds of people gathered around the tree. A faint, staticky voice droned, "testing one two, testing one two," over and over, followed by a loud squeal from the PA that made the fine VA fillings in my molars ache. The kids covered their ears and begged to be lifted up so they could see the tree. Riley hoisted Annie onto his shoulders, and when Lillian reached down for Carleton, I snatched him up over my head with one motion and set him into place on my shoulders. Lillian smiled and said something to me, but another blast of feedback nearly drove the crowd to its knees and I never heard what she said. Carleton grabbed his ears and kicked me in the solar plexus so hard I thought I might drop him.

The tree, at least thirty-feet high, was festooned with coils of wires snaking up its trunk and around its crown. Many of the lower branches had been pruned away, I guess, to keep kids from climbing it—the kind of dare I would have accepted in an instant twenty years before. A young kid, maybe twenty, scurrying around the stage turning knobs and tapping his hand on microphones, was being taunted by a crowd of drunks gathered under the bank marquee. I watched a cop saunter toward the hecklers, but they stayed far enough away to make their point without a confrontation.

A man made an announcement that the switch would be thrown by a special guest who would be arriving on the stage "In just a few brief moments." I adjusted Carleton's weight on my shoulders and asked him if he could see.

"Yes," he said, "But I got to pee, bad."

"I'll take him," Lillian said.

"It's fine," I said. "I'm sure we'll find a bathroom at city hall, or at the police station."

Lillian reached up and patted Carleton's face. "Be a good boy for Uncle Ize," she said.

As we made our way toward the lights of city hall, I wondered how we'd ever find our way back to the others. Though I thought we'd come late, a least a thousand folks must have streamed in after we did: locals, hill people, the subdivision crowd; it seemed to me that most of the county must have turned out. Carleton kept telling me he had to go bad, and I implored him to hold on, fearing feeling his urine flowing down my neck at any minute.

"I got to hold onto my wee wee," he said, "Or I won't be able to hold it."

"Grab it good," I said, much to the delight of the two teenaged girls struggling past us in the opposite direction.

When we'd fought past the back edge of the crowd I lowered him down in front of me and we made tracks toward the police station, Carleton running with one hand on his crotch. I picked him up, careful to hold him away from my body, and ran up the ten steps to the front door of the station two at a time. I opened the door and we stepped into the bright light of the front desk. The cop on duty, a creased woman about forty, glanced up and before I could say a word she noticed Carleton's right hand clutching the end of his penis through his black dress pants, pointed down the hall and said, "Third door on the left."

Between us we managed to get his pecker out of his pants before he let loose. I pulled up his jacket, sweater, and shirt, and was lifting him from behind, trying to help him aim at the urinal. I have experience in trying to focus an unsteady stream toward its destination, but I'd forgotten that kids as young as Carleton have a different arc than a healthy drunk does. His aim was fine, but he was coming up short and peeing on the cracked tile floor. I hurried him closer, but part of the cause of his weak stream was that he hadn't quite gotten all of his equipment free, the band of his underwear constricting his flow. He plunged his free hand into his shorts, and, once loose, peed with the full force of youth against the porcelain, the back splatter spotting his pants.

When he was sure he was done I set him down on a dry spot near the sink and told him not to move. Taking this literally he stood by the sink, his penis peeking out of his fly, his pants mottled with spots, holding up his shirt and coat tails, watching me cover the puddle on the floor with piles of paper towels, and push them around with my boot heel.

I felt my guts roil, imagining someone finding me wiping up a mess on the floor, while he stood there with his willie out to the world. It would be my kind of draw to be figured for a pervert when I was as innocent as Carleton. The fact that we were only twenty feet down the hall from the dispatch office added to my jitters. I shoved the wet towels into a trash can, washed my hands three times, and helped Carleton wash up and get tucked back together.

I thanked the woman cop at the desk as we passed toward the door. "Got my own," she said without looking up. "Enjoy the show."

I knew it was not likely that we could find Lillian and the others until the show was over, but I knew that Riley would wait for us at the truck. We'd done that as kids, making deliveries. It is best, when selling hooch, to have two drivers. That way, if one of you gets in trouble, the other can spirit the load away. I told Carleton that we should stay on the steps where we could see better and where he'd be near the bathroom if he had to go again. He wanted me to put him on my shoulders, but the whiff I'd gotten of him made me realize that he'd gotten the front tail of his shirt pretty good, so I told him to wait until they were ready to hit the switch, not that I knew for sure that there would be a countdown, but I figured I'd get some feeling of when the switch would be thrown.

Carleton was just starting to whine about wanting to see Lillian when the PA began to play A West Virginia Christmas is the Best There is, by Sparky Stiles and His Hilltop Hollerers. It's an awful song, and Sparky Stiles is a dreadful singer, but he comes from Lanks Holler, and was married into the Cooleys so he was related to a sizeable chunk of the crowd. He'd been on the Opry once, where he sang his one almost-hit Mountaineer Forever, and had since managed to make a living playing hillbilly bars and fairs. Sparky would never make you forget Kathy Mattea, or Little Jimmie Dickens, or any other of our state's great vocalists, and I couldn't believe we'd been standing in the cold waiting for him, of all people, to flip the switch, but there he was, rhinestones and beer gut, waving and bowing to the crowd, and being escorted by the mayor to the back of the stage to illuminate the square.

The streetlights went out and a spotlight picked up Sparky

and the dignitaries. With my drunk's eye for kindred souls, I intuited that Sparky was less than a full shot short of falling on his ass. The PA squealed again and the crowd booed. Sparky doffed his Stetson and waved it above his head, like a guy at a baseball game does to get the crowd excited. The mayor read a proclamation giving Sparky the keys to the city, though it was clear to me that he'd have had a damn hard time getting them into a lock, and asked him to, "Please do us, the citizens of Blissfull, the honor of lighting this year's tree to herald in the Christmas season."

Sparky, soaked in the spirits and of great cheer, ripped off his hat again and waved it over the crowd, as if he was blessing us. This seemed to dizzy him and the mayor seized him around the shoulders to save our portly hero from the indignity of falling off stage. I swung Carleton up over my head, careful not to set him on my shoulders, and he squealed, "There's a cowboy up there, Uncle Ize. Where's Santa?"

"I don't know," I said. "Maybe he'll be along later."

I couldn't tell if it was the mayor or Sparky who actually touched the switch, but the lights came on and there was a rush of applause, followed by a chorus of screams. When my eyes became accustomed to the light, it was apparent that Sparky was down on the stage. When the drunks under the bank marquee realized that Sparky had passed out, they began to yell and hoot, as if he'd broken a world's record or performed a miracle before their eyes, clapping and shrieking with as much zeal as the fat ladies at Star of Morning. Carleton yelled, "Did someone shoot the cowboy?" but, before I had to think of an answer, a vintage, open-cab fire truck, with Santa riding shotgun in the place of a Dalmatian, crawled into view, its lights strobing the dark. Santa waved to alternate sides of the truck, and a half-dozen women dressed as elves tossed candy to the crowd. Carleton had become too heavy to hold over my head so I lowered him to the steps and told him that we'd try to find his folks and sister.

The crowd was packing in toward the stage and the cops, who'd been directing traffic around the square, began to shout through bullhorns that people needed to stay back. We only moved thirty feet when the tide of the crowd turned and we were pushed back toward city hall. I was struggling to walk alongside Carleton and keep a hold of his tiny hand, but as the mass of bodies collapsed back on us I had to pick him up again. My arms ached, in part from all the wood I'd split, as I held him out away from me like a leaky bag of trash. His shirt had come untucked, exposing his stomach to the chill and I knew he was getting cold. I took him back into the police station to fix his clothes and he began to wail for his mother. As I struggled to get him put back together he said he was scared that we'd lost her. I tried to explain to him that we'd meet them at the truck and that they wouldn't leave without us, but then he began to cry about not getting any candy from Santa. I offered to get him a Snickers bar from the vending machine, but he wasn't buying. The woman cop was laughing. "How old is your boy?" she asked.

I said, "He's my nephew." When she asked him his name it grappled in my belly and I prayed that he'd only tell her his first name, but he said, proud as he could be, "Carleton Butts, and I'm ten."

The cop stared at me with a look I'd seen on Blissfull cops' faces my whole life. First, there's the glimmer of recognition, then a flicker in their eyes when they figure out which one you are, and then the smile that lets you know they know all about you. "You Riley's brother?" she asked.

"Yes ma'am," I answered, mad as hell with myself for having to be polite, and feeling as humiliated as the old black guys that used to work at The Blue Seal feed store must have felt, forced by convention to remove their hats when they talked to whites and required to call every woman over ten miss or ma'am, and every boy over sixteen sir. I'd never learned to grovel, even when it might have saved me a knock on the head or a night in the slammer, and the cop's smirk galled me.

"Sergeant Amy Wright," she said, stepping out from behind the desk and offering her hand to Carleton. I have done well by cultivating a healthy distrust of the law, but Sergeant Wright was playing her best Officer Friendly—showing Carleton her handcuffs, and asking him if he wanted a copy of the DARE poster hanging on the wall behind us. I knew that Riley would be wild if he found out we'd been talking to the law so I said to Carleton, "Your Mama and Daddy are waiting for us in the truck."

"Thought I saw your brother's truck at the shop," Sergeant Wright said.

"He's got a brand new one 'cause the old one's broken," Carleton said, "It has seats in the back for me and my sister."

I watched the information percolate into the cop's brain and, despite my misgivings, I lifted Carleton onto my shoulders and spun toward the door. "Thank you, Sergeant," I said, the stench of the kid's clothes in my nose, "Have a nice evening."

"Be seeing you," she said. "And be a good boy, Carleton."

CHAPTER NINE

While Riley and I lack the vocal chemistry of the Osborne or Louvin Brothers, acts Mama used to hear broadcast on WWVA, we have honed the ability to impart information to each other without saying a word, and Riley read the fear in my eyes as soon as Carleton and I got to the truck. He stepped away while Lillian was strapping the kids in to their seats and stared at me, but I just said, "Carleton wet himself a bit in the police station."

"He ain't the first person to do that," Riley said. "He need to change before church?"

"I'd recommend it," I said.

Lillian had smelled the problem and before Riley could suggest going home and changing, she'd already made that decision.

The clear night had grown cold, the day's heat escaping into the ladle of the big dipper hung in the northern sky, and the kids, even with a nap were cranky. As the heat in the cab rose, so did the smell from Carleton's clothes. When Annie held her nose and pointed at him he burst into tears and when she showed him the fistful of penny candy she'd scooped up off the square while we'd been in the police station he began to wail in earnest, and I felt some of the family cheer wearing off of the evening.

"Share some with your brother, Annie," Lillian said.

"Why? He stinks," she answered.

I waited for Riley to say something, and was relieved when he simply said, "Do as your mother says, Annie. Santa is watching."

It worked. Annie parceled out a few pieces of candy to her brother and he quit snuffling long enough to chew them, then held out his tongue to show us what he'd done.

"Carleton, swallow," Lillian said.

He made an exaggerated gulping noise and the back seat went quiet. I was trying to find a way to delay telling Riley everything that had happened until after Christmas, so as not to compromise what might be his final chance to work his mountain magnetism on Lillian. But I knew he'd get it all out of me like he'd always done when we were kids.

At the house, I hopped out and helped Lillian down while Annie undid Carleton's seat belt. "You come inside too, Annie," Lillian said, "and go to the bathroom while I change up Carleton."

"I don't have to."

"Try anyway," Lillian said.

"I don't have to," Annie said.

"Ann Elizabeth Stalls Stubbs, you will come in and go to the bathroom or all you'll find under the tree will be a lump of Forsyth Trace coal and a switch. Get inside now."

Annie hopped down from the truck and ran into the house muttering to herself. "I'll be right out," Lillian said, and went inside.

I gave it to Riley as best I could.

"Nosey bitch, that Wright," Riley said. "She ain't from around here, and thinks she's some special shit 'cause they let her dress up and play cop. Carleton's got a fucking bladder the size of a walnut, I swear. Ain't your fault. I can't seem to teach him to pull his damn pecker out far enough to piss in the pot. Don't say nothin' to Lillian."

I almost buckled with relief.

If Lillian needed any more proof of Riley's undying love for her, the fact that he'd even set foot in the St. John's of the Mountains Episcopal Church, no less agreed to attend Christmas Eve mass there, should have cinched it. St John's, everything Star of Morning is not, is a fieldstone and granite edifice with a three-story steeple containing a carillon that tolls away on the hour, and plays three hymns every afternoon at six.

Inside the church, the gleaming oak pews were cushioned, and there were plush rails to kneel on, which is something the Episcopalians seem to favor as they bob up and down like drowning men. The guy I took for the minister sported a long robe and spoke with a Yankee accent, or maybe an English one, but he was certainly not a West Virginian. The cars in the parking lot were new, most of them foreign, and some of them were bigger than my old bedroom in Holyoke.

We had to sit near the back even though we arrived ten minutes before the service began. The organ was up above us in what Lillian said was a choir loft. I'd never been in a church down home where you couldn't see the organist or the choir, and when the St John's organist let loose the whole place shook like a rail siding beneath a runaway freight.

Right at the stroke of ten a group of people in robes, some of them holding what looked like smudge pots, others with books clasped to their chests, and some younger kids, holding large white and gold crosses and mounted banners, assembled by the back door near where were sitting.

I leaned over to Lillian and asked, "Who's the minister?"

"Father Helms, he's called a priest here," she said. "He's the guy with the white hair."

I hadn't known that Episcopalians had priests, but I knew they had money because most of the top mine brass, especially the northerners, had belonged here. I thought for a moment of the old Catholic priest I had remembered earlier who'd helped me through another Christmas, but the Episcopal priest said, "For unto us a child is born, this day, in the city of Jerusalem," and before I could find the right book from the rack in front of the pew, Lillian had pulled me to my feet and the whole place was singing "O Come All Ye Faithful," except they were singing in Latin.

We spent the next forty-five minutes popping up and down like a stick floating in a quick trace. We'd stand, kneel, sit, sing and those who knew the drill answered everything the old priest said. I'd never seen as many fur coats before in my life, nor had I smelled as much alcohol in any bar I'd been in. The congregation sang loud and on key, belting out the hymns with a tipsy fervor, but they didn't move around like the Star of Morning worshippers. Part of it was a lack of room, but I suspect that many of the women didn't want to mess up their hair, and some of the men looked like those really uncomfortable kids who hang by the punch bowl at junior high dances.

The calisthenics lasted an hour, and for the duration four shepherds, three wise men, and a Mary and Joseph stared at a doll in a corncrib set up in the front of the church below the altar, none of them speaking or moving. Lillian explained to me later that what they had created was called a tableau, and after that I understood the reason that the adults could stand stock still during the carol singing was rooted in their early training posing as nativity figures.

After midnight, the kids asleep, the radio on low, Lillian and I were sitting on the living room floor passing presents to Riley to place under the tree. When the kids' stuff, and the gifts Riley and Lillian had gotten each other, were arranged the way he wanted them, I pulled my gifts from under the couch. Lillian peered at me, one eyebrow raised, as I passed the wrapped boxes to Riley.

"I had some money saved," I lied, "From the funeral home. I kept it hid in case you wanted me to leave. These aren't much," I said. "But I want you to know how much I appreciate you'all letting me stay here."

I was stunned when Lillian spoke first, "You're kin, Ize."

Christmas broke white, and, for the first time in years for me, sober. I rolled on my side and wriggled my left arm, which had fallen asleep, the tingling ebbing its way down to the tips of my fingers before disappearing. Easing into wakefulness, I recalled what an old drunk, who claimed to have been a professor, said to me in a bar in Holyoke. He maintained that Christmas is a time when we get a fleeting glance at how we were before we forgot the things we all knew at birth. I was never sure what he meant by that, and though I should have been as happy as I'd been in a very long time, as I remembered those words, I couldn't shake the fear that the good times would sour in an instant.

I drifted back toward sleep, and daydreamed about Sergeant

Wright and a posse of feds busting down the door, trampling the kid's gifts, splitting the boxes I'd given Lillian with an axe, and I suffered a vision of a bullet ripping through Riley's chest, soaking the shirt I'd given him a deeper red. The violence of those images conjured the manifold sorrows of Christmases past, when, as if he could not bear sustained amity in his house, the morning's calm erupted into a shit storm with the Old Man yanking away one of the small toys Mama had gotten me or Riley, denouncing it as a "Goddamned waste of my hard earned money," in retaliation for an unperceived infraction of his rules, or an imagined disrespect of his wishes.

As I blinked my eyes against the past, I detected the faint glimmer of the tree ornaments and the soft shine of the silver bow on my gift for Lillian, and I ached more than ever to believe that I could walk around with my Christmas boots on and not feel like I had to tiptoe.

The hard dark of the predawn glinted in the slit of glass I could see through the part in the living room curtains, and, in the abject silence, I heard Patches groan as he wobbled to his feet and recoiled his bony frame to lie back down. Carleton babbled in his sleep, and the stove ticked as the last of its heat escaped. Shaking the sleep from my legs, my blankets skittering to the floor, I remembered the shrink in Beckley who told me that to achieve any sense of self-worth, that I had to stop trying to win the favor of a man who was both dead and impossible to please when living. Peering over his half glasses, he said, "Get rid of the guilty baggage and useless anger your father left you," suggesting I could make all the necessary changes in my life as easily as changing my shorts. "You have to begin with a belief in yourself," he'd said, shutting his notebook on the day's session. "Without that, your father wins."

Despair, the old priest had told me, was the greatest sin, because it meant that you believed there was no hope, which denied God's very existence. I told him that I had tried as hard as I knew to change and to be changed, but that I could never make the right choice. He told me that until I was sober and willing to hear what God was telling me, that I wouldn't know when my prayers were answered. Well, I thought, lying in the creaky darkness of the only home I have ever known, I am sober and willing, have given my soul to God, and I'm still fucking terrified, shit scared that I am in the middle of the dress rehearsal for more heartache than I could ever hope to bear.

As I was filling the stove with kindling, Roxie whined, and I let both dogs out into a fine dusting of new snow, the stars and moon still sharp in the sky above the hills.

Lillian hugged me and told me I was sweet and that she loved me to death when she opened the cedar boxes. I told her I didn't know how the nameplate should be initialed and when she said, "I've about made up my mind on that," and smiled at Riley, I felt my eyes well and I held her to me. When I stepped away, Annie said, "Don't cry, Uncle Ize," and Carleton jumped on top of me wearing his new Batman cape, shouting, "Only I can save you now."

I glanced over at Riley, leaning in the kitchen doorway watching us. His happiness tore through my guts like a jagged knife, because I knew he was one run in with the law from losing Lillian and the kids, his new truck, his thirty acres, maybe his life, and I'd never known a bootlegger or grower to get away with it forever. Even if he had enough stashed to last a long time, I feared he'd get bored or angry, and be tempted to backslide like a faltering drunk, and work deep into his trade again, and I worried, for a greedy moment, that I would lose his family as well. Living on the edge of violence leaves you raw and sore, and I knew how quick I'd been to explode in the past when that soreness got chafed. I hoped Riley had found his own peace in his family.

Lillian had looped red bows to the collars of both dogs, who napped on the hearth, and their snoring and the light streaming in the window lulled me into a half sleep.

We opened presents and ate, the adults sprawled across the floor in the bright morning light, the kids frantic. A few sheets at a time, Riley crumpled the wrapping paper and cardboard into the stove, in which he'd made a roaring fire that heated the room summer-hot. When he'd open the door for the second it took to tender the colored paper to the flames, the deep blue of the coals flashed against the black back of the stove, like a rainbow against the dark clouds of a thunder storm.

By noon, the sun had softened the snow and the kids and I made a true West Virginia snowman with coal for eyes, a corn cob pipe that Riley had in his bureau, and an old felt crusher that we tied to his head with a scarf. We tromped paths in the dooryard where we rolled the three big snowballs to make the body and head, and Carleton raced over them in his heavy boots, his Batman cape trailing behind him like a sail, chasing bad men and slaying evil criminals. Annie sculpted the arms, packing loose, wet snow around two pieces of kindling I'd stuck into his sides, and tried to fashion mitten hands on the ends. Sometimes when I peeked at the window I'd see Lillian and Riley watching us.

That night, the kids fell asleep on the couch before eight, dribbles of drool on their cheeks, and surrounded by their toys. Lillian cleaned away the last of the leftovers from Christmas dinner—the like I had never known before in that house, the kind shown in holiday spreads in the magazines at the VA, turkey, mashed potatoes, gravy, rolls, sweet peas, boiled onions and pumpkin pie. Riley fiddled with a new diver's watch that Lillian had given him, figuring out the date and stopwatch functions without reading the directions. I wanted to leave them alone, and I asked if I could borrow the truck to go down to the Star of Morning, where I knew they'd be having a service.

"Don't get bit," Riley said as he tossed me the keys.

The service was over when I arrived. I sat in the truck. Reverend Willis was standing outside the door bidding good night to his flock, hugging the women, shaking hands with the men and tousling each child's head. He held his Bible in his left hand, shaking and petting with his right, stooped a bit, as if he'd walked a long time in the heat and his balls had been rubbed sore by old, dirty pants. Bumming, it had been a curse, and my scrotum was polished and hard from wandering the streets looking for an out-of-the way alley or clump of trees to crash in during the days when the cops made me move on. I eased the truck up to the curb fifty feet from the church door and watched the last of the congregation step into the night, their breath rising in ghosts against the faded brick.

The final two people to emerge were Lorena and her mother, who hobbled with a cane I'd not seen her use when I'd been at the house. Reverend Willis hugged them both and when they'd gotten into their car, he walked back inside the church. I watched the windows darken as he switched off the lights, saw Lorena and her mother settling into their seats in the cold glow of a streetlight. Lorena hunched over the wheel and turned the key, but I heard no sound and none of the running lights came on. I rolled down the window to listen and heard the final groan of a dead battery. Lorena smashed her palms on the steering wheel and thrust open the door. Before she could knock on the Star of Morning door, I was out of the cab calling to her.

"Need a jump?" I said.

Lorena turned on her heels, and when she saw who had hailed her said, "Well, if you aren't a welcomed sight. I left my damn lights on."

"Do you have cables?" I asked.

"No," she said. There's some at the house, though."

I drove Lorena and her mother, who told me she'd been hit with gout and gone to church be healed, to her house. Mrs. Whipple was friendlier than she'd been the last time I'd seen her, but I knew that meant little. She'd become obliged to me in her mind, and I could tell that she wasn't sure she liked that. It looked as if, though she stared me in the eyes, that she saw my father. I almost saw him myself in my reflection in the rearview mirror, and I tried to say little as I could.

Lorena and I searched her garage until we found the cables snagged up with some old pick-up tie downs on a shelf on the workbench. I wondered which of her ex-husbands they'd belonged to, and I wondered how he'd let her go, or how he'd left her. I'd lost Lorena once, or maybe I'd never really had her. Perhaps I was only as lonely as she was, and just as invested in finding some happiness on our rock-rich, pleasure poor, ridge.

Lorena told me that her youngest twins were with their grandparents for the night and that her oldest were with their father, and that she was worn out from staying up half the night assembling bicycles for the young twins, cooking two meals, and taking care of her mother who could barely walk. "She won't eat what she should and gobbles all of what she shouldn't, and she won't give up her toddies. All the laying on of hands can't cure that stubbornness," Lorena said, reminding me of what the old priest had said to me. We jumped the car and I followed her home. In her driveway, Lorena said, "I'd invite you in, but Ize, I'm wore down. Call me and we'll decide where to go." Before I could answer she'd put her hands on my shoulder, risen on her toes and kissed my cheek.

CHAPTER TEN

When winter arrives in the north, it hunkers down and gets comfortable for months, but in the south, even in the mountains, it gets up and goes away for a day or two each month. Warm thermals mount the dark hills and send the ditches into song. The snow melts in the open spaces, clinging only to the highest dark hills where the sun's rays can't find it, and in the brief hours of winter daylight, there is enough warmth in the wind to make you think spring is hours, not weeks away.

Lillian moved her things back into the house, Riley making two runs in his truck to fetch them from her apartment, but even though her lease didn't run out until May, she made Riley nervous as hell by not trying to sublet it. I could see the uncertainty in everything he did. Like the Old Man, Riley was a good hunter and when he was tracking game he didn't rush the process. The Old Man taught us to drive the prey into a place where they had limited options for escape, so I understood that Riley was hoping that they'd make it until Lillian's lease was up and she'd be less likely to take off over something less than life or death. He played the odds all the time. To make it appear certain he really did want to make a go of his thirty acres as a timber lot, he spent two days marking trees and laying out where he wanted to build his dream home. The day after Christmas, he took Annie and Carleton with him, and showed them the trees he said he'd use for their new house. He even lent me his truck to visit Lorena on New Year's Eve, our first time together, as she'd had to cancel our previous date to take her mother to the emergency room when she'd complained of severe pain in her leg.

For New Year's Eve, we'd made plans to go out to a dance and dinner at the Mountain Manor Banquet Center and Motor Lodge, but her mother's gout was worse, and two of her kids had come down with the flu. Lorena was crying when she called me up to say she couldn't go, but I was just as glad to not have to worry about dancing. I never got the hang of it, especially when you hold the woman and dance together. I can hang dance, where you just sort of shuffle around clinging on to each other, but all these line dances that I see people doing when Annie watches country and western videos on TV, baffle me. I know it goes back to all the awful days in gym class when Mrs. Gordon made us square dance. If I hadn't already learned the stupefying effects of booze before those first awkward classes, I'd have soon found out. I was so clumsy she made me take my sneakers off so I would be less likely to hurt any of the girls by stepping on them, and I had to "dip for the oyster and dive for the clam," in my hole-plagued socks. Besides, I knew that even the non-alcoholic punch at the party might be spiked and I couldn't risk falling off the wagon by mistake.

Another thing that fretted me was the possibility of seeing someone I knew, someone who'd remind me of some stupid thing I'd done, something that might embarrass Lorena, too. It might have been the tenuous truce between Lillian and my brother, or my natural belief that I do not possess the courage to fight my demons, but I was heart-scalded any time I pondered falling from Lorena's grace.

We ordered dinner from a Chinese place near the mall, the only place we found open, and Lorena rode out with me to pick it up. She sat like southern girls do in the middle of the front seat, on an angle with her legs to the right of the shifter. I felt so good I damn near started crying.

When we'd eaten and she'd settled her mother in a recliner with her bad leg raised even higher with a pillow, we sat there in the living room until Mrs. Whipple began to doze off. Her mother had described all her pains and disappointments to me, and I guessed that was to make it clear to me that she'd prefer I was not another of her life's cruel vexations. I've never mastered the art of conversation. The VA shrink said that was because the development of my social verbal skills had been stunted by fear, first of my father, then of my teachers, but I've considered that for long hours and decided he's full of shit. As soon as most folks know something they're overcome by a rioting urge to let the world know about it. I was never that way. Too much of what I knew was best kept to myself.

Once, in the eighth grade, we had a quiz on Civil War battles in West Virginia, and I was the only one who got all the questions right. I know that if any one near me had done as well, that Mrs. Cathcart would have accused me of cheating, but no one else got even half of them correct. She'd given us the test because when she'd asked us aloud about them, no one had raised a hand. "If you knew the answer, Isaac, why didn't you say so?" she said. I just shook my head and muttered, "I don't know."

When Mrs. Whipple's snoring became deep and regular, Lorena and I slipped into the kitchen. I began to believe that Lorena was getting as squirrelly as I was, because she eased real close to me at the table and held my hand as she told me how hard it was trying to be a good mother to four young ones and her mother. The kids were in the basement watching videos, and they raised a mighty hell when Lorena went down to tell them that it was bedtime. The older twins were incensed at having to go to bed at the same time as the younger ones, but as they'd been the ones with the flu she wanted them to get their rest. I knew she was worried about going back to work after the holiday with the kids sick and her mother gone lame.

When the kids were asleep, or at least quiet, upstairs, and we could hear that her mother was still snoring, Lorena led me downstairs and we did some hang dancing to the radio. The music was from an oldies station, a mix of Christmas songs and New Year's Eve heartbreakers, loneliness and joy squeezed into the same tiny radio waves. As close as Lorena held me, she had to know how I was feeling. I'd noticed that since I'd quit drinking I'd been getting better blood flow, or my mind was imagining my dreams in full Disney color, and between Lillian and Lorena my privates were a constant source of irritation. I'd been taking more showers than I had in my life, and not just cold ones.

The basement of Lorena's house had a wet bar, television,

VCR, stereo and some kind of a game system. There was a couch, three old easy chairs, and a low table. Lorena pushed the table in front of the couch so we had room to dance, and I suspected so we wouldn't just fall onto the couch by mistake. Still, I had the feeling that old willie might get some relief from the way we were dancing. I screwed up my courage and bent down to give Lorena a kiss, my eyes closed and an image of her in my mind from years before at the creek. She turned her head. "Not here, Ize," she said.

I didn't know what to say. It was too cold to go parking and we couldn't go back to Riley's and have a roll on the couch. I thought about suggesting a motel, but before I could come up with anything, Lorena said, "We'll ride over to Beckley next Saturday." Though I wasn't sure what going to Beckley had to do with having sex, I was too afraid of saying something that might ruin my chances, and just said, "Sure, Lorena."

At midnight we watched the ball drop. My balls, tight as a crab's ass, and that's waterproof, ached inside my jeans. Lorena squeezed my hand as Dick Clark counted down the seconds, and when the fireworks began, she leaned over and kissed me. "Be patient, Ize," she said. "You better go now."

It was like being fired. You don't argue, just draw your check and move on. Lorena said goodbye at the door. She looked weary, and as always when I see a beautiful woman yawn, I got turned on. As I trudged out to the truck, I wanted to look back, but I was afraid she wouldn't be there. As I got to the cab door, I couldn't help myself and I glanced back. The hall light was on and I saw Lorena behind the storm door, smiling.

CHAPTER ELEVEN

The Thursday before Lorena and I were supposed to go to Beckley, I walked into town on one of those days winter had headed off up north. The kids had started back to school, and I'd been alone in the house for a few hours, while Riley was marking trees and Lillian was at the hospital. Though Riley never said a word to me, and Lillian was as sweet to me as she'd ever been, I felt like I ought to at least look for a job so as to pull my own weight, and because I worried that, with little to do, I would be sorely tempted to back slide.

It was almost fifty degrees, the sun, though low in the sky, warm on my face. I'd rolled up my shirtsleeves and was carrying my jacket over my shoulder by the time I reached Star of Morning, where I found Reverend Willis out front. He was dipping a giant sponge into a five-gallon bucket of soapy water and rubbing it into the van's tired body, humming a hymn I recognized, but whose words, at first, I could not remember. A garden hose snaked across the sidewalk from inside the church, the water running clear into the gutter and gurgling into the storm drain at the corner.

When Reverend Willis saw me, he dropped the sponge into the bucket and wiped his hands on his pants. "Good morning, Ize. The Lord has blessed us with a fine day," he said "Lorena says you're going to Beckley with her on Saturday. I appreciate the help, and I wanted to clean up the van before you guys took it over for tires."

Though I had no idea that we'd be going in the church van, I acted as if I were in on the plan from the beginning. "We're looking forward to it," I said, "I'll do anything I can to help."

"I know that, Ize," he said, reaching into the bucket for the sponge. "I've had an appointment for two weeks to get some work done on this old van, but I've also been asked to preach a special service Saturday, and I believe the Lord would want me to do that. Lorena has the list of things we need at the church that she can get cheaper over to Beckley. My friend Dale Casper has a garage and he'll lend you a car while he works on this old road warrior."

While Reverend Willis soaped and rubbed, I followed with the hose and rinsed. The sun blazed across the shiny parts of the van's hood, and the water in the gutter ran like molten steel. He took great pains to clean the tires and then he brought out a small vacuum cleaner on a long extension cord and sucked up the grit from the floor and between the seats. We dried the van off with some old towels that said, Mountain Meadow Campground and Motel. I guess I stared too long at the faded blue letters, because Reverend Willis said, "I use to preach revivals there, before it closed. When the man who had it went bankrupt, he gave me fifty of those as souvenirs. Too thin for a body to use now."

When the van was dry and as shiny as she could be without a coat of wax, I drained and coiled the hose. Reverend Willis took care to dry the side- view mirrors well, then dumped the water from his bucket into the gutter, wrung out the sponge and the towels, stepped back from the van and said, "I don't believe any amount of work will make her look any better than she does, Ize. Mind giving me a hand lugging this stuff down to the basement?"

"Be glad to," I said.

It took my eyes several seconds to acclimate from the bright sun of the morning to the darkness of the basement, though Reverend Willis, unfazed by the transition, moved about the room with the dexterity a blind man who'd memorized its every corner and obstacle. As I set the bucket and the coiled hose up on the workbench by the sink, he rinsed out the towels and hung them on a rack in the corner beside the serpent boxes, all the time singing the hymn he'd been humming when I arrived –The Strife is O'er the Battle Done, the sound of his voice setting one of the snakes to rattling. "Someone likes that one," he said. Then he laughed, not a chuckle, but a deep belly laugh, as if struck by a revelation. "Make a joyful noise unto the Lord and the serpent sings too," he said. "Don't Satan beat all?"

I knew he hadn't really asked me a question, so I didn't answer, but I did notice that the minute he stopped singing the rattle ceased, too.

We trudged upstairs into the church and sat on the stage sipping spring water. I think he knew what I'd come to ask, but he was going to make me ask it, not from spite, but because he knew it was best for me. When I had one swallow left, I said, "I'm looking for work, and I don't have a real good history here. Do you have any advice?"

"Advice I can give you, Ize, but I can't offer you a job. I can ask around and I know that there are often jobs at the hospital, and at the mall, custodial work, honest if not glamorous, but the Lord doesn't care about glamour. That's prideful. In fact, He warns against vanity and pride, which He says, Goeth before a fall. And He also tells us that it is easier for a camel to pass through the eye of a needle than for a rich man to enter the kingdom of heaven. My advice is to be humble and honest. Buy a newspaper and look to see who is hiring. It won't be much, but every step you take toward a better life, will be a step closer to happiness."

I thanked him, and he saw me to the door. "You and Lorena can come for the van anytime after seven," he said as he let me out into the sun.

"We'll be here," I said.

The gutter had dried. The van shone in the sun, the lettering brighter, the hubcaps gleaming and the sidewalls of the tires black as hard coal. I ambled down to the Rite Aid and bought a newspaper and a ballpoint pen. In the past, I'd found work by showing up at temporary agencies, something Blissfull did not, in my experience, have. The pay from those jobs is shit, but most guys there are looking for enough work to get a flop and a bottle. I got my better jobs, like the one at Plourde's, from a VA counselor, which would require an appointment and a ride to Beckley during the week.

I lounged on an iron bench by the memorial honoring the Civil War dead from our town, and read through the classified help-wanted listings. Reverend Willis was right, there wasn't much, but there was a half page notice that there would be a special employment section on Saturday. I took that as a hopeful sign, sat a moment with the sun on my face, then folded up the paper and strolled over to the City Hall to visit Lorena.

She wasn't at her window, and when I asked where she was, one of the women said, "She's gone home to look in on her mother and the two of her kids that are sick." All the joy of the morning sagged away from me. I feared two sick little ones might mean we weren't going to Beckley after all, and an old pain ran into me, the feeling I'd get when I gave up on sobriety and flung myself into a bottle, drinking my way into oblivion, getting drunk enough to forget why I was getting drunk. "She mostly gets right back, just uses her ten minute break is all," she said. "You'all can wait for her, less'n I can help." Though I knew Lorena would be in a hurry when she got back, I decided to wait.

Two minutes later, Lorena rushed back into the office and disappeared behind the partition without noticing me. I waited until she appeared at her place and had removed the "Use Next Window Please" sign, then sauntered up as if I was a customer. Her face lit up. "Hey," she said.

I leaned into the window and said, "Just what are we picking up in Beckley?"

"You been by Star of Morning?"

"I helped wash the van," I said, as if it were a secret.

"I got a long list from Theo. It'll take most of the day," Lorena said.

"Do I need to pack a lunch?" I said.

"That will not be necessary, sir. Now may I help you with anything else," she said, her smile about to slit her cheeks.

"Will you be receiving callers tonight?" I said.

"Not between Mama and sick kids no," Lorena said. "See you Saturday morning."

"Star of Morning at about seven?" I said.

"That will be fine," she said. "Have a nice day, sir."

CHAPTER TWELVE

Lillian volunteered to work doubles on Saturdays because she got overtime on top of the weekend pay rate, so she was not inconvenienced to drop me at Star of Morning at quarter to seven. It was chilly and overcast, the sky threatening snow, and I was glad that we'd becoming back from Beckley with new tires, as I had noticed when washing the van that the old ones were near as slick as the stones in a slate trace. The streetlight in front of the church glowed a soft yellow and I waited on the sidewalk peering at the shadow my body cast on the church wall. At five of seven, Reverend Willis sprung out of the church carrying his Bible and a small briefcase. "Morning, Ize," he said as he handed me the van keys and slapped a hand on my shoulder, "Praise the Lord if I don't feel a spell of good preaching on me today." He glanced up at the sky and said, "May be some snow, but this afternoon I'm preaching to a group of businessmen from around the area who are recommitting their lives to Jesus, and I feel the sweet warmth of The Holy Ghost upon me this fine day." He turned to face the church door and said, "You know what, Ize? I expect this old building might see a soul or two saved from eternal perdition today."

Around Reverend Willis, who always knows what to say, I get tongue tied, as if my mouth was full of cotton or fishhooks. "I hope so, Reverend Willis, I do," I said.

"Lord willing," he said, spinning back to face me, "I have taken part of my text from Mark three verse seventeen, because it pertains to the story of Jesus sharing a meal with the tax collectors and sinners. Those who are well have no need of a physician, but those who are sick; I came not to call the righteous but the sinners. That is a powerful image for me. Jesus eats with the sinners and not the righteous, for it is the sinner who needs His care and His love. Even at His final meal, He broke bread with the ones who would deny and betray him. Ain't that some real love?"

Again, I didn't know what to say, and when I did not reply,

Reverend Willis grinned, spun around twice and let out a whoop. "Get thee behind me, Satan," he said as he laughed from his gut.

I tried to weigh just how much of what Reverend Willis was saying was directed at me, worried that he expected a response, but as soon as he'd stopped laughing he said, "The other scripture I intend to explore with these men is from the Old Testament, the book of Amos, one of my favorite prophets. Let me show you." Reverend Willis opened his Bible to a page he'd marked with a piece of a bank envelope and said, "Amos is explaining to the people that God is about to rain down great sorrows on them for their many wickednesses. He says here in chapter seven verses four through six, Hear this, you who trample on the needy, and bring the poor of the land to an end, saying when will the new moon be over that we may sell grain again? And the Sabbath, that we may offer wheat for sale, that we may make the ephah small and the shekel great and deal deceitfully with false balances, that we may buy the needy for a pair of sandals and sell the refuse of the wheat? You know, Ize, the businessmen of these times do the same thing, give too small a measure for too high a price, exploit the poor and their ignorance of such things."

That part I followed, at least Reverend Willis's explanation, and I said, "It never did seem to me that the poor had much of a chance in this life."

"But this life, Ize," he said, "Is transitory. In the next life, the poor, if they believe, will be lifted up." He clapped a hand on my shoulder and said, "Lord, I do feel a spell of preaching coming on me."

When Lorena arrived she swapped her keys with Reverend Willis in case he needed her car, though he said he was going inside to pray for strength and inspiration for his afternoon's work. He hugged us both and retreated into the church. I headed for the driver's door, but Lorena said, "I looked you up on the computer. You don't have a West Virginia driver's license. I'll drive."

I felt like I had on New Year's Eve. I couldn't fight it. I'd been fired again, this time from a job I never got to start.

Instead of heading up Steadman's Grade toward the interstate, Lorena drove through the square and south onto Valley Avenue. Before I could ask why, she said, "I can leave my mother alone, but not with the kids."

I wondered if this was a test. "Are they coming with us?" I asked, trying to sound open to the idea.

"No. Lord no. I need a break, too. The older kids' daddy is meeting us at the mall to take them for the weekend, and the little ones are going to their grandfolks," Lorena said, as if she were explaining a secret. I tried not to show my relief, but I feared she sensed it.

I sat over by the door. When Blissfull men ride, they do that. Only women sit in the middle unless there are three up front. I didn't get out at the house except to open the door for the kids to get in. Scrubbed and polished, they each toted a knapsack and wore school day clothes. As I watched the four towheads bouncing on the bench seat in the rear view mirror, I hoped that Reverend Willis had ordered new shocks as well as tires.

We dropped the boys at their grandparents, who lived in the same development as Lorena, and then met Hiram, the girl twins' father at the mall in front of the store where I'd bought Lillian's Christmas present.

Hiram was a short, sinewy man with a terrier's neck and shoulders wide enough to land a plane on, who told me to call him Bud, "'Cause all my friends do." He sported a gray brush cut and chewed on a toothpick, and though he tried staring me down, I've had enough practice at being invisible that I allowed his gaze to pass through me and into the bustier display at Victoria's Secret.

Lorena knelt down, kissed the girls goodbye, and made them promise to behave for their father. "They always mind me," he said, as Lorena stood up, "but I do need to drop them off early Sunday, 'bout two-thirty."

I watched Lorena's eyes narrow as if she wanted to scrap with him, but she took my hand and said, "That's up to you. I love having them with me," and yanked me toward the exit.

As Lorena raced up the long climb to the interstate, flurries, spit from a low line of black and blue clouds, drifted across the road, and I recalled the night I'd ridden home in the van, stepping inside to its warmth from the wind riddled on-ramp in Holyoke, recalling how the wind whistled in the vent windows. I remembered how sweet the accents of home flooded my ears that night, how unhurried the long trip felt though we drove all the night, stopping twice, once for gas and the other time to check the oil—the moment I gave my life over to a new power. I'd never felt as holy. When Lorena waved to a driver going the other way, she said, "That's Mrs. Linsbury from work, I love her to death." It reminded me of how the Farrell kid, who'd slept most of the way, kept saying, "Jesus oh Jesus," when Reverend Willis told him about my anointing. Midway up the grade a semi, brakes burning, rolled by, and I recalled the smell of the motor oil smudge on my forehead and how it lingered on my shirt long after I wiped it off with my sleeve, when Patches came running up to me in the road.

More than anything, as the shuddering van growled up the grade, I considered how for a long time, whenever I'd left Blissfull, it was for months or years. The idea of running over to Beckley and back heaved me back to a time before I'd ever had another home. I wanted to believe that it was something Lorena and I might do into our old age, but the darkness of my natural instincts raked my spirit, and as Lorena eased onto the highway, I peeked over my shoulder into the back of the van. I saw two serpent boxes, a pillow, some blankets, and a sleeping bag, reminding me that in a few months Reverend Willis would be making his serpent-selling trips north again. For the first time in days, I felt the whirlies welling up and closed my eyes, but when I did I was confronted by the ghosts from the halls at Plourde's and opened them again.

"Falling asleep?" Lorena said.

"No, just a bit of the whirlies," I said, "I'll be fine on the highway."

"Still get them?" Lorena said.

"Not as often as I used to," I said, uncomfortable lying to her, but not wanting to get into a discussion about them either.

"This old van can't be helping it none," Lorena said.

I closed my eyes again, but a picture of the serpent boxes and the sleeping bag was tattooed to my eyelids, causing saliva to invade my mouth like it does in anticipation of a deep pull on a bottle. I prayed in fervent silence that I wouldn't be riding back to Holyoke alongside the Farrell kid because Lillian had left Riley again, or I had managed to wear out my kin welcome by plunging off the wagon.

It took us a bit to locate the garage where we had the appointment as it was stuck off in an old residential section of Beckley that neither Lorena nor I knew. I felt my balls tighten and my stomach quake when we passed a sign for the VA Medical Center and Veterans Avenue. I thought about the shrink there who'd insisted that my problems were rooted in my trouble with my parents, and that I was running away from them in liquor. I'd thought he was full of shit then, but as I gazed at the blue and white road sign for the hospital, I began to wonder if he wasn't right. I felt as if West Virginia, my town, my ridge, and the mountains were where I belonged, if I could just discover my right to my piece of them.

Dale Casper's garage sat on a small rise next to his peeling shotgun house. He was bent and tilted to his left at the waist, and wore galluses and a VFW hat. On the back wall of the office he had a hand-lettered sign that read,

No Credit. No Two Party Checks.
All Work Done By The Book—The Good Book.

As he limped behind the counter to get a work order, Dale appeared to be about fifty, but he was one of those guys who could have been ten years either side of that. I didn't ask, but he said, "Rock slide, twelve year ago. Crushed my hip. Got the same thing as that colored fellah, Bo Jackson, who played baseball and football. No blood to the bone. VA put in a new hip, but too much else was wrecked."

Dale tossed me the keys to his car, a late seventies Cadillac Sedan De Ville, so we could run errands while he worked on the van, but Lorena snatched them out of my hand. Pointing with his bent index finger he said, "Rides good, that's important to me. She burns a bit of gas, but no oil. Big trunk, too, though I might could give you'all a pick-up if you need it."

"This will be better than fine," Lorena said, "We're obliged to you."

We spent three hours riding around Beckley visiting hardware stores, super markets, and Wal-Mart, filling shopping carts with paper goods, canned food, candles, batteries, cartons of spaghetti and tons of stuff I don't remember. Lorena ordered me around each store in a way that made me sure she'd made this run before. When I finally asked her what we were doing, she said, "We're here to re-supply the church, pick up Star of Morning's donation to the Blissfull Food Pantry, and to stock up for the Spring Prayer Week and Revival."

I noticed, when we were checking out at Wal-Mart, that the MasterCard we were using belonged to the church. I wouldn't have figured that a storefront church could have one of those and when I asked Lorena about it, she said, "Reverend Willis has money. He supports the church. The poor folk don't know it or don't want to know it, of course, they believe in miracles."

I digested that for a while, unsure if I liked the taste. As the son of a bootlegger, and the brother of man who used a coffin that was supposed to contain the earthly remains of his mother to import drugs and rifles, I began to wonder how selling snakes could make you rich. I chewed on that as we stuffed the last of what we'd bought into the trunk and backseat of the Cadillac.

When Lorena pulled into the garage lot, I said. "Where'd Reverend Willis get this money?"

"He had it when he came to West Virginia. My sister never told us; maybe he had insurance on her. It doesn't matter. He's a good man and he helps the poor," she said. I could tell from the tone of her voice that Lorena had no more to say on the subject.

When we returned to the garage, the van was still on the lift. Dale was looking under the chassis with a work light and running a rag over the exhaust system while muttering to himself. When he saw us he said, "Ten more minutes. Make yourself at home."

We sat on two leather chairs in the waiting room, leafing through some greasy shop-worn magazines, *People*, *Field and Stream*, *Popular Mechanics*. When Dale entered he said to Lorena, "She's set to go. Tell your brother-in-law that I had to replace the shocks and that he should really think about trading this in while it's got some value. She's sound enough for now, but old."

"I'll let him know," she said placing the credit card on the counter.

Dale pushed the card back. "Bill's taken care of. You might want to head back. I smell snow."

In sobriety, I found an improving keenness of my mind. It was good to realize that I'd not left all my critical brain cells in a puddle in my sitting-in-the-gutter-days, and we weren't in the van half a minute when I asked Lorena how Dale knew she was Reverend Willis's brother-in-law, if she'd never been to the garage before. Lorena looked me dead in the eye. "Because he's the guy who helped Theo after he spent the summer praying in the hills. Dale was up in the hills berrying when he came across Theo. Besides, I didn't say I'd never met him, I just said I'd never been to the garage," she said, but I wasn't buying it. When he'd pushed the credit card back at her, I was sure it was an old practiced routine, like offering a cigarette to an old friend who's quit. It's friendly and allows him to refuse with dignity and still let you light up. "Actually," I said, "you didn't say anything about it until we were looking for the place."

Lorena slapped the wheel, hard, and then pushed her arms forward and locked her elbows. "Still a damn bootlegger, aren't you, Ize?" she said spitting each word out like a bitter seed. "I've met Dale, but I'd never been here before. Okay?"

Fired again, I said, "Didn't mean to pry. I was trying to make conversation and we both know I was never good at that."

"Conversation is fine, Ize, but cross-examination is not," she said. Her eyes told me that she didn't want to continue on the same line of talk.

It was almost three when we began to find our way to the highway. In the shadows of the hills it was already dark, though sundown was still an hour away. All day flurries had wandered down the sky, but as we left Dale's garage it began to snow in short bursts, never quite coating anything. Lorena switched on the radio and hunted for something she liked, settling on a station that was having a salute to Loretta Lynn. They played *Coal Miner's Daughter*, then the one about not "comin' home adrinking with lovin' on your mind." I thought of how my mother could have written that one after one of the times she'd tried to fight off the Old Man when he was roaring. As I thought about Mama, young and not yet broken, I hoped that at least some iota of her ash and bone had washed into the sea.

Lorena hummed along with each song, not speaking to me, as I wondered if I had said something fatal to my hopes of rekindling my chances with her. She kept her eyes on the road, now empty of traffic save for a few big rigs and the occasional car crammed with guys who seemed to be enjoying the time-honored tradition of spending a Blissfull Saturday afternoon going nowhere.

From the highway to home, you have to cross Battle Ridge by one of two routes. The most direct is Steadman's Grade; it pulls hard up the ridge to the interstate, and seems to plummet down the hill on the return trip, or you can go by a county gravel road that winds slowly up the ridge like a coiled rattler. In winter, locals use that route if the grade is at all icy, because, though pulling up the grade isn't often difficult, the descent is rail-straight with no places to pull off.

Lorena chose the county road. In the hills it had gone dark

and the clouds, still spilling intervals of snow, grew black as a tornado sky. After a little cluster of houses that had gone up near an old abandoned town, she pulled the van off onto a side road I did not remember ever driving over. I didn't ask her why she taken that route, as I was coming to learn that the best way to get along with my old girlfriend was to say as little as possible. We'd gone a mile, maybe two, it was hard to tell as slowly as Lorena was driving in the dark, when she pulled into the dooryard of an old farmhouse, shut off the lights, but left the motor running.

She turned to face me and said. "This used to be owned by my second husband's parents, the ones you met this morning, before they moved to town. Ain't no one coming up here anymore, least this time of day." Lorena opened the driver's door and said, "Coming?"

I hopped out thinking we might be going into the house, but she met me in front of the van, took my hand, and led me to the rear door. She wrenched it open and, hauled herself up into a narrow space between the empty serpent boxes and the back seat. Pushing the bags and boxes of supplies aside, and spreading the blankets on the bench seat, she said, "Hop in, Ize, the cold's not doin' either of us any good and we don't need the exhaust in here."

Lorena unzipped the sleeping bag and began to shed her clothes. When she said, "We won't be any colder than in that old creek," I nearly gelded myself getting out of my jeans. Every spare inch of the van, except the seat, was stuffed with the supplies we'd bought in Beckley. My hands fumbled with my belt, and Lorena laughed out loud when I got my zipper stuck. "Hold still, I'll fix it," she said. I would have cut the damn jeans off me, but she unsnagged the zipper and tugged my pants and shorts down. I felt foolish half stumbling out of them with her sitting on the seat stark naked in front of me, but as my eyes got used to the light, I could make out that Whipple smile that had beguiled me as a kid, and I gained control.

There wasn't much room on the seat, but Lorena's body felt as familiar and friendly as it had when we were kids. I nosed in her hair for the scent I remembered, and even if it wasn't there I would swear now that it was. I was so afraid that I'd last only a second that I tried hard to make her come with my fingers, but just like in the old days, she preferred to have me on top of her, those lanky Whipple legs squeezing me like a boa constrictor. It was only when we were rocking so hard that I heard the van springs squeak that it occurred to me where we were and what we were doing and how unholy that seemed, but those qualms passed as Lorena began to move faster and to announce her pleasure in my ear, and when she screamed, "Yes Jesus, oh sweet, Jesus," I was right behind her.

Our exertions had fogged the windows. The van idled on, the heater throwing that musty heat that cars have, and the sleeping bag Lorena had pulled tight to us, lay soft on my back.

I wanted to speak or cry, but I feared moving any muscle, especially my mouth, afraid to ruin the profound sense of relief running through me like a prolonged shock. Lorena must have sensed it. "You can breath now, Ize. It's okay."

"Lorena," I said. "I don't want to say anything wrong."

"I imagine I'm remembering the same things you are," she said. "I don't know where this is going, but I'm willing to let it go a bit longer to find out."

We lay warm, sticky, and quiet for a long time, until she began to shiver from the cold. When we'd dressed, I wiped the rear window glass with my shirtsleeve and peered out at the night. A half moon had risen and the tiniest trace of snow rimed the road. The wind was up and the branches of the trees cast crazy lines on the ground. Had I died at that moment, the devil would have greeted a smiling man.

Lorena drove me home in the van. I argued that I should help her unload it, but she said she and Reverend Willis could do it, and that there was no telling if the special service was over. "If they're still testifying, I'll switch with him in the morning and there'll be plenty there to help. You might be there, too," she said.

Lorena wouldn't come into the house, though she did step out of the van to absorb the view from the ridge, and I knew what she was thinking. I slumped against the hood, staring at the glow of town, wondering whether I belonged to it or if my world ended at the tarred road. Lorena had a house and kids and a job. I slept on my brother's couch and had quit the only decent job I'd ever held for more than a few months. She'd done better than anyone would have guessed a Whipple could, but I was about what folks had figured I'd be. Lorena stood straight, arms across her chest, the wind tossing her hair around her face, abiding in a world naturally hers, humming, though I couldn't tell what song.

The aches of Lorena's life were chiseled into her face in a hard way, like so many women who'd suffered as she had, and when her natural cheerfulness deserted her I could detect some of the still tender wounds in her eyes. After she'd taken in whatever it was she was looking at, Lorena kissed me. I felt my bones shake and I was inspired to jump back in the van and give the new shocks another workout, but when I started to kiss her back, she backed away, put her finger to her lips, and said "If I don't see you tomorrow at church, call me at noon. Maybe you can come for dinner, before the kids get back." I nodded, not sure I had permission to speak. "I had a fine day, Ize," she said, hopping up into the driver's seat, "But I got to go."

I waved as she headed down the hill, the new tires spilling sand and pebbles into the night behind her, her brake lights flashing as she swung the van around the heaves and potholes, until she'd disappeared from sight. I leaned against Riley's truck. The moon was rising and the stars were dimming. I could feel the heat escaping the earth and the night settling its cold blanket on the ridge.

Riley and the kids, who were watching a movie, didn't look up when I opened the front door. "Lillian's gone to bed. She ain't slept in almost two days, and there's some dinner for you if you're hungry," Riley said.

"You've been gone all day," Annie said.

"I know, honey," I said. "I had to go to Beckley."

"With Laura Whipple's mommy?" she asked. "Laura and her sister go to my school."

I don't remember how I answered, but it was the first time that I'd considered that Annie and Carleton might have friends off the ridge. I knew that when they stayed in town with Lillian they played with neighbors, but I hadn't thought about school friends. I hit me that I'd been thinking of Lorena and me as we were as kids, about the only friends each other had, forgetting she'd already had two husbands and given birth to near as many children as her mother.

My stomach growled and I realized how long it had been since I'd eaten. I sat at the table and stuffed myself with cornbread, fried steak, and green beans and studied Riley and the kids, who sat rapt by a movie about a family lost on a mountain in a storm. I thought of Lorena staring out across the ridge and I thought of how we'd been kids trapped on a mountain ourselves, free to wander the hills and ridges, but trapped just the same. I'd left. She'd stayed and been the better for it.

I washed my plate and cleaned up the table. When I was putting the leftovers into the refrigerator, the dogs showed up at the door barking to come in. Riley and the kids didn't hear, still mired in the movie, whispering to people to "watch out." They didn't budge when the door opened and a bitter gust scoured the room, and Annie barely moved when Roxie stuck her cold nose against her hand. I wondered if I was becoming invisible again, the way I used to in cities up North, someone to step over, or to avoid in a doorway, or whether I was simply home.

When the movie ended the kids went off to wash up, and I was struck by how quiet they were, but I guessed that Riley had made a point of saying how they had to be sure not to disturb Lillian. I noticed how hard the kids, even Carleton, tried not to get Riley or Lillian riled, and I knew it was because they were hoping that they'd stay together. They came out a few minutes later in pajamas and smelling of toothpaste and soap. Annie kissed me goodnight and said, "I love you, Uncle

Ize. Sleep tight," and Carleton added, his Batman cape trailing him, "Don't let the bedbugs bite." Riley followed the kids out of the living room to tuck them in, and when he came back he was holding the classified section of the paper where I'd circled some of the help wanted ads.

"Ize," he said, "Lillian and me were talking. We know you want to pull your own weight, so when we move to the new place; you can take over this one. Soon, I'm gonna start cutting logs for the house, clearing the lot and road. I'll need help." He paused and stared at me a minute. "With me?" he asked.

I nodded and he started in again. "So, I see no sense in paying someone who ain't kin to work with me. I'll hire you, and that way if Lillian is at the hospital and the kids need tending, you can help with that, too. They like you."

Riley stopped and waited for me to reply. I said, "I'll help that way if you'd like. I was gonna try and get a job so I could get a license and some kind of beater once the weather gets better."

Riley smiled. "My old wreck is at Earl's garage. He's waiting on a part, but it'll run soon. I'll give it to you if you'll take this on. Look. I can't spend a whole lot of cash that the world can see, but you I can pay under the table. Besides, there is one more score we can make, and you'll have all you'll need for a long while." My butt puckered up tight. Riley must have read my face because he said, "Don't get your nuts in a knot here, okay? Hear me out."

I sat back in the chair and let him go. He told me that he'd been waiting for the right buyer to come along and take up the last of the Old Man's best, which they'd hidden far up on the mountain, near Mama's grave. He said that he had been aging the whiskey in bottles, sealed with a bond. "Ize, there's 150 cases. Each bottle will fetch ten bucks. A dollar for each year it's aged. One-twenty a case. In case you've forgot how to do the math, that's eighteen grand, minus expenses. 50/50. It's the Old Man's stuff, so it's half yours."

"Who's gonna move it?" I asked, "And what expenses?"

Riley whispered, "Keep your voice down. It's going to

a certain friend in Detroit who moves a little whiskey to the immigrant community up there," he said, smiling when he said immigrant.

"We getting cash, pills, or guns, Riley?" I said, with deliberate sarcasm.

"Cash," he said, glaring at me for a minute, the same way he did when we were kids and he was daring me to do something crazy.

"Riley," I said, "It's your business now. I'll help with the house and the trees and the kids, but this is your business."

"Damn it," he said, his voice low so as not to wake Lillian or the kids, "I need your help. The shit's stored where the Old Man left it. I can't get it alone, or risk anyone else seeing it, except our client—an old and trusted friend. This is the end of it. No more still, no stash, no reefer, but we can't waste all that good whiskey either. That'd be sinful." Riley slumped back in his chair. He fastened his eyes on me waiting for an answer.

I'd been played like a foul-hooked fish. Riley was giving me a choice, get on board or move along. With Riley, you don't talk things out. He draws the line and you decide which side you're on. I searched my mind for some way to wriggle out of his trap, but the thought of leaving Blissfull and Lorena robbed my courage. "I've been hearing a different angle on sin, recently," I said. "But I'm obliged to you." I hoped that by saying I felt beholden that Riley might at least tell me think on it, but he smiled and said, "Kin is kin, little brother," and shook my hand. He popped up, shut off the TV and said, "I'm headed to bed. I'll let you know when we're gonna start on the house."

It was only nine-thirty and I was fully awake. I tried to watch TV, but I'd been out of society for so long that none of it made any sense. Even the basketball teams were different from the ones I remembered, and I'd never cared much for that on TV anyway. I never got the same feeling as I did watching Malcolm play in the high school gym—the sneakers squeaking on the wood floor and the hoarse cheerleaders voices' urging the crowd on.

I dug out my Bible from beneath the couch, blew off the

dust, and sat at the kitchen table reading it. I'd begun to skip around, just open to a passage and begin reading. I found that I really liked the Proverbs and Psalms, because they were short and had no begats and begets.

I opened to Proverbs 13:12. Hope deferred makes the heart sick, but a desire fulfilled is a tree of life. I studied on that one awhile. I decided that I liked that verse and I wrote it down in the tablet I kept in my backpack. I thought about Lorena and the desire fulfilled in the Star of Morning van, and my full stomach, the kids kissing me goodnight and telling me they loved me, Lillian calling me kin, and Riley giving me his truck, though I realized that I was obligated on that one, and I felt blessed. Blessed the way Reverend Willis says it, not the way teachers used to say it in school, or politicians say it on TV.

It somehow didn't feel wrong to be thinking about Lorena and those lanky Whipple legs locked around my back and the springs squeaking beneath us, as I read more Bible verses. Everything I read began to seem like a sign, like the ones Reverend Willis says are yet to be known.

About midnight a storm rolled in on the ridge. It began as a clattery sleet, but soon snow was falling thick and fast, swirled by gusts that rattled the windows. I would read a verse, consider it, then close the book and my eyes, and open it to a new place, and without looking put my finger on a new verse. I swear that ten minutes into the storm I hit Psalm 147 verse sixteen. He gives snow like wool; he scatters the hoarfrost like ashes. I closed my eyes again. Snow, Mama's ashes, the creek, Lorena's nakedness all flooded into my mind and heart and I began to cry, not sniffle, but sob like a little kid who's been hurt in a way that stuns him but doesn't want anyone to see. I set the Bible down and sat wiping my eyes with napkins and thanking Jesus, Reverend Willis, Lorena, and even Riley.

In the morning a fresh eight inches of powder lay drifted across the ridge. I didn't hear the kids and Lillian get up, stirring only when I smelled coffee and heard the pop of bacon in the pan. I knew that we'd stay on the ridge and that I'd likely have to call my regrets to Lorena.

CHAPTER THIRTEEN

A week later, the snow gone and the creek near its bank with a thaw, Riley and I sauntered down to the garage to retrieve his old truck, which had been ready for almost a month. We walked from the gravel into town, because Riley didn't want to arrive in his new rig when he owed Earl a wad of cash. Earl was pleased to see him, but pretty hot as well. "Next time, Riley, I have to charge interest and storage. I did the work prompt and fair, and I had to get the parts up front."

"I know, Earl," Riley said, as he began to count out a bunch of small bills, laying them on the counter, "But work's been slow and with Christmas and all I've been tapped. You're a good old boy to be so patient. It won't happen again. I got a new wood lot and Ize is gonna help me get some orders filled soon."

"Wouldn't have any of the Old Man's best around would you?" Earl asked. I couldn't tell if he was serious, but Riley acted as if he was.

"Those was old times. I don't even make a batch for myself anymore. I'm out of the business. I got kids and…well, I just got done with that." The pause hurt me to the quick because I knew he'd meant to say, "And a wife," but couldn't.

Earl smiled and counted the bills. He started to get some change, but Riley said, "That's for storage, Earl."

"Next time," Earl said as he pushed the change across the counter to Riley, and I couldn't help but remember Dale Casper's hand doing the same thing with Reverend Willis's credit card. Sometimes it's those local rituals that let you know that you're among your clan, as that professor might have said. Besides, if Riley had given Earl the money he'd not be beholden to him anymore, and Earl, who had to know about the new rig, preferred to have it that way.

It took me two tries to pass the written part of the driver's test. I'd assumed, since I'd been driving since I was a kid that I wouldn't need to study. The second time I looked at the book. Riley's old truck was legal, but I took the road test in his new rig because he worried that a light or signal might conk out at any minute.

The freedom of having wheels was difficult to adjust to. I kept forgetting I didn't need to walk, or ask to borrow Lillian or Riley's rides. I began to see Lorena several nights a week, usually at her place. Her mother's gout was better, but she kept being struck with new ailments, and she didn't like Lorena out at night, especially with me. Eyes betray all but the best poker players, and Mrs. Whipple's were as cold as a Massachusetts midnight in January. The good thing was that she still liked a stiff toddy and soon after the kids were asleep, she'd be sawing logs in her chair.

Lorena had overcome her aversion to having sex with me in the house, but only in the basement. We'd clear the couch or the floor of the kid's toys and light a fire in the woodstove, and though we'd start out talking and reminiscing, we eventually got to teeth- shaking sex, the kind of furious thrashing I figured we'd left behind at the creek. It was odd making love to Lorena in the dark where I couldn't see her face well. I tried to remember if we'd ever made love in the dark as kids, and the closest thing I could recall was a diamond-hard autumn morning when we slipped into an old barn near her place. Lorena had worn an overcoat that had been her father's that hung almost to her feet and a pair of woolen hunting socks pulled up to her knees under her jeans. For weeks afterwards I could feel the scratch of that wool on my back and the chill of the dark barn on my backside as I lay in my bed reading the dictionary or one of my English assignments.

When we weren't so out of breath from stifling our voices and heaving our bodies that we could converse, I told her about working with Riley on his new house, which he kept saying we'd get to any day. Lorena seemed pleased by the news that I would have a job. To keep her mother happy—who still regarded me with all the affection of a disturbed rattler—I drove her and Lorena to Star of Morning each Sunday morning.

I also stopped into to see Reverend Willis each time I went to town. No matter how fidgety I'd be, he had a way of calming me. And I was more anxious than I'd been in a long time, suspicious of any good fortune. If he was at the church, and he generally was, I'd show him the most recent verses I'd written down and we'd talk about them. He'd always show me some wisdom I'd missed, or he'd ask me to think of one of the verses in some way I hadn't considered. If I hadn't been so fearful of the serpents he handled, I might have studied to be a signs preacher myself.

Before I met Lorena's kids, Pervis Meeker's little sisters, June and Joanne, were the only twins I'd known. No one had ever been able to tell them apart and they made no effort to make that possible. Every time I saw them they wore the same outfits and for as long as I remembered, they had identical pageboy haircuts. When one twin needed glasses, the other got ones with clear lenses, so they looked the same. They were a year ahead of me in school, and when they left for some egghead college in Pennsylvania the gossip was that they were going to be roommates and take the same courses. They both became doctors and moved to Ohio. In a few years, they made enough money to move their parents to Florida, so by the time Riley's buddy, Pervis, went to seek his fortune in Detroit, the Meekers were a memory in town.

Lorena's kids were different. The older girls, Laura and Lucy, were built more like Hiram. The younger ones, the boys, Leonard and Lucas, inherited the long-legged Whipple genes. The boys took to me quickly because they were about Carleton's age and size so I could rough house with them, which most boys enjoy, and I knew the kinds of things boys their age liked to laugh about. The girls were different. They resented me being around, not because they worried about me taking Hiram's place; hell the guy who did that, Lorena's second husband, was gone as well, but I think it was because they were in a struggle for their mother's attention, and I was one more burr under their saddles. Between the time Lorena spent waiting on her own mother, tending to the boys, who being younger needed more of her time, and the hours I took up, I guess they felt they were getting the short straw.

The girls weren't like Annie, who could amuse herself or play with Carleton, and I understood that. All the houses on Lorena's street seemed to have kids. There were swing sets and jungle gyms in the yards, and even in winter bicycles and pedal cars in the driveways. They had never needed to learn how to be alone, the way you do on the ridge. It was different for Lorena, having all her sisters and the freedom to come and go as she pleased, but for most of the hill kids, you are either by yourself, with your kin, or with the dogs. Though Lorena's girls were standoffish with me, at least I could tell them apart, unlike Pervis's sisters. Lucy wore her hair short and curled it with an iron, while Laura tied hers' back in a long ponytail, which her brothers loved to pull. They never wore the same clothes, and Lorena said they had different friends at school. I couldn't remember the Meeker girls ever having any friends except for themselves, even though Pervis was one of the most popular kids in school and they lived in town.

I tried to get the girls to warm to me, but I didn't try to bribe them with gifts, because Lorena kept saying they were spoiled. "Hiram buys them every damn thing they want, then sends his support checks a month late," she told me one night as we were lying on the floor in her basement, "He plays games with them, like he does with all his grown women. He's a sugar daddy one minute then threatening to smack them in the head the next. But he lays a hand on those girls and I'll feed his dick to him."

In my life, the moments I'm proud of are fewer than those I wish I had back, but I have never raised my hand to a woman. Lorena's words silenced me. I was as afraid to say the wrong thing, as I was to say nothing. It wasn't just Mama's trials that made me that way, and it wasn't just that she'd said only a coward hits a woman, but I knew from my own wounds what that sort of shit does to you—I have no taste for blood.

A VA shrink said my Old Man beat Mama because his Old Man had beat his mother, but that's bullshit. I've been beat. Beat so raw my ass bled, smacked so hard I couldn't see from an eye for a week. It wasn't the blood or the pain, but the way it made me feel, as if I was all those things the Old Man said I was, lazy, stupid, a sissy. I used to think that if I had fought back that he might have stopped beating on me, but I never could.

I held Lorena close to me and I said, "I would never raise a hand to you. Man who would is a coward."

Lorena rolled to me and looked into my face. "Ize, that is a beautiful thing to say, and I believe you," she said. "I've never detected any meanness in you, not ever."

I lay still and Lorena got astride me and guided me into her. "I want to feel you in me deep as can be," she said. She bent down, kissed me and said; "Don't close your eyes until you can't stand it anymore. I want to watch your face." Lorena bent over me, palms on the floor beside my shoulders, elbows locked, her face inches above mine. We kissed and I started to move my hips, but she said, "Be still, let me do it." I tried not to close my eyes, but it was unnatural. Lorena increased her pace, her Whipple smile exploding just above my face, then she rose up straight and crossed her arms over her chest. I reached for her butt and held it in both hands, feeling every muscle rocking in a quick circle. I was holding my eyes open and looking at her, looking at me. "Come on now, Ize," she said her voice hoarse and high.

I gave myself over to her and closed my eyes and we must have gotten there about the same time, but I was seeing colors and forcing a scream down into my throat so as to not alert her mother. Lorena had lowered her face into my shoulder to muffle her own joy. No one, even those feeling the anointment at Star of Morning, had ever felt closer to God than I did at that moment as Lorena wept into my ear, "Ize, you are a good man, Sweet Jesus, a good loving man," and pounded my shoulder with her fist.

That night I stayed later than I ever had. I worried that Lorena had to be at work in the morning, but she was as talkative as I'd ever seen her. She told me how Hiram. whom she never called Bud, had turned mean on her after the girls were born, then about Roger, her second husband who died in a wreck after they were divorced when the boys were only four. She told me about how much the grief of seeing the boys so hurt nearly killed her, and how when her sister died she thought about finding an old mine and curling up and dying there. "That's why I am loyal to Theo. He cared for me and never made me get baptized or anointed. He said that the Lord would lead me if I was willing to follow," she said. "I am not a believer, there's too much sorrow in this world for me to believe that anyone has a plan for it, but I am grateful to Theo."

I toiled up the ridge after midnight, Riley's old truck fighting every bump and heave, the night dark and moonless. I thought over what Lorena had said, and I understood it. The Reverend Willis was like a cool stream on a hot day. He flowed; his words, his walk, his smile, all seemed to be headed somewhere, like a leaf bobbing over a riffle in a creek. Though I'd been to his service each Sunday, he'd never beckoned to me, or asked me why I had never come forward, or if my intentions with his sister-in-law were honorable, or any of the things I feared. No, he flowed and what flowed from him, even when he was sweat-soaked and anointed and holding a snarl of serpents up to the Lord, made people feel alive and loved. In the most emotional moments, the musicians cranking up the decibels, the congregation testifying and singing and shouting, the serpents moving and coiling around a worshipper's arms, there was a serenity and security that radiated from Reverend Willis, and each week it brought me more comfort.

The winter remained fickle, a few days of cold and snow, the temperature dropping into the single digits at night, followed by the sun and open fields and thawing snow banks. In early March a foot of wet snow gave way to cloudless blue and winter receded to the north, blowing up over the ridgeline and beyond the summit of the mountain.

We began clearing Riley's land. He'd marked the trees for the house with yellow paint, and the others he wanted to take down with white. His plan was to drop the ones for the mill to debark first, then skid them to the roadside, before clearing the actual lot. Years before, he'd bought an old skidder from a logger who was quitting the business, and had plenty of saws, chains, peaveys and cant hooks for his firewood business, so we had all the tools we'd need.

Riley was a man possessed by the notion that he had a plan that was working. Lillian was attempting to work regular hours at the hospital, which he'd taken as a good sign, trying to get home by three, just before the school bus toiled up the ridge. The problem was she was an emergency room nurse and emergencies don't arrive on any schedule. Riley dutifully watched the road, and on the days that Lillian couldn't get home for the kids, I quit as soon as I heard the school bus turn into the gravel so the kids wouldn't be alone at the house.

Riley was nervous, near the point of paranoia, that Sergeant Wright was looking to trap him with his drug money and when we arrived at the site one morning to find the skidder had a flat, he used that to his advantage. We could have waited to get it fixed, but Riley had me help him jack it up, crib the wheel, and drive into town to get it repaired at Earl's garage. Earl is more than a bit suspicious by nature and Riley played him like fiddle. When Earl asked about the skidder and how the house was coming, Riley laid out the best-concocted story I'd heard in a long time.

"Earl, I owe it to Ize. If'n he hadn't have come home after saving his money and offered to buy the old place from me once I got the new one built, I'd have had to work a whole bunch more years to build Lillian her dream home. Kin is the one thing to count on," he said, and then he bear hugged me and let a tear slip out of his left eye. He made sure that Earl saw him wipe his cheek, though he pretended it didn't happen. I was impressed, but it also reminded me of the way he turned Mama's dying into a big score. I loved my brother; we had too much history to not be bonded tight as wet leather, but he scared the hell out of me, too.

I knew that the story would be in every café and bar in

town, so I asked Riley as he was tightening the lug nuts on the skidder wheel what the details were. "Nothing special," he said. "You saved a wad of cash up north and came home with it in your pack. Heard I had these thirty acres and after that the folks will assume the rest. How and where you got the money makes no difference." I also knew that it would satisfy Earl's curiosity. He could understand a man moving down the ridge if his own kin was taking over the family homestead, more than he might have understood Riley selling it to a stranger, especially a place as haunted with legends as ours.

The beauty of most of Riley's schemes is in their simplicity, and that they work. If he really had a hundred thousand bucks stashed, he could make that last a lifetime, and with just a little honest work he could lower suspicion to a point where no one in Blissfull would much care to know the finer points of how he got by. He would always be a bootlegger's kid, and that is enough to make anyone but the law give you room. Still, he would bring the 150 cases of whiskey up on the mountain that he said we'd need to move as soon as the weather was right, and that seemed to be small potatoes compared to what he had. I knew Riley was capable of deceiving anyone and, that kin or no kin; he'd lie to me in a New York minute.

We worked hard into April clearing the lot. Once the timber for the house, which Riley had come to call a "deluxe log home," was skidded out to the road, we hauled it to the mill to be debarked and dried. We cleared the rest of the trees and bushes for the driveway and the house site, and bucked it up for the stove.

Riley taught me how to dig out the stumps with his backhoe. It was muddy, dirty work, and I was glad for the days that Lillian worked late, so I could get cleaned up and catch a quick nap on the couch while the kids played, before I visited Lorena. She noticed how my muscles were getting hard and how the last traces of my sloppy drunk's paunch had melted away.

We worked six days a week. On Sunday's, I went to Star of Morning. If Lorena had the kids she made dinner at her place. When she didn't we rode around. We got adept at making love in the truck, cab or bed, depending on the weather and the remoteness of the place we parked. It was vastly different than the riding I'd done as a kid, no beer between my legs, no whiskey, no hitchhikers, but it brought the same peacefulness to me. I never sat a horse, but driving a truck is, I imagine, not all that different.

Lorena sat in the middle of the front seat of the old truck, which Earl had been slowly fixing up for me, and I drove for hours, my hand on her knee when I wasn't shifting, and her head against my shoulder. Once we drove out to the old farm where we'd parked in the van, and we got out and wandered around the overgrown dooryard and alder-choked apple orchards. We damn near broke through the rotted boards hidden beneath some thatch grass that covered the well. Lorena told me that she hoped she could buy the place some day and fix up the house. "I think the kids, especially Laura and Lucy, would understand me better if they could live out here for awhile," she said.

A thought tore through my heart, and I wanted to ask her to move up on the ridge with me when Riley had finished his place, but I realized that our old place was too small and shabby, and haunted by too many ghosts to ever be Lorena's home. "I'd like to live somewhere like this, too," I said. "I don't think it ever leaves you."

Lorena didn't say a word, but she leaned into me and held my hand.

The place was too high on the ridge to have yet greened like the valley, but the apple trees sported tiny buds and the weeds along the road had new shoots rising from their winter-dead clumps. A squirrel chattered at us from a tree, and turkey buzzards and hawks rode the thermals above us. The sun was high and my sore muscles were grateful for its warmth. Lorena circled her arm around my waist and when she looked at me I could see in that Whipple smile what she had in mind. I knew the seat of the truck wouldn't do, and the bed was muddy and filled with gas cans and peaveys and crowbars. "I want show you something," she said, and led me around the back of the house along a path defined by flat rocks sunk into the ground. They weren't the fancy stones they make those long college walkways out of up north, just the rocks that grow here in West Virginia.

The hillside had been recently timbered so you could see well beyond the ridge, and a long rocky field fell away down a steep hill. A deck had been built onto the back of the place, and it looked sturdier than the house itself. Midway down the field there was a small pole barn built into the hill. Lorena took a key from the pocket of her jeans and said, "Let me show you the barn."

The grass was wet and slick, our shoes sunk in to the stubbly field making sucking sounds as we took the next step, and little rivulets of water made furrows down toward the woods, where an unseen trace babbled. Lorena opened the barn. Inside was one large room with a concrete floor that had a diagonal crack in it, that stretched from a weep hole in a depression in the middle of it. A few hand tools hung on the back wall, and a little light snuck in through two small windows in the gables. Along the far wall Lorena pointed out some folding lawn chairs. "Ize, get two of those and let's sit outside a minute." I found the two best chairs and dusted them off with my hand as best I could. The barn was musty, the webbing of the chairs flecked with mildew, the metal rust splotched, and I sneezed as I tried to blow some of the dirt off the seat.

I brought the chairs outside and hunted a bit for a flat spot where I could set them beside each other. Lorena was scanning the horizon, shielding her eyes from the sun. She spun toward me as if she was going to ask a question and I froze. Her forehead was worry-lined, and she had her tongue between her teeth, the tip touching her top lip, as if she was trying to find a way to say something unpleasant. Finally she said, "Ize, I need to say a few things, and I don't want you to say anything until I'm done. You fine with that?"

I nodded, thinking I wasn't supposed to speak, and riven with the dread that I was about to be fired.

"Sure now?" she said.

I nodded again, and croaked, "Sure," the word catching high in my throat.

Lorena shuffled her chair closer and took my hand. She said, "Ize, before I can let this go any further, I need to say some things to you, and you might get mad and you might want to stop seeing me."

I shook my head, no, but she said, "Don't say a word, don't move, don't smile or frown, just listen, please. I was some wild with you and with more than a few boys later on, but I never cheated once on either of my husbands, while we were together. Hiram drifted off after the girls were born. He likes them young and carefree. I threw him out after he hit me across the mouth and punched me in the stomach so hard I blacked out. He has a meanness in him I'd been warned about. He been married once before, and his wife had called the cops on him, but he convinced me she was a drunk and that she'd made it all up—hell I wasn't so hard as I am now—and I believed him. Still, with him gone it was difficult trying not to lose the house to the bank, taking charity and food stamps and WIC vouchers, but I swallowed my pride."

Lorena paused, but her eyes told me she wasn't finished. "Every time I looked at Mama, I saw how hard it was for a woman with kids, especially one with girls, to find a decent man, and I married the first one to come along who was willing to take on my kids and me. Roger wasn't like Hiram. He never raised a hand to me, he worked hard, he wasn't much of a drinker, but by God he was a dog. He'd chase any skirt that would be caught or chase him back. He was a college man and worked as an inspector for the state. He visited any place that served food—schools, restaurants, hotels, and he spent a couple of nights each week on the road." Lorena's eyes were like two red slits, and fat, slow tears slipped down her cheeks. "Lord this is the hard part, but I'll get through it, don't say a word, please, Ize, I have to say this. He came home one Friday and asked me how I was feeling. I told him I was fine and he said 'really, everywhere?' and I said yes. We'd fought over him seeing other women, but I had four kids and they were all little. I couldn't lose him."

Lorena tapped my wrist with her fingers. She looked up and began nodding her head. She put a finger to her lips, then said, "He said he'd given me a dose of clap he'd picked up from a woman he'd met in a bar, and that I had to see the doctor. I was humiliated. I cried for three days. I took bath after bath and I felt filthy to the bone. I was breast-feeding the boys and I switched them right to formula. I felt like my insides were full of poison. I went all the way to Beckley to a woman's shelter to be examined. Even when I was well, I kept begging them to test my blood again. I had the kids tested even when they told me they were fine. I threw up everyday. I got dehydrated and had to go to the hospital for an IV. Lillian was there, and she took all the information about the antibiotics I was taking and I had to tell her what happened."

Lorena cleared her throat and started in again. "Roger left and lived awhile in Morgantown. I divorced him a few weeks before he got killed in a wreck. The kids got left some money, but not as much as if he'd died when we were still married."

Lorena stared at the ground, her knees jiggling, hands shaking, and then gazed up at me. "Ize, I've been hurt so hard that I can't be hurt anymore," she said. "I won't bear for a man to hit me, or cheat on me, or leave me. If we go on, there are no more kids, I've seen to that." She paused to gain her breath and swallowed hard. "I don't think I could help you if you backslid, Ize, I'm out of real courage." Lorena leaned forward to take my hands in hers. "I like where we are, and I like where it seems we're going, but I have to be honest and say that my track record and yours aren't exactly full of promise."

I waited for Lorena to say more, but she sat holding my hand, switching her gaze from me to the mountains across the valley, to the sky above us. I blinked hard, fearing that no matter how much I knew I should speak that I didn't know what to say. The breeze stirred and my mind roared. I whispered, "Lorena, I love you." I wanted to add something about gathering our sorrows together, and burying them where they won't come back, but I settled for, "If we'd have stuck together a long time ago, we might have been spared a world of hurt. I have my faults, but I swear I will never again touch a drop of liquor. I'll love your kids as if they were mine, and I won't interfere."

For only the second time I could remember, I'd said the right thing. Lorena hurled herself on me and the old lawn chair collapsed beneath us. She was crying, hard, chest- wracking tears, but she kept saying, "Hold me, Ize."

Ella was like that, crying when she was happy. We'd spend a sweet, sober afternoon at her place, and as it got dark and I'd be heading back to Plourde's, she'd sit on the bed, legs dangling, a sheet gathered around her, with silent tears flooding her eyes. When I'd ask what was wrong, she'd say she was happy and that it scared her. I was scared, too, with Lorena, as we lay on the wet grass, her body heaving against mine. I wondered if I had promised something I couldn't give her, and I knew that if I broke her heart that I would find that mineshaft and hurl myself toward hell.

CHAPTER FOURTEEN

We had two warm dry weeks in mid April and Riley had the foundation poured. He had led me to believe that the logs we'd use to build the house were the trees we'd cut, but it turned out that he'd bought precut logs from the mill, in a numbered kit, and had swapped some of the cost in fresh timber. It was one more reason that I kept hoping the whiskey deal would be forgotten. It wasn't that he lied, Riley enjoyed telling me, but did, on occasion, he allowed, rearrange the facts. When the logs were delivered, we laid the two-by-eight sills on the foundation and fitted the cross beam in its pockets.

Now that it was warmer, Lillian had arranged for the bus driver to let the kids off at the new place after school. Carleton was in pig heaven, sitting up on the skidder or the loader pretending to drive, his Batman cape, which he kept religiously in his backpack, flying in the spring breeze, or riding on Riley's lap as he used the backhoe to position the logs for placement. Annie enjoyed the first few days, but soon wanted to be home with the television, and took to sulking by herself in a thicket where she'd made a hiding place.

One Saturday afternoon Lorena brought her kids over to see what we were doing. Lucy and Laura, at first suspicious of Annie, were soon following her around exploring the place, while Lenny and Luke climbed over the skidder and the backhoe with Carleton. Riley spoke to Lorena with the familiarity of an old friend, asking about her mother, some of the folks he knew at the City Hall, and finally about her sister, Leotta. "She's a nurse's aide in Bluefield. Married an insurance man. They have two kids. She's in touch."

I love that phrase and I've never heard it used the way we do beyond Blissfull. "She's in touch." It means more than that, it means that even though we don't see each other that we are still kin, still blood close. But it also means, to use one of Reverend Willis's phrases, that there is no enmity.

Lorena asked me if we could drive the kids up to her old

173

place in my truck, as she worried that her car would bottom out.

My brother should have been a poker player or a lawyer, as he never misses an opportunity to ingratiate himself. With a completely friendly expression he said, flipping me his keys, "We're at a good place to stop, Ize, take them on up in my truck. I'll take my guys home in yours and we'll clean up. Come by in a hour or so. Why don't you and Lorena and the kids come out with us? We're gonna meet Lillian at The Steak Barn for dinner."

I turned to Lorena and said, "My treat, I insist." I'd never been that pushy with her, but she smiled and said, "Sure."

As the six of us squeezed into the truck, I was aware of all the land mines I had to avoid. First there was the smokehouse, then the sadness Lorena might feel around the old place seeing as how it was so tumbledown, and then later there'd be the unease I knew Lorena would feel around Lillian. Lillian would see Riley's too-happy family smile and she might step back a bit from his mountain magnetism. I had to clean up as well, and having all those kids at the house while I showered worried me a bit.

If Lorena felt any sadness at seeing her childhood home she hid it well. She laughed a lot and showed the kids around the sagging house and roofless barn though we didn't dare go in either building. I showed the kids where the porcupines had gnawed on the outhouse and where the raccoons had nested in the roof of an old shed. When we got near the smokehouse, I spooked the kids by telling them that porcupines and polecats favored such places because of the smell the hanging meat left behind. We stayed until evening was falling, and the mountain shadows made that part of the ridge sunless and dark.

I eased the truck over the rotting humped logs that Lorena's father had once made into a corduroy road from the Whipple place clear up to the ridge road, imagining the days and hours it had taken a man and a mule to skid those logs into place. The girls laughed and bounced in the rear seats and the boys, while Luke perched on Lorena's lap and Lenny sat between us up front. The girls asked about bears and porcupines in the outhouse and Lorena told them a story about being a little girl and going out to use the outhouse on a cold night and seeing a bobcat dragging a rabbit through the snow, describing its eyes as blue lights and its paws as the size of a man's hand. The kids asked her if she was scared, and she said, "I was too frightened to be scared," and they began to laugh again.

I felt like the pall of my past, the curse I'd felt the Old Man had stained me with, was lifting off me like the morning fog, until I turned in the driveway and saw Riley leaning back against my truck talking to Sergeant Wright and another Blissfull cop. I killed the engine and stared at Riley who was smiling as if he was being paid a social call. As we got out of the truck, the kids spilling ahead of me and rushing to greet the dogs, Sergeant Wright nodded and said hello to me. I said, "Hey," and the other cop nodded without a smile. He was a tall pimply kid, who clearly wanted to look tough. Wright turned to Lorena and said, "Hello Lorena, hello kids. Remember me?"

Luke eyed her for a bit and said, "You're Officer Friendly, the no drugs lady."

I thought I'd be sick when she smiled at the kids and started to sing some little ditty about saying no, and learning to grow. After she tousled Carleton's head, and he'd run to his father, she said. "We'll be in touch, Riley. Thanks for the time."

Lorena's kids ran off to explore the place with Annie, but Carleton stayed fixed at Riley's hip. Lorena waited a second for Riley to say something then said, "I'll go see after the kids."

"Pervis Meeker got himself shot and killed, sitting in his car at a traffic light." Riley said. "Problem is, he had an envelope with twenty-thousand dollars in it with my name and address on it."

"Shit," I said. "What'd you say?"

Riley chuckled. "All I could think of on short notice. I told her that I'd stayed with Pervis in Detroit and that Pervis told me that he had made some whiskey with the Old Man just before he died, when the diabetes had gotten his legs bad.

Said it was aging in a special place and that he could get twenty bucks a bottle in Detroit for it. Said I couldn't believe that. I told her Pervis said he knew where it was, and that he'd be coming back to get it and that he'd give me my share."

"She believe it?"

"I doubt it," Riley said, "but it might be worth it to tell her where it is and let her make a big splash. I'd rather cut off my nuts than give her the satisfaction of ruining all that prime whiskey, but Lillian is more important." I tried not to smile, but Riley saw it in my eyes. "Women, God gave them what he did so they could rule the world," he said scratching his chin.

I studied my brother's eyes to see if he was as sure of himself as he acted, but there was nothing to read. "I was in the shower when she knocked. That little peckerhead with her was snooping around the back, and he's goddamned lucky he had his piece on his belt, or he might be in hell now. That bitch is dangerous 'cause she ain't that bright," Riley said. "I'll handle her. You get washed up and I'll find Lorena and the kids."

When I stepped onto the porch the shadows covered the dooryard and most of the field. My wet hair was suddenly cool against my scalp and I realized that I was past due to have Lillian trim it up for me again, like she'd done before Christmas. I drove Lorena and the boys down to her car in my truck and Riley took the three girls in his. I asked Lorena if she wanted to ask her mother to come with us and she was clearly pleased. "She'd like that," she said, "Though it sure as hell won't help her gout any."

We were late meeting Lillian, and I could see from a distance that she was less than pleased, but when she saw the whole mob of us, and Lorena's mother hobbling along with her cane, wincing every few steps, her frown lifted into a smile. "Hey, Lorena," she said, "This your momma and kids?" Lorena smiled and squeezed Lillian's hand. "This is my family," she said, and she turned to smile at me. Then she held her mother's hand and said, "This is Ize's sister-in-law, Mrs...?"

Lillian took Mrs. Whipple's hand and said, "Please call me

Lillian." I fretted that the sister-in-law line might unbuckle both Riley and Lillian a bit, and I stapled my gaze on their faces for a moment, detecting, to my relief, no offense.

It took a bit for the hostess to snag a table for eleven, and the kids were getting restless, but when we got seated we were in our own side room at one big round table. The kids each chose the Bronc Buster Special, steak, French Fries, salad and rolls, and were delighted to be allowed soda or milkshakes. No one ordered any liquor, and I wondered if that was for my benefit, or because Mrs. Whipple had declined first.

Dinner was cruising along, Riley and Lillian careful to include Lorena's mother in the conversation, the kids eating and giggling, until Carleton said, "Mommy, Officer Friendly came to our house."

Riley didn't flinch. "Yes she did," he said, "And Daddy is going to help her find something she's been looking for a long time. But, it isn't dinner conversation, Son."

"Okay, Dad," Carleton said.

Lorena had asked me a few questions on the ride down the hill to get her car, but I couldn't say much, and while we were waiting on the porch for her mother to change and for the kids to use the bathroom, I'd offered her a misleading, but not wholly dishonest sketch of the whole affair, as I understood it. I noticed Lillian staring into space and Lorena's mother glare at Riley, who responded by asking to be passed the salt and by praising his steak. It was a great performance, a testament to Riley's ability to make the best of a bad hand.

After dinner Riley trailed me to Lorena's house in the truck, while Lillian and the kids drove home in her car. We were crammed into Lorena's car, which had front bucket seats, and was thus a constant logistical problem for her when she had the four kids with her, because only one could be up front, leaving an odd boy or girl in the rear. This time I rode in the back with the boys and Lucy, Lenny on my lap.

I knew I'd have to let Lorena in on the reason for Sergeant Wright and her sidekick's visit, and I didn't want to be around when Riley explained to Lillian his version of the facts, so I told Lorena that I'd be back by for her later. I hopped into Riley's truck after helping Mrs. Whipple to the door and saying goodbye to Lorena. He was singing to himself as we pulled out of Lorena's yard and onto Carolina Drive.

"Ize, I think we're about to have what Mama used to call a red letter day."

"Seems like we could be in for a shit storm, too," I said.

"We caught a break here. The money they found on poor Pervis was from the sale of Mama's house. She'd been dead longer than I let on. Almost two months longer. Pervis had always kept in touch with her and her new husband. She'd have him over for Thanksgiving and feed him decent food. When she took sick he told me 'cause she didn't want me to know. Mama knew, from Pervis, that Lillian and me had broken up, and she didn't want to be a burden on us. Her husband died a year before she did. It's his ashes we put in her family plot. I still got Mama's in my closet. I couldn't just rush her home and into a hole, but I had to bury that box. Did you really think I'd bring Mama home with that shit?"

"Then Pervis was on the other end of that radio call the morning the guys came for the pills?"

"Still got some brain cells left, bro," Riley said.

I burst out laughing. "Her husband ain't in that box either. I was afraid of Mama being there so I put his ashes in the creek, by the bridge where Malcolm died."

Riley laughed, too. And pretty soon he was slapping me on the shoulder and hooting like a kid on his first drunk. He told me how Pervis helped Mama sell her place and move into an apartment, and that just before she died, when she was in a hospice, she gave him the envelope and asked him to give it to me.

"Me?" I asked.

"Mama said you was a lost soul, and that if I had the place, you should get something, too. She had no idea what you were doing. I just told her you were working up north. She'd had a rough enough life, first the Old Man, then giving us up, then losing a husband she loved. She deserved better."

I was as confused as I had ever been. I knew Riley had a plan for all this, but I was baffled as to what it could be, and was turning that over as we arrived at the house. "Come in while I get some of this explained to Lillian before you go off to Lorena's," he said, and while he revealed his idea to his ex-wife, I began to understand.

It took Riley a full ten minutes to convince Lillian and I that he was certifiably crazy and brilliantly clever. He was going to march into the Blissfull City Hall and announce that he knew where a huge illegal stash of whiskey had been hidden years ago, and now that his father and poor Pervis Meeker were dead, he felt it his obligation, as a reformed man, to help the police locate the 150 cases of well-aged hooch. He told us that Pervis, for all his recklessness, was nearly illiterate, and as he said we knew, no moonshiner ever wrote anything down anyway. What Riley didn't tell Lillian was that the money found in Pervis' car was intended for me, or where it came from. He told her the story he'd told Sergeant Wright about it being a blood debt.

I realized that this was overkill, but he didn't want Lillian to know something the cops wouldn't know. She sighed and said, "I just hope this isn't some con, Riley. If you're into anything like the old days, the kids and I will be gone, not just from this house, but from this town faster than flushed shit."

"Lily," he said. "I'm doing this for us."

I don't know whether it was calling her Lily, or the conviction in his voice, or the little catch in his throat, but I caught her eyes and saw that she believed. Mountain Magnetism.

It was after ten when I got back to Lorena's. She was a harder sell than Lillian. She'd always lived in the same town as Riley, and his reputation was that he could look you in the eye, pat you on the back, and lift your wallet in one motion. Still, she was willing to be made a believer, she said, but she was tired and feeling bloated from her period. She thanked me for dinner and for asking her mother along. "She may never like you, but she may stop being so suspicious of you. She got hurt every time I did, and blamed herself. You understand, I know," she said.

That Sunday, the Star of Morning was as loud and full as I had ever seen it. The roads had dried up and the hill folk who didn't have a signs church on their ridge rolled into town. Stove-up old miners, arthritic hill farmers, and some folks too old to work, crammed the room in a humid cloud, and the windows and doors were wrenched open to the spring day. Young girls in long dresses and boys in ties and creased black pants filled the chairs and aisles, giving each other shy looks and nods, and getting reacquainted after a winter apart.

Lorena was fidgety and we left early. She said she felt poorly, and even though her kids were gone until late, she didn't want to go for a ride, or go out for dinner. I sat with her and her mother in the sun in the back yard of her house. Lawn mowers droned in the afternoon calm, and kids rode bikes up and down the street. It was warm enough for the neighborhood boys playing, "make it you keep it" basketball across the street to take off their T-shirts.

Mrs. Whipple lay in a lounge chair with her foot up, drinking ice tea, which she kept adding sugar to, and reading *The World Weekly News*. Whenever she'd get to some story about babies with three heads or who were half wolf and half human, she'd read it aloud, look at me and say, "So many amazing things in this world," her tone and expression inviting comment. Each time I said, "Yes ma'am, that is so."

Lorena laid her head against the back of her chair and kept dozing off, waking up when her sunglasses would slide down her nose. I watched the boys playing ball and the sun move across the mountains, feeling my old invisibility creeping into my heart.

Finally, Lorena, after waking for about the tenth time with a start said, "Ize, honey I'm not very good company. I'm going in to lie down." It wasn't as bad as being fired, and she had called me honey in front of her mother, which she'd never done before, but as I walked Lorena to the house, I asked her if she was all right.

"I've got cramps, and a headache. I'm tired and I need a nap. If I feel better I'll call you later," she said.

Lorena kissed me on the cheek at the door. "My breath must be awful," she said, licking her teeth, then glancing back to see if her mother was still reading, laid her palm against my crotch and said, "We'll be back in the saddle by Tuesday, baby. I promise."

CHAPTER FIFTEEN

We didn't work on the house on Monday, and true to his word, just after the kids got on the bus and Lillian sped off to work, Riley said, "Let's go make that fat-ass, lesbo Sergeant's day, brother."

Like I'd told Reverend Willis, when I was on a jag, or had the DTs, I'd seen some weird sights, but what I saw that morning in the Blissfull Police Station beat all. Riley marched up to the front desk and asked for Sergeant Wright and the cop on duty said she'd be in at nine, a half hour's wait, so Riley said to him, "Call her, tell her Riley is here to see her and I'll bet she'll be right along." The cop, a morose-looking guy in his mid-thirties, shrugged his shoulders and sauntered back to the desk. Over his shoulder he said, "Have a seat. I'll see if I can reach her."

Ten minutes later, red-faced and gasping like a beached trout, Wright hove into the station. When she asked Riley what he wanted, he said, "Is there somewhere we can have some privacy?"

Wright summoned her little toady, the one that had been snooping on the ridge, whose name we discovered was Patrolman Carr, to fetch us coffee. Hearing his name, I damn near laughed out loud, but Sergeant Wright was being hyper-professional, acting like a TV cop, efficient and wary. She shuffled us into what she called an interrogation room, a small room with a table and six chairs which was the same one I'd been held in to wait for the Old Man to come get me the time I'd stood on the hood of the car as we circled the square. When we were seated, she asked if she could tape what we said, so she'd get it just right. Riley said, "Oh there's no need for that, I'm sure, but do as you wish."

I thought Wright might piss her pants right then and there, though I hoped Riley wasn't overplaying his hand. She fumbled with the microphone and the tape recorder, her trembling fingers unable to slip the cassette in cleanly. Riley said, "May I," and taking the tape from her, clicked it into the machine and pushed the record button. "Want to check the level?" he asked.

"Test, test," Wright said, adjusting the knob. "Go ahead Mr. Butts, but please remember that you're not under arrest nor obligated to say anything you don't wish to."

"Sergeant Wright," he said, "Anyone who has lived here for any length of time is aware of my late father's professions. One, of course, was whiskey making. He also poached game, and late in his life was involved in the marijuana business. This caused my family, along with his drunken beatings of us all, to disintegrate. My mother, once she knew my brother and I would be safe—this involved a wrench I laid into my father's head—moved to Detroit for her own safety. My brother and I eventually fought the Old Man to a truce, though Isaac will tell you that he struggled with alcohol problems until he recently became affiliated with a local minister who has helped him leave that behind." Riley paused, "Am I going too fast?" he said.

I was dazzled by this opening act, though I felt the onset of an attack of the whirlies as my heart quickened.

"No, Mr. Butts," Wright said, "You'all are doing fine. Continue."

I got a little nervous then. Riley was playing her like a fish, but I knew she could spit the bait anytime, and I hoped that he wouldn't underestimate her. I figured that being a woman in the cop business wasn't easy. The fact that she was as homely as a dog's ass couldn't have helped either.

Riley cleared his throat and sat up in the chair. "Please Sergeant, call me Riley," he said. She nodded and he leaned over the table, clasped his hands together, and spoke directly into the microphone. "One of my father's associates was the late Pervis Meeker. Pervis had been doing me a great kindness by looking in on my mother in her final years, especially once she became ill with cancer. When I went to Detroit to fetch my mother's ashes, I saw Pervis for the first time in many years and stayed at his home. I thanked him for his kindnesses and he said that he owed my father a great debt. Apparently, you folks in the police department were once close to finding a large batch of high-grade whiskey distilled by Pervis and my father. They hid it in barrel kegs in an underground cavern where the temperature is relatively constant, summer or winter. It was to set for at least ten years." Riley drew a deep breath. "When the heat got heavy, my father suggested that Pervis move away. It was only supposed to be for a while, until the trail got cold, but Pervis found something else to do in Detroit, and the whiskey was left to age. My father got diabetes and had several amputations before he died, but he and Pervis were able to bottle and band the whiskey before he passed on." Riley cleared his throat and took a sip from a bottle of spring water that Wright's stooge had brought along with the coffee. He sat back as if he expected Wright to ask him a question.

When she said, "Continue," Riley got right back into it.

"The Old Man contacted Pervis before he went off to hell," Riley said, dragging hell out for effect. He told him, Pervis imparted to me up in Detroit, that when he could, Pervis should move the whiskey in Detroit, and split the money with my brother and me. I wanted no part of it. I worked for the Old Man when I was a kid, so did Ize, you know that, but we've had nothing to do with that in a long time."

Wright started to ask him a question, but Riley raised his hand and said, "I think I can anticipate what you might want to ask. Please allow me a few more minutes here."

I was hooked, even if Riley seemed to be giving my inheritance away before my eyes. If he fucked up, I might be headed to the pen as an accessory, but he was on fire, as smooth as Reverend Willis with a coil of serpents and the spirit on him and all the while Wright was scribbling notes and swilling water.

Riley spun the rest of his tale quickly. He told Wright that Pervis had promised him twenty thousand for the stash, though he couldn't imagine why, and that he'd given him a vague idea of where it might be hidden. "I'll take you up that way, if you like, but I don't know for sure where it is. What I do know is this," he said. "That money is the Old Man's and I don't want it around my family."

I was stone impressed. If Riley weren't my brother, I'd have nominated him for some civic prize. He could have made a saint weep. But I saw that Wright wasn't sold.

Pretty soon he was telling his tale again, to the chief and the detectives, and I could see that Wright was resenting the fact that as the brass got involved she was getting squeezed out. I also wondered why she'd shown up at the place instead of a detective. It wasn't as if she been around a long time and knew our family, but I assumed that Riley had been correct in his assessment of her ambition.

In the Old Man's time, bootleggers always dealt with the same locals, and the revenue men only got involved if they thought you were big time and sending stuff into other states. Of course, down here the states are all hunched up against one another, and making a run into Virginia, Kentucky, or even North Carolina wouldn't take all that long. The Old Man was wily though, he'd take a little less profit if he could make local deliveries and let someone else haul it out of state. The other thing about the locals was that they'd be happy to leave you alone if you played by some basic rules. Don't sell to kids, was rule two, which came after what ever financial arrangements had been made, but just as important was this: No matter how prosperous a moonshiner was, he could never be conspicuous about it. "Fastest way to the pen is acting proud and uppily," the Old Man told me once. "Got to know your place."

As Riley was running through his story a third time, and keeping to his script with amazing precision, the chief scribbled some notes on a pad and showed them to the detective. The detective shoved the pad back over to the chief and I felt a cold terror rip through me when the chief said that Riley might want to check with an attorney. Riley stared at him blankly, and I knew that meant he was worried. Then the chief said, "You boys might be entitled to that money." Riley waited what seemed like a few seconds too long until he said, "There must be a charity in Detroit that can use it. I have no claim to it."

I breathed a little easier until the detective said, "The DEA may have an interest in it from what I can discover." Even Riley seemed to flinch a little at the mention of the Feds, but he played it well. "I wondered how Pervis lived so well," he said. "But he was very kind to my late mother."

The cops all looked at one another and then the detective said, "Of course any money given to your mother, if it was from the sale of drugs, or any property purchased with that money, might be subject to Federal forfeiture. He went on to explain that the Feds could seize anything, anybody owned, if they thought it was purchased with drug money. The chief added, "Illegal whiskey is the same thing for these purposes."

Riley never broke a sweat. "I have my tax returns, and my copy of the deed which gave me my place when my father died. My mother's estate is in probate in Michigan, she died without a will far as anyone knows. She had little left. I believe that she gave it all to Pervis. He'd been more like a son to her than I was, and I regret that now."

I saw why Riley believed in his mountain magnetism. He'd have had Sergeant Wright out of her pants in two minutes if they'd been alone, even if she was skeptical of his story. He had all the charm I never found and I had no idea where it came from. The savvy and ability to think a few moves ahead might have come from the Old Man, and his survivor's instincts from Mama, but the smooth, disarming tone of his voice, the honesty in his inflections, and the unflappable expression on his face was original. I was so stunned by his performance that I recalled something I'd read in Newsweek or Time up in Holyoke about a white South African couple who had three black children. Some gene or trait had reared up from their past, and the article said that such things were more common than most people knew. If some genealogist had at that moment told me that my brother and I had descended from Patrick Henry, I'd have believed it with the certainty with which Reverend Willis embraced Jesus.

We stayed long enough for the city to buy us lunch and for Patrolman Carr to fetch a pile of county maps. Riley studied them for a while and said, "I could show you better. I can't read these so well." I could tell that Riley was having second thoughts, buying time, and I sensed that the cops were onto that as well. Without warning, though I suspect they had a signal for it, they all got up, shook our hands, thanked us for coming in, and said they'd be in touch.

In the truck, Riley was fidgety and pale. "That fucking detective knows too fucking much," he said. "Pervis might have fucked up on me." When I didn't say anything he said, "That DEA shit was for my benefit. Pervis had been moving my stuff for a long time. If they were close to getting him, they might have me as well. Least you're clean."

Anyone but a local might not have fathomed what my brother had just said. Saying I was clean meant he wasn't, no matter what he might be offered, going to implicate me in anything I'd helped him with since coming home from Holyoke. It also meant that if things were going to get ugly that he'd warn me off before the bullets started flying. I knew it also gave me some responsibilities to Annie and Carleton, and, in a way, to Lillian as well. As cowardly as it was, I began to think again about calling Mr. Plourde and begging him for my old job back. I've always run, and when that has been your history, making a stand is scary as hell.

CHAPTER SIXTEEN

By Tuesday we were celebrities. Someone at City Hall had leaked the story to the Crier Gazette, and even the Beckley papers and TV had the news. We got so many calls that Riley quit answering his phone. At first it was kind of cool to be known for something other than being the spawn of the Old Man, like being in the Chamber of Commerce, or on the school board, but the downside was that Lorena was growing distant. We weren't back in the saddle Tuesday. I saw her, but she was remote. She said she was tired, that the first warm spells always made her sleepy, that she'd perk up soon.

On Wednesday we had two visitors at the new house. The first was a reporter who said we could make a bundle by giving our story to him exclusively and letting him see the stash first, so he could take pictures and write a book about it. He tried to tell Riley that someone would stumble on the whiskey before, in his words, "Blissfull's five and ten cent Dick Tracys" found it. "You don't want to end up holding the bag like Geraldo do you?" he said. I had no idea what he meant, but after Riley ran him off he explained it to me. Which led to a good laugh, because the only thing we'd ever seen the Old Man read was a Life Magazine article about Al Capone that he kept in his bureau. He admired Capone because he'd made so much money on booze. I think the Old Man would have liked to have been big time, and I know he learned his trade from the old time guys who distilled the stuff during prohibition and the Great Depression, some of whom allegedly moved up north and lived in style on the profits.

The second visitor was Reverend Willis. He spooked Riley more than the reporter had, and before I could put down my tools he made an excuse to drive up to the house while I took my lunch break.

Reverend Willis and I sat on the tailgate of my truck and I shared my sandwich with him. He said a little prayer, a grace, before we ate, and I detected some agitation in his voice. After he'd chewed a bite he began to speak in soft tones, his eyes fixed on mine. He advised me to let my brother do what he thought he had to do, but that I should be mindful of Lorena and her feelings. "You seem very good for each other, you both have known sorrows and trials, and you have both been lost and come home to the Lord. It might be on your mind already, but you cannot ask Lorena to give her heart to a man who might wander off the righteous path and into wickedness," he said. "You need to consider if you should make her your wife in the sight of God and man, and lead a life as free of sin as you can, so as to help her raise those kids as good Christians."

This wasn't the way Reverend Willis had spoken to me in the past. He sounded weary as a Sally preacher, as if his heart wasn't in it. I looked at him and said, "I care deeply for Lorena, but we need more time. She's been clobbered too many times before. If I rush her, I'm afraid I'll lose her."

Reverend Willis smiled and he clapped me on the back. "All I ask, Ize, is that you think of her best interest. I am very fond of my sister-in-law."

I remembered something from the Old Testament about a guy named Onan and obligations to sisters-in-law, or something like that, and for a moment I wondered if he had feelings for Lorena as well. We ate slowly and he asked me what I'd been reading in the Bible and I told him I was rereading Genesis. "I can follow those stories best," I said.

"Have you reread the story of the first Isaac?" he asked.

"Yes," I said.

"It is the greatest story of faith in the Bible, Ize," Reverend Willis said. "Yes, Jesus gave His life for us and God gave His son, but God can do all, and Jesus was of God. It is the redemption we all need to be saved, to be cleansed, to accept Jesus' sacrifice, but Abraham was a man and God asked him to kill his son. The son he had waited his scores of years for, to sacrifice him with his knife, like a beast or a bird, and burn him on an altar, and Abraham was willing to do that, because he was a man of faith. He knew the terrible power of that faith." Reverend Willis paused and tossed a piece of his bread to a chipmunk that was nosing in some brush. "The Bible teaches us that there is no greater thing than to lay down your life for another, but that is nothing compared to what God asked of Abraham," he said. "He asked him to take that life he loved the most dear. God may not call us to do that anymore, but He calls us to serve in many ways."

Reverend Willis finished his half of the sandwich. I offered him some water from my jug and he drank it. He set the jug down and put a hand on my knee and looked me full in the eye. "I will be gathering serpents soon, and I would like you to come with me," he said. Before I could reply, he said, "Think on it, pray on it, ask the Lord and you will know."

Reverend Willis slid down off the tailgate and headed back toward the road with the gait of an old man, picking his way carefully along the rutty driveway. He stopped and looked back. "This is a beautiful place for a home," he said, and opened the door to the van.

When Riley came back he asked me what Reverend Willis wanted. I told him it was just a pastoral call, a visit to see how I was doing.

"You see him every Sunday, don't you?" Riley said.

"I don't speak to him," I said. "The service goes on most of the day. Lorena and I never stay the entire time."

Riley mused on that a bit, then said, "This place won't build itself."

We spent the afternoon placing the joists for the second floor. The logs were numbered and notched, so I lifted them up to Riley with the loader, and he guided them into place and nailed them off. I was getting good with the loader, and I thought about those ads on the backs of matchbooks with numbers to call to learn to drive trucks or run heavy equipment. Everyone I knew growing up could run a tractor or a backhoe, but more importantly every man knew how to fix one. Riley's loader had been the Old Man's, and I know he didn't get it new. It ran a little rough at first, but like any geezer who needs to stretch his muscles and oil up his bones each day, once she began humming she ran strong. The skidder was just as old, but it was dented up and riddled with white blotches where Riley had sanded down a layer of rust and slapped on fresh primer.

The place was beginning to look like a house, and when the kids got off the bus they pestered Riley to show them where their rooms would be. He pointed to the second floor and said, "You'll each have a big room on the second floor, and there will be a bathroom up there, and Mommy and I will have a bedroom downstairs with our own bathroom, and there will be a living room and a dining room. Upstairs there will be extra storage places, and in the basement there will be a washer and a dryer room and a room just for the TV and stereo, called a family room. I'll show you the pictures."

While Riley showed the kids the awful brochures that came with the kit, I sat on the skidder and drank the last of my thermos of coffee. It wasn't real hot, but it was strong, and I needed a boost. I'd already seen the pictures, a father, mother, older sister and younger brother, a yellow dog and a calico cat, thick carpets and new appliances, two cars, a station wagon and a sedan, in front of the optional two-car garage with upstairs office capabilities, and they made me as baleful as Ella's tears. She'd been on that bed in Holyoke crying because she knew that whatever it was that made the two of us find each other was the same thing that would divide us. She must have known then that she'd go back to her home ridge, and that I'd either do the same or die on some Yankee street on a winter night. As I watched Riley showing the pictures to the kids, I knew that what they were seeing wasn't what they'd live. There might be new appliances, but not all at once, and there might be new carpets, but they'd have to come in installments, because he was still a moonshiner and the Old Man's advice to not look too prosperous or uppity burned in him as hot as blazing anthracite. If he showed his hand, if he built his monument to Lillian, the feds would take it all from him.

I wondered how many years he could keep the dream of this palace in the hills alive enough to hold his family together, just how long his mountain magnetism could work its charm, and I wondered if he hadn't over-played his hand with the cops. I heard Annie ask if the barn cats from the home place could move to the new house. "No," Riley said," We'll get you a house cat, one you can pet and play with. I promise."

The word promise caught in my chest. Riley had enough promises hanging out that he was beginning to sound like he was running for governor, and I knew in the darkest places in my gut that he'd have a hell of a time delivering on most of them.

On the way up the hill, the five of us in Riley's truck, the kids were badgering him with questions about when they'd move and what color their rooms would be, and Riley kept saying that he didn't know those things for sure, and that the colors were up to Lillian. "Will Ize live with us?" Carleton asked.

"No son, he's gonna live in our old house. That way you can visit him there and it will be like having two houses."

It was tough enough hearing Riley promise to do things himself, but making promises to the kids on my part was worse. I loved his children as if they were my own, and that meant that disappointing them in a big way would scald my heart. Our childhood had been a string of broken promises and false hopes, and I couldn't bear to hurt Riley's kids, so when Annie said, "Is Daddy right, Uncle Ize?" I answered, "Yes darlin', he is."

Lillian was sitting on the porch facing the sunset. She had on shorts pulled high on her legs to maximize the tanning potential, I guess, a halter-top, and dark glasses. She waved as we pulled in and sat back in the chair lifting her feet off the floor. I am ever struck by the perfect symmetry of her legs and the beauty of her face. As soon as I was in earshot she said, "Call Lorena, Ize, she's hoping you'll come to dinner."

The kids rushed up on the porch to hug their mother and I went in and phoned Lorena. One of the boys answered, I could tell them apart on sight, but never on the phone, so I said, "Hey, partner is your momma home?" He didn't answer but I heard him holler, "Mom, it's Ize."

It took Lorena a second to get to the phone and she sounded out of breath, but when she started to speak I swear I could see those Whipple eyes and that Whipple smile over the phone lines. She asked if I could be at her house by six, and when I said yes, she said, "See you later, cowboy." My heart soared.

After I showered, Lillian insisted on trimming up my hair. She had me sit out on the porch in the chair she'd been in when we'd come home, with a beach towel over my shoulders, while she snipped away. It was a warm dusk, and while she was evening out the front of my hair, five deer skittered across the road below the house. For a moment, Roxie, who was sleeping by my feet, lifted her nose into the wind, but gave no chase. Lillian patted my head and said, "You're presentable now." She lifted the towel, walked to the edge of the porch and shook it out. "Lorena is a nice girl, Ize. She's had some real hard breaks. Two shithead husbands, and the caring for her mama. Give her my best."

"I know, Lillian. I even know what you know about what Roger did to her. She says you were kind to her," I said.

"Go on to dinner, Ize," Lillian said, laying the towel over the railing. "Some things are best left resting. I'll run you down to your truck."

The sun was going down; purple shadows mottled the road. If I hadn't memorized the heaves and bumps, potholes and washouts, I might have busted an axle on my way down the ridge. Earl had rebuilt much of the front suspension, but the truck was old. I tried to be kind to her, but the spring was running in me, same as in the creek, and I felt for the first time in years like I had some choices. I ran without headlights until I got to the pavement, same as I did as a kid on all but the rainiest nights. My eyesight wasn't as keen as it had been then, but the thrill was the same.

My spirits dropped a little when I saw the Star of Morning van and a red pick-up parked in Lorena's driveway. I smelled a barbeque and picked out a thin streak of blue-gray smoke rising up above the roofline, and laughter coming from the backyard. I walked around the house and saw Reverend Willis, Lorena, her mother, and the kid, Lucius Farrell, who'd been with Reverend Willis when he picked me up in Holyoke, sitting around the picnic table. The kids were playing on the swings or running along the fence line between Lorena's and a neighbor's place with two kids I didn't know.

Lorena bolted right to me, gave me a kiss, and grabbed hold of my hand as hard as she ever did in church. "Hey, honey," she said. "You know everyone here."

Reverend Willis came and gave me a hug, and Lucius shook my hand like he was meeting me for the first time. "Glad you could come," Lorena's mother said. "I fixed some special food just for tonight."

Suspicion welled up in me the way my guts used to after a night of drinking, and I felt my mouth get watery. I muttered my gratitude for the invitation and slapped at a mosquito, spreading its blood along my wrist. Lenny and Luke ran over and asked me to come see a dead bug they'd found in the side yard and I was quick to oblige. The insect was snared in a spider's web that hung between the end of the fence and a laurel bush, lit by the rays of a street lamp. It looked like a June bug, but its wings, which were half opened, were a deep black, almost purple, and it had a yellow line on its back. The girls, and the two kids I didn't know, who turned out to be neighbors, stood next to me while I squatted and studied the insect.

"What is it?" one of the neighbor kids asked.

"I don't know. I've never seen one just like this, but it's some kind of June bug," I said, trying to sound like I knew something. "You could put him in a plastic bag and take it to school and ask your science teacher. He or she might know."

Laura said, "I'll bring it for show and tell."

The kids tore into the house, and I had to go back to the others. Reverend Willis asked me what kind of bug it was and I told him I didn't know, and that the kids were going to ask their teacher. He said something about God's vast menagerie, but I was trying to figure out if this little party had to do with gathering snakes, and if it did, how I was going to excuse myself from that mission. Lorena, or maybe Reverend Willis, I thought, was putting on the dog. Thick steaks sizzled on the grill, and the table was piled with salads, plates of cornbread, bowls of beans, and pitchers of iced tea and lemonade. I offered to help Lorena fetch things from inside, but she said, "Just relax. Keep Theo and Lucius company, and keep working your charm on Mama."

Once the food got to the table, Reverend Willis said a long grace and I could see that the kids were getting itchy to eat. When he finished, Lorena fixed plates for the boys, while the rest of us filled ours. The adults sat at the big table, Lorena's mother at one end so she could keep her leg raised, and Reverend Willis at the other, while the kids ate at another smaller table next to us. I had Lorena on my left and Lucius on my right, and as he's left-handed, we spent the meal bumping elbows.

Between bites, Lorena kept her right hand below the table on my thigh, lightly scratching her nails on my jeans. She kept popping up to help the kids or to settle them down when they got loud. As the night got darker it grew cool, and the flames from the citronella candles Lorena had lit before we sat down shot jittery shadows across the table. Lorena put on a sweater, and brought her mother an afghan and a blanket for her leg. Reverend Willis, who was wearing a dress shirt with the sleeves rolled up, let them down and buttoned the cuffs.

When we'd finished dinner, everybody except Mrs. Whipple cleared the table, and we all stood in the kitchen wrapping up leftovers, washing or drying the dishes, or putting them away. We had dessert, vanilla ice cream with hot fudge, in the house, the bugs having become fierce and insistent. The kids went down to the basement, and the rest of us sat in the kitchen. Lorena said, "Anyone want coffee?" but she had no takers. I began to feel like one of the people in the brochures Riley had been showing the kids. Everything in the kitchen was color coordinated. Lorena and her mother had enough matched dishes and glasses to serve twelve people, and I shuddered as I remembered all she had gone through, that allowed for that.

I knew Reverend Willis was a man who rose early and turned in early, too, and when it got to be eight-thirty, and Lorena was beginning the battle to get the kids washed and in bed, I figured if he was going to ask me about snake hunting, that he'd do it soon.

Instead, he asked me how the afternoon's work had gone, and when he did, I saw Lorena give him a hard look. "That's a beautiful place for a home, plenty of good wood, and your brother will have a great view of the valley when he takes down a few more trees. When do you expect to be done?" he asked.

"I don't know. Riley has to go slow. It's expensive, even though he traded out some logs for part of the kit. We'll be at it a long time, I think."

I watched Reverend Willis digest what I had said. I hadn't said a word of untruth, but worried that if confronted with the need to stretch the truth to him, that he'd sniff it out in a second. "Life is not a race," he said. "Victory is not always to the swift. Too few people forget that there is no value in gaining all the riches of the world, if you lose sight of God's will and kingdom. I have held riches in my hand, but been richest when I gave them away." I'd never seen his eyes as cold, or as fixed on me before. Lorena squeezed my leg. "I wish you boys luck," Reverend Willis said, "But the hour is late for me."

We all got up when Reverend Willis did, which is another gesture peculiar to Blissfull, no one sitting when the preacher is standing, except in church, and while he hugged each of us, Lucius made the rounds shaking hands. When they'd both driven away, Lorena asked me if I would keep her mother company while she got the kids settled. I sat in the living room with Mrs. Whipple. She'd waited until Reverend Willis had gone before she'd made her toddy, and I was glad to see her finish it and make another.

Lorena was a long time getting the kids quieted. The boys persisted in hopping out of bed and hollering from the top of the stairs for a drink of water, and the girls hollered that the boys hollering wouldn't allow them to sleep. It was only when Lorena promised to make their bottoms hurt, that the house got quiet.

By nine-thirty Mrs. Whipple was out in her chair and Lorena and me were downstairs and back in the saddle. By ten we were lying on the floor having what was beginning to feel like a quarrel. Lorena had asked me what Reverend Willis had come to see me about and I told her the same thing I'd told Riley, that he'd come to see how I was doing. Lorena had the same reaction. "He sees you every Sunday, and if you'd fallen off the wagon he'd hear that. He hears everything. That man knows more about the people in this town than anybody but God himself. He ask you about us?"

I was at a crossroads. If I said yes, then she'd know I'd been holding something back. If I said no, she'd keep prying until I said yes. I said. "He said how fond he was of you and the kids, and how he wanted to be sure that I understood how hard things had been for you..."

"He should have kept his mouth shut, preacher or no preacher," she said rising to her naked knees and leaning over me. "My damn mother's been talking to him, and that's what all this was about tonight, I can feel it. What I can't figure out is why she invited that homely Farrell kid. He gives me the creeps."

I relaxed. I was glad to see that Lorena had had no hand in the evening's plans, but I relaxed too soon.

CHAPTER SEVENTEEN

The next morning we'd hardly begun working when Reverend Willis pulled up to the new place. He eased out of the van and picked his way to below the spot where Riley and I were using a pair of peaveys to roll a second floor gable log into place. He stood patiently shielding his eyes from the sun and watching us work. When we'd sistered the log into place and nailed it off, Reverend Willis strode up to the edge of the house and said, "It is a truly wonderful thing to see a home being built in the old way."

"It's a kit," Riley said. I don't know why Reverend Willis spooks Riley like he does, but I am sure that Reverend Willis sensed it because he said, "I won't keep you long, but I was wondering, Ize, if you might be spared tomorrow afternoon?"

Now Riley was in a true bind. If he said no, he ran afoul of a preacher who could denounce him to his parishioners and that would make life less pleasant for us all, especially me, as Lorena's mother would pitch a fit about me. If he said yes, we'd lose a full day on the house because it wasn't work you could do with one man. And, if he said yes, without asking me whether he should or not, he ran the risk of pissing me off, though that was the least of his worries. One thing about Reverend Willis is that he knows the old ways and the traditions, the customs I guess you'd call them, and he had played his hand well.

Riley hedged his bets. "Might could, if it's important."

He'd thrown the ball back to Reverend Willis, but he was used to having his faith tested, so he said, "I need a hand gathering serpents. The sun and the temperature will be right from mid-morning on."

He'd done it. I was trapped. He'd asked me for a favor knowing I felt beholden, even if it wasn't a particularly Christian thing to do, in front of someone else. Even though Riley was my brother I was in a tight spot.

"It this takes two men to work these logs into place." I said, "If Riley can spare me, I'll go."

"I understand," Reverend Willis said. "It's up to you."

He stood looking at me with the soft kindness I was used to seeing from him. I looked at Riley for help, but he gave me a look that told me I was on my own.

"I guess I could leave about eleven, let us get a half a day in, if Riley says it's okay," I said.

Riley nodded and my heart sank. "Try not to get him killed," Riley said. That, too, was tradition. He'd let Reverend Willis know that he felt taken advantage of, and by mentioning death to a man who'd lost his wife to snakebite, he was flexing his own mountain mean.

"I believe that the Lord will protect us, and I am obliged to you both. I will come by here at eleven," Reverend Wills said. "If we can take your truck, Ize, that would be a help, as we needn't walk so far."

I nodded yes and Riley said, "Where you headed on this hunt?"

"Bald Max Ridge, up yonder," Reverend Willis said, pointing up the ridge.

"In that case," Riley said, "We can all go in my truck. The four-wheel drive will get us up to the top of the ridge, right to where the Old Man used to say a crazy woman drowned. Just one thing though. No snakes at my house."

"You needn't do that," Reverend Willis said, "But you are welcomed, and the offer of your truck is most Christian." He paused a minute and gazed back up the ridge and said, "And I would bring no serpents into your home."

Reverend Willis strode off toward the van, turned and shielded his eyes and said again, "I am much obliged."

I'd about shit my pants when Riley said he'd go. As a kid, he'd killed his share of snakes, and I knew he hated them as much as they terrified me. When I asked him why he'd offered to help, he said, "That old boy has a weird look to him. He looks, acts, and smells like an old whiskey man to me. I bet he figures he can find the Old Man's stash for himself."

"Riley, the man doesn't drink anything except pure water," I said.

"And you never met a 'shiner didn't drink?"

I stewed on that a moment, and after we'd gotten back to work, I said, "I think you're wrong about him, Riley. If he was searching for your stash, why would he want me along?"

Riley stood tall and declared it time for a break. We sat on the tailgate of his truck and had some coffee and pie. "It's like this, Ize," Riley said. "That old boy lived in the hills for a whole summer. He went out for a walk with 'bout nothin' with him and wanders around 'til the end of August. He goes over to Jolo, and then disappears. When he returns he's got money to start his church and get that van all painted up. Now he damn sure didn't find any gold up there. He was up to something. I've known plenty of preachers, sheriffs, and other pillars of this community who ran a little hooch." He paused a moment and laughed. "Hey. Remember when the town voted to allow liquor in restaurants? Whose shorts were in the biggest twist about that? The preachers and the whiskey men, Baptists and bootleggers cozied up together. Only guys like the Old Man who had a good trade with people who preferred the homemade weren't worried. Who knows anything about this guy, except what he tells them. I don't know what snakes go for, but he didn't get rich on selling them up north—which can't be legal by the way. But I do believe this; what the Reverend Theobald Willis does, and what I do, ain't much different."

"Snakes in church are legal in West Virginia," I said.

"But I'll bet you my left nut it ain't legal to sell 'em out of state," Riley countered. "I think he was hoping to get up on the ridge with you and see if you shied from goin' anyplace particular, or if you tried to stay away from some part of the woods. He'd figure you to know where the stash is—like I said it's best you don't."

"I thought you were gonna lead the cops to it if they asked?" I said.

"Or someplace like it," Riley said.

"You believe that Reverend Willis wants to find the whiskey first?" I asked.

"If that brain of yours ain't too shot, think on it some."

Riley crumpled up a napkin and fired it into a pile of slash. "Let's get after this, especially since we ain't gonna get shit done tomorrow." I pondered what Riley had meant when he said, "What I do." It might have been a figure of speech or a slip of the tongue, and the way Riley put the whole affair together made more sense than the way I'd been looking at it. Except for the old jobs I had when I came home from the service, the temporary stuff I did between benders, or my job at Plourde's, most of what I'd supported myself doing was illegal. It stung a little to think that Riley might be right, that there was some kind of a con going on at Star of Morning, but I'd seen people saved, and I'd seen real pain swept away, if only for hours or days at a time. I'd found dignity and life with Lorena. I'd begun to feel like I wasn't the shit most folks scrape off their shoes. I wanted to defend Reverend Willis, but I didn't want to argue with Riley, because he'd cut across a nerve in me and I was afraid that he'd say something else that would make me more suspicious, and being suspicious never served me well.

That night I didn't tell Lorena I was going serpent hunting. We about shook the foundation of her house, and I stayed past midnight, lying on the floor in the television's mute glow, aching to ask her more about Reverend Willis and her sister and the money, but I knew that if I lost her I'd run right back to the bottle and I knew that might mean the end of me—an unidentified transient buried by the county.

Riley and I started work at six, and though my mind and body should have been bone weary from a late night, I was surging with energy. We'd spied a herd of deer grazing among the birches in the overgrown fields by the old Whipple place, and watched a bear cub scamper up a tree by the washout along the creek, the sow rearing up on her hind legs to regard us passing. We laughed about the time I hit the tree with the Old Man's truck, and, for a moment, though I should have been relaxed, was sure that all the good things I had were about to washout as well. I had no particular reason to be mournful; uneasy, scared maybe, but not sad, and I was.

Reverend Willis showed up at eleven sharp and he wasn't

dressed for snake hunting. He had on running shoes instead of work boots, a white dress shirt, regular, gray pants, and was bareheaded. Riley and I both wore logger's boots, jeans, a ball cap, and had heavy work gloves shoved down into our back pockets. Riley wore a Bowie knife sheathed at his hip and had a pistol and holster in the truck's toolbox.

Reverend Willis fetched a pair of snake sticks and two heavy burlap feed sacks out of the van and laid them in the bed of the truck. When Reverend Willis asked, "May I ride up the ridge in the truck bed so as to enjoy the view?" Riley answered. "Fine morning for it Reverend."

We crawled up to the end of the road, Riley careful not to jounce Reverend Willis, passing the rebuilt wall blocking the entrance to the road to the grave with the stranger's bones and the traces of the stepfather we'd never known, and I wondered if their spirits were comparing notes on Mama, finding that thought a comfort for my churning guts and racing heart. Peering through the cab's rear window I saw that Reverend Willis was sitting with his back to the cab, and I envied him the view of the valley unfolding before him as we climbed the ridge.

Riley rolled to a stop at the edge of the creek where it could either be forded or crossed by stepping from boulder to boulder. He buckled on his pistol and took a pair of sunglasses from the glove box, while Reverend Willis tossed me a bag and a snake stick and the three of us started walking, him in the lead.

Bald Max is one ridge, or fold, over from our ridge, and it sets low behind ours so it's darker and can't be seen from the valley. The creek runs off it and into a little saddle on our ridge then down the mountain, and, as I hoped my stepfather found out, eventually into the ocean. I imagined his bone and ash racing through the New River Gorge, tumbling through the roiling water, having one hell of a fine ride, but I wasn't even sure which river the creek emptied into. When we began to make our way across the creek by jumping between rocks, I realized that Reverend Willis's work pants were lighter and less restrictive than my jeans, and marveled at his agility.

It was near noon when we stepped through the break in the ridge and into the narrow valley between us and the hump of Bald Max. Staring across the short expanse of scrubby pines and boulders, I could not recall how long it had been since I'd been in that saddle or the valley, but I knew that as sure as I'd walked every inch of it as a kid, I'd never found a cellar hole, or heaved up stone wall, or any sign of humans having lived there. It felt good to be taking long strides through the woods, passing through clearings where the land was too rocky for big trees and the sun poured in, or through dew-drenched ferns hidden from the light by the evergreen canopy. I watched the way Reverend Willis walked, never looking down, humming, his sack on his shoulder, using his snake stick as a walking cane. It would have been more peaceful though, if Riley hadn't kept playing with the snap on his holster.

We trudged across the valley for about ten minutes as it fell away from us down a long hill, hawks riding the warm thermals above us, birds scattering ahead of us. Just before we reached the base of the low ridge, Reverend Willis veered left toward some ledges and my heart galloped. I had forgotten why we'd come, and as we angled toward those rocky places where I expected rattlers lived, it came back to me and I lagged behind.

Riley, who'd been trailing me, strode by and caught up with Reverend Willis. "We headed up along the top of that ledge?" he asked, pointing to a sunny flat spot among the rocks. Reverend Willis stopped and rested a moment. "Later," he said, "but I want to skirt them off to the south a bit. There's a trail, mostly overgrown, that winds up the backside of a low hill. We'll look there first."

Riley didn't say anything and we pushed on. Passing through a dark stand of pines, and then a grove of hardwoods pushing out new half-opened leaves, Reverend Willis spied the trail, no more than a deer run, and we waded through some new grasses and thick brush to reach it. Riley dropped off the pace and whispered to me, "That son of a bitch is headed right for the damn stash. Those ledges we passed have got to have more snakes than any we'll find in these woods."

I was spooked. The gun made me doubly nervous, but we kept walking until we were through the woods and standing in the shade of some tall pines on the edge of a cliff. As I'd never been to that place before, I looked around to memorize the lay of the land. Riley, I could tell, knew the place well by the way he looked only at Reverend Willis. I was breathing harder than either of them, not because of the climb, but because I hoped that Riley wasn't about to do something crazy. I didn't like the way he kept his hand on his holster or the way he'd unlocked it. "I believe there will be serpents sunning below us," Reverend Willis said. He bowed his head and began praying "Dear God, Lord in heaven, we ask that You and Your Son, our Savior Jesus Christ, protect your servants, Theobald, Isaac, and Riley, and deliver unto us, if it is Your will, serpents. Amen."

Reverend Willis took ten or so steps to his left, dropped his stick and bag, and began to ease into a crack in the rocks. He put his arms on the sides of the crack and lowered his body out of sight, as I moved over to get a closer look. As he worked his way down, I understood why he wore sneakers. He got a better grip on the ledge and made almost no sound. It was a ten-foot drop to a spot where a broad ledge, ten feet above another, jutted out. When he touched down on the first ledge, Reverend Willis looked up and said, "Come on down, Ize."

I have no idea why I went after him. I didn't dare look at Riley; I just followed Reverend Willis's lead. I tossed him my gear, and though my boots didn't feel the rocks the way his shoes did, I did manage to work my way down the crack and land next to him after stretching my arm muscles to their maximum. He handed me my stick and bag, picked up his own, and pointed with his hand to a group of snakes lying half coiled on the rocks to our right. I froze. I suddenly wondered how we'd ever get up that crack with two burlap bags full of timber rattlers, but Reverend Willis said, "Watch me and believe on the Lord. He will never fail you if you believe on

Him." I couldn't move. "Praise Jesus," he said, louder than I would have thought necessary, and moved toward the snakes. I'd have thought that you would want to sneak up on them from behind, but Reverend Willis walked right up to them, all the while singing, "What a Friend We Have in Jesus," at the top of his lungs. Maybe he shocked those serpents into staying still, or maybe God froze their rattles, but he looped up three as quick as you please, dropped each one in the sack, without one of them shaking a warning, but missed the last one as it slithered down into the rock. "Praise God, for he has blessed us today. Three fine serpents on our first try," Reverend Willis shouted, loud enough to have it echo in the valley. He was grinning like a poor boy with a candy bar, and it seemed as though he shed ten years in two minutes. My legs were trembling, and my stick was rattling on the ledge. Riley who'd been watching from above hollered down, "I ain't never seen anything like that in my life. Reverend, you are either crazy or blessed."

Twice more he found snakes on the ledges, and soon he'd put five in his bag and four in mine. He declared his captives to be enough for one spot, then tied the necks of the two bags together. From deep in his pants pocket he pulled out a roll of twine, tied one end around a small rock and the other to the top of the serpent bags. He tossed the rock up to the top of the ledge and said, "Sometime when you feel the spirit, when the anointing is on you, you'll do what I have done. God alone can bring the Holy Spirit to you, but only if you pray and believe on Him."

Riley hauled the serpent sacks up while we climbed back up. Going up was easier than coming down as I could see better and get a better purchase with my feet. I was glad that I had worn gloves, and when I got to the top of the ledge, I felt as good as I had in a long time. Though my heart was speeding, my breath came easily, and I was more excited than afraid. Don't get me wrong, I didn't want to get any nearer to those snakes than I was, nor was I sure that I could carry them out.

I didn't have to. Reverend Willis handed me both sticks and

asked me to coil up the twine. He hefted both sacks over his shoulder and began humming. "Won't they strike you through the bag?" Riley asked. "Not if I can keep humming in the key of B Flat, and the Lord stays with me," he said.

Reverend Willis never did stop humming, and though I heard a rattle or two, and though he nearly fell a few times in the woods, tripping on roots, and stumbling beneath the load, he was untouched. It took three quarters of an hour to get back to the saddle where Riley had parked the truck. Reverend Willis rode in the back with the serpents, and Riley and I kept shaking our heads at what we'd seen.

Riley crept down the road. He'd never have admitted it, but I smelled fear on him. He made frequent checks of the rear view, and kept the slider in the back window of the cab cracked enough to hear Reverend Willis's voice as it hummed hymns. At the new place, he let the truck roll to a gentle stop.

At the Star of Morning van, we watched as Reverend Willis loosed the snakes one at a time onto the ground, picked them up with the stick and dropped them in separate serpent boxes, the brass fittings and nail heads gleaming in the high sun. He never stopped humming that hymn, except for a quick second now and then to tell us what he was doing, and he had no trouble with any of the snakes.

When Reverend Willis had boxed his catch, he thanked us, clasped Riley's hands in both of his and said, "It was kind of you to save me all that walking, and to take time from this house you are building. I pray that the Lord will always bless it, and your family."

"No problem, Reverend," Riley said. "That was without doubt the finest snake catching I've ever seen."

When the van disappeared, Riley said, "Watch out for him. He's a snake catcher and a snake oil salesman if I ever met one. Before he dropped down onto that ledge, the two of you were standing not ten feet from where that whiskey is hid. I bet he went up there today to see if we'd let on. He's looking to get his hands on it. I don't care if I don't get a dime from it, especially if it throws the cops off me, but I damn sure ain't letting no snake handler steal from me." Riley snapped his holster shut and my heart sank into my shoes.

"Why haven't the cops asked you to take them up there?" I asked.

"Likely they were building a case against me and Pervis, and now that he's got himself killed, I am all they got. Still, I have an idea or two."

We worked for an hour, but neither of us had any heart in it, and Riley decided to pack up early. I took my truck up to the old place to be there when the kids got home. Riley went into town and fetched a pizza for dinner.

I didn't see Lorena, needing to sort out what had happened in my own mind, before I told her about it. I phoned and told her that I had to watch the kids, and Riley took advantage of that to drive around planning his next move.

I wanted as much as anything for Reverend Willis to be a true believer, to have been gathering serpents and not looking for the whiskey, but Riley had instincts I never had. In school, he knew which boys were queer, and which teachers you could run a game on, and which of the lunchroom ladies would give you a free ticket if you told her you were hungry and had no money.

He came in around ten and went to bed. I turned off the light and tried to sleep, but was wide-awake when Lillian came in after midnight, though I pretended to be out cold.

CHAPTER EIGHTEEN

I don't know how long after I awakened that I lay in bed thinking about what to do about my new life and its terrors, but I'd reached no conclusions when Riley rousted me. When she'd come in the night before, Lillian had taped a note to the refrigerator that it was fish sticks day at school and the kids wanted a sack lunch, so Riley had made them ham sandwiches with mustard, and given each kid some cookies and an apple, as well as a dollar for juice. I'd never seen Riley make the kids' lunches before and it touched me. I wanted to go off for a long walk, but I figured that as soon as the bus came that we'd be back at the new place. However, the Blissfull Police Department had another plan.

Detective Burleson called at seven-thirty and asked for Riley. I could tell from just his end of the conversation that they wanted to take him up on his offer to look for the whiskey. An hour later Riley and I were riding over the same roads we'd ridden the day before, but instead of a signs preacher and serpent-hunting gear in the bed of his truck, we were trailed by three state police Ford Explorers, a Blissfull version of the same rig with Sergeant Wright at the wheel, and a four-wheel-drive van with two K-Nine Officers and dogs trained to sniff out drugs and explosives.

Riley was loving the attention until we stopped at the creek. We hadn't been out of the truck ten seconds when Burleson dropped to a knee by the rear wheel and said, "You were up here yesterday?"

"My brother and I drove Reverend Willis of Star of Morning Church up here to hunt for snakes for his services," Riley said.

The look on the detective's face was worth all the churning my stomach had been doing on the ride up. "You boys snake handlers, too?" he asked.

"No," Riley said. "Reverend Willis helped my brother quit drinking. We're obliged to him. His old van never would have made it here, so I offered to get him this far. I imagine you'll

208

see our tracks across the valley. We went over to Bald Max, which is where we're headed today. My father was mean as a snake so I wouldn't be surprised to find that whiskey hid right in a rattler's den." Vintage Riley, but not what I'd had in mind for the morning.

There were twenty-four humans and four dogs, so it took us much longer to get to the ledges than it had the day before. The cops, dressed in uniforms or fatigues, were quickly red-faced and panting from the heat and the rugged terrain, especially Sergeant Wright. Riley stayed out in front and when we got to the deer run up toward the ridge top and the ledges he yelled to the dog handlers to watch out for snakes, less of a warning, I knew, than an attempt to ratchet up their fear of such things.

I've seen only a few more absurd sights in my life than two dozen people and a double brace of dogs standing on a cliff top staring down into a series of ledges all waiting for someone to tell them what to do. The dogs were sitting alongside their handlers, their tongues lolling and dripping saliva. The state cops were staring up at the mountain peaks, and the locals were gawking at Riley. He waited a long time, then said, "Well boys, if this is the spot, you need to get down on that next ledge. Work your way north about thirty yards and look for a hole big enough for a man to crawl in and hope it don't start to rattle when you poke your head in. Reverend Willis captured several serpents there yesterday."

The first thing that was apparent was the dogs would be of no use unless they could be lowered down onto the ledge, and the dog cops tried to figure out a way to make slings from their belts, but after nearly losing one of the big German Shepherds over the edge, they abandoned that idea. The second was that Riley had an alibi, albeit a bizarre one, if there was no whiskey found—he wasn't the only one who knew the location, though the Old Man and Pervis, who had known, were dead.

The chief huddled with the state cops and then came back to Riley. "How did the preacher get down to that ledge," he said. Riley walked them over to the ledge and explained it to them. Then, in great detail, he told them how many snakes he'd captured and how he'd been singing at the top of his lungs, and how he used the twine and a rock to get them back up to the top.

I was hoping that the chief would order Sergeant Wright to go down on the ledge, but two of the younger locals, including Patrolman Carr drew the duty. You'd think the police would have a physical fitness test of some kind, but I guess they don't. Carr and the other young kid, Bigley, struggled like catfish on a creek bank, thrashing and cursing about risking busting their arms, until they managed a slow slide down the crack to the ledge. I was hoping that the snake that had slithered away from the group Reverend Willis had snatched up would crawl out on the ledge, but all the commotion they were making, as it was likely in the wrong key, would have scared off Satan himself.

The chief bellowed at them to use their flashlights as they moved along the face of the ledge. The ledge was about four feet wide, but you'd have thought they were on a tightrope the way they inched along the rock. I knew damn well they would have shit their cop blues right there if I'd hollered, "Rattler," at them. After about ten minutes, Bigley yelled out, "Think I found it." After that, all the state cops and two of the dog cops made it onto the ledge and they took turns peering into the hole with their lights. "It's one hell of a good-sized cave," one of the state guys said, "Big as a banquet room."

The first one to crawl in was one of the dog cops, a tall thin kid, maybe twenty-five. He took off his baseball hat, and I could see that his hair was cut as close to the skin as it could be without being shaved. He was inside about five minutes, and all the cops at the entrance were calling to him. When he came out he was holding an envelope in a plastic bag, and a bottle of whiskey. "There's one case of these bottles in there," he said, and this typed note that says, "I never steal all a man has. It ain't signed."

I got to thinking about that reporter, Geraldo, and then I

had the same thought I was sure the cops were having, that Riley had moved the stash, or sold it, and then I wondered if Reverend Willis had stolen it, and then I wished I was anywhere but where I was. The cops played around for a few hours, collecting pieces of broken bottles in little plastic bags, and shining their lights into the cave. I tried to read Riley's eyes, but his face was as blank as a fresh page in a new tablet. The detective grilled him about who might have stolen the whiskey, and he said, "Unless Pervis had already got it when I saw him, I can only guess that maybe he got liquored up and let the location slip out."

The cops kept up a full court press on us for three weeks. We'd go down to the new place and they'd show up mid-morning with questions, usually the same ones they asked the day before. Twice, two black detectives from Detroit came and asked us about Pervis. They didn't seem interested in us, more amused that they were where they were than anything else.

Riley figured, and I thought he was right, that they were trying to find Pervis's suppliers. Riley and Pervis had a simple set up. Riley grew, tended, and harvested the weed, about half an acre a year, and Pervis picked it up. "I burned the shed and the field after the last harvest. I'm out of that," he told me after the Detroit guys left the first morning, "With dogs they might get a trace, but nothin to get me any time. They'll make tax trouble, but I guess we'll be all right." The way he said we was a bother.

On the first Thursday in May, Reverend Willis came by the house while we were sheathing the roof. We'd been expecting Hal Grimsley, a plumber from town, so when we heard the Star of Morning van coming up the road, we assumed it was him and climbed down off the roof. As soon as Riley saw the van, he scampered back up the staging and began nailing off the plywood on the backside.

I expected that Reverend Willis might want to go serpent hunting again, but he had come instead to ask me to deliver a

211

few boxes of serpents to Pennsylvania for him on Saturday. "A brother in Christ from Maine, Billy Parsons, who is building a signs community there, will meet you at a diner in Lancaster at five o'clock. I'll give you directions. I can't go myself because I'm preaching at a camp meeting near Bluefield, and he can't come a different time." He spoke to me like I had already agreed to go, and when I said I was supposed to help Riley, he said that Lorena had said she'd go if I couldn't. For the first time since I'd met him, I doubted with some conviction that he was telling me the truth, and I wondered why he couldn't send Lucius Farrell, or some other Star of Morning regular. I knew Lorena was as fearful of snakes as I was, so I couldn't believe he'd ask her. "I ask because we need the money," Reverend Willis said, "I usually have to drive the van to Maine. Billy is meeting me more than half way."

He had me, and I was pissed off that he knew it. When I said I'd go, he hugged me to him, then stepped back. "Ize, you must remember that what we are doing is illegal in the eyes of the law," he said, "And I know that you have not felt anointed to handle. You may say you don't want to go, and I will bear you no malice."

I shrugged and said, "I'll do it. Maybe Lorena will ride along with me."

Reverend Willis lingered a moment and looked around at the woods like he had the day he'd come to ask me to hunt snakes with him, and he said the same thing he'd said then, "Beautiful place for a home."

I told Riley that I couldn't work on Saturday and he assumed that I was going hunting with Reverend Willis. When I told what I was doing, his face cracked open in a jaw-splitting smile and he said I should figure out how the business worked too, "See if it was worth getting into, Ize," he said. At first, I thought he was kidding, but knew he was serious when he said, "Find out exactly what he gets per snake." Though I vowed I would, I had no intention of learning any of the details except by accident.

Lillian had been working all the overtime she could get,

and we'd been hard at the house every day. Things at the old place, like laundry and groceries, had been neglected and that morning there had been nothing to make a lunch with, so I'd offered to go into town and get us some po' boy sandwiches from Fat Eddie's Restaurant. We'd just climbed down from the roof and Riley said, "Not for me, Ize. In an hour it'll be too hot to lay tarpaper. You go in to town and I'll go home and see if I can't get a few things done before the kids get back."

We picked up our tools and I headed to City Hall.

It was always strange for me to see Lorena at work, dressed up, make-up on, standing behind her window, or sitting at her desk, reading glasses perched on the end of her nose, or talking to the people who came to see her. It was as if she was a different person then, not full of the Whipple enthusiasm, and I realized that for most people, those who have regular jobs, that part of their life doesn't breed perpetual enthusiasm. I'd always figured when we were kids, that she loved her time with me because it was so unlike life in that broken-down farm with all her sisters. As soon as she saw me her face lit up.

She was with a customer, and I was going to leave, but when he bent down to sign something, she held up one finger, meaning that I should wait. When the man left, she put her next window please sign up and hurried from behind the counter. When she got to where I was standing by the office door she took my hand and said, "Come with me a minute." She was nearly running as we went down a hall and into a small room with a table piled with maps and folders. Her face was ashy and drawn, her eyes red, as if she hadn't slept well.

Lorena took both of my hands, looked down at the floor then directly into my face and said, "Did Theo come see you?"

"He wants me to make a delivery to Pennsylvania," I said.

"I know," she said. "He came to me first, and asked if I could do it if you wouldn't. Makes no sense. He's got a congregation full of snake handlers who'd do anything he asked."

"I've thought of that, but I said yes because I owe him."

"Ize, he gave you a ride home. You quit drinking 'cause

you decided you had to. I owe him for what he did for us after my sister died, but it was hunting those fucking snakes that got her killed. I adore Theo, but a preacher of all people, ought not to make folks feel beholden to him."

Lorena could curse with the best rummy I'd ever known, but she rarely says fuck, and at work she was particularly careful not to sound rough. "I'll go with you, but just this one time," she said letting go of my hands.

"Who'll look after your mother?" I asked.

"Theo's arranged for some of the old biddies from the church to stay with her, 'stead of getting one of their men to tote the damn snakes. Hiram has the girls and the boys will go to their grandparents," she said. "Ize, I don't like this, not the cops getting into your brother's business, or the way Theo's been acting. When school is out I want us to go away, take a vacation. I can't remember my last one. The girls will be at Scout camp, and the boys go to their grandparents for two weeks at the same time. I'll get a nurse for Mama if I have to, but let's go away, somewhere cool. I'm worn down, Ize."

Lorena slipped her arms around me and leaned into my chest. "I swear I could fall asleep right here," she said. After a few seconds she pulled away and said, "I gotta get back."

CHAPTER NINETEEN

At six-thirty Saturday morning it was a hazy, wet, seventy-five degrees and headed higher. I picked up Lorena and we swapped my truck with Reverend Willis. The serpents were in separate boxes, each one with a tiny padlock whose key was taped to the side. Reverend Willis handed me a large manila envelope with Billy Parsons written on it in his scrawling hand, and said, "God Bless you both. The tank is full, and the credit card is in the glove box with the registration." He patted his shirt pocket like a man looking for his cigarettes or a lost list, then reached into his hip pocket and pulled out a small notebook and pen. "Keep track of what you spend so I can reimburse you," he said. "And don't push the old van too hard. She needs to last us a while yet. I'll be here on Sunday, all day. We can swap vehicles then."

We said goodbye, and Lorena and I took the cooler she'd packed from the bed of my truck and stowed it in the van along with a small duffel bag, her purse, and some pillows and a blanket she'd brought so she could sleep. Though Reverend Willis had given me directions, Lorena had gotten her own off her computer at work from AAA to ascertain the best routes to Lancaster and the alternate roads around construction, and she'd taped them to the dash.

At the top of Steadman's grade tufts of white fog stole across the road, and I could see that it had recently rained. As I hit the interstate I noted that the van had turned 120,000 miles, which was almost six thousand more than it had on it when we'd taken it to Beckley to be worked on. I knew that Reverend Willis faithfully visited the sick, but I wondered if he hadn't been running snakes some as well. When I got the van up to speed, and had discovered to my delight that the air-conditioning worked, Lorena snuggled down in her seat and said, "Wake me up when we get there. It's 388 miles and it should take us six and a half to seven hours."

She slept soundly most of the two hours to Lexington, snoring at times, and shifting in her seat only once or twice.

I was glad I had decided to make the trip, I think as much because Lorena and I would be together for so long without any kids or her mother, and because, though I had illegal cargo, I was driving with a valid license for the first time since just after I'd gotten out of the service. But most of all, I'd been entrusted to do something by someone who would have every reason to be suspicious of me. Granted, Lorena was a kind of insurance for Reverend Willis, but as pissed as I'd been that he'd made it near impossible to refuse the mission, he had asked me for a favor and trusted me to carry it out, and that was more than anyone had done in a long time. I felt like I did when Lillian began to trust me with the kids, and as I looked at Lorena with a line of drool on her cheek and a few strands of her hair caught in it, I wanted to cry.

At Lexington, Lorena woke up and we stopped to pee and top off the tank. When I signed the credit card slip for the gas, I realized that it was the first time I'd ever done that. "You've moved up to the big kid's table," Lorena said, when I replied that I wasn't sure what she meant, she explained it to me.

The ride up the Shenandoah Valley is as pretty a drive as I've ever made. When I'd come home from Holyoke, we'd driven most of it in the full dark of a winter night, the mountains deep shadows then. Now, though the haze made them look as grainy as a stag film, they loomed over us like leaping whales, and I was beyond glad to have Blissfull in the rear view.

I kept the van at seventy, which meant that most of the traffic flew past me, and that when I got behind a semi on a hill, I had to either wait to get to the top of the grade or slip out into the fast lane and hope the cars that raced up onto my tail didn't hit me before I could ease back to the right. I watched the temperature gauge because I knew from my time in the motor pool that using the air-conditioner strained the engine. Lorena, now that she was awake, was on fire to plan a vacation with just the two of us. "First two weeks of July. I want to go where they have nice beaches and lighthouses and seafood restaurants, and motels with pools. I want to go out to movies, maybe even a drive-in if we can find one, but I don't want to go to Florida."

"We could go to Cape Cod, in Massachusetts, or Rhode Island, they're nice," I said.

"North Carolina, New Freakin' Hampshire, I don't care," she said. "I want good food, good weather, and no serpents. Can you arrange all that?"

"I can guarantee everything except the weather," I said.

"I want a nice big bed," Lorena said. "So big it doesn't matter which way you're lying down, you don't hang over it. We've been seeing each other since Christmas, here it is almost end of school and we haven't been in a proper bed."

There it was, in her eyes, the Whipple enthusiasm, and we had four or five hours ahead of us, and half a dozen serpents six feet behind us. "I'm hot," she said. "I'm going in the back to change."

I looked in the rear view while I tried not to run off the road. Lorena stripped off her jeans and T-shirt and fished a sundress out of her bag. Her sitting on the rear seat in her skivvies was as sexy a sight as I can recall ever having seen. When she climbed back into her seat, I said, "We could drop these serpents off, turn right around, head back and stay the night in a motel."

"Save your money for July. And anyhow what's Theo paying us for this? He gets a hundred a snake."

Though I had discovered the answer to Riley's question, I was unsure if I'd tell him. "I didn't ask to be paid," I said. "I don't want to be beholden to him. If he pays me it's harder to say no if he wants me to make another delivery," I said.

"He offered me expenses and a hundred dollars," Lorena said, "but you're right about being beholden to him. Grateful is fine, indebted is another thing."

When we'd been headed east from home to Lexington, the sky behind us had been dark, and thunderheads had been building. Soon after we got on 81 and headed north, the front caught us, and we slowed down in several downpours, semis blasting by us and nearly drowning us in their spray. We saw a few flashes of lightning, and heard long rolling grumbles of thunder. I got off onto Route 11, which parallels the interstate, when we got caught in a squall and a traffic jam behind an accident. A few miles later we found a scenic overlook and stopped for lunch. The rain had abated to a mist, and I turned off the van and opened the windows.

The front had just about moved through and the thunder was a faint boom off to the east. We were overlooking a field of cows and across a flat, broad section of the valley to the mountains beyond. Lorena had packed a huge lunch, and we sat for half an hour eating chicken wings and carrots and cold slices of apple pie. She ate with her feet up on the dash and her seat slid back, and I kept staring at her legs and bare feet, trying to remember her as the skinny kid I'd first made love to. I wanted to take her into the back of the van and make love right then, kiss every dimple and curve of her body, but I didn't know if I could get her naked back there with the serpents. Sure, she'd changed earlier, but I didn't know if I could get her to shed that last layer in a picnic area in a church van in the company of six rattlers.

Lorena finished her pie, tipped up the last of a bottle of root beer, and began putting the food back into the cooler. When she'd finished that, she said, "Ready?"

I leaned over and put my hand low on her belly and kissed her on the end of her nose. "Want to crawl in the back?" I asked.

Lorena didn't answer me at first, then said, "Ease the seat back." When I did she leaned over me and opened my belt and fly, threaded her fingers in through the slit in my shorts. "You can repay the favor later on," she said. "You'll be beholden to me."

The diner was just north of downtown Lancaster. I'd been told that Billy would be there ahead of me, but we arrived an hour early. Lorena wanted to get some coffee and a dish of ice cream, so we went in and sat at a booth. I'd parked the van as far back from the entrance as I could, but where I could still see it. We had a college kid for a waitress. She was wearing a dark blue T-shirt that said, F&M Field Hockey and she told us that stood for Franklin and Marshall College, which she said was down the road a mile. While we drank our coffee and Lorena had her pistachio ice cream, I scanned the lot. Reverend Willis had said that Billy would be driving an old bread truck with, Full Gospel and Sword Tabernacle, lettered on the side.

We'd paid our bill and were walking back outside when I saw the truck pull into the lot and park near the Star of Morning van. I had a picture of Billy, taken in the winter, that Reverend Willis had given me. In it, Billy had been standing next to a woodpile surrounded by snow, with mountains in the distance behind him. He was wearing an open parka, plaid shirt, wool hunting pants, and a Red Sox baseball hat. When he got out of the truck in Lancaster, I could see that he was bald, and paunchier than he'd looked under his winter clothes.

"Billy Parsons?" I asked.

"Isaac Butts?" he said.

"Yes," I answered, "And this is my friend Lorena Whipple."

Billy had no desire to linger. He took two grain sacks that said Finestever Wood Stove Pellets from his truck and had me open the back of the van. He looked into the screened openings of each box and said, "Look like fine serpents. Our brothers and sisters will be filled with joy to see them. Please tell Reverend Willis that we are most grateful and will keep him in our prayers."

Billy put the serpent boxes into the sacks and slid them into one of the bread racks in his truck. He had me sit in the passenger's seat as he drew a wad of bills from a bank bag and counted them out on the console. "There is seven hundred here. The hundred I owe from last November, and the six hundred for today. It's like Theo prefers it, tens and twenties." I could see Lorena sitting in the van, and I wanted to get out of Lancaster as quickly as I could, but Billy insisted I count the money after he'd done it twice.

"It's all here," I said.

219

Billy handed me the bag and said, "You can keep it in this." I zipped the bag closed and opened the door. "I hope we'll meet again. Come see us in Maine," he said.

"Been a pleasure," I said.

I've held more money in my hand, and committed bigger crimes, but I'd never felt as uneasy after a deal was done. When I'd made runs for the Old Man, I'd been plenty nervous until the job was complete, but once I had the cash, and I was sure the law wasn't waiting in the shadows to grab me, I'd get an adrenaline spike and my heart would start to throb like a pounded thumb. It's the only thing I've ever known to be as good as sex.

I stashed the money in the glove box, and we turned back toward Blissfull. Lorena offered to drive, but I wanted something to concentrate on, so I said, "After a bit." We ate dinner as we drove along, Lorena biting off pieces of chicken and feeding me with her fingers. I knew that if we didn't hit any traffic jams, or more storms, that we might make Blissfull by midnight. As we got deeper into Virginia I could feel the mugginess coming back, as the heavy smell of thick southern fields streamed in the open windows. Lorena played with the radio, but all she could find were preachers and country stations that weren't to her liking.

I pulled off to get gas and use the restroom at the big interchange in Staunton. A cop had been riding in the right lane behind me for four or five miles and it was affecting my driving. I found myself speeding up and slowing down, getting paranoid that he was following me.

Lorena bought us coffee and candy bars. "Energy food," she said as she handed me a Snickers. "Why don't you pull down to the end of the lot so we can drink this before we get back on the road," she said.

I crawled along past a long line of idling semis to an open spot. We drank our coffee and then Lorena began to make up a pallet on the long seat. The Star of Morning van has a curtain you can draw so no one can see into the back of the van from the front window and each of the side windows has a sun shade. Reverend Willis said he lived in the van for six weeks while he was working on the church. He said he often rested in the day because he'd be up all night working and praying, and he didn't want folks to see his serpent boxes if they should wander by him while he was sleeping.

We rocked the springs some, but we were both tired and we fell asleep, Lorena on the long seat, and me in the driver's seat, which reclines. I woke up when a huge rig pulled in alongside us in the night, and the drivers stepped outside to stretch and have a smoke. I was only awake a few minutes, and when I next awoke the sun was up.

Blissfull lay gray and rainy before us as the van rolled down Steadman's Grade, the new tires singing on the asphalt. More than six months of sober living had made me partial to cleanliness, and I resented the dirty itch plaguing my skin and the musty tang in my mouth, which recalled the roiling stomach and dull throb of a hangover. As many days as I'd been on the bum before, neither brushing my teeth for weeks nor changing the clothes nearest to my skin for days at a time, you'd think that I wouldn't have been as bothered by one night in the van as I was, but the smell of soap and toothpaste were something I associated with Lorena and being home and happy. Though I backed off the gas whenever I found myself speeding, I ached to get out of the van and away from anything to do with snakes for a while, wishing that Lorena and I had our own place, a big bed with a canopy like Riley and Lillian's, our own closets, toothbrushes in a holder by the sink, favorite chairs in a room with a TV and a VCR, and a place to play all her records and CDs, a side of the garage for each of our cars, and a side of the bed with pillows to our liking, and a clock and a night table. I wanted towels with our initials on them, and for her kids to call me Daddy, but most of all I wanted to wake up easy with her next to me, and not have to hurry home, and to be able to make love with the lights on, or in the daytime. I wanted to see her as naked as she'd been in the creek, so I could kiss every sweet inch of her skin, from the soles of her feet to the top of her head.

I had never in my life felt that I could ask a woman to marry me, and knew it wasn't the time or place to ask Lorena, but as the road leveled out into the valley, and mist coated the windshield enough for me to crank the defrost and wipers, I swore to God that I would do anything He asked of me, if He could see His way to keep us together for all of our time on earth. I realized that I was feeling things I'd been too afraid or too drunk to feel for a very long time, and I prayed, really prayed, to a God I had never much believed in. My hands rattled on the wheel and my scalp tingled like I'd washed it with one of those shampoos they give you at the VA when you come in with your head all scabby. The tires whined and I swear that I heard way off in the distance angels singing the hymn Reverend Willis crooned to the serpents, What a Friend we Have in Jesus. I peeked over at Lorena who was gazing out the window at the rain and the fog banks on the hills and I said, "Lorena, I love you."

She turned to me, squeezed my hand and said, "I love you too, Ize." I about caved in on my heart.

The last woman to say that she loved me was my mother, the final time she'd left Blissfull for Detroit, and I'd never told any woman other than her, including Ella, that I loved her. I kept asking God if I had the right to be happy, if I'd atoned for enough of my many sins to have a chance with Lorena, a chance to live like the people I'd never believed I could be a part of. Lorena had made it off the ridge, though she'd been stomped on, betrayed, and had had to claw her way along. She'd proved that it was possible, and I hoped that she'd let me claw along the rest of the way with her.

I thought about Bob from Kroger's and I wondered if he'd slept with Lillian and if he was as on fire for her the way Riley was, and if he was sending her flowers or calling her at work or driving by the hospital to leave notes on the windshield of her car, now that she'd returned to the ridge. The voices kept rising as my mind replayed the memory of Reverend Willis striding along that skinny ledge, singing at the top of his lungs, charming the snakes with his thundering voice, and slipping the wire over them as if they were waiting for him.

Near the bottom of the grade I saw a snake flattened by countless wheels and I tasted the cold skin my Old Man had pushed up against my mouth. I shuddered, and groaned audibly. Lorena turned and said, "You alright?"

I tried to answer but the words caught like a fishbone in my throat. The soles of my feet and the small of my back itched. I squirmed in the seat and said, "My stomach's a little sour. Must have been all the bad coffee."

"Want me to drive?" Lorena said.

"No, I'll be fine," I said, though I was unsure I would be. I didn't have the whirlies, at least not as I'd had them in the past, but everything beyond the windshield began to shimmer and twist: the solid line on the road, the distant Blissfull skyline; a dispersing vapor trail on the horizon, the dark spots in the clouds coiled into serpents and snakeheads. I tried to calm myself, as if it were the DTs, but I still trembled. I sang Jesus Loves Me to myself until I came to stop in front of Star of Morning.

Though services had not yet begun, parishioners were arriving and we didn't go in. I couldn't have dealt with Reverend Willis just then, something I felt badly about, and something that scared me a little, too. Whenever I'd even had an inkling of having a drink, I'd gone to see him and the craving passed without any discussion of it. I was afraid that, keyed up as I was, that I might ask him something to injure our relationship and I couldn't face the thought.

I left the van keys in the ashtray, the place I'd discovered mine in my truck. I threw the cooler in the bed and we piled the rest of our gear on the seat between us. I was still shaking. I tried not to let Lorena see it, but she asked me again what was wrong. "It's an old ailment," I said. "If I sit too long, my leg shakes. A VA doctor told me it was poor circulation, but that it might get better over time without booze. Mostly it has."

There was no one at Lorena's house. Her mother had gone

to church with Luella Cullin, the woman who'd been looking in on her, according to a note on the refrigerator. It was the first time that Lorena and I had been alone there, but we were both too tired to play. I peed, washed my hands, splashed my face, and gargled a mouthful of toothpaste.

"Ize, this feels good, but you gotta let me go at my own speed," Lorena said as she let me out. "Call me later on," she said as I sprinted out to the truck, the rain falling again in earnest, slanted in a cool wind.

Roxie and Patches were the only ones home to greet me. It was pouring too hard for Riley to work on the roof, and I guessed that they'd gone off shopping or to eat somewhere, because Lillian's car was in the driveway. I let the shower run over me until the hot water was almost gone. I turned the cold on full just to feel it sting my skin. It was if I'd shed a layer of tough old skin, skin hardened to prevent any sensation from getting under it, except oblivion. I liked the new skin and I slapped my left ass-cheek to see if it hurt. I imagined Lorena asleep on her side in a white nightgown, drool on her cheek, and the covers kicked half off. I tried to sleep, but I couldn't. The rain came harder and a wind roared up the valley and drove it against the windows. The dogs barked on the porch and when they came in and laid down on the floor, they smelled, as wet dogs do, like a drunk's old socks.

I was proud that I'd done my job without messing anything up, and was glad that I could report to Riley that snakes were a small-time business, that it wouldn't be worth his while. Then I suddenly remembered that I'd left the money in the glove box and the van unlocked. I grabbed a slicker of Riley's and ran out to my truck, and started for town. I cursed my stupidity, though I didn't think anyone would steal from a church, then I remembered the times I'd pinched money from a collection plate, or from the candle box in one of the Catholic churches up north.

It was there, in the bag, still zipped up. I didn't know what to do. I couldn't go inside and leave it in the free will offering, but I didn't want to take it with me without leaving a note, and I didn't have anything to write on. I sat for half an hour, hoping the service would break up, but I could hear the singing and testifying even with the rain drumming on the hood of the truck. Finally, I tucked the bag into my pants, pulled my shirttail out and went inside.

CHAPTER TWENTY

On Tuesday, Sergeant Wright, Carr, and a State Police Detective named Burns, a short guy with glasses who looked like the professor who'd come to school to teach us about our Scots-Irish heritage, were at the new place at eight. Burns told us that the State Crime Lab had been unable to lift prints off the plastic bag the dog cop found in the cave or off the note inside. Since they didn't have any prints and as they'd taken mine, Riley's, and the Old Man's on more than one occasion, I could tell that they were fishing to see if we had any ideas about who might have stolen the whiskey. Burns said, "If you have any idea who stole the whiskey, you'd be best advised not to pursue any revenge."

Riley said, raising his arms as if surrendering, "It isn't my concern, detective. I've told everyone that from the start."

They didn't stay long. They spent more time asking about how the house kit worked than anything else, as if Riley's response had disarmed them, but just when it seemed that they were about to leave, Burns turned to Riley and said. "Detroit says Meeker was shot in a drive by. They seized the money. If you want it you'll need to go to court."

Riley was as cool as a March morning. "Look what whiskey has done to my family," he said, bulling his neck and clinching his fists. "I don't want the money. Ize and I are all the blood kin we have, except for my kids. Pervis has been shot dead, and you guys are coming by here most every day. Seems we'd have no peace in this world if we had all its money."

Burns seemed to take offense, hunching up his shoulders and sucking in his gut, but I thought he might just be one of those little guys who has to act tough, the guy who starts most all of the bar fights I've ever seen, the puny mutt who wants to piss on the big dog's sign, and, loaded with enough liquid stupidity, throws the first punch, or calls out the biggest guy in the joint. "This will be a nice place to live, if you get to finish it," he said. "If you financed any of this with money from drugs or illicit whiskey, the state can seize it under Federal and State forfeiture laws. I must advise you that we'll be looking into that, too, Mr. Butts," he said.

Riley, who'd been leaning on a shovel, stood to his full height. "Detective, I've been living under suspicion for my whole life on account of who my Old Man was. You go on looking. I ain't afraid. My lawyer is Cal Tuggle. He does my taxes every year, and I have filed them faithfully. I'll take you down to the bank and show you that I have eleven thousand dollars in my passbook. My wife is a nurse in the emergency room and she works hard. We were broken up for awhile because she got tired of being looked down on. We're trying to move on here and start fresh."

Burns smirked. "Mr. Butts, if you have nothing to hide, as the saying goes, you have nothing to fear. I'll let you get back to work, but I imagine we'll be in touch."

Wright and Carr pissed me off more than Burns. He was doing his job, and he was one notch better at it than the Blissfull bunch, but the local yokels acted like the kind of stupid, slack-mouthed, southern cops they have on TV. Grinning and shuffling their cop shoes in the dust, they acted like the kind of fools that Yankees conjure in their minds when they hear the words, West Virginia; the kind of moment when they drag out all the incest and hillbilly jokes, the kind of ribbing that I grew less able to tolerate each time I heard it. Long after they were out of sight I flipped them the bird and heaved a rock out onto the road.

"Assholes," Riley said. "I'm going into town to see if I can talk with Cal. They ain't fucking around now, and we got to be ready." The word we, as it often did, unsettled me. Riley knew I'd be loyal, but he'd also said that I was clean. "You only got to say that you brought six thousand home with you from up north. I need to account for that much unearned cash. Cal says that they won't do anything to you except maybe make you pay some taxes, and that it ain't enough money for them to get riled over. I'll show them that much, and say it was a payment on the old place. Can you do that?"

Riley had done what Reverend Willis had done when he

asked me to go to Pennsylvania, posed a question that wasn't multiple choice, though to an outsider it might not seem to be the case. Before, I would have said yes, grabbed my pack and some hooch, and headed for the highway, but I believe that Riley, who can read a man as well as anyone I've known, intuited that Lorena had too great a hold of me for me to light out. "I can say that, Riley," I said, "And I will. Only thing I ask is that you let Cal coach me some."

"He will, brother," Riley said, "I assure you of that. But we got to keep this from Lillian. I don't want to spook her."

A week later we were in Cal's office with a woman, Karen Shields, from the IRS; a state lawyer, Wendell Hills; and, for a few minutes, Blissfull's own chief of police, Fred MacDonald. For four hours they poured through all of Riley's records and tax forms, and I think that only the IRS agent, Cal, and Hills, had any idea what was happening. Cal was great. He acted pissed off the whole time, which he could do, and Riley and I sat stone quiet as a pair of mutes. We were packed into the conference room at Cal's office, which he'd insisted to us was part of his strategy. On his own turf he could play the host and have his secretary and his two young partners bring around coffee and doughnuts, and bottles of Yankee spring water, but spend the entire time being as inhospitable himself as he dared.

From the start I could see that Hills didn't like the IRS agent, because she kept saying that everything was in order. She was a pretty dark-haired girl, a little heavy and short-legged, but her voice was smoky and low, and she had a sexy gap-toothed smile. On the street, I'd have taken her for a bank teller or school principal. Hills was a well-freckled, sandy-headed beanpole, with hands near large enough to palm a basketball, and a hoarse voice, thin as an old man's.

Cal was deferential to Shields. He answered every one of her questions politely, and a few times when she was looking at something she wanted him to explain, he'd get up, walk around to her seat, and lean over her shoulder to see what she was reading. When Hills asked him a question, Cal would ask him to pass the paper over to him so he could read it.

We'd started at eight o'clock, and by eleven-thirty I had begun to forget that they were going to get to me at some point. I'd been letting my mind and my eyes wander, gazing out of the window and across the square toward City Hall trying to picture Lorena behind her window, or working at her computer. I knew she'd been searching for vacation ideas during her lunch breaks, and that she'd decided that she wanted to see New England, fueled by a mighty desire to view Plymouth Rock and the mansions in Newport, Rhode Island. When she asked me for my opinions, I'd answer that I would go anywhere that would make her happy. That wasn't enough for her, and each night when I'd go over to see her she'd have printed out pages of information on places to stay and visit, or gotten vacation kits from The Chambers of Commerce in Vermont or Connecticut. It had been so long since the future had a real meaning to me that I didn't know how to plan for anything, but I tried to make her believe that I was as excited as she was to go.

Lorena had the mileage and travel times calculated to the half hour, and had planned possible routes that avoided the interstates and were marked as scenic on her maps. A few nights she didn't want to make love, and we'd sit upstairs at the kitchen table pouring over her stiff new Rand McNally atlas, sipping coffee, and talking about the trip.

I was startled from my daydream when Hills said to Cal, "Can we take a break and get to your other client next?"

"How's ten minutes work?" Cal asked.

"Fifteen," Hills said.

"That'd be fine," Cal said.

That was the last inch Cal gave Hills. When he'd spoken to me alone in his office a few days before, in preparation for the meeting, Cal had said that above all, I wasn't to argue with anyone. "I'll do the fighting," he said. "You stay calm, and don't try to impress anyone." I'd seen him just once before, and the only thing he'd asked me was if Mr. Plourde had paid me by check. I told him that he did, and that I had an apartment. He asked me if I had a bank account and when I told him that I cashed my checks at a bar, he said, "That is perfect."

Riley had been right. Hills didn't seem to care about me. I was, as I had been most of my life, the four-inch bluegill you curse for stealing your worm then toss back into the pond. Shields spent more time with me. I don't have Riley's personality, his mountain magnetism, and she was all business. She asked me if I understood that everyone has to file a tax return even if they don't earn enough to pay taxes. I said, "That's been explained to me by Cal. He wanted me to meet with you to figure out how best to get me back into the system. That's why I came, to make a fresh start."

I saw Cal smile when I finished saying, word for word, what he'd told me to say. "We can arrange a time to do that," Shields said. Then turning to Cal she said, "Counselor?"

"When we're done here, we can a find a time that's good for both of us," Cal said.

"Then, the IRS is satisfied," she said.

Cal looked at Hills. "And the state?"

Hills flopped a long yellow pad down on the table. "At this time, we make no forfeiture claim. However, there are matters being adjudicated in Michigan, which may rekindle the state's interest in your other client."

Cal took a deep breath. "My client has been forthright and forthcoming. You sir, and the State are abusing your powers, and this can only be considered harassment. You have, along with the state police, the Detroit police, and our local police, been out to my client's home on numerous occasions. He has been interrogated several times over a matter he brought to your attention without the aid of counsel. Mr. Butts, in endeavoring to help you locate a stash of illegal whiskey, has been as cooperative as anyone could be. I must insist that this matter be considered closed."

Hills stood up. "I remind you, counselor, of the gravity of interstate trafficking in drugs and that all profits from the same are subject to seizure."

"I do not need instruction in the law, sir," Cal said. "I believe our work for the day is concluded."

Hills and the others, except for Shields, left. She and Cal made an appointment for two o'clock to meet with me and get me back in the system. Odd as it seems, I was thrilled. Paying taxes was something that the Butts had avoided as much as possible. That's one of the things that moonshiners get popped for, not paying the taxes on the sale of spirits, which is why Riley had always paid some, though never on his whiskey or pot sales. He was clearly the best criminal in the family, and avoided most of the stubborn traditions that brought so many people like the Old Man down. He'd never given the government their full share, but he'd always given them enough of a taste to keep them at bay until now. The only thing that would sink him would be to lose Lillian, or to have the cops find his cash, and I was overjoyed not to know where it was hidden.

Cal offered to take us all to lunch, "Thank you, but it's against rules and protocol," Shields said, regarding her watch. "Back here at two sharp okay with you?"

"We'll be here," Cal said.

Riley, Cal, and I decided to drive out to Billy Ed's Barbecue on Lake Harris, as it had recently opened for the season, where we could get a quiet table, it being a weekday.

As soon as we were in Cal's car, Riley began firing questions. "What the hell happened in there," he asked. "Did we win or lose?" The old we tightened my gut again.

"Right now we've fought'em to a draw in your case, and by three o'clock, Ize will be out of the woods, if I am any judge of character. I don't know as I would want to know every detail of your finances, Riley, and if you were in something big with Pervis they might have you yet, but I think they won't be pursuing this much longer. They say dead men don't talk, and as smart about keeping his mouth shut as I believe old Pervis likely was, the cops will be sniffing each other's asses in a blind alley soon enough."

"How damn long 'til we know?" Riley asked.

"Can't say," Cal said. "Cops can be patient. If the local boys smell forfeiture money this may take a bit to end, but I suspect that if the state gets out they'll forget it soon enough as well."

Riley was in such a black stew at lunch that you'd have thought he was having his final meal. "I should have never gone to those bastards in the first place. I should have let them keep fishing," he whispered to Cal.

"Hard to say, Riley. You may have overplayed it a bit, but as your lawyer, I'd have advised you tell the truth as asked for it."

I resented Riley bringing me down with his snarly attitude. I was as high as you get on the third stiff one, as full of hope as I'd been since I walked up the ridge the week before Christmas, unable to keep my mind from imagining lazy days at the beach with Lorena, and nights in a motel bed.

When we got back to Cal's office, Riley said to him, "I'm goin' home. What time should I be back to get Ize?"

"I'll run him up the mountain when we're done," Cal said. "As soon as our IRS lady is happy, I'm going out to the club and knock a few balls around."

Cal laid out my life to Shields, how I'd been in and out of VA hospitals and how I'd become a Christian and had been sober since November, and how I had a "fine lady friend who works at the courthouse," and was getting my life straightened out. Shields took lots of notes on one of the same kind long yellow pads Hills had scribbled on, the kind made in a factory in Holyoke where I'd worked some weekend nights on the cleaning crew. After a bit, she fetched a calculator out of her briefcase and punched some numbers into it while studying a book with tables and columns of figures. While she worked the calculator with her fingers, she chewed her pencil, and each time she punched up new totals the calculator whined out the results on a curly paper and the bracelets on her right arm jingled like a wind-chime.

Finally she said, "Mr. Butts. You need to get back into the system. You need this so the Social Security people will know about you and so you will be eligible for benefits when you retire. You need to pay your taxes so that you don't end up a delinquent, or, if you don't file, become subject to fines and possible jail time. Had you filed taxes most of these past years, you would likely have gotten most or all of what was withheld returned. However, as you have few reliable records, the government cannot assume this to be true. Do you follow me?"

I told her I did, but I noticed that she wasn't smiling like she had been and I was getting the willies about the whole process. "If you will pay the IRS five hundred dollars, and promise to file a good faith return for this past year, which your lawyer will explain to you, we will grant a one time amnesty to you. If, however, you fail to file in the future, you will give up that amnesty and we will be free to do a full and thorough assessment and audit of the previous seven years." Shields didn't look at me but at Cal.

"Ize, this is more than fair. As your lawyer I would advise you to accept Agent Shield's offer."

"I do," I said.

Cal laughed. "You're not getting married here, boy. A simple yes will do."

Taking a page from Riley's book, I added, "God bless you both," and turned to shake Shields' hand.

Five hundred dollars to the IRS, and a thousand to Cal from Riley and me, and I was almost a full-fledged, tax-paying, flag-waving, proud veteran of the United States Army, and by God, full-blooded West Virginian and American citizen. I ran to City Hall and told Lorena the news as quietly as I could, my voice cracking and the sweat running down my back and into the crack of my ass, and then I raced back to Cal's office so he could run me home.

When I got there Cal was on the phone. His secretary told me I could have a seat and wait for him, but I told her I'd wait outside. I plopped on a bench and looked at the square. I thought about all the people I could remember who'd gone from Blissfull, by death or by design. There were the dead: Malcolm Greaves, my parents, Pervis, Lorena's father, a sister, all gone before their allotted four score and ten years as Reverend Willis says; and the living, like Fred and his family moved to Orlando, the Meeker twins, doctors in Ohio. I tried to see each one's face as I recalled them. Not a one of them, had they given it any thought, would have believed that I'd make it past thirty, or that I'd ever be sober. Even Mama would have been shocked to see me sitting on that bench wearing clean jeans and a dress shirt and a decent sports coat, my boots polished, hair combed, the stink of the streets and flops scrubbed out of every pore in my body.

I felt only a little guilty about how uncertain things had turned out for Riley, because I wanted to enjoy what I had. The sun was hot but I didn't care, nor did I mind the muggy, diesely, smell of the square. If I had risen from the earth at that moment, I would have looked down on Blissfull and believed that I was leaving a place where I belonged.

Cal honked to me from his Jeep and I got in for the ride up the ridge. "You caught a break, Ize," he said. "I'm glad. But I'm gonna give you a piece of lawyerly and neighborly advice. The old days are gone. These guys play for keeps now, and you can't get the old wink and a nod deals from these local boys that your father and his generation could. The old family alliances are gone, too. I can't think of five guys from high school that I see anymore. Lorena Whipple is a fine girl, tough as granite. Between the two of you...well let's just say you both been beat on and beat down. Think of the future and don't be a fool."

I didn't say anything because I sensed that Cal's little sermon wasn't over. I looked out the window so as not to see his face. "Riley thinks he's smarter than everyone else," he said. "He can get away, for a time, with fooling Blissfull's finest, but he better be careful with the rest of them. I know they've been out to the sawmill to check on his dealings with the house. He appears to have a lot of on-hand cash for a guy with such a small time business. I know he got the old place clear and that Lillian makes a decent buck, but even I can see that it doesn't add up. I've lived here all my life and I understand that kin is kin, but stupidity is kin trouble all the time."

"I'll bear it in mind, Cal," I said, "I appreciate all you've done as well."

CHAPTER TWENTY-ONE

School ended at noon on a Thursday. Riley and I were at the old place cutting up a big maple branch that had crashed down across the driveway in a thunderstorm the night before, and Lillian was hanging sheets on the line. We glanced up when the school bus gasped to a halt and the kids shot out, their arms full of drawings and papers, and shrieking "No more books, no more school, no more teacher's dirty rules."

As Carleton and Annie spun and danced through the driveway's shadows, I thought about Lorena's four towheads, and about our vacation moved up to begin in a week and a day. We had a plan to drive to Maryland after she got done at the City Hall on Friday afternoon, and then spend most of two weeks driving up the coast as far as Bar Harbor Maine, finding places to stay as we went, so we wouldn't be hurried. Lorena had located a deal on a rental van that we could sleep in if we had to, and she'd borrowed some camping gear from a neighbor as well, having backed off a bit from her original vision of king-sized beds and lavish hotels with pools, in favor of AAA bargain motels and campgrounds. "I have been so damn few places," she said. "So I want to see as much as we can. Each night, while we sat at her kitchen table and her mother slept off her toddy, she'd bring out her checklist of things to have as the trip began, and instructed me on what I should bring with me. Though I wondered how we'd get it all in the van, Lorena insisted there would be plenty of room.

She'd gone so far as to inform her mother, in front of me, when she complained that it was a public disgrace to have us go off together, that the Mountain Sunshine Home had openings for seniors on Medicare saying she'd, "Be pleased to pick up an application any day on my lunch break." It was the first time I'd seen Lorena get sharp with her mother, and couldn't tell if she did because she was softening her up for the possibility of my becoming a permanent figure in Lorena's life, from weariness, or because of her excitement at going on vacation.

I leaned against the front of my truck watching the kids tossing papers in the air and giggling as they tried to catch them; happy as any kids could be, Roxie and Patches barking and chasing them in circles, and I remembered how much I'd hated some classes, but how much I'd liked being in school. On school day mornings, Riley and I crept out of the house as early as we could and sauntered up the ridge at the end of the day, hoping we wouldn't meet the Old Man, or find Mama waiting to warn us off to the woods.

Annie was singing a ditty that went, "School oh school is such a bummer. How I wish it was always summer." For Riley and me, summer had meant endless drudge if the Old Man was around, and even if we got out of the house before he could chain us to some task, he might whip us when we got home for not being at his beck and call. I'd always wanted to know that sense that kids have that summer has finally come and that there will be only warm sunny days, time to swim and fish, or hunt up berries, or shoot crows, things we did, but never without a sense of dread. How many times had I heard some ruined old drunk crying in his beer about how much he missed being a barefoot kid in the summer doing what he pleased? I couldn't count, but I couldn't understand his sorrow either. For me summer had been one long game of hide and seek, where no one calls, "all ye all ye in free."

The kids and Riley went in to have lunch, while I sawed up the rest of the branch and considered the job of felling the rest of the tree. "Kids had a swing on that branch once, an old tire and some rope. If I'd have known she was so rotten I'd have never allowed it," Riley had said, before we'd begun bucking up the branch. "Something happened to them or Lillian, I don't know what I'd do, Ize." I'm used to Riley's voice changing tone from sentence to sentence, bitter as a winter creek then warm as a sun burnished rock, in seconds, but there was a resignation in his voice that shrunk my guts. I knew that cornered, he'd be as dangerous a man as any I had ever known, including the Old Man.

I knew that inside the house the kids were laughing and

that Riley was bound to be mugging it up while he helped them get lunch, and I wondered where that came from. I could never amuse the kids the way Riley does, nor can I act as clownish as he can.

After lunch Riley and I drove Carleton and Annie down to the new place and let them run loose. The walls were up, the roof shingled, and the kids got a kick out of looking up through the chimney and arguing if it was big enough for Santa Claus. Beyond that, Riley had stopped working on it. He'd been taking more logs to the mill, unloading them cheap to get cash to pay the plumber and electrician. The work hadn't been going well for other reasons. He'd blown a fuel pump on the skidder and wrecked a tire on the loader. He knew that he wasn't taking in enough to show the feds if they looked into his books again to cover what he'd have to pay out. When he tried to swap the electrician five cords of firewood for what he owed him, the guy refused.

As we stood in the front room, Riley told Lillian that we might have to close the place in and wait until the next spring to finish it enough to move in. I know he told her in front of me so she'd have time to cool off if she was mad, but she put a hand on my shoulder and said, "You'll be on the couch a little longer, I guess."

"Unless he takes up residence in Pine Hills," Riley said.

I didn't answer.

The kids were tearing around on the first floor and climbing the ladder up to the second. My brother had sent a shot across my bow. He'd get decent money for the old place if he sold it, more than enough to finish the new place. It was the kind of small farm that professors buy to spend their summers fixing up, or doctors buy for weekend getaways. He had more than a hundred acres and a long stretch on both sides of the creek, the kind of place fly fishermen and hunters covet. I was entitled to half, but I didn't really care. For every good memory I had of that old farm, I had a hundred butt-puckering nightmares.

It seemed to me that I was being squeezed on every side, except Lorena's, and I knew she was going to see how our trip went before she gave more of herself to me. I could have said to Riley to sell the old place right then, but I couldn't bring myself to do that.

Saturday, Lorena drove me out to the rental place to see the van she'd ordered for the trip. She'd gotten an AAA bargain price of four hundred dollars for the two weeks. The salesman explained that there were cheaper vans, but this one had captain's chairs up front, seats that folded into a bed in the back, air-conditioning and a six-speaker stereo that played tapes and CDs. It was an automatic, which I never did like, silver and gray, and the odometer showed only 3000 miles. For an extra ten bucks we could get a roof storage bin with a lock, which Lorena declined. "We can park right on the ocean," she said, "And fall asleep to the waves."

I didn't have the heart to tell her how private Yankees are about their shorefront, and I knew that she had brochures from some campgrounds in Maine with "sea view sites," so I squeezed her hand and said, "This is great, Lo."

The next morning, I picked Lorena up at eight-thirty to go to Star of Morning. I hadn't left her house until after one the night before and hadn't wanted to go to church at all, but as the congregation, after a spring infusion thinned out in the summer, and as no one had felt the anointing in three weeks, and thus no one had handled, which seemed to weigh on the worshippers, I felt obliged to add myself to the meager crowd.

Reverend Willis had not flagged in his preaching despite the diminished attendance. Each Sunday he stood at the pulpit and exhorted us to believe and within a few minutes he was bathed in sweat and his eyes were flashed with his faith. I was ever astonished by how much of the Bible he'd committed to memory. I had stopped studying mine, though I would open to a random page and read now and then before going to sleep.

We sat near the rear of the church, though it wasn't a third full. We had never stayed to the end, and as Lorena's mother had not come with us and had the kids until the day we left for our trip, we'd planned to leave early again.

Reverend Willis had taken Luke 6:32 for his text. I opened my Bible and, as Lorena looked on, I read:

If you love those who love you,
What credit is that to you?
For even sinners love those who love them.

"Who doesn't love being loved?" Reverend Willis cried out, holding his Bible above his head with one hand and wiping the sweat from his face with a handkerchief he held in the other. "What you must do is learn to love those who hate you, who revile you, who steal from your gardens and larders, love the ones who speak ill of you to others, love the back biters and the blasphemers and sodomites and the wicked, because God loves them all. He hates their sin, and He has smitten them with His mighty sword, but it is because He loves us. He made us in His own image as we know from Genesis, and He delivered us from Pharaoh's yoke, as we know from Exodus, and He gave Moses the laws and commandments to give to us, and His greatest commandment was to love others as we wanted to be loved, and to put no God above Him, who gave us His perfect love. And then as the prophet John told us in 3:16, This God so loved us that He gave His only son so we might be redeemed, be saved from sin, free from Satan—get thee behind me devil, be free to love our enemies. Praise God," he cried. "Can I get a witness for Jesus?"

The congregation answered him, praising God and shouting "Amen." The service felt different than it ever had. The musicians were playing a little quicker and the rhythmic clapping was louder, even though there were fewer hands at work. Though the crowd was small this was definitely the varsity at their best, their energy contagious.

When Reverend Willis asked for those who wished to be healed to come forward, only two approached the pulpit and they were the same heavy old women who would swoon at his touch, then rise to do the Holy Ghost dance. Reverend

Willis preached harder, quoting Mark 16 and Revelations, and as his voice got raspier and louder, he suddenly fell to his knees and began praying, "Of God, Sweet Jesus, Maranatha, Jesus come by here, help the afflicted, those who believe in Your love and power, strike down our fear, I praise You, I praise You, oh God, oh Jesus, thou art my rod and my staff, deliver us from our sins, unworthy as we are." He knelt with his head hung down, silent. The musicians played on. Lucius Farrell was acting as an assistant and he lugged one of the women onto the stage. Reverend Willis jumped to his feet and in as loud a voice as I've ever heard, screamed out, "Get thee behind me Satan," and he began to do a little dance, waving the air with both hands, as if his backside was on fire.

Lorena pulled me close to her and said, "Ize, I'm afraid. Something feels wrong."

I asked if she wanted to leave, but she shook her head, no.

Lucius and another young man were assisting the second woman to the stage. Reverend Willis was off to the side. He had tears rolling from his eyes and sweat dripping off his nose. Rather than present herself to be healed, the first woman grabbed two serpents from boxes, a rattler and a copperhead. She lifted them out and held them above her head like the Episcopal priests had done with a bright silver chalice on Christmas Eve, and when the second woman rose from the stage she fetched two more. I'd never seen four serpents out at one time before unless Reverend Willis was handling, and Lorena was shaking and crying and holding me around the waist.

Lorena would say later that she saw it in her mind a full minute before it happened. The women were spinning in circles, and the older of the two let go of a long tawny rattler that flew through the air and landed on Reverend Willis, who was standing with his eyes closed, his hands above his head. The serpent sank his fangs into his shoulder and he sank to the floor. Lucius ran to him and grabbed the snake behind the head and wrestled his fangs loose. Blood seeped quickly through Reverend Willis's shirt. Lorena was sobbing and screaming, "No Theo, oh God no," over and over.

Lucius wrestled the snake into a box. The musicians ceased playing, but Reverend Willis cried out, "Make a joyful noise unto the Lord, and they plunged back into the hymn. " He rolled to his side, and then stood. "Forgive me Lord," he cried and sat down on the edge of the stage facing the congregation. Women were moaning and shrieking and several men were hunkered around Reverend Willis on the stage. Lorena and I surged forward and I heard an old woman ask Reverend Willis if he would go to the hospital and he shook his head no. "Trust on the Lord," he cried.

I followed Lucius and two other men as they carried Reverend Willis to his room. He had a bed, a chair, and a trunk, not much more than a jail or monk's cell. His clothes hung in a small, doorless closet. He refused ice for the wound. Lorena held onto me, her eyes emblazoned with fear, and every fiber of her lanky Whipple body shuddering.

When the room became too close with people, all praying and begging God to save their pastor, Reverend Willis sat up a bit. "Does it hurt bad, Reverend?" Lucius asked.

"It does," he answered. Then he grimaced and cried out, "Heal this sinner God, if it be Your will."

At that moment I understood that he could die. I'd had that nightmare where Riley got shot, and I'd had any number of bad dreams about my own death, but I'd believed Reverend Willis invincible. How could a man who sang serpents into submission be bitten by one? The woman who'd lost hold of the rattler could be heard beating her fists on the stage and calling out to be forgiven in a hoarse, mournful wail, choked with tears. I'd never seen a snakebite before and only when Reverend Willis tore away his shirt did I see the two swollen places where the rattler had sunk into his shoulder, and the broken piece of the serpent's fang that stayed behind. "Earvin," Reverend Willis said to one of the older men near him. Yank out that tooth, will you?"

The old man fished a pair of glasses from the front pocket

of his overalls and a jack knife from his hip pocket. He put the blade up against the side of the fang and his thumb against the other and tore it loose. "He bit you deep, Reverend," Earvin said. "Sure I can't at least get you some ice for the swelling?"

"I must bear this, Earvin. I want you all except for Lorena and Isaac to go on home and pray for me."

"Shouldn't we stay a little while yet, Reverend? Just a while to see how bad the bite is?" the old man asked his voice rich with respect.

"I am in God's hands now, Earvin. You all go on home and pray. Love thy neighbor as thyself."

I had no idea why Reverend Willis had asked for us to stay, but we stepped aside and waited for the others to leave. The woman who'd lost the serpent insisted on coming to the room, and the Reverend Willis told her that what had happened was God's will and that she should go in peace. "I thought I felt the spirit anoint me, but there was fear somewhere in the church," she said. "I've handled so many times and nary been bit. Oh God forgive me, Jesus forgive me."

Reverend Willis raised his good arm and said," Verna, I love you and Jesus loves you. Go now and let me rest. Pray for me."

Lorena sat on the bed holding Reverend Willis's good arm. She begged him to go to the hospital. "My sister would be alive if she'd been able to get to a doctor. There is no sin in living, Theo," she said, her voice breaking.

"Lorena, I cannot do that. God has given me a trial. He will give me no pain I cannot endure, or He will call me home. I am a believer, not just in the signs, but in all of His mercies. I am going to ask Isaac to do me a favor, and when he tells you what it is, I ask that you help him. First, I need to be sure that he and I can speak alone for a time. Please go out into the church and see if everyone is gone, even from the sidewalk."

Lorena bolted out and I could hear her open and close the front door. "They're all gone, Theo," she said, when she came back.

"Now I would ask you to go, too. Isaac will be along soon."

"I don't like this, Theo," she said. "It's not like you."

"Please, Lorena, trust me. I want to live. I want to live to be a very old man, and to love again and have babies and grandbabies, but this is up to God now. I must be with Isaac, alone."

The mention of children and the tenderness he'd always shown Lorena unnerved me for a moment, and even though he'd counseled me to treat her honorably, I feared that his sin might be that he coveted her for himself.

Lorena looked at me with both terror and surprise. I said to Reverend Willis, "Can't she stay?"

"No, Ize, she can't," he said. As he tried to sit higher on the bed, his face contorted and his teeth ground against each other. "Dear Jesus, sweet Lord," he said softly, "The old serpent bit me deep."

Lorena, after a pause, ran from the tiny room, and we heard her leave by the front door. "She won't go home," I said, "She'll be sitting in the car. I give half an hour before she storms back in here. She's petrified that you're going die. She loves you Reverend Willis, we all do."

"I know that, but loving me is easy," he said, gasping through clenched teeth. "What I am going to ask of you is not. Do you remember today's text?"

I nodded.

"Ize, I am going to tell you something you need to know, and I hope that when I have that you can still love me. Don't say a word, please, until I am done. I want to say this now, in case my time on earth is about done."

"You needn't tell me anything. I'll do what you want, because of what you've done for me, and for what you mean to Lorena."

"Hush, son," he said. "Give me a drink of water from that glass on the windowsill." He drank the glass down. His voice was gravelly and sore, and he began to speak like a man who was about to tell a long story.

"When I met Lenora, I was living a life of sin. She had run away from a mean husband and heartbreaking poverty. She wasn't like Lorena. When Lorena got kicked, she kicked back, refused to be held down. Lenora rolled over and got kicked some more. If she hadn't been afraid that her husband would have killed her the next time he got angry, she'd not have sought my protection." He paused and adjusted himself on the bed.

"I had turned from God. I had left a family, just walked away, and I have to this day, though I have searched for them, never found them. A wife, and a boy. For a long time, four full years, I drove once a week to Kentucky to look for their relatives, and to ask about them, but no one would say where they went. I cannot blame them for if any man mistreated those he loved, I did."

I wanted to interrupt him and tell him how I understood cowardice as well as any man, but when I started to say something he said, "You promised to hear me out."

He asked for another drink, and carried on speaking as if he had all the time in the world. "Lenora and I weren't hunting serpents for church when she died, we were collecting the early buds on a cash crop of sensimilia. She stepped on a snake deep in the woods and I couldn't get her out in time. I can't say as I loved her until she knew she was dying, and she pleaded with me to carry her faster, and I heard her beg God not to let her die. She called for her mama and her sisters like a little girl. In my most tormented hours I hear those cries as if she were here. Even when I knew she was dead, I kept running down the mountain for the road. Some can survive the serpent's bite, but some, even the saved, can't. It is one of God's mysteries."

I must have looked dead myself, because Reverend Willis ceased speaking for a moment and stared at me. "You all right, Ize?" he asked.

"Fine," I said, though I felt a case of the whirlies coming and when I sat down on the bed beside him, he groaned.

When he'd rested a minute he began again. "You know from Lorena that I brought Lenora's earthly remains back here, and after a while I went up on the mountain, often blind drunk, and began praying to find my way. I spent the summer wandering the hills hoping I would find God or get so lost as I'd die myself. The problem is, you cannot find God when you have no hope in your heart."

He stopped and held his good hand to his shoulder, which had continued to swell and darken. "Remember you told me, Ize, that an old priest told you that the greatest sin was to despair? I believe he was right on that. I came off the mountain and went to Jolo where the signs believers are many, and I prayed with them and I handled, because I knew that I had to do that for Lenora, but I wasn't yet saved. I visited Lorena and Hiram, and they offered me a home, but I went back to the hills. I hunted for serpents day and night. I would catch them and handle them and let them go."

He reached with his good hand over his chest and took my hand. "Then," he said, "I found the whiskey in that cave, even more, I believe, than your brother may have told you about. I gave into that temptation. I went to Tennessee and brought back three old associates of mine with me and we stole all but one case of the shine."

He paused to gain his breath as mine quickened.

"Took us days to get it out. We made a killing. I took my cut of the money and drove to Biloxi, Mississippi, where I sinned assiduously. I fornicated, cursed the Lord, defiled my body with reefer and liquor, and I despaired of ever feeling whole again."

He shifted his legs and bit down on his lip. I moved toward him, but he waved me away, and asked me to stand. I began to wonder if I would ever be free from the Old Man's curse. Before me, perhaps dying of a snakebite he wouldn't have tended to, lay the only man I'd believed holy since the old priest up north, and he'd been no better than me.

Reverend Willis's voice grew stronger. "But the Lord had a mission for me. I woke in the night with my body surrounded by flames, foul smelling and hot, but they consumed nothing. I realized that God was showing hell to me. Above me I saw my wife and my child and Lenora, all crying and pointing at me.

My entire body was riven with a pain worse than this serpent's bite. I tried to get out of bed, but some force, which I know now was the Holy Ghost, the Almighty Word, pinned me to the sheets. I wrestled it like Jacob, and in the early morning not only my hip, but my ankles and wrists were tender and weak. It was still dark when I crept out of my motel room and stared over the water. I limped down to the beach, all the time the wind seeming to follow me, and I looked up to see a star, one star, winking through the glow of the sunrise and the streetlights. The tide was out, ebbed as low as I had fallen. I bathed in the coolness of the water and the heat of the pain was lifted and I prayed to God all that day and the next night, on my knees in that filthy motel."

"I collected all the cash I had stashed from my dope-growing days and came back to Blissfull a reborn, but not yet a born again, man. I was most prideful driving into town with the van lettered, Star of Morning Church, Blissfull, West Virginia, on the side. But I knew I would start the church, help Lorena and her mama—Hiram was gone by then—and work, slave if need be, to repay the Lord's kindness in sparing me. I have been blessed, but keeping silent while the law has squeezed your brother is sinful, and I believe that the Lord is paying me for that sin. If I live, I will tell the authorities what happened."

"There's no need to do that," I said, and he didn't shush me. "Riley will be fine. I won't tell him."

"No, Ize, I need to tell the truth. I've been lying about too much for too long."

He was still a while and then he said, "My Lord this hurts, Ize, take my hand in yours and let me squeeze it."

Though he seemed to be bearing down, his grip paled to the squeeze Lorena had given me when the snake struck him. I gave him more water, and I asked him again if he might like some ice, but he said, "No."

"Should you sleep?" I asked.

"In a bit," he said, shifting some in the bed. "Isaac, I need to ask you this favor. I need you to make a trip for me."

I didn't answer, waiting for him to speak.

"You are too sharp not to have noticed how many miles I'd put on the van between the time you went to Beckley and now. I have learned where my wife and child are. They have gone a long way from Kentucky, and they live not far from Billy, in a city in Maine, Lewiston. I have an address, and I need you to take them a letter and some money. I don't know their circumstances, or if Lou-Ann has remarried. You told me you once had a Kentucky girl, so you know how fierce they can be."

"I'll do that gladly. Lorena and me are going on a trip up…"

"I know, Ize, she told me. If that were all I had to ask, I would have asked that when she was here. I need you to deliver some serpents as well."

For the first time I argued with him. I knew he was snake bit, and I knew I might be denying a dying man his last request, but I asked him how he could ask that of us when this meant so much to Lorena.

"Ize, Lorena will do it. I never helped her in order to make her beholden to me, but she will feel that way. I'm may be dying, it's in the Lord's hands now and I ask you to do this for me even if I have forfeited the love you once had for me."

"I can't lose Lorena," I said to him. "A few months ago I was living over a funeral home in a cold Yankee city, drinking enough to kill off the demons, and not too much so I lost my job. If you and Lucius hadn't stopped, I might be dead, or back on the bum. Every time I feel clean, I get asked to get dirty again. I wish you wouldn't ask this of me."

"I wish I didn't have to," he said. "Let me sleep, Ize. If I die, and you can see your way to heeding my last wish, the instructions, the letter, the money, and directions, are in the money bag Billy gave you, and that is in the trunk at the foot of the bed, shoved down into a gray, woolen sock. And one more thing. If I go, please write down what I have told you on a tablet you will find there. I have signed the last sheet."

Reverend Willis drifted off and I sat beside him on the bed him while he slept. Twice he cried out in his sleep, saying

Lou-Ann and Lenora's names, and crooning "Sweet Jesus." Lorena stole back into the room, as I knew she would do, and her eyes were as red as the garnets we used to gather on school field trips where they'd blasted a seam of granite to carve the interstate through the mountains above Steadman's Grade.

Lorena and I argued about calling for a doctor, or asking Lillian to come down, but in the end I owed Reverend Willis his wish to put his life in his God's hands without my interference. Lorena mopped his brow and washed the wound, and though he stirred he didn't wake. Lorena left to get her Mama and kids their dinner and I asked her to call Riley and Lillian and tell them where I was.

Reverend Willis slept until it was near dark. I left the light on in the room so I could read my Bible, and I was so deep into the story of Samson, that I didn't hear Lillian come in.

I looked up, but I didn't need to ask why she came. She knew not to call the ambulance. When I first began going to Star of Morning she told me that she'd seen a few handlers who'd been bitten. She warned me that most signs people won't seek medical help, and refuse the ambulance when it's called. She snapped on some gloves and examined the wound. "It's deep. He's in good shape for a man his age, but he might not make it. I can get Dr. Crowley; he's a new guy, to look at him. He gets off duty in the ER in a few minutes and he said he'd come over."

"I'd appreciate it," I said. "I'm scared for him. Lillian."

"I won't run down a man's religion," she said, snapping off her gloves, "but handling rattlesnakes is plum-assed foolish if you ask me."

Dr. Crowley was one of the doctors who pay off some of their medical school debts by working in under-served areas of Appalachia. He was the kind of guy I'd figured Lillian might've left with when his tour was up, good looking and likely to be well off when he relocated to Atlanta or Charlotte, or some place up north.

He looked Reverend Willis over and said, "I would get him

to the hospital. Even if he lives, and that is at best 30-70, he might have long-term paralysis, or even lose his arm. I can't make him go, but a next of kin could request we take him against his will if he's delirious."

"He has no kin here," I said.

Dr. Crowley touched Reverend Willis's shoulder and he woke up with a shout. "Get thee behind me Satan," he said, but he didn't seem to know where he was for a minute. Lillian took the phone from Reverend Willis' bedside table and put my hand on it. "Please," I said. "These people don't believe that anyone but God can save them."

"If He is so all fired powerful why'd He let him get bitten?" she said.

I pondered that for a moment, and I wondered that since he hadn't been handling, and that the woman had accidentally let go of the rattler, if there was some technicality in play that would allow me to send him to the hospital. "It's what they believe," I said. It wasn't what I believed, but I couldn't summon the courage to betray him.

Reverend Willis got his bearings and twisted himself up to a sitting position. The wound was oozing and it smelled like the matted wet leaves I turned over in the fields to find fishing worms as a kid. He tried to shout, but his voice was wheezy and weak. "I will have no doctor but the great healer Jesus Christ Almighty, Son of God, Redeemer of Man. If it is my time, then I pray that God will deem my soul worthy of the kingdom of heaven and everlasting life." I could see the light that shone in his eyes when the spirit was on him, and I believed that his time had not come.

I sat with him all night. Lorena brought me dinner and a thermos of coffee. She sat with me and asked me to tell her what he had said. I told it to her as best I could, and she hardly spoke, though she snuffled and cried and kept saying, "Oh Theo." She left just after midnight, her face as puffy as if she'd been hit, her eyes dark and narrowed. Ladies from the church came and prayed over him, as he slept. Earvin sang into his ear for an hour and as he went to leave he told me he had sent for a man, "From over to Jolo who has prayed many to health."

By two, I was alone again reading in my Bible while Reverend Willis dozed and mumbled in his sleep. I jumped in my seat every time he cried out. It sounded at times like he was speaking in tongues, while other times he seemed to be telling someone to look out, or commanding Satan to get behind him.

A few times I was sure he had died. He'd gasp and then I wouldn't see him breathe for a long time and it scared me way it used to when Lorena would take a deep breath, grab hold of her nose, and submerse herself in the creek to rinse her hair. I knew she'd hold out as long as she could, and I knew deep down that she was always treading water just below the surface, but I still got panicky when she'd been out of my sight for a long time.

Sleeping in a chair can be worse than not sleeping at all. Anyone who has bummed hard and passed out in the weeds, or in an awkward position on a steam grate knows this. The ache and numbness can take hours to go away, and if you get a crick in your neck it might be there for days. Thugs will look for that if they think it might be worth it to mug you, because you can't turn to see who's behind you.

At six, Lorena was back looking only slightly better than Reverend Willis, her eyes as hooded as a cobra, and even with her make up on she was washed out and pale. She stood over my chair kneading my shoulders and neck. "I didn't sleep," she said. "I've cried so hard that my stomach feels like I was kicked by a damn mule. I'm sick of snakes and death and this place. When we take our trip, let's look for a new place to live."

It took me a few groggy seconds to realize the enormity of what Lorena had said. How she could convey so much in so few words astonished me. Unless I was a complete fool, I realized that she was thinking about us in permanent terms. I could not think of what to say, so I reached up and took her hands for a second. "Dollar for your thoughts," she said.

"Lorena," I said, "I'll be happy anywhere you are, and I've got plenty of things I'd like to leave buried on the ridge."

She kissed the top of my head as her hands wrung the knots from my sore muscles. "Ize?" she asked. "Does it seem possible that we were who we were as kids?"

I knew what she meant, and I told her that I wasn't sure. "Sometimes it seems as though we're still wet from skinny-dipping, and sometimes I feel like we just remember the two people who did those things. It does seem to me that you are the only person who knows the good in me, and you know it better than I do."

"Theo knows it, too," she said. "Only us who've been down so hard by life can see those things. I know that most boys around here thought me and my sisters was just some bony hillbilly sluts, and that you and Riley were common. I guess I stayed just to prove them all wrong, and because Hiram came around and knocked me up. Getting married seemed somehow to shove all the mean shit I heard as a kid, all that crap written on the walls about me, right up the asses of some of those stuck-up bitches who were still hanging out in the bars, or flirting at church like a dog in heat, to find a husband. But even then every man just used me up and threw me away. I never feel like you look down on me, and you seem too happy when we're making love to be using me. I've been crying about Theo, but I've been crying about us, too. I need us to work."

I stood up and held her so hard I could feel her heart rap against my ribs. The closer I clutched her the harder she sobbed and I couldn't tell if that was a good thing. I knew that I needed her the same way a man needs to breathe. If I left Blissfull alone, I knew I would backslide, and that would mean an ugly, lonely death. The best end then might be a VA ward and liver cancer.

We stood swaying and rocking as if we were hang-dancing in a crowd until Reverend Willis woke up screaming. His eyes were open, but he shouted like a drunk having a nightmare--his words fuzzy and choked back in his throat. He came to slowly and sat up. He stared up at the ceiling, said our names, and then fell back. I was sure he was dead.

Lorena searched the wrist on his good arm for a pulse. She kept calling out, "Jesus, no," and, "Theo, please don't go, not now."

I heard voices in the church and ran out to find Earvin, a half-dozen of the Star of Morning ladies, and a bent old man in stained coveralls, stooped and lined with age, who carried an ancient, worn Bible in one hand and a cane in the other. "I believe he's dead," I said.

The old man and Earvin shuffled into the room, and Earvin pulled Lorena away while the old man put his head to Reverend Willis's chest. Then he put his nose right on Reverend Willis's and touched his tongue to Reverend Willis's forehead. "He hasn't been called home. I believe the Lord will spare him, but he needs our prayers," the old man said, and as he spoke the old ladies knelt on the floor and started to pray, all at once calling out to God, and saying different words or singing.

I gathered Lorena to me and brought her out into the morning. The peaks of the hills were cloaked in a single, gravid, blue-gray cloud, the top humped and ragged, and the bottom as level as the Kansas prairie. Below that, thin wisps of fog rose and fell on the ridges, and a light mist wet the town. The morning traffic sputtered and droned as the lights around the square switched from blinking to red and green, and the first pedestrians pushed the buttons at the crosswalks. A whiff of diesel floated down the sidewalk from Main Street, and the queasiness in my stomach, from a night of coffee and little sleep, rioted and burned.

Lorena and I leaned on each other and against the front wall of Star of Morning. I smelled honey-scented shampoo in her hair, and its sweetness calmed my stomach and tempered the pounding in my head. "I love you, Lorena," I said. She turned and nestled into me and said, her voice muffled against my chest, " I love you, Ize. I didn't mean to make you say it to me, when I said I needed this to work."

"I wanted to say it, but I wasn't sure you'd want me to," I said.

"We were always better at showing our feelings than we were talking about them," she said.

CHAPTER TWENTY-TWO

He didn't die, and by Wednesday, though he was still in great pain, and his sick arm hung at his side, it was accepted by the believers at Star of Morning and the man from Jolo, that Reverend Willis would live. There was a constant vigil at the church, with the regular Star of Morning people and serpent handling believers and holiness people from all over the area coming by with food and prayers. The inside of the church resembled a shelter I'd stayed in once in North Carolina during a hurricane with blankets and cots everywhere, and kids playing on the floor or racing around chasing one another. The place had the air of a picnic or what I had imagined a church social would be like. I came every day, but I didn't like to see Reverend Willis surrounded by so many people when I thought he should be left alone to recover.

Thursday morning I was having breakfast on the porch steps with Lillian and telling her about how the man from Jolo said that Reverend Willis was out of the woods now, but she said. "He could still die from gangrene, be permanently paralyzed, and, then he might recover, no one knows that yet. You can place your bets with those old snake handlers if you want, but I'd get him to a doctor. He's tough, but that bite was deep."

When I didn't respond she said, "You and Lorena still going on your trip?"

"We're planning to leave tomorrow," I said.

"Riley and I may go away for a few days as well," she said, "Take the kids, if I can get the time off, but he's worried about leaving the place. I hope to hell he isn't lying to me about having any damn drugs or moonshine hidden around here, or any other damn place, because I will be gone for good, and the kids will vanish with me—way gone."

"I think he's telling the truth," I said. "He may have more trouble with the tax people, and this thing with Pervis could get dicey, but Cal thinks he's okay."

Lillian glanced up from her eggs with a flinty stare. "You've

255

been away awhile. I wouldn't put it past Cal to be up to his neck in something with Riley. I love your brother," she said, "but I love my kids more, and I'd say that if he were here this minute. Riley's problem is that he's a kid—worse than Carleton sometimes. Carleton will want something he can't have, or I won't let him have, and he keeps banging away until he gets his way, or I threaten to warm his skinny butt up. Riley is the same way, except he's too big to spank."

This was the first time Lillian had been so forthcoming with me, though I'm sure Riley had endured her riot act a multitude of times. I sat back and said. "He knows this is his last chance, Lillian, he's told me that a hundred times. If he isn't free from all the old stuff, he's trying to get free of it." Omitting for the moment the bones we'd buried with the ashes, I said, "He'd do anything to keep you."

"We'll see about that," she said.

She was right. Riley had gone to the new place to cut more firewood. I wasn't sure whether he'd been spooked by the all the attention he'd gotten from the cops and the IRS, or if he was just looking for something to do that would look like gainful work.

"He isn't gonna finish that house by selling firewood," Lillian said, "And I'm not naïve enough to think that he hasn't got the money stashed to finish that house and build another. It's also clear that he wants this place to stay in the family. What I don't know is how the hell he thinks he can pull it off, and I'm getting weary of living in the dark on a bagful of promises."

"I think he's trying to be smart about things," I said.

"Smart-assed," Lillian said, and then she laughed. "One thing is for sure, if anyone can wriggle out of a mess, it's your peckerhead brother, God love him."

I finished my toast and coffee while Lillian quartered a grapefruit half and pulled the fruit from the peel with her teeth. As she chewed each piece, I watched her jaw work, and her eyes scan the view from the porch. The morning was warm, drier than it had been, and the valley rolled out before us. "I never tire of this view," she said. "If you pass a day out here, you still can't see it all, there's too much."

"I know," I said. "I used to sit here with the dogs in the early morning when I was real little, smaller than Carleton, trying to memorize the way things looked. A thousand times I've sat somewhere away from this ridge and tried to recall every detail, but I'd never get it right. I could always see the red glow at night, and the shadows on the road like they are now, but most of it would just run together."

Lillian stretched her legs, the skin brown and smooth beneath the hem of her nightgown, and yawned. "If you and your brother can keep out of mischief, maybe we'll sit up here as old farts and remember how it was now. I got to get to work; I should be home by five. Riley said he'd be back in the early afternoon. That work for you?" she said, as she got up to go inside.

I was glad to have the kids because I didn't want to be at Star of Morning, so I said, "I have no plans until Lorena and I fetch the van."

I carried the dishes to the sink, but I didn't wash them until Lillian had showered. She came out into the living room brushing her wet hair with one hand and putting things into her purse with the other. I imagine that there are women who feel the need to put on make up, or style their hair before they go out into the world, but Lillian is afflicted with no such vanity, which is her beauty. Running shoes, hospital greens, and long wet hair, might not flatter some fine-looking women, but Lillian could stir lust in a man if she was wearing greasy coveralls and a bandana. Lorena is never as sure of herself. It may be because she was so skinny and pale as a kid, but she seldom lets the world see her in the rough.

I glanced at the clock as Lillian left and saw that it was already seven. As a kid, I'd only slept that late on a summer morning when I was sick. It wasn't only the Old Man's moods that got me out of bed, it was the fact that the ridge is its most beautiful around sunrise and sunset. Some folks like the early morning for its quiet, but on the ridge it was always quiet, except for when the Old Man was roaring.

I made a second pot of coffee even though my pulse was racing and I feared that a vessel in my brain might rupture at any minute. I knew that I would have to make a decision on Reverend Willis's request by nightfall. Lorena was being no help. She said that it was up to me to decide on the serpents, because I was the one who had been asked to deliver them, when I'd tried to get her to be the one to say no to the request. We'd planned to sleep in the van quite a few nights, and serpents don't make the best company, even when they're locked in their cages. If you've never heard a rattler's tail going at full speed, you've not known full fear.

I sat back out on the porch with Roxie and Patches and stewed on the situation. I thought I could tell Reverend Willis that since God had healed him, that he might want to deliver the serpents himself, but I knew there was no way for me to prevail against him in an argument. I considered telling him that we didn't have room, but a half-dozen serpent boxes don't take up much space, and he'd just give me one of his sermons on the burden of possessions. The more I thought about it, the more I realized that this was a test of my loyalty and that angered me. I was grateful, but I didn't feel beholden. I resolved to just not stop by the Star of Morning until we returned, and to say that I'd decided I couldn't do it, and that I didn't want to bother him with my reasons while he was recovering. Though it didn't feel right as I tossed that option over, and I was haunted by a feeling that I would give in, I decided that I had decided.

Riley came home at noon. He was covered with wood chips and sweat, and he took off most of his clothes on the porch, much to Carleton's delight and Annie's chagrin.

"Daddy you are filthy," Annie said holding her nose and enunciating each word, "You're as dirty as a pig."

Carleton laughed, and when Riley began to snort like a mad old boar, the two kids collapsed into laughter. He snorted and stomped around on the porch, the whole place shaking under his weight, and the chips falling from his hair, and the more he clowned the more the kids shrieked. After a few minutes,

Riley plopped down on the steps, but Carleton badgered him to, "Be a pig again."

"Daddy's tired," he said. "I've been cutting wood all morning. After I shower we'll eat. Maybe Uncle Ize will get lunch started."

The sun had climbed high enough to burnish the ridge, so we ate inside where it was cooler, Riley having set the fan to oscillate air across the kitchen. The kids gobbled their food and endeavored to cajole Riley into some more horseplay, but he told them to go outside so, "Me and Uncle Ize can talk."

I remembered what Lillian had said about Carleton and Riley, as Carleton pitched a fit about Riley not playing with him right that minute. Riley didn't put up with it for a second. "Go outside or your bottom'll be sore till school starts," he said, "I'll come out and play later. Go."

Carleton backed out the front door, arms crossed and pouting, his lower lip stuck out far enough to trip on if he'd been walking forward. Annie asked if she could play in her room, but she scampered out the door behind her brother when Riley said, "What'd I say, girl?"

The door had barely shut when Riley said, "Cal came by. He says that the Detroit shit with Pervis is still a problem, but that the feds don't think I'm worth pursuing. The locals and the state shitheads are threatening to seize the new place on the grounds that it was bought with drug money."

"Fuck," I said.

"They offered a deal, but I'm shit scared that Lillian will explode about it."

I couldn't believe that the man sitting in front of me was the same guy who'd been making us all laugh fifteen minutes before, his face was ashen, his left leg jiggling so much that the kitchen table vibrated. I hadn't seen the look I saw in his eyes since we were kids and he'd just had the skin near-flayed off his ass with the Old Man's belt.

"What do they want?" I asked, my voice shaking.

"Even though they got no proof, not a fuckin' shred of proof, they want twenty grand and a plea of nolo contendre to possession with intent to distribute. That results in no jail time, but a record. It'll be all over the papers, Ize. She'll be gone like last year's leaves."

I knew he was right, but I lied. "I think you've worked enough charm on her to make this work for you," I said. "Offer accepting the deal as final proof that you've gone straight."

"Nice try Sherlock," my brother said, "That'll fly when cows do. She's too smart."

"Cal have any other ideas?" I said.

"He says we might win in court, but if we turn this deal down that they'll come after me, hammer and tong, in his words, and dig until they've crawled up my ass and out my nose. He said they'll harass Lillian and the people she works with. The fuckers. Either way I lose her."

We sat a long time. Every few minutes one of us would curse, or would start to say something, but mostly we sat and thought on it. I was sad beyond sad thinking about breakfast and the things Lillian had said about taking the kids and going away. I knew she'd do it. She was wounded and cornered by her own stubbornness, but she'd been burned. Unlike Lorena, though, she was still up for a fight, a down-in-the-dirt-tussle, and she'd have all the cards. It may be because Lillian has so much kindness and sweetness in her heart that she comes up so vicious when she reaches down for some fight.

Fred had an old terrier named Max. He looked like a tired, grade school, reading book dog, but if you startled him awake when he was sleeping, he'd tear a chunk out of any man, woman, or child. Lillian was the same way. Once, when I'd been drunk and passed out on the couch, she'd come to drop the kids off for the weekend. She tried to wake me up and I swatted at her. I didn't connect, but I brushed her chest. She grabbed my feet and pulled me off the couch so I landed on my back. I cracked my head and saw stars like I've never seen on the clearest winter night.

Before I could recover she was kneeling on my arms and cussing me out, her face inches from mine. She called me "a no-good-peckerheaded-hillbilly-goat-fucking-piece-of-shit," and a host of other things I can't now recall. When I left home that time, I figured that I would never get back into her good graces, and though I had, I knew there were no third chances with her.

Riley leaned over, his elbows flat on the table. "I'm gonna take the truck into town to wash it," he said. "The cocksuckers gave me until Monday to make up my mind."

I sat alone in the kitchen as a terrible dread that I recognized all too well swept into my heart. My mouth watered and I fought the lure of that first good gulp of an epic drunk. Sadness squeezed me like a python. I saw ghosts in front of the refrigerator; Mama, the Old Man, and someone it took me awhile to recognize as the old priest who'd told me to never despair. I closed my eyes and I saw Ella, the way I'd first seen her, holding a cup of coffee with an elegance that was as out-of-place in that Holyoke diner as a stray dog in church. I wanted to talk to my mother and I wanted to tear the shit out of my Old Man for making me such a coward, so damn afraid to do what I knew I should do. I wanted to tell the drunken son-of-a-bitch that all his beating on me hadn't made me tough, just scared, scared that there was no reason ever to feel safe in this world. But nothing in the house, palpable memories or visions, terrified me as much as the bottle of bourbon in the cupboard.

It was a new fifth, Lillian a modest imbiber, and Riley near a teetotaler, and less than an ounce was gone. The glass cool as snowmelt in my hand, the bottle balanced and snug as I gripped the neck, I was delighted to not have break the seal. I twisted off the top and raised the bottle above my head, the light streaming in the kitchen window splitting the amber into a prism on the refrigerator, the rainbow spilling over Carleton and Annie's drawings and report cards. My arm trembled and a few drops of the liquor shipped over the rim and onto my shirt cuff and wrist. My skin burned as I set the bottle on the table. I stared at the spots staining my shirt and a vision of the serpent's punctures in Reverend Willis's shoulder raked my eyes. I shook my head like a prizefighter stung by an uppercut, and glanced out the window at the sound of one of the kids squealing. Annie and Carleton were squatting beside each other peering into the stump of the maple we'd taken down, Annie pointing at something I couldn't see. My stomach roiled. Lorena had told me she could have no more children, and though her kids were warming to me, I could not imagine them loving me, and, as Carleton and Annie played, they seemed destined to be wrenched from me as well as from Riley.

I opened my wallet and edged my finger along the cool plastic of my first credit card, an equity charge card, which meant that even though I had no credit with anyone, as long as I kept money in an account at the bank, I could charge against it. Lorena and I had waited on a bench for most of her lunch hour one day, while a short woman, drenched in perfume, helped me fill out the application form. I had five hundred dollars worth of credit and we planned to use that to rent the van, but I began to wonder how far I could run on that much money. It was mine to spend until I used it up and the card was denied.

I was ahead for the first fucking time in my life, and I wanted to quit right then. I flicked the tip of my tongue into the neck of the bottle, the deep, caramel scent invading my nose. Then, in a moment of terror, screwed down the top. I was unsure if I had actually touched the bourbon, but I knew that I had tried to do just that, tease myself, less as a test and more as a justification to buckle beneath my sorrows and dread. When I realized that I hadn't, that I could place the bottle back in the cupboard without even a shot, I felt liked I'd kicked the Old Man's ass.

Riley returned from washing the truck and slumped at the table. "Ize," he said, "I love my kids so bad, and Lillian is the only woman I can imagine living with. If I lose them, I'll put one slug into the back of my throat, and you can feed me to somebody's hogs. If I lose them, I'm no better than the Old Man, and no better than what's been said about me since I could crawl."

I tried being brave. "Bullshit, Riley," I said, "We ain't neither of us him. Lillian may rip the skin off your balls, but she loves you and the kids too much to bail on you. She can work anywhere, and if you have to leave, we'll sell out and all go. What the hell has this ridge done for us?"

"Lily can be fierce. Remember when she lugged you off the couch and tore you a new asshole?"

"That was different. I'd been bowl-huggin' drunk around the kids," I said, but I knew where he was going, and that he was right. If he wound up in the paper or on the news, the last thing he'd see of Lillian was her backside heading for somewhere with a hospital and a beach.

I couldn't look at Riley, and I didn't dare speak or move, because that might start him back to worrying. We sat, quiet as we used to be when we were riding around on a Saturday, Riley chewing his lip, me drumming on my thigh with my thumbs, until he slapped the table so hard he tipped the saltshaker over.

"Hot-fuckin' damn," he said. "I got an idea. Watch the kids. I gotta see Cal." He didn't wait for an answer, just ran into his room and came out a few minutes later, tucking in his shirt and combing his wet hair with his fingers. "I'll be home soon as I can, Ize. I may be able to save my ass yet."

Riley's enthusiasm should have made me feel better, but the old blackness had engulfed me and I couldn't muster the optimism to swim all the way up to the surface.

I went out to the porch. The kids were trying to induce the dogs, who'd crawled into a burrow they'd dug under the barn on the first hot day of summer, to come out and play fetch with them, to no avail. Carleton gave up, and though Annie persisted a bit, they both asked if they could come inside and watch TV. I knew that Riley or Lillian would have said no, but I said yes.

When Carleton and Annie began to fight over what to watch, I sat between them on the couch and told them that I would pick the show and that they were free to go outside if they didn't like it. I felt bad that they only had each other. If they'd both been either boys or girls, they might have liked being together better than they did. Annie was bossy, but I couldn't blame her, as she was practically her brother's mother at times, and, when she didn't like any of the choices on the tube, he wouldn't go outside without her.

I decided we'd watch "The Price is Right." Our other choices were a talk show where they were discussing the secrets to a good sex life, which seemed inappropriate for the kids, and another show with two smug New Yorkers talking about Notre Dame football and the Academy Awards.

To my surprise and pleasure, the kids got into bidding on the prizes. Their guesses were as good as mine, though we all missed every item by a mile, and I remembered how a guy I'd picked apples for in Vermont one summer told me that, "If you have to ask the price of something you can't afford it."

A chesty, blonde woman won a washer and dryer and a year's supply of something that eliminates static cling, and a lanky black man with graying hair won a car by spinning a wheel, and when Bob Barker pointed to the left side of the stage and a leggy brunette opened a curtain to show a little Japanese sedan, he almost fell down. When the camera zoomed in, I saw a shine in his eyes like one of the Star of Morning ladies doing the Holy Ghost dance, and the spirit the anointed have when they raise a serpent above their head.

I had to get up three times to pass gas, my guts as balky as if I'd been on a binge, each time afraid I'd shit myself, so I sat on the toilet choking on my own smell. It didn't smell like shit, but like despair or fear, like the smell of old guys on the VA cancer ward with only a few weeks left.

I don't know how I beat the urge to have just a few hits from Lillian's bourbon, but I did find myself humming a melody I'd heard Reverend Willis hum. Finally, I tried to pray while I sat between the kids and watched the credits roll, while Bob yucked it up with the big showcase winner. But I hadn't learned how to do it, how to beg God for a favor, when I still couldn't imagine deserving one. Instead, I prayed for Reverend Willis, Lorena, Lillian, and the old priest. Then I asked God to be kind to Mama, and though I had been taught by Reverend Willis to pray even for those who did not love me, and for those I wanted to hate, I could not pray for the Old Man. I soldiered on thinking of folks and the more people I remembered to pray for the better I began to feel, so I added Lorena's mother, and her kids, Riley and his kids, and then added a special prayer for Ella.

The kids were playing marbles in the dooryard when Riley got back two hours later. He was as wired as he bounced in the door as he'd been depressed when he left. "I don't know why I pay my god-damned lawyer so much money, Ize," he said, flinging open the screen door. "Sometimes Cal ain't got the brains of a worm."

Riley could have been a lot of things, even an attorney, except that by tradition the Butts family has had as little to do with any faction of the legal system as possible. Riley's face was flushed and overwhelmed by a grin. "I told Cal to counter-offer," he said. "I told him I'd pay the twenty grand, but that I'd insist that it was cash left to me by our departed father, so I had not made any of it illegally. Therefore," he said, with a sweep of his hand, "No forfeiture."

"What'd Cal say?" I asked.

Riley clapped his hands and hooted. "First, he says we got one problem. That being that if the cash was the Old Man's it would be in old bills. So I told him I could cover that and that I'd admit to moving some it around in the bank over time."

"Doesn't the law call that money laundering?" I said.

Riley didn't answer that. "Cal liked it," he said, "He's setting up a meeting."

I knew I was only getting Riley's version of the conversation, but as lopsided as it was my brother is neither prone to exuberant exaggeration nor self-delusion.

"Cal say what the chances were your plan will work?" I asked.

"I told you," Riley said. "He likes it. You'll like it, too, when we get the new place done and all this shit is over."

I didn't answer him, and I declined his offer to ride over to

Beckley to buy some new saw chains, because I figured he'd rather ride alone and think out the fine points of his new plan, and because he'd said nothing to lift the cloak of self-pity I'd drawn over me. Besides he didn't want my two cents, just my approval.

"Suit yourself," he said as he left. "If you're not coming, I'll leave the kids here."

As I heard Riley drive off, I knew I should have felt a little better, but I didn't. Cal would have been straight with him and maybe Riley had hit on something, but I was reluctant to let my spirits improve. Mostly I was fearful of being on the road with Lorena when Riley's house of cards collapsed, when he'd be the most inclined to lose his nerve and strike out at his enemies, but, having whipped the bottle again, nothing was going to prevent me from taking Lorena north.

CHAPTER TWENTY-THREE

Lorena was so tickled to be going to pick up the van that I was sure she'd pee her panties. The cab of my truck reeked of grease and bar oil, and the fact that it was well over ninety and I had no air-conditioning made her jitters worse, because she'd just had her hair done and didn't want me to run with the windows all the way down.

Our appointment was for six, but Lorena was bound and determined to get there as soon as we could, so we found ourselves sitting in the waiting room at High Ridge Motors and Auto Leasing cooling our heels while the only salesman on duty took a young couple for a test ride in a used Ford Ranger.

Lorena snuggled next to me on the fake leather sofa, shaking like she used to after the first swim of the summer. She pawed at my hand and talked non-stop, asking me if I brought my credit card while assuring me that she had the traveler's checks, and reminding me that she wanted to eat lobster and see a moose in Maine. When she added that she had her mother resigned to our leaving, I began to fight my way out of my funk.

I stared at her legs, jiggling up and down, toes pointed on the floor, and realized that we hadn't had sex in days, and as I glimpsed her flex her calves and felt her fingernails graze the back of my hand, my gloom dispersed. Feeling the heat in her skin, I considered that she might be right about finding a place to start over. I had no idea what I'd do there anymore than I knew what I'd do if we didn't go, but I was going to hold on to her with the same strength I'd used to keep my bottle out of the hands of another desperate rummy on a hundred black nights.

When the paperwork was signed, the salesman showed me where to park my truck. "Since we won't have to plow while you're gone," he said, as if he expected us to laugh, "you can take the keys with you."

I have to admit that driving into town in that shiny van

with Lorena beaming beside me was as fine a sensation as I'd ever experienced with my clothes on. I still felt invisible in Blissfull, even after Riley's brush with celebrity, but Lorena waved to everyone she knew on the street or in passing cars, the Whipple smile seared into her face.

At the square, I had to wait for three stoplight changes as a farmer had stalled his tractor and couldn't get it to start. While we idled, Lorena said, "We need to see Theo before we leave. If he passed while we were gone, and I hadn't seen him, I'd forever regret it."

The gloom returned. I had hoped that we'd just go to her house, pack her gear, drive up to the old place, grab my things, and I'd be able to convince her to head north and spend the night in the van. The last time I'd been at the Star of Morning, Reverend Willis had been cheerful and in much less pain. He was propped up in his bed talking with the ladies who were still sitting vigil with him and working a tennis ball in his hand to get his strength back. I feared that he would convince Lorena to deliver the serpents.

In the previous months of sobriety, the blessings of a dried-out brain had become apparent to me, but the more alert I'd become, the more suspicious I became of things I would have ignored or not sensed when I was drunk. I was mortified to have wondered if Lorena and Reverend Willis had been closer than either had let on to me, but Lorena never called him Reverend Willis, always Theo, and she was the only one who did. If she knew, and I had no way of knowing if she did, that her sister had been bitten while pulling buds off premium reefer and not gathering serpents for religious purposes, her affection for him seemed out of place. On the other hand, I'd been thinking that if she cared for him in a romantic way there had been nothing to stop them from marrying, as they'd have hardly been the first in-laws in Blissfull to tie the knot.

At the Star of Morning, the crowd had spilled out of Reverend Willis's room and into the main part of the church. There were more little kids than I'd seen the last time, and more young couples, most of whom I didn't recognize. The old man from Jolo was sitting with Earvin whittling ash sticks into some kind of toy, strips of bark and wood flying before them and landing on a sheet on the floor. It had become more like a wedding reception than a vigil with tables of food and cases of spring water set up in front of the stage.

As Lorena and I approached Reverend Willis's room, the people parted the way as if we were dignitaries or the law, and I felt as if a clammy hand had clamped itself to my neck. We had to squeeze by an enormous woman who was praying out loud, her hands waving above her head, and sweat running in gouts down into the deep folds of her chins. The room smelled better than it had in days, but the stale scent of old sweat and tired breath hung in the air and the white walls seemed tinged with blue.

Once we'd struggled through the door, we pushed back against the wall, waiting for Reverend Willis to look up. He was holding hands and praying with two of the old ladies who knelt on either side of the narrow bed, and his eyes were slammed tight, his voice raw as a crow's. "Heal us Jesus, God Almighty we thank You for the promise of everlasting life. Amen," he said.

Once Reverend Willis locked his eyes on us, I knew what lay in store. I hated myself for having neither the resolve to say no, nor the courage to say yes. I decided to let Lorena do that. After blessing the old women, he asked everyone but Lorena and me to leave the room. I expected him to tell me to open the trunk and dig out the instructions, but he instead instructed Lorena and me to stand beside and take his hands, me the weakened one.

"Ize, Lorena, I am going to ask a favor of you, but I want you to hear all I may say, before you give me an answer," he said. "I may yet be called to my judgment. As I have no assurance of heaven, and I fear Hell with every fiber of my soul, I ask that you help me atone for my sins. If you have the love for me that I believe you do, please hear what I have to say."

He shifted on the bed and, with his strong arm, pushed

himself upright. When he spoke again, his voice was strong but low. "In our church, we do not hear confession like that old priest you met up north, Ize," he said staring at me. "We confess directly to God, and only God. We believe, and I am certain this is true, He can, and will forgive us for the trespasses we make if we truly repent and truly believe. I wronged my wife, I abandoned my issue, I fornicated and stole, and I desecrated this earthly body that God gave me, this very temple for the Holy Ghost. Now, the poison of Satan is in me, and I have to make peace with the Lord, or perdition awaits me, the everlasting fire of Hell." He paused, moved his gaze from me to Lorena and back to me and said, "Ize, help me to stand."

He felt small, almost without weight, as I locked my arm under his, reaching around his chest, avoiding the shoulder where he'd been bitten, and hoisted him upright. It was obvious that he had once been a strong man, especially in his forearms, and as he straightened, the muscles in his abdomen pulled his gut taut. With my help he shuffled to the front of the bed and stood before the trunk. He was naked save for a pair of worn white shorts with a button fly. "Lorena," he said, as if he was winded, "Please open the trunk. There is a gray woolen sock with a red toe on the bottom of the trunk. I believe it's at the back on the right side. I'd be obliged if you'd pull it out."

Lorena knelt down and rummaged in the trunk among Reverend Willis's clothes until she discovered the sock. It looked like a Christmas stocking from a catalogue, except that a string had been tied around the top of it. I'd seen thugs use an old sock like that filled with rocks to roll drunks in the skids and outside bars. "Lay it up on the bed, please," he said, "And untie the cord. "

Lorena stood up, closed the trunk, and placed the sock on the edge of the bed nearest Reverend Willis. "Go on and untie the cord, Lorena," he said. "Dump out what's inside for me."

Lorena untied the knot and turned the sock upside down, but the only thing which fell out was a small pocketknife. "Help her, Ize," he said. While Lorena held the sock at the toe, I fished out three rolled-up manila envelopes, a small white envelope stamped with the return address of a motel in Biloxi, a pocket New Testament, and a hand gun.

Reverend Willis stared at the things on the bed for some time before he spoke again. Worry crowded Lorena's face, and I saw that she was as weary from the rollercoaster ride Reverend Willis had us on as I was. I was as angry as I was confused, but to my surprise, calm. When Reverend Willis had said nothing for several minutes, I thought he was working us up like the congregation on a hot Sunday morning. Finally, Lorena said, "Theo, you still with us here?"

"By the grace of God I am, Lorena. One of these envelopes goes with the serpents to Billy Parsons. One goes to my wife, if you can find her, as does the New Testament, and one, the one with nothing written on it, is for you to open after the serpents have been delivered. The gun is to be thrown into the ocean, or dropped into a deep river. That must be done discreetly. In the little envelope you'll find the directions to where I believe my wife now resides, and a number to call to meet up with Billy, as well as instructions for tending to the serpents so they will reach him in safety. Please do not open your envelope until you have left Billy."

It just came out of me, and as much of a shock as it was, it felt good. "I won't agree to that," I said. "A gun that needs to be dropped into the ocean doesn't seem like the kind of thing I should be carrying around. It isn't fair to Lorena, either. I don't want to deliver the serpents, but I will do that. What I won't do is risk Lorena's freedom. Think of her kids and her mama."

Reverend Willis shrugged and turned to me, his eyes pleading, his face cracked with sorrow. "Isaac, I believe that I was sent once to find you, that God told me to pull off at that exit in Holyoke to find food for Lucius and I, and that even the time I first saw you drunk in the ditch that God was leading me to you. You do not owe me for the mercies of God, but I ask you to help me in my time of need. This is not about the money for the serpents. This is about my soul, my desecrated and sin-ridden soul. I have prayed each waking minute since

I was bitten, and I have come to believe that our Lord has led you back to me to help with my redemption. My sins are my own, but my redemption is in your hands."

My own soul was torn between believing that he was running a game on me, and a gnawing belief that I had to follow the mission through, and my mind raced back to the morning Lorena and I had taken the van to Beckley, when he'd told me about Jesus eating with the sinners, and how he even ate his last supper with those who, in the end, denied and betrayed him.

It was no different than falling off the wagon. Each time you know it might end in a flophouse with a roaring headache, or on the street with some cop kicking you to move along, or in the weeds with piss-soaked pants and shit-striped skivvies, or in the VA with a shrink and weary nurses trying to hydrate you to live again, or the morgue. All poor choices. The first belt goes down and there is a rush, not only from the booze, but from the adrenaline. A mighty adventure is about to begin, and you're signed on until the boat limps back to port or founders on the rocks and you go down with it. "Explain the gun," I said.

"I cannot do that, Ize. I am begging for all of eternity. The Lord can forgive any sin, and as I have prayed through this torment I have seen those signs. What I cannot do is make my sin your sin, and to explain this gun would do that," he said.

He staggered a step toward the bed and braced himself against the trunk lid with his good hand.

"I'll take the gun," Lorena said, her eyes fierce and her breathing heavy. "Isaac, we will not discuss this."

I've never been a good gambler, nor known the thrill card players say they get when the stakes are high, and though I wanted to stand my ground, I realized as we stood in the weak light of that bare room that the only thing I could not lose was Lorena. "The gun I will agree to," I said, "But no bullets."

Reverend Willis smiled, not the pleased kind of smile that wrinkled his face when he'd captured a serpent, or won a point in a discussion or disagreement, but a kind, grateful smile, the smile I'd seen in Lorena's eyes when I'd held her to me in the soft moments when our hearts quieted and our breath came easy on the heels of bone-rattling loving. "No bullet shall ever enter this weapon, again," he said.

Reverend Willis shuffled to his closet and reached down among the shoes and yellowed cardboard boxes on the floor. When he drew himself up, he grasped an aged attaché case in his good hand. "Take this with you," he said. "It locks. The combination is OXI, the last three letters in Biloxi.

Lorena placed the envelopes and the gun in the case, shut the lid, and locked and unlocked it a few times. Reverend Wills tried his best to encircle us with both arms and ask us to pray with him, the smell of his wound lightly masked by aftershave and sweat. I closed my eyes and though I heard his voice, my mind blocked out his voice. I had my own praying to do, but I couldn't find the words.

When he'd finished praying, Reverend Willis hugged us both and ask for Lorena to help him get back beneath the covers. When I asked why he needed the blankets drawn up when it was so hot in the church, he said, "To sweat out the serpent's evil," and closed his eyes. Nestling his head into the pillow, his eyes shut, he said, "Go now. Godspeed. Believe on Me says the Lord, and ye shall have ever-lasting life."

When we left Reverend Willis's room, the church was empty save for Earvin who'd stacked the serpent boxes in the back of the van, lashed them together with ratchet straps and tied the bundle to the legs of the rear seat. I told him that he couldn't do that because the seat would be folded down as a bed. He glared at me as if to warn me off such a sinful notion, but I didn't care. I just wanted to see Blissfull in my rear view as I headed up Steadman's Grade. Earvin rearranged the boxes so they would be secured to the inside handle of the rear door, which we had no intention of using. "The serpents will not need food or water until they are delivered to the believer at the other end of the trip," he said. "But be sure this stays locked or a sudden stop might cause the handle to open."

I liked Earvin enough, but I didn't like that he knew about

Lorena and I having the serpents with us, and he'd clearly been told where they were headed or he wouldn't have mentioned how long they could go unattended. The difficulty with being sober is all the chaos. In drunken oblivion, the sounds and the smells and the fears are subdued, muted, off in the distance like the call of a hawk, or the scent of new grass, the haunted pull of the past. Too many things I would have given no second thought to had I been drunk unnerved me, and I knew that my only hope to conquer my uneasiness lay in the ultimate success of two weeks on the road with Lorena.

CHAPTER TWENTY-FOUR

It was full dark Friday by the time we hit the interstate. Hiram had been late getting the kids, and Lorena wouldn't leave until he'd come for them. Part of this was not wanting to rile her mother, part that she had no faith in Hiram. When he did show up, I knew she wanted to cuss him out, but Lorena never fights her battles with him in front of the kids or me.

The van ran much smoother and quieter than the Star of Morning's clunker, and the dashboard looked like some thing from Star Trek. I played with the cruise control until I got the hang of it, and set it at seventy-four. Lorena fiddled with the radio and CD player, and then the air-conditioning. She switched on the dome light and pulled the manual from the glove box so she could read up on the other features of what was called the cabin. She located the vanity and map mirrors, the emergency tool kit beneath the passenger seat, and the electric controls to raise and lower the seat, pushing hers forward and back and playing with what was called its lumbar support system.

As a kid, I had envied boys like Malcolm Greaves who had a car they kept shined up, and who drove around with good-looking girls. I figured they got to feel things I'd never feel, and though my mind was pestered by the serpents and the gun, Lorena sitting beside me, her feet up on the dash, her dress at mid-thigh, singing along to the radio and going over the next day's itinerary, as she called it, was as powerful a rush as I'd ever known. Feeling like you belong in the world, and that someone else knows it, lifts your step, and I found myself sitting tall in the seat and feeling that I had the right to be there. I knew in my gut that this was one of the times in my life that I could not call attention to myself without peril, but I felt too good not to strut a little.

Our first night of sharing the van with the serpents was spent in a rest stop near the Virginia border. We'd planned on going further north, but the ebb and flow of the day had worn us both out. Lorena fixed up the bed, while I stepped out and stretched my legs by walking down to the tourist information center. I brought back two cold bottles of spring water and a complimentary Virginia is for Lovers bumper sticker. It turned out to be a noisy, truck-infested spot, and as the night wore on we both tossed around. We'd fallen right off to sleep, but a couple of kids, laughing and clowning a few spots over, woke us both up and Lorena snuggled close to me. She was sleeping in a large T-shirt, emblazoned with Wild Wonderful West Virginia across the front, and I thought of how that described her, especially when she'd been that skinny kid on a leeched out farm. I felt for her breasts, her skin warm and smooth and she gave me a slow, musty kiss, as she began easing her arms out of her sleeves. I shucked my shorts and fused my belly to hers. "Slowly," she said, "We've got all night for this, because I sure don't think we'll get much sleep." Lorena doesn't just hold onto you, she tries to absorb your entire body through her own thin frame. She's bruised my ribs with her knees, because her legs are so strong from tramping all over the ridge as a kid working that bony side hill farm, and because she loves sex. She told me once, "Ize, it's something I'm good at."

When she came, she was on top of me and she buried her face in my shoulder about as deep as the rattler had put his fangs into Reverend Willis, muffling her pleasure. Though I quickened my pace, she rolled off of me and tugged me on top of her, locking her legs around me and spurring her heels into the small of my back. She had me so tight I almost couldn't move, but then she began to rotate her hips like the blades of a giant ceiling fan coming up to speed. I still couldn't move too much, but I didn't have to. Though we had better shocks and springs than the Star of Morning van, the vehicle was rocking and the serpent boxes, though not the serpents themselves, were rattling against each other and the rear door. When Lorena went over the top the second time, I thought she'd broken my back. She slacked a little and I pushed for glory until the world exploded into millions of dots of color and I heard my voice calling her name.

We spent the next night in Delaware at a nice motel near the beach. Before going to bed, we got some take-out barbeque and parked the van in a lot over looking the water. It was high tide, the beach swallowed up by the ocean. We sat with the windows open and listened to the rush of the water onto the sand and the funny sizzling sound it made as it retreated. Lorena insisted on wading into the surf, holding the hem of her dress high up on her legs. She looked as beautiful as she ever had, not in the perfect way Lillian does, but at that moment, sexier. Lillian is so good looking sometimes she makes me feel clumsy and ugly, while Lorena can make me believe that I deserve to be with her. As she played tag with the waves, I remembered being at the mall with Lillian and the kids, and noticing the men ogling her and then glancing at me and shaking their heads, no doubt wondering if there was any justice in this world. With Lorena, out alone, or with her kids, people assume we're together.

The trip from the rest stop had been easy and short, but the lack of sleep the night before had sanded down our energy pretty thin. Lorena dried her legs off and we sat in the van until the sky was a soft red and the sea as dark as a bottle of tawny port. "Red sky at night, sailor's delight," Lorena said. "I have no clue what it means, but I'm happy, Ize."

At the motel, for the first time in our lives, we made love in a bed, a bed so big we could lie across it and not hang over the edge, and I could taste traces of the ocean on her skin. This time, when Lorena came, she cried.

We left the motel just before check-out time at eleven, and though it was Sunday morning, the traffic was heavy all the way to New Jersey. We were surprised to discover that there is no north to south interstate in Delaware, Lorena having somehow missed that in her research, and that giant chicken farms abound along the flat plains.

At the New Jersey border, Lorena decided she didn't want to drive on the turnpike so she ordered me to turn off as soon as we crossed the state line. We started out following route 40 east, but soon Lorena was hollering to me to "hang a right," or "go left at that sign," until we were riding across a vast swamp that felt as southern as South Carolina or Georgia. Battered bungalows and trailers shot up out of the scrub or hunkered back in the piney woods, and we rode for miles without a sign of a store, or gas station, though we did pass several small, weathered churches with hand-painted signs announcing the topics for the weekly sermon. Satan Doesn't Fear A Dusty Bible, and, There's Only One Kind Of Insurance For Life Everlasting, are the two I remember. As it was the Sabbath, the pocked-dirt parking lots were full, and cars spilled along the shoulder of the road in each direction.

It was the only place in the north that I'd seen the wariness you see on the people from the deep hollers—that mix of suspicion and anger and shame. Lorena said, "Man, these are swamp hillbillies if I've ever seen such a thing in my born days." I laughed because I get a kick out of her when she speaks like the high mountain people. I don't believe she was making fun of them as much as laughing at herself for being a hillbilly at heart.

It wasn't until we got gas at a town called Red Lion that it hit me that we were in the north. The gas jockey was a short, barrel-chested guy with a turban who made change from a wad of greasy money he kept in the front pocket of his baggy work pants. He was flying around serving a station full of cars. When I offered to pump my own gas, he said that was against the law in New Jersey, which seemed particularly odd to me because in my experience Yankees have more self-help stores, gas stations, drive-up banks, and the like than southerners do. I'd been in small towns in the north where every restaurant was a fast-food joint, not one diner or hole-in-the-wall coffee shop like down home.

I memorized Lorena gulping it all in, the machine-gun speech, the nasally accents, the frantic pace of everything, cars weaving in and out of traffic, flipping their lights at you to pull over so they can pass you even when you're going ten better than the speed limit. As Lorena's eyes raked across the traffic and the sights, I wondered if she was still thinking about us leaving Blissfull for good now that she'd begun to taste and feel and hear the north. She'd made three calls from the motel, one to each set of twins and one to her mother, and I knew that no matter how much you may think you want to quit the mountains, escape the suffocating and judgmental eyes of Blissfull, that your ridge has a pull as powerful as any there is. It's like a great rubber band that stretches away from home as far as you want it to, but tugs just enough to remind you that you are hewn from that stony soil, and that it is the place you should be laid to rest. The only other people I'd met like that were New Englanders, so it must be in the rocks.

Being naïve to the ways of Yankee traffic, we managed to find ourselves crossing the George Washington Bridge at four o'clock on Sunday afternoon in the summer. In the Star of Morning Van, I'd have been afraid of a boil over in such a big jam, but the temperature gauge didn't move a notch as we inched along, over the course of an hour, to the tollbooth. Once we were on the bridge, I eased into the right lane and Lorena stared at the Manhattan skyline. She made me promise to take her there sometime, and I said I would. I was paying so little attention to the road, my eyes focused on her slack-jawed gaze, that I nearly wrecked merging into the proper lane for Connecticut.

We had reservations at a place in New London. I've stayed in motels, hotels, flophouses, rooming houses, and a few other establishments that let beds or rooms, but the Graceful Tide Bed and Breakfast was a first for me. It was like being invited to someone's house, except that you had to pay. Our room had a high, narrow antique bed with a canopy, two tall dressers, a clothes rack, an ancient steamer trunk at the foot of the bed with a sign on it that said, "Extra Quilts," and an upholstered, high-backed wing chair. Lorena was over-the-moon, but I was afraid to sit down as the whole place reminded me of a dollhouse. We could walk downtown, and when we did we found a small bar and restaurant, Dutch's, and had big burgers and fried clams, with little salads and iced teas.

Strolling the streets after dinner, I realized that for Lorena it must have been like being in a foreign country. We nodded to a black woman sitting on a bench holding hands with a white man, something you still aren't likely to see in Blissfull, and later passed two men sauntering arm in arm along the street. A group of kids went by speaking what sounded like French, and later an Hispanic man, disappointed to discover that we weren't locals, pulled his car to the curb and asked us for directions. For some reason that made me think of the serpents and the gun, and my guts tightened as I wondered if I had locked the van. Not wanting to panic Lorena, I told her I needed to pee and we ambled back to The Graceful Tide.

We spent Monday and Tuesday in Rhode Island, swimming and sunning at Misquamicut Beach and staying in a state campground. Though the van heated up in the day, the night sea breezes cooled it down and we never did unpack the tent. Lorena favors strapless sundresses so she won't sport the classic red neck tan like me. Working with Riley had bronzed my face, arms and neck, but the rest of my skin was the color of clotted milk. Lorena slathered me in sunscreen, and bought me a straw hat that came with a picture of a rooster sitting next to a sunburned woman in a red bikini with a caption that read, "There's Only One Kind Of Rhode Island Red I Want!" As soon as my skin showed the slightest evidence of the sun's rays, she'd grease me up again. If I protested she'd threaten to pull down my trunks and coat my bare ass with it as well. I couldn't help but indulge her every time that Whipple enthusiasm invaded her face.

I guessed that I looked like a rube tourist, but I was ecstatic to be with Lorena and away from snakebites, the law, and Riley and Lillian's tinderbox. I considered calling Riley, but if I didn't get an answer, or if I did and it was bad news, I knew it would ruin my mood and I owed Lorena better.

When we left Rhode Island on Tuesday morning, it was misting and dim thunder rolled to the west. I turned the wipers on and figured out how the set the speed so they cleared the window just about the time they needed to. Lorena fell asleep soon after we were on the highway. She'd put on jeans and a sweatshirt and brought a blanket up front with her, which she'd wrapped up in before buckling her seatbelt.

The rain turned steady and the horizon disappeared. The air got steamy and I considered turning on the air-conditioning, but I was afraid it would make Lorena cold. I kept the window cracked enough to let the air circulate without letting too much water in.

Lorena woke up when I stopped quickly to avoid plowing into the last of a line of cars that had slowed for a squall. Each time I had to brake hard, I'd peer in the rearview mirror, or look back over my shoulder to see if Earvin's straps and knots were holding, as a few times the jolt had jostled the boxes enough to set the rattles going and quake my stomach.

A few minutes later we slowed to a stop. Emergency lights flashed behind us and I knew we trailed a wreck. A dread settled on me and though I tried not to let it show by whistling and making small talk, Lorena smelled it out like a hound on a convict's trail. She reached over and said, "You okay?"

"I'm sick of this damn Yankee traffic," I said. "Other than that I'm fine, you?"

Lorena didn't answer at first. She unhooked her belt, unwrapped herself from the blanket, and said, "Soon, we'll have done what Theo asked of us. After that, you don't have to do his bidding any more. You won't owe him an earthly thing, and neither will I." She re-buckled her seatbelt, tossed the blanket into the back, opened the window and stuck her head out as far as she could. "Rain feels good on my face," she said. "According to Triple A, you get off at the next exit."

Yankees have even more sayings about the weather than southerners. Phil Godreaux, one of the undertakers at Plourde's, was from a little town near Madawaska Maine, which he showed me was at the far northern tip of the state. As a kid he'd spoken French at home, and he and Mr. Plourde's grandfather, who, though he'd long retired, came to the home most days, used to blabber away in it for hours. Phil said that in Maine there were two seasons, winter and the Fourth of

July. Mr. Plourde used to say that in Massachusetts, there were four, "Before winter, winter, still feels like winter, and road construction." I was beginning to understand the construction one. I'd just about get up to a speed where I could set the cruise control, when we'd be narrowed into one lane. Lorena had hoped to be at out motel near Bath, Maine in the early afternoon, but the rain and the traffic and the construction were slowing us down and sapping our energy. I knew her heart was set on a lobster dinner in a restaurant overlooking a blue ocean, but purple clouds were draped low across the sky, obscuring the hilltops, and idling in traffic, we couldn't feel any breeze. "Fuck," she said, when just after we'd gotten rolling we drifted to a crawl again, "We'll never get there like this."

"If we can't go out tonight, we can do it on the way back," I said. This caught Lorena as funny.

"You looking on the bright side, now there's a change," she said. "I'm getting squirrelly is all, Ize. I'm worried about the kids, not that there's any reason for it, worried about Mama, Theo."

"But not us, I hope."

"Not at the moment, baby," she said.

"Still thinking about leaving Blissfull?" I said, not sure I wanted to hear the answer, but feeling she'd invited me to ask.

"I don't know if I could live up here, but Rhode Island was nice. I like the ocean, and as much as I'd miss the sunsets in the hills, and the colors in the fall, I could learn to live at the beach."

"Warmer in Carolina or Georgia," I said.

"Then next vacation, we'll go there," she said.

The traffic broke up when we got into New Hampshire, and I pulled off at an exit to get gas. While I was filling up at a Sunoco station I'd found by wandering into Portsmouth, Lorena scoured the coolers for the makings of a lunch that we ate as we drove. I'd done almost all the driving, and we were both happy with that arrangement, because it allowed Lorena to navigate and absorb everything she could see through the van's spacious windshield. Lorena's a great driver when she knows where she is, but in unfamiliar territory she slows way down, and forgets to signal turns. Not signaling put her in good company up north, especially in Massachusetts, but damn near got us run over a few times as well. I drove over the big bridge that crosses the Piscataqua River into Maine, a bottle of spring water between my legs and a ham and cheese sandwich balanced on the console, Lorena feeding me chips and bites of pickle and feeling as high as a bank robber getting away.

Each mile north pulled us farther from the storm. By Portland the sky was lifting. A wind came up, enough to rock the van and make me put both hands on the wheel, and by the time we found our motel, the sun had almost broken through the haze.

When we signed in, the desk clerk looked at the card I'd filled out and told us he was a West Virginian, too. "From just south of Frostburg, Maryland," he said, which is a part of the state I don't know much about. He was wearing a shirt that said, Bowdoin College, and hearing him pronounce it, I was glad I hadn't tried to say it first. He said he would be a senior there in the fall and that he hoped to go to law school after that. He was agreeable in the way southerners are, but his accent was Yankee and polished, and the last subject I wanted to get into a discussion about at that moment was anything to do with the law or lawyers. I didn't take a liking to the kid, but Lorena pumped him for a good place to eat and he told us that one of his three summer jobs was washing dishes at what he called a lobster pound that he said had, "The best deal on the peninsula."

I had no idea what peninsula he was talking about, but Lorena was willing to trust his judgment as a fellow West Virginian, even one who sounded like he was from Pennsylvania, so we him asked for directions. He said, "I get off here at six. You can follow me if you like." Lorena allowed that would be fine, though six seemed a trifle early to me for a romantic dinner you'd been planning for weeks, and she introduced us by our first names. He told us his name was Thad and handed us our room key. "Room number Twenty-six. You can reach it by going down the hall to the right here," he said pointing the way, "Or you can park down at the end of the building and enter through the door there. All rooms are entered from the inside hallway. Ice machines on every floor by the stairs, and the pool closes at nine on weekdays."

The first thing Lorena did in each motel room was put her bag on the floor by the left side of the bed, use the bathroom, lie down on the bed and pronounce it comfortable. Then she would get up, throw open the curtains so she could see the view, and adjust the air-conditioning to her liking. I'd been living on my brother's couch for so long that the rooms we'd rented embarrassed me. I felt as if I was waiting for the real owner to show up and toss me out on my scrawny, hillbilly ass.

We settled in as much as you do when you're only staying a night. It isn't like you need the drawers in the bureau, or all the hangers in the closet, so I generally put my shaving kit on the bathroom counter, and my bag on the floor, unless they have those collapsible luggage stands.

The room faced the pool and looked across the parking lot to where the land rolled away downhill toward the water. Across the bay, another strip of land was emerging from the haze, and a few boats sailed between the necks, their white sails and hulls visible against the gray and silver clouds. The water reminded me of the signs on the highway bridges as we'd passed over rivers, Piscataqua, York, Mousam, Presumpscot, Royal, and I shivered as the memory of those rivers conjured up the gun in the van. While Lorena had been showering in the bathhouse at the campground in Rhode Island, I'd examined it, discovering the danger in it and the likely reason why Reverend Willis wanted it gone. I know rifles from being a mountain kid and from basic training in the Army, but Reverend Willis's pistol was the first Glock nine millimeter I had ever held. A seething terror had welled in my guts as I recalled that it was the type of gun that the Detroit cops said had killed Pervis Meeker, and the fact that it held no clip offered me no great comfort. I shook to think that it might help to explain the miles on the Star of Morning Van, and Dale Saunders easing the credit card back at Lorena, and Reverend Willis being so concerned about Riley getting harassed by the law, but most of all it surely might explain the fear of Hell in Theobald Willis, Signs Preacher.

What I did not know, even if all my considerable conjectures were correct, was how Lorena or Riley might be involved in all this. If I was granite certain they were clear, I might have risked breaking every code I'd been raised by and given the gun to Sergeant Wright, handing her the biggest bust of her career, but I couldn't risk that and Reverend Willis, if he were the con man Riley thought him to be, had damn sure banked on just that. Any way I tried to cast it, I might have been abetting Pervis Meeker's murder and the thought riled my belly like dry ice.

I'd been staring out the window turning over Reverend Willis's speech to us before we agreed to make his delivery for him, especially the part where Lorena said we wouldn't discuss it anymore, when she came up behind me and put her hands around my waist and fiddled with my belt buckle.

Later, while Lorena showered, I called Riley collect, which is how I've made most every call I've ever made home. Annie answered and it took her a few seconds to understand what the operator wanted, but eventually I was put through and she said, "Hi Uncle Ize, where are you?"

"I'm in Maine honey, way up north. Have your Mama show you on a map."

"She already did last night. You're coming back aren't you?" she asked.

"In about ten days, Annie. I promise. Is your Daddy there?"

I heard the phone clatter against the wall and Annie run out onto the porch. And holler, "Daddy, it's Uncle Ize. He's in Maine."

Riley assumed that something was wrong. "What's the matter, Ize?"

"Nothing," I said. "What's up with Cal?"

"Looks good. Gonna cost me a bundle, but the Old Man takes the fall. I get hit with tax penalties, but I've explained that to Lillian."

"She's okay with that?"

"She was hotter than a pissed-off panther for two days, but she's coming around. She ain't looking for a new apartment at any rate. You'll be on the couch a while longer unless you take up housekeeping with Lorena."

I've never been particularly adept at small talk, and I truly despise talking on the phone. When I can't see someone, I don't get enough from what they're saying to judge what they're thinking and I don't care for that feeling at all. "Riley, I need to ask you something about Pervis," I said.

"You on a cell phone?"

"No," I said.

"Still, don't be a damn fool, Isaac. I got nothin' to do with what happened to Pervis, but you just bringing it up can cause me trouble. Hell, this phone might be tapped for all I know. You need to ask me something wait 'til you get home. Bye."

Riley hung up. I don't think he was as angry, but he was surely at the end of the conversation. I couldn't make up my mind whether he was telling me the truth, but I realized that I might never have been able to do that anyway. Sitting on the edge of the bed stewing about the complications in my life, I realized that it was time to finish what I'd begun, that I had to dump the gun, deliver the serpents and the envelopes, and pray that Lorena loved me and wasn't a mere confederate in a scam to save Reverend Willis's ass.

I heard the shower stop, and Lorena singing, and I knocked and asked to come in. The sight of her wet nakedness sucked the wind from my lungs. For a second, I was back in the creek. The glaring overhead light and white-tiled walls reflected her tanned skin and bleached-bone teeth. I kissed her minty mouth and held her warm, round cheeks in my hands.

Lorena adored dinner, though she was pretty messy with it. She ordered the bigger of two sizes of lobster, and a second order of steamers. Seeing her thin, Whipple face grinning over the top of her paper bib, I had to hold back tears. The kind of joy radiating from her eyes isn't something I've seen that often in my life. She said she loved the food and the view of the harbor, and she said she loved me, but all my uncertainties about Reverend Willis invaded my mind in a flood of gut-clenching fear. I knew that I had to know, and I could think of only one way to find out so I reached across the table, took Lorena's buttery hand in mine and asked her to marry me.

She stopped in mid bite and fixed her eyes hard on mine. "Ize, I love you more than any man I have ever loved. I've told you that I can't make the wrong choice again. I'll drown myself if I have to go through the hurt I've been through again. If you can swear to me that you will never touch another drop of liquor, and that no matter how old and creased this face gets, and no matter how saggy my boobs are, or how many varicose veins I have on these skinny old legs of mine, that no matter how hard it may be to help me raise four kids and tend to my Mama, who will never cotton to you so long as she breathes, that you will love me and stay with me, the answer is yes. But if you find any weak spot in your heart, I beg you to tell me now, and I'll be content to go on as we are, until either we drift away or that doubt dies."

My heart told me that I knew, and I said, "Knowing all those things, I want to marry you."

Someone watching us from across the restaurant might have thought we were having a fight the way the tears were running down our cheeks. Lorena's paper bib was soaked and she'd balled up half the napkins in the holder. I used the back of my hand and the sleeve of my T-shirt. Lorena stopped crying for a second to laugh. "You have got to be the only man in the world that proposed to a woman who's just got her period in the middle of their first vacation. We are a pair. Guess we always have been," she said.

We held hands across the table while our tears dried. Lorena looked absurd sitting in her wet bib picking at a mound of damp napkins and finishing her second bowl of clams. The empty lobster carcasses and shells overflowed the extra plates the waiter had brought to us. Watching the waiters and waitresses scuttle around the room, I recalled a time I was working as a dishwasher in a decent restaurant in Ohio, when I'd been asked to come out into the dining room with all the staff and sing Happy Anniversary while a cupcake with a single candle in it was brought to a table where a couple were celebrating their tenth. When Lorena excused herself to the ladies room, I wondered if I should ask the waiter for something like that, but I was afraid that if Lorena cried anymore she'd be as dehydrated as the rummies at the VA.

I paid the bill and left a good tip, not so much for the service, but because it seemed right to remember what had happened between Lorena and me. Passing the kitchen I saw Thad loading plates into a dishwasher. I would have felt sorry for him, but he was a college kid and it wouldn't be his life's work. I waved to him and he came over to see how we liked our meal.

"Best one I ever had," Lorena said.

We stayed up until after midnight talking and making plans and promising to be patient with each other. I held my hand on Lorena's stomach as we lay in the dark and she reached into the fly of my shorts. "There's no need for that, Lolo," I said.

"You haven't used that name since we were kids, Ize. I thought you'd forgotten that you called me that."

"I forgot very little about you," I said, "Though I wish I could forget a little more about me sometimes."

I felt her lips press cool on my chest, and I wondered for a fleeting few seconds if we'd become like the bitter old people I'd met from time to time, the ones who bitch that their wife doesn't want to make love, or that their husband wants only to sit in his bass boat and drink beer, but I decided that we could never be those people, because we'd beaten all the bitterness that could be expected of us and only a secret could hurt us now.

CHAPTER TWENTY-FIVE

Lewiston was easy enough to find and didn't look any different to me than Holyoke, New Britain, Nashua, or any other northern mill town I'd seen in my travels. Finding Reverend Willis's ex-wife in the Rising Sun trailer park was another story. We had his directions, but they weren't very good and we were forced into stopping at three different convenience stores before we found someone who set us straight. Even then, we were faced with a maze of dirt roads named for trees that seemed to have no pattern to them. Our directions only took us as far as the park itself and no one we stopped to talk to was any too enthusiastic about giving a couple of southerners any information.

Finally, we pulled up by a unit where a guy with a long gray beard and ponytail was polishing a Harley. I'd stopped because he had a Stars and Bars on one of the handlebars, and though I'm not one to fly it, or have ever owned one; I figured that if we had any chance it would be with a fellow southerner.

I told him who I was looking for and he said in a heavy French accent, "Her name's not Willis anymore, it's Brouillard. She married my cousin. They live in Auburn. What you want with her?"

It dawned on me that I had no answer for that question, so I just said, "We have a package from her ex-husband we promised to give to her."

"You can give it to me," he said.

"I can't," I said. "I have to deliver it to her."

"Suit yourself, you know Auburn, eh?" he said.

"No," I said.

He turned to Lorena and after looking her over he said, "You?"

"My first time in Maine," Lorena said.

"I draw you a map," the man said, " If you got a pen."

He sketched a map on the back of the envelope I had for Lou-Ann, and went over the directions five or six times each time adding landmarks and approximate distances, as if just recalling them, and I tried to make a note of them. We thanked him and wound our way out of the park

I knew we wouldn't arrive as a surprise, and when we found the house on a side street near the river, Lou-Ann was waiting for us along with a surly-looking boy of about sixteen. He was trying to look tough, his arms folded across his chest, and his feet spread shoulder width apart. He hadn't outgrown the gawky stage, and his fierce face would have been comical if its fire hadn't paled beside the rage in his mother's eyes. I pulled the van to the curve, and rolled down the window.

"Lou-Ann?" I asked.

"Mrs. Brouillard will do," she said.

"I have an envelope from Reverend Theobald Willis that he wanted me to give to you," I said in as friendly a way as I could as the boy cracked his knuckles loud enough for me to hear over the purr of the van.

"Reverend, so that's his new con is it? Tell that worthless son-of-a-bitch that I don't want anything from him, and no one in my family does either."

I didn't know what to do next, but Lorena got out of the van and went to the sidewalk. "Ma'am," she said, "Theo has been snake bit bad. He might make it and then again it might go septic on him and he'll die. He gave me and Ize this envelope to give to you and the boy. He told me that he'd sinned awful against you, and that he deserved to suffer for what he'd done. He's a man of God now. If you can't forgive him, at least take the envelope so we can have leave of our promise to him."

My heart sunk. Lorena had just told the woman something I thought only I knew. In my heart, I cursed Reverend Willis for playing us off against each other. If I hadn't heard Lorena say that she loved me, I'd have believed that she was using me as well. Every muscle in me spasmed at once and I could hear myself pant.

Lou-Ann stepped toward the curve, holding her hand up to the boy not to follow. She recognized a custom in Lorena's formality. I don't think a Yankee could quite have understood what had happened. Lorena had made taking the envelope from her a simple obligation to one who had gone to great trouble to make their word good. "I have no malice toward you," Lou-Ann said, accepting the envelope from Lorena. "If he lives, you tell him that we want nothin' to do with him and if he dies the devil is welcomed to him. I appreciate you'all coming by, and I bid ye good day."

Lorena got back in the van and we sped off. "You hear her say, 'bid ye good day?" she said. "That woman is a long way from home."

"When did he tell you about Lou-Ann?"

"He didn't. I knew he had a family once 'cause he carried pictures in his wallet. I guessed the rest. Don't have to be a damn detective to figure that out. The boy looks just like him."

"You didn't listen at the door when he told me?"

"No, Ize, I listened at the damn window. I don't lie to you, so don't get me cross. Look. When Theo stayed with Hiram and me after Lenora died, I washed his clothes and his wallet fell out of his pants. I saw the picture; I took it out and on the back it said, Lou-Ann and Teddy. In that picture the boy was maybe two. He looked just like him. Think, Ize. He's worried he might die; he knows she hates him and he had us right willing to do his dirty work. Theo's a good man, but he sure as hell ain't a saint. Who is? You got to learn to trust me."

"I trust you, Lorena, but I don't trust him anymore and that scares me."

Lorena kept trying to explain things, but the more she spoke the more doubts I had. When she stopped long enough for me to speak without interrupting her, I said, "I'm sorry."

"For what?" she said.

I answered, "Because it felt like we were having a fight."

Our instructions for delivering the serpents were vague at best. We were supposed to drive to Rumford, a town out in the western Maine mountains, and call Billy Parsons. I'd lived in a motel in Rumford for a month once while working on a cleaning crew at the paper mill in neighboring Mexico. Our gang had been over in the White Mountains of New Hampshire for a month before that, working in Berlin, and in Westfield, Massachusetts before that, but I remembered Rumford because the rank smell of the Mexico stacks left me perpetually sick to my stomach. We worked the night shift cleaning machines and workrooms, and spent the days sleeping and drinking. I got fired for being loaded on the job, and in the dead of a winter night hitchhiked to Portland, where I holed up at the Sally for a week before heading out again.

Lorena tried to navigate us out of Auburn and between her studying the map and me watching the road we found our way onto Route 4. We weren't supposed to make the delivery until the next day, but I was hopeful that Billy would take the serpents off our hands a little early. The afternoon was cool and even along the highest peaks there wasn't a cloud. The Maine sky is a harder, richer blue than I've seen anywhere else on the east coast. The hills at home are foggier, which is why along the way from Virginia to Georgia they're called the Smoky or Blue Ridge Mountains.

I called Billy's number from a gas station near a series of enormous waterfalls on the Androscoggin River that nearly drowned out the ring, but got no answer or answering machine. We sat in the van gaping at the river like the tourists in West Virginia do at the New River Gorge; log trucks and semis toiling past us from time to time blocking our view. A sharp breeze blew the smoke from the mill's stack away from us, and I tried to imagine how beautiful a spot it must have been before anyone had tried to make the river work for them.

Lorena looked up O'Neall's Corners on the map and suggested that we could drive as far west of Rumford as Bethel and find a room. We drove by a slew of motels, many advertising "Canadian Money at Par in July and August," though several still had out their, "Skiers Welcomed," banners, until Lorena decided on The Madison, a place with a restaurant that sat on a small hill above the river east of Bethel.

After dinner, I tried Billy again with no luck. Lorena called home. I always left the room when she called home, so I'd miss the row if she were fighting with her mother. I went to the van, closed the curtains, and took the gun out of its hiding place. The Androscoggin looked like as good a place as any to dump it, even though the stretch behind the motel didn't appear from a distance to be that deep. Still, I wanted the pistol out of the van. If it was the gun that sent Pervis Meeker to his grave, it was part of mountain mean, just like him. Not that he deserved to be shot, but he'd gambled some high stakes and lost. What still stumped me was how he'd been on the other end of the radio with Riley when the guys from Virginia picked up the pills, and how Riley said he'd been looking in on Mama, and yet when he turned up dead, Riley hadn't seemed all that broken up over it. "Pervis must have fucked up," was all he'd said.

I took the gun and the towel back to the room. Lorena was still on the phone, and I was able to figure out that she was arguing with Hiram about the girls having seen an R-rated movie. She said she'd seen it and it was okay with her, but he must have been putting up a struggle on the other end because when Lorena saw me she lowered the receiver, made a gun with her hand, stuck her pointing finger in her mouth and feigned pulling the trigger. "Well, Hiram," she said. "I let them see a movie that was R-rated for violence, and they see you lead an X-rated life, so we're even. In your house, it's your rules. I've got to go. No bye, I'm gone." Lorena flopped back on the bed and patted her stomach. "What was I thinking when I let him slide his sorry thing between my legs? At least God gave me those two girls for my suffering."

"I'm going to toss the gun in the river," I said.

"That's a hell of an opening line," Lorena said, rising up on her elbows. "You sure this is a good spot?"

"When it's dark." I said, "We'll go for a walk, skip a few stones, throw a stick or two into the current, and send this piece to the bottom. You know why Revered Willis wants this gone?"

"Your guess would be as good as mine," she said. "He didn't say."

I closed the curtains, flipped on the overhead light, and stood by the bed. I held the pistol up and said, "This is a Glock nine millimeter. Pervis Meeker was killed with one of these. Pervis was in Blissfull in December. Just a few weeks after we took the van to Beckley for tires and such, it had nearly six thousand more miles on it. Reverend Willis said he'd been going over to Kentucky looking for his family."

"So?" Lorena asked.

"Lou-Ann didn't say anything like, 'How'd you find us?' or 'How'd he know I was up here.' I find that odd. I don't care where she moved off to, if she has kin in Kentucky they're bound to be in touch." I paused a minute to let what I'd said steep. "Reverend Willis seems mighty upset that my brother is being hassled by the law." I said, "And he says he's bent on helping Riley out, a guy he claims he stole booze from. If Riley believed that our dear preacher had ripped him off, he'd have dead sure killed him. He's got that much of the Old Man in him."

Lorena sat up on the bed; the Whipple smile had vanished and a shade of pure dread, pale and ashy, had taken its place. "Ize, what are you saying?"

"I'm saying that Reverend Willis hasn't come clean with us. If this is the gun that killed Pervis, no matter who pulled the trigger, then he asked us to risk a hell of a lot more than the trouble we'd be in for ferrying a few snakes up here. Hell, the money in that scam is nothing to a guy like Riley, or Pervis, or our dear Theo. We don't know what was in that envelope we gave Lou-Ann. It might have been pure coke."

"Ize, you're losing your grip. She didn't even want the envelope in the first place."

"I know, but there is too much that I can't figure out. This sounds like one of his sermons about, 'The many signs we have yet to come to know.' I'll ditch this gun and I'll deliver the serpents, but I will not have any more to do with him. He'll get us into something, Lorena, that'll ruin us. I couldn't bear that."

"You are coming ragged at the ends," Lorena said, storming into the bathroom and slamming the door.

When Lorena is pissed off she gets stone quiet, and trying to get her to tell you what is making her angry if she doesn't want to is as impossible as an August snowball fight in Miami. While I waited for her to cool down, I flipped through the channels with the sound off and counted the perforated dots in a ceiling tile above the bed. I began to see that even if the rest of the trip went without a hitch we weren't out of the woods. If we left Blissfull, we might be setting ourselves adrift in a sea of regret, and, if we stayed we'd have to fashion a private life in a world invaded by ghosts and occupied by people who would always know something about us that could be used to compel us to do their bidding. I even questioned whether Lorena was mine, or if I was another disaster whom she'd allowed to slip his willie into her. After ten minutes of silence she said, "If we're gonna do it, let's go now."

We picked our way to the banks of the river like any couple in love might, sauntering and holding hands. I stopped to pick up some sticks, and Lorena pulled up a long piece of grass to chew on. Mosquitoes swarmed around us as the evening gathered and we drew closer to the water, the current burbling and making sucking sounds around the rocks, the moon reflected in the slow pools against the far bank.

I tossed a stick into the water and waited for the splash. I had second thoughts, thinking I might have been better off to have waited until the morning when I could have seen how deep the water was. Lorena picked up a rock and flipped it into the current. I was about to heave the gun in when I heard a rustling in the grass. I froze, but when I twisted around I saw three deer, a buck and two doe, edging toward the dark river. Lorena and I held our breath as the buck nosed the wind, and then led the doe into the current.

Reverend Willis would have seen it as a sign, but to me it was dumb luck. The deer splashed into the river and swam for the far shore, landing twenty feet downstream where they bolted up the far bank and shook the river from their backs. The gun caught a flash of moonlight and splashed in midstream, tremoring ripples in the light.

I called Billy all morning to no avail. When it got to be near check-out time, we went to the desk and booked the room for another night. It wasn't the beach, but it was a better place than the van to sort out all the demons and deceptions that had followed us from Blissfull. I could tell that what I'd said the night before had shaken Lorena, and while I would rather have been gang-buggered in the weeds by a bunch of hobos than hurt her; I knew we had no chance if we let too many things go.

Bored, we took a ride toward Bethel. Afraid to spark an argument, I said little, other than to point out the ski runs on the mountains, now green slashes among the trees, and the shapes of clouds. I knew the gun was eating at Lorena and I figured that if I could put her mind at ease about it that her mood would brighten up. I apologized for not thinking to have dismantled the damn thing and thrown parts of it in every river we'd crossed since we left Blissfull, and assured her that it would rust away long before anyone found it, especially as no one would be looking for it in the Androscoggin to begin with, but Lorena, remained somber and mute until blurting out, "It'll be this way, Ize. If you're ever linked to the gun, I'll say Theo gave it to me for protection 'cause he was worried about Hiram hurting me or the girls, but that I was so frightened of it that I begged you to go with me and dump it in the river."

I told her that wouldn't be necessary, but she insisted, and the worry ebbed from her face. "I swear life is a trial," she said, "and the best you can hope for is a hung jury."

I didn't reply and a few beats later she said, rubbing her stomach "Ize, you are a good man, and these are the worst cramps I've felt since I was fifteen."

We stopped at a tourist center in Bethel to buy some aspirin and water and Lorena bought a huge folding map of the area, which we studied in the van while we ate lunch at a take-out joint.

I finally got through to Billy at two o'clock that afternoon.

CHAPTER TWENTY-SIX

I wasn't happy with Billy, because he insisted on waiting until nine o'clock to meet us. In fact, the way he spoke to me made me wish I had the gun back, and loaded. When we'd met him in Lancaster, he'd seemed like any religious type, humble, low-key, but on the phone he'd been almost manic, like he'd been swallowing reds and gulping bourbon shooters. He said he'd meet us in the parking lot of a bar in Bethel, and that he'd be driving a blue Ford pick-up with a load of cordwood in the back. He said he'd drive through the lot and that I was to just pull out behind him and follow him. "It's as far back in the woods as anything you know, and I know where you're from," he said, with more than a little menace in his voice. I tried to suggest that the less remote, more open our rendezvous, the less suspicion it might arouse, but he insisted we'd meet where, "I always meet Theo."

Lorena kept saying things to ease the tension: "A few more hours then we're done," and "We'll be back at the beach tomorrow," but her face told me she was as skittish as a November buck and as unconvinced of a smooth transfer of our poisonous cargo as I was. Though I was riven with guilt to feel it, her fear made me trust her.

We sat in the van at The Sunday River Brewing Company too amped up to even listen to the radio, our eyes following each car in and out of the parking lot. Billy had only said the truck was a blue Ford, no tag number or anything else to identify it by. A state cop cruised through the lot and Lorena shuddered. I ached to summon up my old whiskey-runner's cool, but it had deserted me years ago. When I was a kid, I could be calm, almost sedate, in tense situations, I guess because I believed that I had nothing to lose, but that had changed.

At nine-thirty, half an hour late, Billy rocked through the lot and I was alarmed to see that he wasn't alone. A kid, maybe twenty, was riding shotgun with a ball cap pulled low over his eyes. Lorena kept the dome light on, following our progress toward Billy's preferred rendezvous on her map. We left the pavement west of Bethel and began to wind up into the mountains on a series of old tote roads. In places the road was dusty and I had to trail farther behind the truck than I wanted to. Though the moon was up, there was little light in the mountains' shadows.

The night cooled as we climbed. We'd long since left any roads on Lorena's map, and trying to read it in the low light, with the van jouncing over rocks and bumps, she said had made her queasy. "We've got no choice but to keep going now," I said.

Lorena clicked off the light. "I'm going into the back to get my sweat shirt," she said, "I'm frozen bone cold."

She was crawling back between the seats when I saw the moose, a few seconds after Billy should have. I jammed on the brakes and swerved left to avoid the body flying over the front fender of his truck, as several pieces of wood bounced out of the bed into my path. I heard Lorena fall back against the rear seat, and yelp with pain.

For a second there was silence, then Lorena screamed. "Ize, oh God, Ize help me." I turned on the dome light, but I'd already heard the problem. The rattler was shaking faster than my heart was racing. Lorena was pinned under all but the top serpent box and most of our camping gear. The top box lay broken around her, and a yellow-brown serpent was raising its head and nosing her fear. Outside Billy and the boy were cursing unlike any Holiness people I have ever known.

I tried to calm Lorena by telling her to be still and silent, but when the serpent coiled up on the ground cloth, dark against the silver foil, flicking its tongue to divine its surroundings, she called to me again, this time in a low shudder.

With all the dust the truck had been kicking up I'd had the windows rolled up, but Billy and the kid heard Lorena's screams any way. Seeing the rattler flicking its fangs and coiling down onto itself, I cursed the stupidity of not bringing a serpent stick. I eased the driver's window down and called out to Billy to bring me one, nearly bursting his eardrum, because though I had not seen him in the dark, he'd been pressed to the van window.

"What the fuck are you two hillbillies trying to do, call every cop and warden in Maine? It's just a young moose. Tell your girlfriend to get over it."

"Listen, asshole," I said, "Lorena is pinned under half a ton of shit because you couldn't keep from hitting that damn moose, and one of the serpent boxes broke loose. Get a serpent stick and catch him."

Billy hung his head and swore. "Jesus fucking Christ, what next?" He looked up at me, his eyes wild with rage and said, "Snake handling is your gig, right? I buy them delivered."

I knew I'd been had, but I said, "You're the one with the church, not me; you're the signs believer."

"What I believe in is the inherent meanness in West Virginia and Pennsylvania rattlesnakes. They're better than pit bulls or rotties at guarding what's mine. I been buying them from Ted Willis since long before he became Theobald The Signs Preacher." He paused as if out of breath and said, "I need these snakes, and what I don't need is to be linked to a snake-bit woman. She dies of a snakebite in Maine and we all have some real trouble up our asses."

Lorena was cringing in the corner and crying softly. Through her tears she said, "Maybe you can come around back and open that door and I can roll out."

"Stay still, Lorena," I said.

Billy stepped up onto the running board and when he did, I smelled the resin on his fingers and the smoke in his hair. A true pro would have been more discreet and that worried me as much as the serpent, who was sitting coiled and only rattling occasionally. If Billy was as reckless as he seemed, killing two strangers might be no big thing to him.

I'd heard of snakes being used to guard indoor reefer farms, and that in some places it's called Doing The Indy, after that Indiana Jones movie. Billy stepped down. "Me and the kid are gonna pull on our fender and see if we can get the truck to run. The snake is your problem. If we don't get them tonight, we can meet up tomorrow," he said.

I twisted my head around to get a full appreciation of the situation. Lorena was on her back, trembling, and clearly trying not to flinch when the snake lifted his nose to the wind blowing in the window. "They're going to leave us here, Ize," she said through clenched teeth. "Don't let me get bit like Lenora, please, Ize."

"I won't, Lolo," I promised, as I eased the seat back as far as it would go. Options stormed through my head. A serpent stick was my preferred choice, because if the rattler struck as I reached for it, it would lunge towards me and away from Lorena, which might allow her time to wrench open the rear door and roll out, provided she could get out from beneath the other boxes and our gear. I also considered waving the map at him in the hopes that it would either cow him or distract him from Lorena. However, the dark was his place.

"Be still, baby, " I said. "How much can you move?"

"A little, I think, but my leg is going to sleep and I don't know if I can get out from underneath all this," she said, her voice a bare whisper.

I heard Billy and the kid cursing and yanking on the fender, and when one of them fell with a crash into the ditch, they both laughed. I glanced out into the beam of the van's headlights as the stunned moose struggled to her feet and wobbled into the woods. Convulsed with laughter, the kid stumbled up from the ditch, and clutching his side, bumped the front of the van. The noise agitated the snake and he began to stretch and rattle.

"Easy, serpent," I said, as I turned over a few more ideas for saving Lorena, but I could tell by the fear in her eyes that she was getting panicky. I thought about a log or a stick that might not only distract the serpent, but which he might clamp into so I could hurl them both out of the window.

The snake stretched toward Lorena and a desperate squeal escaped her throat. "I'm gonna' go for it, Ize," she said, as she attempted to roll over on her side.

"No," I yelled so loud that Billy and the kid stopped

messing with the fender, and hustled toward the van, their boots grinding the gravel. "Be still, I'll get him."

I eased over toward the console, hitting my head on the dome light, and turned the switch off. I knew the snake could find Lorena by smell and by the heat her body gave off, but I hoped darkening the van might calm him. In the sliver of light that filtered in the windows, I saw the snake eyeing me and I was beset by the whirlies, unsure if it was from striking my head or from abject terror.

I've never developed the great voice Mama had hoped would get me and Riley onto the Opry, but I sang as best as I could, "What a friend we have in Jesus, all our burdens he can bear," making up words when I forgot them. I inched toward the rear of the van fastening my eyes on the rattler, and tasting that long-dead copperhead's scales in my mouth. I tried to recall if I had ever seen that particular rattler handled at Star of Morning. Afraid he might be the one who'd bitten Reverend Willis, my balls crinkled like over-boiled peas, but all the same I kept singing the same words over and over, gradually letting my voice get louder like Reverend Willis had done when he'd captured the serpents on the ledge.

The serpent's head swayed a little side to side as I rose up to clear the console between the captain's seats, and when I slid feet first onto the rear seat he faced me. I locked my eyes on him, Lorena praying with as much ferocity as anyone I'd ever heard at the Star of Morning, and felt all the spit leave my mouth.

The nearer I eased toward him, the calmer the serpent held his coil. I wondered if I should grab for it just behind the head, or pick the snake up by the tail as I'd seen Reverend Willis do dozens of times as he spoke or sang to one. I'd never handled a live rattler, and the memory of the few dead ones I'd touched gave me no courage, so I paused for a second to offer a silent prayer, still humming the hymn.

As I glanced at Lorena, I caught the kid peering into the rear window, and heard Billy, leaning in the open driver's window whisper, "Easy now Jesus boy, don't get bit."

I knew I had to keep my eyes open if I was to handle the serpent cleanly, and that if I reached and missed, it was a near certainty that either Lorena or I would be struck. I leaned toward him, within his striking range and began to sing loud like Reverend Willis, praying like hell that I was in or near the key of B flat.

I do not remember grasping the serpent behind his head, only Lorena's shriek as his tail uncurled across her face and he thrashed against me, or how I righted myself after falling over the tent bag, but somehow I held on until I was outside the van. The kid opened the rear door and pushed the serpent boxes and camping gear off Lorena who heaved herself up and leaped out of the van. When she found me, I was standing in the darkness just beyond the beam of the headlights, holding the serpent in front of me and singing to it in as soft and composed a voice as I could muster.

I ordered Billy to take the rest of the boxes and put them in his truck. "There's no room," he said, pointing to the wood stacked in the bed. "Deal is you take them half a mile further on."

"Then make some room," I said, holding the serpent out as if to pass it to him. "We're making the delivery here." As tough as he'd been just a few minutes before, faced with the possibility of being tossed a four-foot rattler, he was pretty meek. Turning to the kid he said. "Make room for our snake friends in the cab."

Billy and the kid unloaded the boxes from the van, handed Lorena a bank sack with Reverend Willis's money, and turned to leave. "We aren't finished with this," I said, "There's an envelope on the dash for you. Get it."

The kid reached in through the window and grabbed it. I stepped toward him holding the serpent, who'd gone limp in front of me, my hands now steady. "Open it," I said.

"It's just a letter," the kid said.

"Unless you're illiterate, read it out loud or I'll shove this snake down to where he'll feast on your balls."

The kid bought the act, and I was elated and relieved that

neither he nor Billy pulled out any heat.

The kid read. "Dear Billy. This is the last I owe you and it will be the last we do business. Killing Pervis was unnecessary. I had always wondered who'd stolen my gun, and when you sent it back to me, I understood how evil you are. I have accepted The Lord and I am trying to atone for my mistakes and sins. The young man, Isaac, and his friend Lorena, who brought you the serpents and this letter, have nothing to do with any of our old business, but I have discovered that the whiskey we stole had belonged to Isaac's brother and Pervis. Pervis wasn't holding out on you, he was trying to pay a debt. The money they found on him was owed Isaac's family." The kid paused, then said, "There's a PS, hard to read, that says, I've been snake bit and may die. I want no debts on my conscience."

Billy scuffed up the dirt in the road. "Well, hillbilly what you gonna do with that old rattler?"

"Let him go."

"Can't live here. The winters are too cold."

"Well, you paid for him. Why don't I just hand him to you?" I said taking a step forward. "You can hold on to him until you get home, then you can let him run around in your garden."

"I got a compound bucket with a lid in the truck. The kid will get it," Billy said, backing away. When the boy didn't move, Billy said, "Go on, Teddy, get the bucket."

"Teddy?" Lorena asked.

"Yes, Teddy. Crazy, love to kill gooks, Teddy. Teddy who pulled my ass out of the fire twice before I saved his. Boy's named for him. Your Theo The Signs Preacher. That man used to smoke more weed in a day than most men could handle in a week, and he used to eat enough speed to kill a grizzly bear. Bug fuck, jungle-crazy Teddy, who damn near got discharged from Quantico before he finished basic. Teddy, who couldn't keep the bad dreams out of his head. Reckless, crazy Teddy Willis, the Tennessee Stud. I love him. My brother-in-arms and my former business partner. He did fine until he took up with this skinny girl he met out in Tennessee. I think she got him headed out on the straight and narrow. When she died, old Teddy come unraveled."

"Lenora," Lorena said.

"That's it, Lenora," Billy said.

"My sister," Lorena said.

Billy's face screwed up in surprise. "Your family ought to stay away from snakes, lady."

The kid returned with the bucket and lid. I'd seen the anointed slide snakes back into a bucket like the one he'd set in the road, but I dangled the rattler over the top for few seconds before dropping him in. The kid slammed the lid on and crushed down half the tabs.

Billy stared at Lorena. "You do look like her, but she was skinnier, hungry-looking."

Lorena didn't respond. Billy turned to me and offered his hand. "You got big balls buddy," he said. "Give the preacher my regards and tell him that I didn't personally cap Pervis. Tell him that if he ever wants to do business again to look me up. Now we got some walking to do 'cause that truck ain't moving and we got to get these snakes to their new home before anyone happens along."

Lorena said, "We could ride you."

"I'm afraid access is limited to where we're headed. Lock them snakes in the cab, Teddy, and let's get going. Your mother will be worried about us."

"How do we get back to the highway?" I asked.

Billy stopped in the road and looked back a moment. "I thought you hillbilly boys never got lost. I hear that you find your way by the sun and the stars," he said.

"I guess I missed that gene," I said, "I been lost plenty."

"Three lefts, two rights, a left, left at the fork."

Lorena repeated the directions aloud until she was able to write them down in the van. When we reached Route Two, I was as elated to see pavement as I'd ever been.

Back at The Madison, we slept the sleep of the dead.

CHAPTER TWENTY-SEVEN

Lorena and I considered moving to Rhode Island, in part because it's a Navy state and we wouldn't have been the only southerners there, but also because there are no venomous snakes, and miles of public beaches. The first week of August we drove up to Misquamicut and camped for three days, each set of twins getting their own tent and me and Lo sleeping in the van, which we'd rented again. The boys developed a quick addiction to Del's frozen lemonade and wet-drip sand castles, and the girls reveled in the attention they attracted from young boys as they paraded up and down the shore in their kid bikinis. The kids struggled at first to understand the locals, whose accent is the thickest of all New Englanders, but like kids most anyplace they soon adapted and had formed alliances with other kids their own ages at the campground and the beach.

Nature did her best to seduce us. Each day dawned bright and warm, a fair ocean breeze moderating the afternoon August sun and a stiffer wind preventing the mosquitoes from swarming our cooking fire in the evening. For the first time in years, I could sit still in a chair and read or doze, and time lost all sense of dread.

The last night, we took the kids to a place called Monty's Clam Shack for dinner and devoured plates of fried clams and shrimp and the greasiest fries I have ever consumed. Afterward, we sauntered along the beach, the girls licking ice cream cones, the boys spooning up their frozen lemonade, and Lorena and I saying little as we listened to their chatter. All the religious people that I have known, Sally preachers, Catholic Priests, the believers at Star of Morning, all describe a peace that transcended them when they committed to their faith. I cannot believe that any sensation electrifies a soul with greater elation, or soothes with as sweet a serenity as that I felt as Lorena and I paused to stare out across the water that evening, as the kids trudged up the beach ahead of us.

But as much as Lorena has come to crave clams and

lobsters, the heat of the beach, and the susurrus wash of the waves on the sand, Blissfull tugged us home.

We got married on a Saturday under a tent on a flat spot at the farm where we'd consecrated our relationship, as Lorena likes to say, in the old Star of Morning van. Reverend Willis performed the ceremony for us at Mrs. Whipple's insistence, though I would have preferred having a Justice of the Peace officiate at the courthouse, and most all of Lorena's kin joined Riley and Lillian and their kids for the service.

It was mid-September, still, the sky specked with slashes of bone-white clouds drifting eastward like errant brushstrokes, autumn's palette firing the far hills. Lorena clenched my hand as we exchanged vows, gripping me as if we were back at Star of Morning and the anointed had opened the serpent boxes. As I slipped the ring on her finger, she turned to smile at the congregation and I knew from a brief flicker of pain that spasmed in her eyes, as she surveyed her family gathered on the bride's side of the tent, that Lenora's absence burned in her heart like a swallowed ember.

I have a job as a landscaper and excavator, working for Earl's youngest brother, Evan, who came home to Blissfull after ten years of running heavy equipment in Florida. With three new subdivisions planned for our neighborhood, the contracts he's working on for the hospital and other commercial clients, and the influx of summer folks, he believes he can make a go of it here. The pay is fair, and allows me to pull my weight, especially now that I am no longer sleeping on Riley's couch. I do worry that with winter approaching, Evan might have to lay me off from time to time, but he's taught me to operate some of his bigger equipment in the hopes that we can get some snow removal work as well.

Though I have become accustomed to living at Lorena's, and the kids no longer see me as a stranger who arrives at their bedtime and is gone when they wake up, we've begun negotiating with the county to buy her old homestead for back taxes. Now when I slide into sleep, rather than passing out, the sounds of the night fade in my ears instead of disappearing like music from an unplugged radio. I miss the ridge, more so than I ever have, the crepuscular serenade and the squawk of dawn, the wind crawling down the mountain through the summer trees and the clack of sleet on the winter roof. As my brain and soul heal, I have begun to understand that the great fortunes of my life may yet triumph over the ragged despair of my past. If Lorena and I can work out a deal for the old Whipple farm, we'll torch the buildings and build a new house in increments. I figure that we'll get a kit like the one Riley bought, and Evan's agreed to swap the site work for some overtime without pay.

Riley and Lillian have endured, despite Agent Karen, who proved immune to his mountain magnetism, playing hardball. He lost the new place, which was sold at auction to a couple from Virginia who plan to live there in the summer, to forfeiture, and the local cops scored two new four-wheel drive SUVS with their share of the money. He used some of what he'd stashed to remodel the old place, erasing, for me, the most lethal vestiges of the Old Man and the fierce memories of Mama's leaving us, which have long abraded our hearts. He raised the roof, put in a full second floor, and an addition that expanded his and Lillian's bedroom. Later we ripped off the front porch, much to the dismay of Roxie and Patches, and constructed a deck that looks out over the valley, in two furious weekends as the hills colored and the leaves swirled around the dooryard. Later, we razed the shed and the barn, salvaging the decent wood for a future garage, and burned the rest.

I've seen, in Lorena's girls, signs of that Whipple smile and it freezes my insides every time I drop them off at a school dance or at the mall to meet their friends, though I know that Lorena has told them the things her Mama never told her. I hope for their sake that their bodies work like their mother's and their aunt's, if they are as reckless as they were when they were young. Hiram, now that I am here, pays them little heed, finding excuses not to take them on alternate weekends, and I think Laura and Lucy have begun to regard me as a stepfather, leaving me hopeful that I will earn their true affection in time.

Lenny and Luke are easier. Tossing a football around with them, shooting baskets, oiling their bike chains, and basic roughhousing bond us. When we're together, I remember how Reverend Willis told me that though my father was dead that I had another one in heaven. At the time that troubled me, because I sensed that he meant that I was supposed to miss the Old Man, and I didn't. Roger, in a way, never existed to his kids, so his ghost doesn't haunt us.

Lorena misses Star of Morning and she's searching for a church to haul the kids to on Sunday mornings. She told me that, "Children brought up with no faith struggle in life," and says that, "When they're older they can choose for themselves." After Lorena asked her about it, Lillian took her to St. John's one Sunday, but Lorena complained that, "A religion that hard to follow isn't worth it." When we locate a new place it won't be a signs church, as we're both plagued by nightmares of the rattler in the van, and neither of us want the kids around serpents.

Signs Believers are sincere, and I bristle when I hear people demean them. I have never detected a scintilla of unkindness in any of them, and I have witnessed a consistent generosity of spirit and a gift for gentleness, not as often present in others. Were I gravely ill, I'd welcome their praying over me as much as a doctor's care, and, in moments of temptation, I've wept recalling the Sundays when Lorena squeezed my hand near to the point of stopping my blood flow at Star of Morning, as Reverend Willis exhorted his faithful to believe. In my inchoate sobriety, Lorena's touch, and Reverend Willis's eyes, steadied me. I would not now claim that it was the hand of God that saved me from the bottle, though I have often said it was, or that it was their faith in me that allowed me to imagine myself as more than a stew bum. Sometimes if I am up late at night, nettled by dark dreams of serpents, I take the kid's boom box out onto the porch and dial in a religious station to listen to those on-fire preachers who say as much with the tone of their voices as they do with the words they shout into the dark spaces of the night.

Though a persistent tingling in the arm pesters Reverend Willis where the rattler sunk his fangs, he's back at the helm of Star of Morning and continues to hunt serpents for the church, but not for sale. I believe that he is a man of God and His Word, a true Believer in the Signs. I have never spoken to him about Billy Parsons or Pervis Meeker, or any of the other inconsistencies about his past that vexed me, nor of the favors he asked of me that have never made sense to me. None of those were explained in the simple note he gave to Lorena and me to read after we'd delivered the serpents. That had simply read:

As in water face answers to face
so the mind of man reflects the man.
Proverbs 27:19

It isn't that my curiosity has abated, but I'm afraid to sunder the remnant bond of our friendship. I have decided that I do not wish to know if he was ever Lorena's lover, for, though I no longer feel beholden to him, I do bear him affection.

After our wedding, Lorena's mother claimed that she could no longer climb the stairs to her bedroom, and began to sleep the full night in her recliner. Lorena and I worked to make the old girl accept me, but I know I look too much like my father and she can never be reconciled to the fact that her daughter had married the bootlegger's boy.

In early October, Miriam Leeks, a widow who once lived in Lorena's neighborhood, invited Mrs. Whipple to stay with her at her apartment at Mountain's Majesty Christian Senior Housing for the weekend. Whether it is from keeping her leg elevated, or the plethora of widowers Miriam has introduced her to, she claims her gout is better and has been attending Friday night dances in their community center. She's on the waiting list for her own place, as much for the company, I am sure, as because she could never live again on the ridge as Lorena and I hope we will one day soon.

Mama got her rest. Riley and I took her up on the mountain in his truck and interred her with the few ashes of her second husband and the bones of the person we'd named "The

Lover." The rifles are also packed away with them. Riley says they'll come in handy if they ever have to blast their way out of hell, but when the heat is off him, I have no doubt that he'll try to move them for a few bucks. He is relieved, perhaps respectable, but I know that he will never be fully reformed.

Of a warm evening, Lorena, the kids, and I often sit with Riley, Lillian, Carleton and Annie on their deck, and watch the evening gather over the valley and hills, listening to the mountains. At first, you don't hear a thing, and then as everyone quiets, a lone whip-poor will, or hoo hoo hoo haw of an owl cracks the stillness, and in the spring, or if it has just rained, you can hear the creek racing down the ridge.

At Lorena's, when I can't sleep, I close my eyes and imagine that I am hovering over myself seeing me, three years ago, standing on the on-ramp in Holyoke as the first flurries began to swirl out of the blue-black sky, and I am singing, but this time I know the words, "Throw out the life line, throw out the lifeline, someone is drifting away," and then I am singing What a Friend We Have in Jesus, and the ramp is full of serpents coiling around each other, the snow clumped like confectioners sugar on their marked backs. I watch myself, thumb out, passed by every car, shielding my eyes from the sand and snow they kick up as they roar by me up the hill and disappear among the taillights of the traffic.

Then, a van stops, and a naked man gets out. It is Reverend Willis, except he has long white hair and a thin beard. He has a copperhead in one hand and a rattler in the other, and a large black snake is girded into a knot around his waist. The tip of his penis is hooded like a cobra, and along each collarbone, which protrude from a pale, sunken chest, twin fang bites ooze blood. He beckons to me without speaking, and as I start toward him I see the shrink from the Beckley VA who told me that all my problems were rooted in my fear of being abandoned standing behind him, and he is shaking his head from side to side and waving me to back away. I move toward Reverend Willis, and I feel the hand of the shrink on my shoulder, and as I turn, I see the Old Man and Mama, and

310

when I look back at Reverend Willis, I see Lorena and Riley and Lillian, and all their voices begin to speak to me at once in the tongues of the angels. At that moment, it ends. And though I have tried to dream this daydream to the end, and to conjure it in my sleep, its conclusion remains a mystery. Then, I slip out of bed, careful not to wake Lorena, and tiptoe to the window to listen for two, poor, skinny, mountain kids making love in a creek, and I am washed clean.

ACKNOWLEDGEMENTS

I regret that I have lost touch with my tenth grade English teacher at Vermont Academy, Mr. David Bain. I hope this book finds it way to him. Sorry it took me so long.

I've learned as much about telling a story from my companions and guides from my music playing days as from anyone, and acknowledge that indebtedness to Cormac McCarthy, Bill Morrissey, Harvey Reid, Paul Geremia, Jim Mercik and Dave Van Ronk. For fifteen years of traveling together in motorhomes, Subaru station wagons, Isuzu Troopers, ferryboats, sloops, catboats, and various other conveyances, and for all the ensuing years of friendship, I offer to my old friend Ramblin' Jack Elliott a copy of this book, my best impression of Pete Seeger and Doc Watson's reaction, and my hopes that he remembers that on his 100th birthday we are supposed to explore the length of Moosehead Lake in his Penguin sailing dinghy. Jack taught me that the story is always worth the wait.

I would like to thank three fine writers, Morgan Callan Rogers, Henry Garfield, and Marc Berlin, whose advice and friendship has been invaluable to me, for taking the time to read and comment extensively on early drafts of this book, and to Jack Driscoll for showing me how a great story breaks your heart.

The idea for much of this book sprung from a trip I took many years ago with my sons Benjamin and Zachary and our friend Barry Ward that included a ride through the mountains of southwestern West Virginia. Barry's observations and ruminations are ever insightful and provocative and I have been the beneficiary of his counsel and friendship for forty years.

My appreciation and admiration go to Brad Barkley, Roland Merullo, Richard Hoffman, Walter Wetherell, and Ann Hood for their sound advice and helpful criticism during workshops on other projects. To B. Lee Hope for believing in me and for introducing me to so many fine writers.

Finally, my deepest thanks to Joan Connor, Mike Kimball, Clint McCown, and, Michael C White, friends and mentors in the truest sense of those words, and writers extraordinaire. Your generosity, patience, and wisdom have meant more to me than you can ever know.

PUBLICATIONS, HONORS, AND AUTHOR'S BIO

Fiction

Nominated in 2008 for a Pushcart Award in fiction, Bruce Pratt's debut novel, *The Serpents of Blissfull*, published by Mountain State Press, is due out in early 2011. Pratt won the 2007 *Andre Dubus Award* in short fiction, and was a runner up or finalist for the 2007 fiction award from *Georgetown Review*, the 2007 flash fiction prize from *Mindprints*, the 2006 Ontario Prize, the 2005 Rick DeMarinis Short Story Award, and the 2003 Fiction Award from *Dogwood, A Journal of Poetry and Prose*. His short fiction has also appeared in *The Greensboro Review, The Boston Fiction Annual Review, The Dos Passos Review, WordSmitten Quarterly Journal, Briar Cliff Review, Portland Magazine, Watchword, The Staccato Literary Magazine, The Gihon River Review, The Dalhousie Review, Puckerbrush Review, Cooweescoowee, Existere, Vermont Literary Review, Hawk and Handsaw, The Blue Earth Review, Diner, Roanoke Review, Potomac Review, The Wisconsin Review, The Binnacle, Apocalypse, Crosscut,* and *Stolen Island Review*.

Poetry

Pratt's poetry collection *Boreal* is available from Antrim House Books. He is the winner of the 2007 *Ellipsis Prize* in poetry, a finalist for the Erskine J. Poetry award from *Smartish Pace,* and his poems have appeared in, *Only Connect*, an anthology from Cinnamon Press, (Wales) *Smartish Pace, The 2007 Goose River Anthology, Revival* (Ireland), *Puckerbrush Review, The Poet's Touchstone, Rock and Sling, Red Rock Review, Crosscut, Iguana Review, The Tipton Journal, The Unrorean, Heartland Review,* and *Wild Goose Poetry Review.*

Nonfiction and Journalism

His nonfiction has appeared in the *Yale Anglers' Journal, Vermont Literary Review, Hartford Courant, Bangor Daily News, Salty Dog, Bangor Metro,* and *Portland Magazine.*

Drama

His short play *Electrolysis* was performed at the 2008 Maine Short Play Festival, and was included in the 2nd Annual Northern Writes Festival. Another short play *Polygamy* will appear in *Literal Latte* in 2009. *Barter* a one-act play was included in the 2010 Maine Play Festival and The Northern Writes Festival.

Bios

A graduate of The Stonecoast MFA at The University of Southern Maine, where he teaches undergraduate creative writing, Pratt and his wife, Janet, live in Eddington, Maine.

Born 1951 Bronxville NY. Pratt grew up in Connecticut and graduated from Vermont Academy in 1969, Franklin and Marshall College with a BA in Religious Studies in 1973, The University of Maine with a Masters Degree in English with a concentration in Creative Writing in 2001, and The University of Southern Maine's Stonecoast MFA with a degree in creative writing with a focus on short fiction, and a concentration in Critical Theory in 2004.